**KATE NIVISON**
worked in various parts of the world for
ten years, after which she began writing short
stories and serials. Her work has appeared in
many well-known magazines (under her Kate
Miles pen name), on TV and in short story
anthologies. Her first book, *How to Turn your
Holidays into Popular Fiction*, was published in
1994, and she also writes travel features.

Now living in London, she is married with three
children, and works in adult education. She still
travels regularly, especially in Africa and the
Far East. Her next project is a round-the-world
trip with her daughter.

Kate Nivison

# TIGER COUNTRY

The Adventure Club
A.001

Aspire Publishing

An Aspire Publication

First published in Great Britain 1998

ISBN 1 902035 02 X

Printed and bound in Great Britain by
Mackays of Chatham Plc, Chatham, Kent.

Typeset in Palatino by Kestrel Data, Exeter, Devon.

**Aspire Publishing** – a division of XcentreX Ltd.

This book is dedicated to all those involved in saving the tiger and other endangered species from extinction.

# TIGER COUNTRY

# Chapter One

The starter was quails' eggs on a bed of winter salad. Fran fielded a wink from Nevil and tried to relax as their guests drifted in. Two days ago when she'd started on the preparations for tonight's dinner party, cookery book in one hand, shopping list in the other, quails' eggs had seemed like a bright idea. Unfussy, yet sophisticated – she hoped . . . Nevil had said tonight was important. But then he always did. So had she hit the right note? Oh, what the hell – they all ate far too much anyway.

There was some murmuring about how pretty the table looked and the usual shilly-shallying as they sorted out who was sitting where from the neat little cards by each plate.

'Right beside our lovely hostess – I'm flattered.' Jeremy Cuthbertson, senior partner of Cuthbertson and Pearts, was in what he would have called good form tonight.

Flattered? Don't be, thought Fran flashing her best smile at the over-pink face homing in on her. Just doing what I'm told, Jeremy old chum. There's a couple of things Nevil wants me to winkle out of you over the coffee, that's all.

But then someone like Jeremy would know that anyway, wouldn't he? Fran's smile softened a fraction. Jeremy wasn't the worst of them.

11

'And quails' eggs! I haven't had them for years.' He beamed. 'How clever. Where do you find them, tucked away out here?'

'Smart woman, my wife. The only problem is getting her down the tree again once she's raided the nest.' You could always rely on Nevil for a good, ice-breaking laugh.

'From the local butcher, actually,' said Fran, wrinkling her nose at him as he helped Mary-Lou Cuthbertson into her seat. Since Mary-Lou was wearing something rather tight in turquoise satin, this was no simple matter. With the Barbie-doll hair, she looked like a mermaid just washed in on the Gulf Stream.

'And ah always thought quails was a kinda fish,' cooed Mary-Lou, to an almost audible wince from Jeremy.

'I know what you mean,' nodded Fran, instantly warming to the girl. 'Like caviar.' Lord – she must be half Jeremy's age. Was she his second or third wife?'

'I guess so,' twinkled Mary-Lou gratefully, and turned her aquamarine gaze on the suave face opposite. Well, she'd had to put Tony somewhere. Tony was the other half of Merrick and Baldwyn, Financial Consultants. Tony was Nevil's business partner, but still unattached in every other sense. Dangerously so. But with any luck, even Tony wouldn't dare flirt with a merchant banker's new wife. Not this particular merchant banker's, anyway. There was too much at stake.

Fran crossed her fingers under the table and nodded to the agency lads she'd got in to serve the wine and generally buttle around. Only three more courses to go, followed by the coffee and liqueurs, and then – get them out of here! Nevil had promised that tonight would be the last 'do' on this scale until after Christmas. He really had promised this time, even agreed to a proper holiday. No business – a real break somewhere well away from e-mail and faxes and phones. Meanwhile, Mrs Francesca Merrick, married to one half of Merrick & Baldwyn, and keeping a discreet eye on the other half, was doing her bit for England and an export-led recovery.

Everything went swimmingly as far as the cheese. She'd already learnt that Jeremy Cuthbertson's bank was postponing further expansion into Europe and looking at the Far East. Hardly heavy duty industrial espionage, but it showed which way the wind was blowing, and might give Nevil and Tony a tiny edge for the rather delicate negotiations that were coming up with Cuthbertson's next week.

Glad of a small breathing space, Fran watched her husband at the other end of the long oval table. In spite of the suntan and apparent air of bonhomie, Nevil still had that strained look about him that she'd noticed more often recently. Of course, it was Friday, and everyone was always pretty knackered by the end of the week. And he'd been home very late again this evening. Almost hadn't made it, in fact. No time for explanations. You had to allow for that too.

Right now he was conducting a lively post-mortem on the gang's last golfing weekend. Golf! Before getting into the deep end of the business world herself, Fran had assumed it was a game for her father's generation. Not a bit of it. Every rising Thirtysomething-in-the-City knew his woods from his irons and belonged to at least one expensive club where deals were wheeled and reputations established over a seemly relaxed round or two. The Japanese and Americans loved it. But this time she wasn't falling for that one. This holiday was going to be miles away from anything green with eighteen holes – that is, if it was going to stand a chance as a second honeymoon.

'Are you into golf, Fran?' Mary-Lou had caught the drift.

For an instant, Fran wanted to grab the girl's elaborately manicured hand and yell, 'No, it's so boring I could scream.' But this was business.

'Let's say I like to keep an eye on the ball,' she said with a smile.

'You always did, Fran. You always did.' That was Tony, joining in jovially. 'Do you know, Mary-Lou, we really miss her back at base.' He glanced up the table to make sure Nevil was listening, then did his vintage Spike Milligan bray. 'Gad, Matilda, how long is it since you left me for that swine?'

Everyone laughed. It was all part of the game, and she knew the rules to this one.

'Absolutely can't remember, Tony dear – and do you know, I don't miss it one bit.'

It was the sort of good humoured banter they wanted to hear, but for all that, it was two years and three months since she'd left Merrick and Baldwyn to marry Nevil and she did miss it quite a lot. Not because of Tony, though. So maybe he had fancied her once. Tony fancied most women – until they started asking too many questions about company liability, tax, and other things mere PA's weren't supposed to know too much about. No, for all his joshing, Tony was quite relieved she wasn't around any more.

And now there he was, reworking some yarn from the Saudi days, while Nevil threw in pained protests about his accuracy. And here *she* was, neutralised – a contented company wife. Like hell.

14

It was time to check the kitchen. The coffee should be on by now, and Mary-Lou wanted decaff.

It probably wasn't deliberate, and Fran certainly wasn't the paranoid kind who thinks people are waiting for them to leave the room before saying things they're not supposed to hear. But she was just on her way back from the kitchen when some ominous phrases from Nevil's end of the table caught her ear.

'So you'll be taking your clubs then, Nev? I wouldn't leave it too long without practising that swing.'

'Do they have golf courses in Colombo?' chuckled someone.

What? She almost said it aloud. *Where?*

Well trained as she was, her feet kept moving long enough to find her chair again. She hesitated a moment before sitting down, trying hard not to stare down the table where Nevil was intent on not catching her eye while quickly changing the subject. He was feeling guilty, obviously. So what was going on? Because he'd been home even later than usual this evening, they'd had no time to talk. Had that been deliberate? And Colombo – where the hell was that? Oh for pity's sake, what excuse was it going to be this time to avoid taking a break?

Pretend you haven't heard, urged a voice in her head – then sort it out afterwards.

'Shall we have coffee in the jungle?' she announced brightly, waving at the new conservatory where some mail-order palms and cheese plants were doing their best to give it a long-established look. Colombo. Wasn't that the drugs place? No, that was Colombia. But it was somewhere with jungle, and not coffee – but tea. Of course – Sri Lanka. Nevil

15

had never been there before as far as she knew. Hong Kong and Singapore many times, various bits of the USA, and the Gulf States - where he'd palled up with Tony. But not Sri Lanka.

She had to force herself to lighten up. Perhaps he'd been cooking up some super-exotic holiday and had wanted to surprise her. If she could hang onto that idea, maybe she could get through the rest of the evening without exploding.

Nevil seemed to take longer than usual, pottering around locking up before coming upstairs. Getting into bed would have made her feel too vulnerable, so she sat at the dressing table idly brushing her hair. As soon as Nevil came into the bedroom she knew her gut reaction had been right. There was guilt all over his face.

'Thanks for everything, darling. It was a terrific evening,' he said, coming over to kiss her.

'Judas,' she replied lightly. 'OK, what's going on?'

'Honestly, I meant to tell you earlier . . .'

'But you somehow didn't have time. So when is this little jaunt?' Suddenly it hit her how angry she was. 'And don't tell me it's only for a few days. It's almost as far as Singapore. You remember Singapore? Last time you were so jet-lagged . . .'

'Please, Fran, not that again! I know it was Alison's wedding, and I did apologise. But this really is important.'

'It always is! Why can't Tony go instead? I was just about to make the bookings. I was thinking of the Western Isles, or maybe Connemara.' She was improvising wildly now. 'It's supposed to be gorgeous at this time of year.'

'Sorry,' he said shortly, in a way that set her teeth on edge. 'I can't pass on this one.'

'So what's the point of having a partner? Isn't Tony up to it? Don't you trust him?' It wasn't something she'd particularly meant to come out, but it seemed safer to take her anger out on someone who wasn't there.

'That's a pretty bloody thing to say!'

Not so safe after all. Now he'd simply write her off as "being unreasonable". 'I know,' she said. 'But that's how I'm feeling about this. You promised, and you need the break, Nevil, you really do. Look at you! You're permanently stressed out.'

'I know,' he echoed, beginning to take off his clothes.

She watched him in the mirror. Not so long ago, the fact that she was watching would have excited them both, but now all she could see was the strain of a so-familiar dilemma in his every movement. To tell or not to tell. If this trip was so important, it usually meant one thing – brinkmanship. No one in their line was very far from the edge these days, and there'd been times when they could have lost everything they'd worked for on one turn of the Market.

'Right,' she said, spinning the seat round to face him. 'Exactly how crucial is this trip? Am I in for any more broken promises tonight?'

This was getting dangerous. When they'd got married, she made him promise, really promise, no more games; there'd be no more high-risk ventures. No more putting the house up as collateral. No more dabbling in off-shore funding on the nod from a friend. At first she'd enjoyed the excitement of it – the elation when a long shot came home. But nail-biting tension and rounds of champagne didn't quite

17

go with starting a family, and Nevil always said he wanted that as much as she did.

'Don't look at me like that,' he said, still avoiding her eyes. He sat down on the bed, reached for her hand, and surprisingly, kissed the palm. A familiar warm, warning thrill shot through her. She wanted to slip her fingers through his hair and make him come to her. Men shouldn't have hair like that. It was so soft and springy.

But he wasn't going to get off lightly this time. 'So it's something big. Something so big I'm not going to like it? Sri Lanka, now let me guess. I know – they're building a new airport, trade centre, Hilton Hotel, huge resort complex, whatever, and someone's over-shot the budget. How am I doing?'

'They've already got a new airport, and a Hilton.'

'Don't quibble. OK, new docks, a dam, any combination of the above. Arab money, Chinese labour. Arab labour, Chinese money – something like that. Some buddy of yours needs bailing out, or he's doing the International Rescue bit and offered you some of the action – at a price that's too high, with people you don't trust. But if it comes off, we can retire to the Bahamas and play golf all day. Am I getting warm?'

'Oh come on, Fran. I said I was never going to get in that deep again. But the contacts are mine, not Tony's, so it's really got to be me.'

By now she wasn't really listening. 'Don't fob me off, I can smell it! It's one of *those*.' It was on the tip of her tongue to say something utterly corny like, 'Daddy always warned me it would be like this', but that would have made her feel ridiculous, and all the more so because it happened to be true.

Dad – oh Christ! He was coming to lunch on Sunday, and she could just see the I-told-you-so look on

18

his face if she let him see how fed up she was about all this.

Nevil dropped her hand, muttering something about her exaggerating, and pulled off his shirt. 'About half an hour ago, you asked when.' He was checking a small sticking plaster high on his left arm. 'That's sore!' The area round it looked pink and swollen. 'Typhoid jab. I called in at the doc's on the way home. That's why I was late. The flight's on Monday, early.'

'You're kidding!' She stared at him, then flounced into bed. 'You're sure you wouldn't like to start packing right now? Oh for goodness' sake, how long for, this time?'

'The thing is, I don't actually know. I've left the ticket open.'

'*What!* Nevil, I just don't believe this. What are we talking about – a week? A month – a year?' She was going over the top again but didn't care. 'And what am I supposed to do, sit here and manicure my toes?'

'I really am sorry about this, Fran. Honestly, it's pretty big – I won't risk it otherwise.'

'Risk what?' she asked sharply.

'Upsetting you like this, of course.'

'Oh great! And you'll make it up to me afterwards, I suppose,' and without waiting for an answer, she rolled over and turned out the light.

The atmosphere wasn't much better next morning, especially when Nevil said he'd have to leave on Sunday night and stay over at the airport hotel because the Monday flight was so early.

'So I'm going to have to drive you there,' she groused. 'Right, that does it. I'm ringing Dad and cancelling Sunday lunch. I'm not in the mood to be

sociable.' For a moment she almost regretted it because Nevil seemed relieved to have been let off
socialising with her father.

'Sorry, Dad, Nevil's having to go away again,' she
found herself explaining in that too-light voice
she'd been using rather a lot lately. Who was she
kidding?

'Everything all right, my darling?' He always
asked. She'd come to think it was his way of saying
that one day he knew it wouldn't be.

'Oh, fine.' She was going to be on her own for an
indefinite period, the longed-for break was off, and
she didn't seem to be even vaguely pregnant yet –
but everything was just fine. 'I'll pop over some time
if I get lonely.'

'You do that,' said the ever-unruffled voice, and
she could almost see her father, trim as ever,
probably in a cashmere as it was Saturday, one
foot propped on his antique desk.. He liked the
best, did Peter Mayers, and made it sometimes a
little too plain that he'd expected the same for his
daughter when she married Nevil Merrick. *Change
the name and not the letter; change for worse and not for
better* . . .

She went thorough the motions of sorting out Nevil's
lightweight clothes, and asked about his golf bag. 'I'll
hire some if I have to,' he said, ignoring the edge in
her voice. 'I'm just popping out for a couple of guide
books and flight fodder from the library, and I'll need
some more malaria pills.'

Later, she picked one up one of the guide books –
*Sri Lanka, the Paradise Isle*. Weren't they all? Maybe
it was, although Colombo itself didn't look particularly exciting. Nevil was booked in at one of the usual

businessmen's watering holes, the sort of place where once you were safely inside, you could be in any big city anywhere in the world. From force of habit she grimaced at the prices. A couple of nights in a hotel like that would cost as much as an entire fortnight's package tour in the resorts down the coast, where at least you'd get to see a few waving palms.

She was about to put it down and start the lunch when, on an impulse, she checked the library date stamp. *Six* weeks from now? He'd actually asked for an extension. Fortunately he was upstairs in his study, somewhere she left severely alone unless the house was burning down. Anyway, it was too late now.

By Sunday she had resigned herself to the inevitable and was feeling a little more gracious. There were lots of women in her position, and many more for whom a chance would be a fine thing. Her friends said the same. Every now and then the absences, the rapid changes of plan and the uncertainty got to you. Then there was a good old-fashioned blow-up. But provided neither of you stepped over the magic mark, things quietened down, you joined a gym, took up golf, or maybe Japanese just to be different – until the next time.

Yet still the feeling nagged that this latest episode had been a step too far and it frightened her. She dressed extra carefully that morning – slim-fit chestnut jersey trousers with a long waistcoat over a bronze silk crepe top – her colours; newbuck ankle boots that had cost the earth from somewhere south of Sloane Square. Nevil liked her to 'look the part', and she enjoyed it, but all her efforts to get rid of a small knot of anger in the pit of her stomach didn't seem to be working.

'Thanks, I'd sooner do it myself,' he said quickly as she made her usual good humoured attempt at wifely fuss over the last minute packing. Maybe he meant to save her trouble, but it made her feel like a bit part in someone else's play.

'Are we having dinner at the airport hotel?' she asked as he was about to disappear upstairs again. It was what they normally did before a trip if time allowed.

He paused only a second. 'I'd just as soon have a snack here and use the time there to get my head straight for the trip,' he said. 'I'll be taking the laptop, and I can make Sunday rate foreign calls on my charge card from the hotel.'

Having little choice, she said nothing, just nodded.

Their goodbyes on these occasions had become more or less routine – quick kisses at the front door, or in the car if she was dropping him off, or at the departure barrier, the 'love you's' and 'I'll phone's'. Then that strange, empty feeling as she realised how much she really was going to miss him. But this time she found herself wanting something more – something to reassure her that everything was still all right; that his distance and preoccupation was nothing to do with her, but only the job.

At the very last moment, as they drew up at the hotel entrance he seemed to respond to her unspoken need.

He leaned over and gave her a lingering kiss, stroked her cheek for a moment as if trying to remember what it felt like and said, 'Cheer up, Fran love. I'll be all right, you know.'

Hadn't he meant to say, 'It'll be all right'? Why 'I'll be all right'?

'I should bloody well think so!' she replied casually

and then, repentant, waited to blow him a kiss as he turned to wave. The taxi behind gave a discreet toot. Why had he said that? Slip of the tongue?

# Chapter Two

Back home, the big house seemed emptier without him that evening than it did during the day when he was at work. Fran thought about a coffee, looked at the time and poured herself a weak whisky and water instead. Very weak. A look at one or two of the older 'business wives' had been a warning on that score. The temptation was always there, though. The constant entertaining, the duty-frees, and then the evenings alone were not a good mix.

Idly she flipped through *Homes and Gardens* until a nice spread headed *Doing up his Den* caught her attention. It was something she'd been thinking about for some time. When they'd moved in, Nevil's study had been one of the few rooms not completely redecorated because he'd liked its crusty feel. Once he'd moved in with all his files, that had been that. Now it was a little too crusty, to the extent that even Maggie the cleaner did little more than vacuum the bits of carpet still visible. Her eyes fell on a picture of a big, black ash desk and matching filing cabinet. Now maybe something like that would look good without spoiling the atmosphere.

Taking the magazine with her she went upstairs to brave the study. If Nevil was going to be away for some time, why not give it a face-lift? She half smiled as she looked round. Nevil's button-down manner and general air of well-ordered grooming did not extend into his workspace. The place was a tip, and Maggie was due in tomorrow.

More out of habit than anything else, Fran went to the overflowing waste bin and tried to push it down. A new carrier bag on the top still held a box and some white foam packing. It was probably some new gizmo for the computer – that kind of thing. Except the picture showed what looked more like a small camcorder, which was odd because they already had one, a very superior model that they'd got for their wedding. Underneath was a smaller box for a mini cassette recorder, and at the bottom was a credit card slip.

'Hell's teeth!' she muttered, blinking at the amount on the slip. It wasn't that they couldn't afford it, but did camcorders and itsy-bitsy cassette recorders really cost that much these days? Clearly, she was out of touch. And what on earth could Nevil want them for?

She had another look. Friday's date, from a shop in Tottenham Court Road. With that detour and the jab at the medical centre, no wonder he'd been so late home, but he hadn't mentioned it. And it had to be connected with the Sri Lanka trip. Slightly bemused, she sat down in his big leather swivel chair and slowly swung herself from side to side. Was that why he hadn't wanted her to help him pack? No, that was silly. She got up quickly. Someone had asked him to bring them out, or they were a present, a little sweetener perhaps. But if they were for presents, why had he removed all the wrapping?

There was of course a rational explanation. Nevil always said that everything he did was perfectly rational. It was just that his view of rationality took on board a higher risk factor than hers. Dad, never one to mince words, had called him a chancer.

But if there was a rational explanation for the impulse purchases, it was not very obvious at three o'clock that morning as Fran lay awake, alone in their king size bed. She never slept very well when Nevil was away, and was trying to put her unease down to that. In the old days, she'd have had to get up for work tomorrow, and there'd have been no time to dwell on puzzles. Now there was.

She was up too early, and found herself looking at the receipt again. Why those items? Why so expensive? It was no good – she knew she was going to ring the shop. Perhaps it was all those years of office work. Someone threw a question and a piece of paper at you, it was Monday morning and you had to take action. The phone number was there. Do it.

So she did it.

'Good morning, I'm making some enquiries about a couple of items recommended by a friend. I wonder if you could give me some details . . .' After years of Merrick and Baldwyn, lying over the phone came easy.

'Ah yes,' said the young man, when she told him the make and model numbers. 'Very state-of-the-art. They're the best we have in the miniaturised line for really good picture and sound quality. Was there anything in particular you wanted to know?' There was a tiny pause. 'We do have cheaper models but under certain circumstances when, er, confidentiality is essential, they're not as effective, if you know what I mean.' He gave a conspiratorial chuckle, and Fran suddenly had a nasty feeling that she knew exactly what he meant.

'I work for an investigative journalist,' she said, feeling her nose to see if it was getting any longer. It was something she'd always done at work, just to show herself that she still knew she was doing it – lying.

'Well worth the expense then, I'd say,' said the young man, warming to his subject. 'Very popular with private detectives and dodgy lawyers. Um, no offence. "Spy in a bag", we call that model in the trade. And the recorder's sensitive enough to be worn under clothes. The cam's even got an infra-red facility for night work.' He laughed. 'Mind you, we just flog'em. What our clients do with them is no concern of ours.'

'No, it wouldn't be, would it?' said Fran and put the phone down as if it had suddenly grown small hairy legs.

So what had she expected to be told – that these expensive pieces of sophisticated hardware were the latest thing for birthdays and christenings? One was the kind of thing that took videos through a hole in your bag, and the other could record a conversation from the comfort and safety of your own underwear! Words like sleaze, corruption, admissible evidence, videoporn, and espionage, came to mind. In the wrong hands, things like these could bring down governments.

Talk about paranoia. Nevil hadn't been gone five minutes – well, four hours, actually – his flight had left at six o'clock – and she'd already got him up to all sorts of villainy.

'Get a grip,' she said to the coffee mug. 'Get a life. Get a cat!'

After a third coffee she settled on something less drastic; short term – call Dad; long term – revamp the study. Dad first, tonight when he'd be home. After all, he'd been done out of his Sunday lunch yesterday. Maybe he'd fancy having something with her instead of eating alone.

'Why not come over to me for a change?' suggested her father. 'I know you have enough of entertaining. I'll ring for a pizza or something. They're always too big for one. Did you say Sri Lanka?'

Which was how she found herself eating garlic bread and a seafood special with extra topping, from best Worcester china in front of a blazing real log fire, being quizzed about the one thing she didn't want to talk about.

'No, I don't think there's "anything more to it", whatever that's supposed to mean,' she found herself saying quite sharply.

'Now, my darling, I didn't mean to imply . . .'

'I should hope not, indeed.' She made a face at him to take the sting out the words.

'Quite right. None of my business, of course. But you did seem to come over a bit indignant about this one.'

'I was. OK, I still am. But I did realise it would be like this when I married him.' And if I didn't, she added silently, it wouldn't have been your fault, father dear. 'Actually, I think I'm more bored than cross.'

A silence fell between them. Fran didn't like to look up, because she knew that if she did, she would see a large bubble over her father's head filled with a cute cuddly bundle in a pram. Hard-headed financier he might be, but he had his soft side. Fortunately he was good at silences.

'I'm sure you've probably dismissed this idea,' he said eventually, 'but I could think of worse places

28

for a second honeymoon than Sri Lanka. Your grandfather was there briefly in the war, you know. He really loved the place – used to make us laugh about how they painted coconut tree trunks black and set them pointing out to sea to look like heavy artillery. Bit different now, though. They're welcoming the Japanese with open arms.'

'And everyone else too,' said Fran, who still managed to be mildly irritated when a note of disapproval tinged her father's voice over anything to do with the Far East. But he was a different generation. Fathers were, and that was that. 'And it's up to people like Nevil to show the flag, wouldn't you say?'

'Oh, absolutely. It's an ideal place, I suppose – apart from a little local difficulty in the North with the Tamil Tigers and what-not. Still, show me a place that hasn't got some kind of terrorist threat these days. Good half-way house between Gulf money and Pacific Rim know-how, but without Indian red tape.'

'It's no good fishing, Dad. I've no idea who he's seeing or why.'

Her father had more sense than to reply directly. He took a large bite of pizza.

'Call me a hopeless romantic,' he said, as he munched, 'but really, why don't you got out and join him? You know where he's staying, and when it's all over, you could take off down the coast for a week or two?'

Fran glanced up. 'Do you know, I suppose I could. It looked rather nice in the guide book.' She grinned at him. 'Dad, you're a genius. Sort of two birds with one stone. OK, blow Connemara. I'll get onto it first thing tomorrow.'

*       *       *

It didn't take long. A package tour was too limiting, but their local travel agent got her an open ticket much the same as Nevil's. 'If it's the Colombo Inter-Continental, I wouldn't bother to book,' said the girl, checking her computer. 'It's the tourist off season anyway, and there aren't any big conferences at the moment, that I can see. Perhaps a fax or something, to let them know you're coming.'

'I want it to be a surprise,' Fran told her. 'And I only need a couple of nights, anyway. Then I'll hop off down the coast to see what I can find, and my husband can come on when he's ready. I'm really going to enjoy this. It's ages since I've done a bit of travelling on my own.'

Feeling very much more cheerful, she decided that she should at least ring Tony and tell him what she had in mind. After all, it was possible he might know something more about how long Nevil's business was likely to take. At the last minute, she hesitated before picking up the phone. Curious as she still was about the surveillance equipment, should she mention it? Better not. With business, you never knew – and much the same applied to Tony.

'You mean, you're going out there yourself?' Tony was following the script as expected. Even so, she wasn't prepared for the sharpness, alarm even, in his voice. 'Fran, I'm not sure that's a very good idea.'

'Why ever not?

'Well, you *know* . . . . Colombo can be a pretty dangerous place.'

'Honestly, Tony, I'm hardly going to get mugged taking a taxi straight from the airport to the hotel.'

'No, no,' he said rather too quickly. 'I mean, the guerillas. The Tamil Tigers or whoever they are. It's not safe.'

'Thanks! So Nevil's in imminent danger of being blown up or kidnapped or something, is he? Anyway, I checked. The trouble's mostly in the North, which is off-limits anyway, and Colombo itself isn't much worse than here in terms of bombs and what have you.'

'I still don't think it's a very good idea. Won't you be bored?' He was scratching around now. 'Anyway, Nev's not going to have any time to go swanning round bazaars and temples and things.'

'I've always wanted to know what you men get up to on these trips.' She was only half joking. 'You wouldn't be trying to put me off for any other reason?'

'Whatever gave you that idea?' said Tony huffily.

Years of knowing you, she wanted to say. 'Anyway, I've already booked the flight. Now tell me, I want to be suitably dressed – are there any Saudis in the group?'

'Probably – it's the usual mixture,' he replied, his mind obviously elsewhere. 'Mainly Chinese. When are you leaving?'

'Early Monday. I'm going to fax the hotel on Sunday to be on the safe side. It's supposed to be a surprise, though, so don't you go spoiling it.'

'Wouldn't dream of it,' he said.

She put the phone down. Five years ago, she thought sadly, she would have believed him.

Sheer excitement and last minute preparations kept her going for the rest of the week. Nevil hadn't rung, but the five-hour time difference could have made it awkward, and she knew if he'd have been coming home so soon, he would have let her know. Thoughts of warm, deserted sandy beaches, rolling monsoon breakers and starry nights carried her along as she packed their beach gear and promised herself some batik wall-hangings for the hall. The study re-vamp could wait.

There was one nasty moment on Wednesday evening – a report of a car bomb in Colombo, with twenty people killed. The Tamil Tigers had claimed responsibility, and the story was linked to another report on the continuing troubles in the north of the island.

'Oh come on, Dad,' she'd said to her father who knew what she was planning by now, and rung up when he'd seen it on *News At Ten*. 'No foreigners were killed. It's not us they're after. And it was nowhere near the central hotel district.' Yet it was enough for her to think that maybe both Tony and her father had a point - that the political situation was worse than she'd thought - but by now it would have taken a full scale state of emergency to put her off.

On Sunday morning she made a quick time calculation and decided to send the fax sooner rather than later in the day to be sure of catching Nevil before he went to sleep. She went up to the study with the hotel leaflet he'd left her, sat down at the PC and switched on.

For a moment it felt almost felt like old times as her fingers flew over the keys. She composed two messages, one was to the hotel management, and the other to Nevil headed, *Surprise!* Then she gave her flight details, adding that she'd make her own way from the airport. That way she wouldn't interrupt his schedule.

As she keyed in to send the fax, it suddenly struck Fran that she'd been so busy that she hadn't checked the machine at all since Nevil had left, either for incoming faxes or for e-mail. She sent the faxes on their way and waited for the 'completed' message, marvelling briefly as she still sometimes did, that her words had now been printed out in a hotel office half way round the world. Then she checked for incoming e-mail and got a surprise.

'Eek!' she squawked to the empty room and glared at the new message accusingly. It was dated and timed last Sunday, just after they'd left for the airport. At least with good old fashioned telegrams, someone used to ring the doorbell. With e-mail, the machine didn't even have to be switched on. Words crept silently down the telephone wires and into the machine at all hours without so much as a chirp or a tring. With Nevil away, she hadn't bothered to check, because anything important usually went to the office anyway.

At first the words on the screen made no sense to her, and she drummed her fingers on the desk, puzzling. The sender was no problem – Brian Gaskill, whom she vaguely remembered as another of the ex-Saudi crowd. The heading was *Tiger Country*, and the rest simply said *Possible tie-in with funding for above. Take care.*

Was *Tiger Country* simply businessman's jargon for a tricky mission, and the whole thing no more than some extra information Nevil should have had? But suppose it wasn't. What was the 'above' that needed funding? Could *Tiger Country* be a code name for some deal or project? One thing was sure, it couldn't possibly mean real tigers – not in Sri Lanka. There weren't any left, and wild life was hardly Nevil's line of country. Tamil Tigers? Guerrilla armies always needed funding – in which case the 'Take care', used so casually these days, might actually be some kind of warning.

With her pulse rate rising, she forced herself to sit back and consider the logic of all this, then told herself she was being utterly daft. At the same time, Brian wouldn't have bothered to send the message if it wasn't somehow important to Nevil. Perhaps she should reply, saying he'd already left but that the message would be delivered tomorrow, by herself.

Feeling a bit more sensible, she typed in a suitable answer and tried to send it, but after several attempts the computer gave up with an annoying 'not found' message. Whatever e-mail address Brian had been using last Sunday, he certainly wasn't using it now. Such things only existed in something called cyberspace, and gave no indication of the sender's true whereabouts, except that it seemed to be outside the UK.

She printed Brian's strange message out, switched off and put the sheet in her hand luggage which was already packed and ready to go. All this had taken longer than expected, and there wasn't that much time left if she was going to sort out the last minute chores and get to the airport hotel for dinner and an early night before tomorrow's flight. Nevertheless, leaving out a note saying, *No milk until further notice* gave her an odd twinge, and, on double-checking all the doors again, she realised that she had absolutely no idea when they'd be back.

'If you'd like something to read, madam,' said the smiling stewardess, 'there's some magazines in the rack. It's a very long flight.'

'It certainly is,' replied Fran. Flying was one of the rare occasions when she regretted being taller than

34

average. Her legs felt like compressed springs, and they weren't even at Bahrain yet. But it could have been worse: she could have been fat like the man in the seat beside her who was into serious overspill. 'Oh yes, thanks,' she added, noticing for the first time that there were other things in the rack by the emergency exit apart from escape plans and duty free price lists.

She spotted a well-thumbed *Time* magazine, South-East Asian edition, and then snatched it out of the rack when she saw that the front cover featured the political troubles in Sri Lanka.

She asked for some water, then reluctantly went back and squeezed into her seat. After five minutes of tight American journalese she began to feel much more clued in on the whole subject of separatist movements in the region. Then a sub-heading caught her eye and almost made her spill her drink. *Who's funding who?* it blared, with a listing of governments, organisations and undercover groups thought to be involved with each group.

Funding? Brian's message had mentioned funding. It had to be a coincidence, she told herself, and really it wasn't much more than a round-up of all the usual suspects – Libya, the CIA, international drug cartels, assorted mafias and the like. For the Tamil Tigers it simply said: *Affiliated ethnic groups on the Indian sub-continent and elsewhere*. Was there more? She returned to the main article again. At the end was a paragraph that put her breathing on hold. *Efforts to stop arms reaching the Tigers northern stronghold round Jaffna have so far been concentrated on monitoring ships and fishing boats using the narrow straits between Sri Lanka and the mainland. The government however is becoming increasingly concerned that outside business interests are being used to launder funds for the guerrillas.* If that wasn't enough, there was a concluding piece about bodies being found in the lagoons round Colombo, mostly of young Tamils thought to have had Tiger connections.

'Another drink, madam?'

'Yes please!' she replied rather too enthusiastically. Fourteen hours of this!

At Bahrain she bought a large bottle of mineral water and a replacement for the magazine now tucked into her bag. The acrid heat from the tarmac took her breath away, but even in the welcome cool of the transit building she couldn't relax. For most of the hour they had to wait, she paced up and down the aisles of duty frees like a caged animal. A tiger? she wondered wryly. She'd always thought them the most wonderful of creatures. But no, right now, anything but a tiger. A small domestic tabby perhaps . . .

There was only an hour of daylight left when they landed in Colombo. By then she had almost convinced herself that her panic at the magazine article had been brought on by being cooped up for a whole day crossing time zones with flickering in-flight movies and grotty airline food.

The noticeable police presence at the airport hardly delayed things at all, and even the death-by-bullock-cart antics of the taxi driver didn't stop her enjoying the ride into town against the pink and violet fantasy of a tropical sunset. All she wanted now was a very cold shower, food that didn't taste of plastic and a good joke with Nevil about her mid-air imaginings.

After the jostling, dusky chaos outside, the lobby of the hotel was a vast, cool no-man's-land of potted palms and gleaming glass. Fran looked eagerly round the clusters of sofas and armchairs hoping Nevil would be somewhere around and by himself so she could run into his arms with a whoop.

When she didn't see him, she made for the reception desk, introduced herself and asked them to buzz Nevil's room.

'Ah, Mrs Merrick,' said the clerk. 'We received your fax of course, but we discovered too late, you see. Most unfortunate. You did not know your husband was leaving?'

'I'm sorry?' said Fran, feeling totally at a loss. 'You mean he's not here?'

'He checked out yesterday morning.'

'*What?* Did he say where? I mean, has he gone back to England? I can't believe it.' Suddenly she felt quite weak.

Under the circumstances, she might have expected a bit more sympathy, but the young man was looking round as if hoping she would go before somebody spotted her spoiling the decor. What the hell was going on?

'Look, I've just arrived. I can't leave until I've got some idea of where he's gone,' she said firmly. 'Did he book a taxi or something? Where to – the airport?'

With almost furtive speed, the clerk checked through a tatty record book. 'Mr Merrick, isn't it? Room 404. He used a hotel taxi, but not for the airport.'

'Then for where?'

There was an embarrassed pause. Damn, of course, he wants a tip, she thought and rummaged in her bag.

'The taxi was for the Blue Peacock. Does madam know it?'

'No, but whatever it is, can I order a taxi there? I mean, is it possible to stay there?'

'If madam wishes,' replied the clerk stone-faced, pocketing the rupees she had pushed towards him and pressing a brass bell button.

'Thanks a lot,' said Fran, not very sincerely. 'And please cancel my reservation.'

It was only a moment before a small, dark-faced plump man appeared. There was a rapid exchange at the desk and she was shown out to a waiting car.

'Where exactly is the Blue Peacock,' she asked before getting in. Colombo had turned out to be a much bigger town than she'd thought.

'Three hundred rupees fare, madam. Too much traffic.'

Was that an answer? She did a quick calculation. It couldn't be very far for that price, although it was still probably too much, but she was in no mood to haggle.

Strangely, the little cabby seemed ill at ease, even reluctant to get back in the cab. 'You from England, madam? You don't know the Blue Peacock.' The last part did not sound like a question.

Curious, and not ruling out the possibility of an expensive goose-chase all over town, she said, 'Why – should I? Is it a good place?'

'It is not a good place,' he said emphatically. 'No good for nice ladies.'

'Oh dear,' she said faintly, which didn't adequately describe what she was feeling just then. The phrase 'I'll kill him' briefly flashed in neon across her mind, while around her, the thick, sticky tropical night was pulsing with alien life forms. Meanwhile, her only human means of connecting with any of this was looking as if he was about to hijack her bags. She had to do something, however crazy, to give herself time to think.

'For four hundred rupees,' she said, 'will you take me to a hotel cheaper than this one,' and she nodded back at the bright lights of the InterContinental, 'but suitable for ladies?'

So OK, first a shower and a change of everything somewhere quiet and not too pricey. Then she'd find Nevil – and *then* she'd kill him.

The little man suddenly broke into relieved smiles and tossed her bags into the car. 'I will show you a good place, madam,' he said. 'Very clean, very suitable.'

And with a lurch, they were off into the teeming, humid darkness.

# Chapter Three

Fran looked at the dark silhouette of the driver's head and tried to remember the last time she had let her life get so stupidly out of control. There'd been that time in Rome, backpacking with Melanie from college, when they got locked out of the youth hostel. Melanie hadn't helped by sitting on the steps and crying, but they'd survived the night by tying scarves over their heads and pretending in very bad Italian to be student nuns from Poland. Even at eighteen, some inner sense had told her that it was no good looking aimless and vulnerable – you had to have a cover story and stick to it, even if it meant doing an all-night crawl of half the churches in Rome, lighting candles and kneeling a lot.

'You from England, ma'am?'

The question startled her, but the next one would be, 'Which part?', so she forestalled it with a cheerful, 'Yes, just outside London.' Her brain was still refusing to come up with anything more, which was a pity, because next it would be, was she on holiday – although by now it must have been obvious that she wasn't with any kind of package trip. So what *would* she be doing here? Apart from looking for her husband, who seemed to have gone missing, care of the obviously disreputable Blue Peacock. Perhaps not the best thing to admit to right now.

'I take photos,' she said, leaning forward. 'For, er, magazines. I was told the Blue Peacock would be a good place – you know – plenty of atmosphere, for taking fashion pictures and so on.'

The driver gave a frantic blast on his horn as they lurched round a wandering bullock and into the path of an oncoming bus with no lights. Fran closed her eyes and gripped the back of the driver's seat. So this was what you got for telling lies round here.

'Ooof!' gurgled the driver and spat out of the window, although whether from relief at avoiding both bus and cow, or admiration at her exciting new profession, it was hard to say.

Encouraged, she pressed on, fishing like mad, 'It's a sort of night-club, is it? Maybe it would be better if I go there in the morning to speak to the manager.'

Fran got the feeling that, had the man been Christian, he would have made the sign of the cross. 'Bad place. Too many lights.' He took his hands off the wheel at yet another hair-raising moment and mimed a kind of mini-Las Vegas of flashing decadence for her, without quite hitting anything. 'Rip-off, isn't it,' he went on, proud of his vocabulary. 'Chinese, you see,' he hissed. '*Criminals!*'

'Oh, right,' said Fran nodding sagely. Was that it? Maybe it was just a sort of clip-joint run by whatever form the Chinese underworld took round here. Triads, or something? In which case the Blue Peacock was probably no worse than a few places in Soho where you could get a mean egg fu-yong and an in-your-face girlie show, and if you didn't upset them, they didn't upset you. In which case, what was Nevil up to? That kind of thing wasn't really his style – as far as she knew.

Oh God, why was this happening? And where the

hell where they, anyway? Better start looking for
street names to remember for when she could get
hold of a map. Anything was better than looking at
the traffic. Even at this time of night, there was
enough manic energy around to light up a city, and
this one could certainly have done with some help
in that department, plus a few other mod cons beside – like pavements, drains and halt signs. Those
signs she could read were either a meaningless
jumble of local scripts or oddly comforting, if slightly
adrift – Brighton College, Melford Crescent, the
Roxy Cinema – *Kensington Gardens?* Neat little con-
vent schools sat primly among panel beaters' yards,
huddled shacks and sandy wastes of market debris.
Here and there, great golden images of the seated
Buddha in bandstand-sized shrines knotted around
with tinsel, rubbed shoulders with larger than life
Sacred Hearts and blue-cloaked Virgin Maries, all lit
up like Christmas cribs against the benighted lanes
off the main road.

Without warning, the taxi took a right into a side
lane whose mud-spattered sign declared it as St
Anthony's Avenue. There was barely room for two
cars to pass without scraping the high, moulding
walls topped with glass on either side. The lane itself
had possibly once had a single strip of tar skim,
judging from the sudden bumping and bouncing.
Fran gripped the back of the seat more tightly, but
then noticed that much of the claustrophobic darkness was caused by overhanging trees. The smell of
exhaust fumes faded and a sudden honey-scent of
blossom caught at her throat. Almost hidden behind
the thick foliage she could see a few lights, of two-
storey houses and bungalows. She relaxed a little.
This was probably the Chelsea of Colombo – the old

colonial civil service area. Maybe after all she wasn't going to finish up as a Foreign Office statistic about what not to do on your holidays.

The taxi jerked to a halt and Fran peered out, relieved to see some kind of low, whitewashed building at the end of a short drive.

St Anthony's Guest House and Tea Garden would not have looked much out of place if suddenly transported by angels back to some Bournemouth of the 1930's. A coat of paint and a bit of dusting wouldn't have gone amiss and the huge fruit bats wheeling eerily in the trees might have caused a few raised eyebrows, but the brass water pots of palms and ferns on the veranda would have gone down very well.

'Nice place, very clean,' said the driver. 'Garden is very good for photos of weddings and all that.'

Agreeably surprised that he wasn't showing signs of following her inside to ask for a commission, she over-tipped him, took his card and went in. Whatever this was, it would have to do, for one night anyway. Inside, the place smelt reassuringly of floor polish or disinfectant, depending on whereabouts you were standing. There was no air conditioning, which she had always disliked, but there were big brass ceiling fans, and the manageress had a warm smile. Fran took to the place immediately and was soon flopped out on the faded cotton quilt in her room, wondering what on earth she was going to do next.

A sleepy girl brought her a tiny brown pot of tea on a tin tray, with two Nice biscuits on a chipped, flowery plate, and Fran felt revived enough to be quite touched by it. This was so much nicer than the InterContinental – or would be, if only Nevil was here. It also made her realise how late it was, because

43

it was pretty obvious that she'd woken everyone up by arriving after ten.

She glanced at the antiquated phone by the bed. There wasn't a phone book, and she'd have to wake everyone up again if she tried to get the number of the Blue Peacock. The last thing she remembered, before the dull thud of jet-lag caught up with her, was watching a pair of geckos mating chirpily on the ceiling and thinking how lucky they were.

She woke still fully dressed, with the sun bright on the walls. Her watch said just after six, but she quickly gave up any attempt to work out what her own biological clock might be telling her to do. This was here, and that was that. Now – one step at a time, sweet Jesus, as the nuns always used to say: shower, breakfast, phone.

The phone book was kept behind the counter downstairs, and it was a simple matter to find the number of the Blue Peacock. In the lobby was a little statue of St Anthony – the user-friendly one who helped you find things. He was gazing in holy wonder at the vase of plastic carnations in front of him. But was he any good at finding husbands? In case he was, Fran gave the tonsured head a friendly pat, and then wondered if she was being condescending. Funny how fear brought it all back. If this went on, she'd be popping into churches lighting candles, or burning incense at roadside shrines – this was not the time to be choosy. Nor the place to ring the Blue Peacock, not with the manageress beaming at her and asking if she wanted to stay another night.

'I'd like to, but I've got a couple of calls to make,' Fran told her, waving vaguely in the direction of her room. 'Is it OK if I let you know by ten o'clock?'

'Is OK.' The smiling face was tilting from side to side in that almost flirting gesture which suited the women more than the men. 'Midday is OK.'

The place was hardly full. A young couple, immaculately dressed and shy with each other had been the only other people at breakfast. Fran had smiled at them. Honey-mooners, probably – how sweet. Staying on another night, if she had to, didn't look as if it would be a problem.

'We have a big reception this evening,' said the manageress, as if reading her mind. 'Wedding – many people.'

But of course, Colombo was not the kind of place where cheap rooms stayed empty for long. Fran nodded, went up to her room and had to uncross her fingers before she dialling the number of the Blue Peacock.

'Good morning to you,' she began brightly, hoping in typical Brit fashion that this would penetrate whatever was being said at the other end. 'I would like to make a reservation.'

It could have been the sound of a European female voice that had temporarily thrown her listener, because the answer, when one came, was fluent enough.

'You want meal and show? For how many, please?'

'Ah – I was thinking of a room. You do have accommodation?'

There was a long pause. 'For special guests.' The accent could have been Chinese. Actually, it could have been any nationality. 'You from a company? We make special arrangements for, ah, business groups.'

I bet you do, thought Fran. Definitely Chinese – or maybe Thai . . . 'I see,' she replied smoothly. She had her story ready now. 'Yes indeed, we're Mayers Asia Ltd., the telecommunications people,' (she'd pulled that one out well – better to use her maiden name than something she might forget later) 'and you were recommended by one of our clients a Mr Nevil Merrick. I believe Mr Merrick is with you at the moment. He wants a meeting with my boss. Could I book him in for tonight. That's Mr Peter Mayer,' (her father, probably still sound asleep back home in Hatfield, would have been tickled to know about all this). 'I'm sure the gentlemen will want to make their own, er, entertainment arrangements with you later. Assuming Mr Merrick is still there . . . ?' She let her voice trail off hopefully, professionally, while un-bidden, an image of Nevil zonked out on tigerskin rug with a red-nailed oriental tart swam before her eyes.

'One moment, please.'

Fran crossed everything again and made beseech-ing faces at the ceiling.

'Sorry, miss,' said the voice, as if sorrow was the last thing on its mind. 'We had no Mr Mellick staying here last night. Maybe he just took in the show. Maybe he liked, and will come back tonight, so your boss can come and find him. We have special business discounts. No need to book.'

'Thanks. There must have been a misunderstand-ing. I'll get onto it.'

Well-trained from years of abortive calls, care of Merrick and Baldwyn, Fran put the phone down with deliberate care to stop herself doing it perma-nent damage. Now what? She was hardly going to admit defeat after just one dead-end call and yet here, where she didn't know the rules . . . But they had phones and faxes, didn't they? Well, maybe not a fax at this place, which was one drawback to all the old colonial charm.

Hurriedly she did some calculations. It was nearly half past eight here. Five hours and a half hours backwards. Weird, that extra half hour. Sugar! It was only three o'clock in the morning at home, and they'd all be still sound asleep. It was ridiculous. How dare they be? She was pacing up and down now. Tony would probably be up by about seven o'clock, assuming he was actually at his flat and not with some female somewhere, but he was bound to check his fax before he left for the office. She knew his number by heart. If he had been in on all this and had been holding out on her, she'd have his guts for garters – at some unspecified time in the future. And when she got to a fax, she'd better send one home and to the office too, just in case Nevil had actually left Colombo last night and was on his way back.

Her notepad was by now a jumble of numbers, half-started scenarios and lists of things she might try. Dad? But what could he do? Amazingly, she found herself smiling. When it turned out, as it almost certainly would, that all this had been a complete waste of time and that Nevil had decided to take a night flight home after a quick drink with some old friends at the Blue Peacock, just to surprise her by coming back early for once, she'd take great delight in telling her father that her trip had all been his fault. Except that it wasn't. They were chancers, all three of them, but each had limits to their lunacy, and Fran felt that this time she had definitely reached hers.

'You can make a fax from Mr Silva's shop on Galle Road, two blocks from the big mosque,' the manageress told her, and produced a hand-drawn,

messily printed and very grubby sketch map showing where they were, although in relation to what,
Fran couldn't quite make out. 'You want taxi?'

She tried to remember the dark lane they'd come
down last night. It wasn't that far from the main
road, and Mr Silva's shop was not even as far again as
that, according to the map. 'About ten minutes to
walk?' she guessed, and the manageress smilingly
waggled her head from side to side again. Fran took
it as a yes. She had three to four hours before anyone
would be awake at home, which took her rather close
to midday and a decision about whether to stay on.

'I'd like to stay another night, please,' she told the
manageress. What the hell – she had nothing much
else to do. If she heard Nevil was on his way home,
why not take another day or so just to say she'd seen
Colombo, and serve him right.

The walk back to the main road cheered her up. The
morning was sparkling clear and it wasn't yet too
sticky. Overhead, the branches that had seemed so
threatening last night threw a lacy veil of shade over
the pockmarked surface of the lane, and the fruit bats
which had flittered eerily across the moon were now
hitched in untidy rows like folding umbrellas in some
derelict lost property office. As she walked, Fran composed what she had to say, in that peculiar style that
was half telegram, half phone call which faxes
seemed to require. For Tony it would have to be
something like – *Urgent – Nevil not at InterCont. Any
ideas where he might be? I'm at St Anthony's Guest House
and Tea Garden, yes really – run by nuns – well, no, but
it's fine, and cheap. Please phone the number below as soon
as you get this. He's not at the Blue Peacock, in case that's
in his contact book, and it had better not be, by the sound of*

*it. I've tried that. If he shows up, give him a kiss and a kick from me. But I need to know what's going on right NOW.*

From home, it was going to sound a bit like the old joke: 'If you get there first, you draw a blue line; if I get there first, I'll rub it out', but what else could she say, except, 'If you're there, for heaven's sake phone.' And if you're not – where the hell are you?

Mr Silva's office on Galle Road – the main road to the south, as far as Fran could make out – turned out to be a tiny room in a Sixties-vintage, single storey concrete block connected by droopy wires to almost every other building and tree in sight. Next door was a place selling TV's, computers and similar electronic equipment of considerable sophistication, considering the surroundings. Roped to the cracked and battered trunks of a couple of ancient neem trees were the metal grills that would protect the plate-glass windows at night, four mopeds, and a greyish, heavily pregnant cow with sad, patient eyes.

The young man in charge of the shop, which also advertised cheap rate calls to almost everywhere and a fax return service, said that for a few rupees extra, someone would deliver a return message to the guest house. He pointed to the mopeds outside.

'Brilliant!' said Fran, and told him this was better than London.

'We are calling this Tottenham Court Road,' replied the young man, who had amazing teeth when he smiled. 'My brother is working there.'

Before walking back, Fran looked in the next shop window and stared at all the camcorders, ghetto blasters and other electronic gizmos on display. Tottenham Court Road. That was where Nevil had stopped off to buy all that stuff he had thought it necessary to take with him on this trip. Surveillance quality stuff. But why?

Thoughtfully, she wandered over to the cow to give it a pat, but drew back when she saw its halo of flies. Poor cow, she thought. The traffic streamed past, but the honey smell of neem blossom – she recognised it now – still reached her through the belching fumes and exhaust heat.

She checked her watch. It would be a couple of hours at least before anyone would reply. Why waste it? Several prowling taxis had already slowed down hopefully at the sight of a lone European on the hoof. So why not go into town and at least get a decent map? It was also beginning to dawn on her that, in spite of her feeling of having handled things pretty well so far, she had really been rather slack. Suppose Nevil's night away from the InterContinental had been just a blip. Maybe he had contacts here and had been invited away for the night and would be coming back. She tried to conjure up the hotel lobby in her mind. For that time of the evening, and for a place like the InterCont, there should have been more activity if they were fully booked, and at those prices, was that likely? What was more, she hadn't even had the foresight to leave a message in case he did came back. There was bound to have been a notice board. But then, she'd been told he'd decamped to the Blue Peacock . . .

The next taxi to come by got a firm hailing, and almost upended itself in its eagerness to stop. On hearing the magic word 'InterContinental', the driver asked twice what she had been charged last night, which in any case would have carried a hotel taxi premium. Some hard bargaining followed until Fran thought she'd got him down to something like a reasonable price. The cow watched them, her flanks twitching, still munching mournfully.

As Fran had hoped, there was a different clerk at the reception this time. Fingers crossed, she made another inquiry for Mr Nevil Merrick, and got the same reply. No further bookings had been made in that name. She asked if she could leave a message on the board and moved towards the coffee shop to think about it.

On her way, crossing the huge near empty lobby she looked round, praying so hard that Nevil would miraculously appear that it almost hurt. It didn't seem right that Nevil had been here – eaten, talked, slept, in this place so recently – and that she couldn't in some way catch a hint of him, just the faintest sense of his presence. She wanted it so badly that she actually stopped half way across and inhaled deeply. But there was only that smell of – what? Coffee, leather, new carpets – that something synthetically, expensively, hygienic that you got in these places. Was it money? Did money smell like that? Perhaps they actually sprayed these places to make them all smell alike. Was there an aerosol spray which smelt like money? When all she wanted was the smell of Nevil, all over her, and right now, badly.

But that wasn't all. Her nose twitched as she padded on over the springy carpet. Lurking beneath the layers of scented camouflage was something else – dampish – mouldy – very faint, but definitely there – a kind of ancient bedrock smell of old forests, ruined temples and animal decay. And it made her shudder suddenly.

Coffee – quickly. She ordered a double cappuccino

and started to write – a chirpy, wifey, 'Hello darling, Surprise! I'm here, Where are you?' sort of note. Then she stopped. They'd give her an envelope for it, of course, so no one else was going to read it. But suppose someone did.

Oh come on, she scolded herself. Don't let's be dramatic here. But seriously, suppose there was any kind of, well – problem. She'd always accepted that there was more going on at Merrick & Baldwyn than they often told her. Much of it was probably harmless, and almost all of it would be boring, but there were some very funny people in business these days. Especially when it came to foreign deals.

She took a gulp of the coffee and almost burnt herself. Not that Nevil would ever do anything illegal – all right, not morally wrong anyway. It was a distinction he recognised, or she wouldn't have fallen for him, she was certain of that. But the line was a fine one, and not everyone agreed where it should be drawn. And some of those people who couldn't see it at all could be very awkward indeed. It had all been said before, by her father, quoting Kipling almost seriously: *Ship me somewhere East of Suez, where the best is like the worst, Where there aren't no Ten Commandments, and a man can raise a thirst* . . . Quoted not seriously at all by Nevil and Tony who'd heard it from Dad, usually when they'd had a few drinks with their pals from the Saudi days.

Yet Nevil had promised her – promised that there'd be no more skating on thin ice. Not promised not to tell her if there was; but simply that there wouldn't be. So why did this trip not feel right? It had never felt right, from the minute she'd known he was coming here. She wasn't normally given to this much nervous tension when Nevil wasn't where he should have been, and that had been often enough. If she'd have stayed home like a good girl, she'd never have known anything about it anyway.

Strangely, that thought didn't comfort her. If she'd caught him out this time . . . No, that wasn't right. She hadn't caught him out at all – wasn't trying to. Yet the feeling was always there just below the carefully polished surface of things, that she didn't really know her husband at all. And if she didn't know him, how could she know his friends?

On the off-chance – the paranoid, long-shot, off-chance that someone who shouldn't might open the envelope and realise Nevil Merrick's wife was around, she carefully tore up the first note. Silly, silly, she recited to herself, but quickly wrote another, briefer version sounding more like a business contact, giving the address and phone number of St Anthony's and asked him to ring immediately. She dithered about giving the address. But then, if she gave only a number, all anyone had to do was ring it anyway, to see who answered. She didn't put her name, just 'F', knowing that Nevil would recognise her writing immediately. He'd claimed often enough not to be able to decipher her strong, slanting scrawl when they'd worked together.

The envelope was duly pinned onto the board. She bought a decent map of Colombo at the hotel shop, and a touring map of the whole island, just to show herself that she hadn't given up on the idea of a trip down the coast together when Nevil finally pitched up. Feeling she'd done all she possibly could for the time being, she decided to get back to St Anthony's, calling at Mr Silva's on the way, and sweat it out until someone made contact.

With a vaguely grim feeling that she might need all

the friends she could get, even if they did charge more, she produced last night's driver's grubby card at the desk, and felt ridiculously glad to see him when he appeared. I'm being pathetic, she thought, vowing that when Nevil did show up, she wasn't going to admit to any of this. In business, you had to do things their way. If you had a bad feeling about something, the rule was that you played it cautiously. But then one person's caution could very quickly be seen as hysterical over-reaction. Of course, she wasn't getting hysterical. She was just being careful, that's all.

A bad *feeling*? What was she saying? In business, it was better not to feel at all.

'Everything very busy today,' volunteered the driver as they ground to a halt for the third time within a few minutes of leaving the hotel. The traffic certainly seemed a lot thicker than an hour or so ago. The next time, they were stuck for almost ten minutes, and the impatience all around was tangible. Two police cars sped past them, sirens wailing. In the stationery vehicles around her, drivers were yelling things out of windows at each other. Probably they were only trying to find out what was going on, but the rapid fire of Tamil or Sinhalese – Fran had absolutely no idea which – sounded more like the beginnings of a riot. Then it struck her that some of it was actually English. She thought she caught the word 'bomb', but couldn't be sure.

Disregarding the heat and fumes, she put her head out of the window and tried to tune in. Rising above it all, more sirens could be heard, and bells.

'Is that a fire engine?' asked Fran, hoping to diffuse the driver's now obvious agitation.

'Fire – big fire,' he told her. A whooping ambulance

went past the other way, but even that side was almost at a stand-still now.

'Oh dear,' said Fran rather limply. The heat inside the car was now quite uncomfortable and she wished she'd had the sense to bring some water.

'You want air conditioning? Please close window.'

She could see that they were in that unpleasant Catch 22 situation of Third World traffic jams. If you kept the engine running for the air conditioning, and everyone else did too, in the end all you breathed was the filth sucked in from everyone else's exhausts. If you shut off the engine and opened the windows, you had to pray that everyone else did the same, or it was just as bad. Behind them was a bullock cart and several run-down looking open pick-ups loaded with passengers muffled against the fumes.

'No, please shut the engine off,' she said.

Outside, others were doing the same. People were getting out and stretching, standing on the roofs of buses, trying to see ahead while continuing to assault each other with machine gun bursts of verbal energy.

Fran opened the door on the shady side, kicked off her sandals and stuck her melting feet outside. She was wondering if she could smell burning in the air, but it might just as well have been simply Colombo in a traffic jam.

'My name is Francesca,' she said, leaning forward and offering the driver her hand. 'My husband is out here on business. Now tell me about your family, Mr Sanjay. And whereabouts do you live? Is it near here?'

Half an hour later they were still in the same place. They were on first name terms, she knew enough about Rajev's numerous family to fill a small book, and she was gratefully sharing swigs of tepid tea from a metal bottle kept under his seat. He was a Tamil, and had begun to show her the difference in the two main local scripts by pointing to shop signs. At this rate, she'd soon be trying out a few sentences.

'This must be a very big fire,' she ventured at last.

'I thought you must be hearing,' he said, waggling his head from side to side. 'It is a bomb, you see. That man over there has a radio in his car. He is telling everyone and blaming the Tamil Tigers. Very bad for visitors.'

'Very bad for everybody. Has anyone been killed?'

'Thirty, he is saying, but nothing is certain.'

'Thirty! Don't the Tigers give any warning, then?'

He shrugged unhappily. 'They are very bad people. Bad for all of us.'

Ah, thought Fran. Divided loyalties.

'You know,' she said. 'We have the IRA. You've heard of them? Well, my mother's family was Irish, you see. She's dead now, for some time, but she didn't like what the IRA are doing. It is a problem, isn't it?'

The plump little man agreed that such things were indeed a problem. He looked at a man with a mobile phone who was relaying some heated information to the people around from the sun roof of his Mercedes. 'He is Sinhalese.' he said without further explanation.

'Speak English, please,' yelled someone in the pick-up behind. 'What is happening?'

'It is a car bomb, in the Fort district.'

'But that's behind us, isn't it?' asked Fran, looking at her map. Fort was the original part of the town, she knew that by now. The main railway station was called Fort, and it was the central commercial and hotel district.

'The police have put road blocks all round. They always do it. They think they will catch them.'

'What is he saying? Is it the government offices they were after?'

'He does not know, but he is blaming the Tigers. So many people are dead and wounded because there was a bus passing.'

Fran thought of the hopelessly overcrowded buses she'd seen, and winced. It was all rather depressing. She looked at her watch. Tony would soon be up, if he wasn't already. How long were they going to be stuck here, for heaven's sake?

As if in answer to her prayers, things suddenly began to happen. Horns sounded, sirens went, and people began to jump back into their simmering vehicles. As if in some sort of tension relief therapy, everyone began to sound their horns at once.

'Galle Road is open,' said Rajev, who obviously knew where the road block had been posted. 'Soon we will move.'

As the taxi began to crawl forward and then accelerate, Fran realised that every piece of clothing was stuck to her all over. Gently she pulled various parts loose and shook them around, pleasantly surprised when she began to dry out quite quickly by the open window.

She asked Rajev to drop her at Mr Silva's. Outside the next door shop, a small crowd had gathered, presumably to watch the news of the bombing on the numerous TV's, even if they couldn't hear it. She went in. A radio was blaring away in the corner. The young man got up excitedly to greet her and said that a fax had arrived and already been sent round to St Anthony's. She paid him, and asked to see it.

Eagerly she scanned the sheet he printed out for

her. It was from Tony, and it read: *Sorry, love, no info here. What can our boy be up to? Maybe something's cropped up. Not to worry – he'll show up when he's ready. Advise you come home soon if you don't find him. Enjoy the waving palm trees while you can. Dull and windy here. Love, Tony.*

Terrific! Fran stared at the sheet.

'Nothing is bad, I hope,' asked the young man politely.

'No, no,' murmured Fran, turning to go. 'I just got caught in a bad traffic jam this morning, and I didn't meet the person I was supposed to.'

'Ah, yes, the bomb. Very bad.' Why was he smiling? Maybe everyone smiled here. The radio was still rabbitting on in excited Asian English. She paused, listening.

'. . . the Tamil Separatists have not yet claimed responsibility, although the kind of car bomb used bears all their usual hallmarks . . .' It was all depressingly familiar. 'It was not clear what was the intended target of the bomb. The car with the explosives was parked outside a well-known night-club in the Fort District, the Blue Peacock, and it is thought that the detonation may have been mistimed. People worried about relatives in the area . . .'

'Are you feeling faint, ma'am?' asked the young man anxiously. 'Shall I bring a glass of water?'

'Yes, please,' said Fran, and sat down hard on the metal folding chair by the counter. 'A glass of water, and I'll be fine. Just fine.'

# Chapter Four

Back in her room, Fran sat on the bed and tried to come to grips with the situation. She hadn't had the courage to tell her new-found taxi driver friend what she'd heard at Mr Silva's, and was wondering if he'd noticed any change in her behaviour. Maybe outwardly she'd seemed calm, but she still felt as if an acid poker was trying to get up her throat. Mechanically, she reached into her medicine kit for some indigestion tablets. Maybe crunching them would make the fear would go away.

It didn't. The more she thought about it, the worse it got. It couldn't be a coincidence, *couldn't* be, that the bomb had gone off outside the Blue Peacock. One of the things her father always said was that he didn't believe in coincidences. Dad's Golden Rules. More often than not, she'd found they worked. So far. They gave a kind of shape to life when it was all looking a bit messy, but if she ever wanted this one to be proved utterly, comprehensively wrong, it was now.

But how many night-clubs were there in Colombo anyway? Quite a few, from the listings in her guide book and the pamphlets she picked up. So why this one, and why now? No matter how she tried to shake it off, an icy suspicion was seeping into her that Nevil's apparent disappearance was somehow connected with the bombing.

If you're in a blue funk, do something. Action, however useless, made you feel less of a victim. Dad again? She knuckled her forehead. What had the radio been saying? But of course, what they always said over things like this. Emergency numbers to contact. Damn! She cast around hopefully for a room radio, but that would have been asking a bit much of a modest place like this. Downstairs then. There'd be one somewhere.

'This is most distressing,' said the manageress, still beaming, but sympathetically, as Fran made her request. 'We have been listening ourselves, of course.'

'You see, I'm a *little* bit worried about my husband. I think he might have been in the Fort area around that time – on business. And I was hoping to meet him this morning. Have they said if any Westerners were among the dead or injured?'

The manageress stopped smiling, took a deep breath and let out an operatic burst of complicated syllables in the direction of the kitchen quarters. There was a pause, then the sound of a door opening, and an older  man's voice answered at some length and at a similar pitch.

'Papa says it is now thirty-two who are dead, and only one is a Westerner. Maybe one hundred are wounded, and one of the serious ones is a Westerner, but a woman.' She saw Fran's face had changed colour and grasped her hand. 'Trust in God. The dead man will not be your husband.'

'No, no,' whispered Fran. 'Of course not. But I have to check. Who can I phone, please?'

'Come,' said the woman briskly and beckoned Fran to follow her to the kitchen quarters.

An elderly man pulling on a shirt over his singlet

and striped *sarama* emerged from a low block that
seemed to double as the staff quarters, judging by the
quantities of bedding and washing around. Inside,
Fran could hear a television, and after a brief conversation in English, the man said he would write down
the emergency number displayed on the screen.

'I don't think you will get through,' said the
manageress. This was a feeling Fran shared as she
thanked them. She and the manageress went back to
the hall phone, where they tried for at least fifteen
minutes.

'But there is something you can do,' said the
manageress. 'This number is almost certainly a
general police number. In our country we also have
the Tourist Police. Maybe by now they will know
who these unfortunate Westerners are. The main
office is in Fort, I think, but there is also one nearer
here, at Mount Lavinia.'

Fran felt the cloud lifting slightly. 'Perhaps I
should just get a taxi there. Maybe they'll be able to
find out for me.'

'Then I will come with you. I am Mrs Marianiya-
gam, but for you people, I think Mrs Mario is easier.'

'That's really very kind . . .'

On the way out, the manageress paused briefly
before the little statue with its plastic flowers and
made the traditional hands-joined greeting gesture.
It looked very like an emergency prayer.

'He is always very good to widows,' carolled Mrs
Mario. Then she paused and giggled. 'That is, I am a
widow - you are not a widow.'

Instinctively, Fran copied the prayer gesture. No
she wasn't, not yet, and she'd be very grateful if
St Anthony could keep it that way.

A taxi took them back onto the Galle Road, heading

south from Colombo. The Tourist Police Office, not very imposing at first sight, was attached to an information centre down a smaller road that led towards the sea. Mrs Mario marched in towing Fran by the wrist like a reluctant daughter. At the desk was a young and very smart-looking policewoman.

Briefly Mrs Mario explained the problem, and it was clear that if the policewoman didn't know the guest house personally, she recognised the breed.

'But of course, I shall do what I can,' she replied in brisk, clear English, and as she looked Fran firmly in the eye, Fran got an immediate sense of keen, almost impatient intelligence. She'd seen that look before – usually in women who were someone's personal assistant, in outfits not unlike Merrick & Baldwyn. It usually meant they were brighter than their bosses.

The crisply uniformed back disappeared into the side office. There was some conversation and the sound of someone on the phone, then the noise of a printer.

The policewoman reappeared with a printout and a notepad, but disconcertingly said nothing except, 'Could you give me a few details, Mrs Merrick – about your husband?'

She's knows something, thought Fran. It's like having to describe your handbag and then say exactly how much was in it, so they'll know – oh God.

'I'm sorry . . ?' Why had her brain stopped working?

'Your husband. Could you describe him for me?'

'Well, he's got brown hair, and sort of greenish-brown eyes . . .'

'I see.' A kind of stillness had come over the police-woman, as if she didn't quite know what next to say.

'I'm sorry, but I'll need something more than that,' she said. 'You see, in these sad cases where there is a bad fire and lots of glass, it isn't always possible . . .'

'Jesus,' said Fran and felt her legs going. The body must be unrecognisable.

'His height. How tall was he? *Is* he?' The policewoman corrected herself quickly. 'Taller than you, maybe?'

Fran nodded dumbly.

'So that makes him very tall, your husband?' The woman was trying so hard to help her. Some part of Fran's brain was still trying to register that, since arriving, she had been very conscious of her height, more so than at home. 'He's five feet eleven,' she breathed. Were they metric here?

The tense, bright face opposite broke into a smile of relief. 'Then you can relax, Mrs Merrick. This victim, the only male Westerner involved, seems to have been a very young man, and possibly about five feet eight or nine. He was wearing sandals and shorts. They think he might have been a backpacker, although his pack is still missing, so we haven't a name. It is possible he was on the bus with the girl who is in intensive care. She seems to be Australian. Maybe he was, too . . .'

'Oh, the poor things!' Mrs Mario was holding a handkerchief to her eyes. 'So young. What of their parents . . .?'

'Terrible,' murmured the policewoman. 'I think we all need a cup of tea.'

She shouted something into the office, while Fran concentrated hard on the grain in the wood of the counter. It wasn't Nevil. It wasn't him. She wasn't a widow . . . Thank you, God, St Anthony, whoever . . . 'Thank you,' she said aloud, while Mrs Mario patted

63

her arm in a motherly way and began chirping away to the policewoman about what the world was coming to and the wickedness of it all.

Almost sick with relief, Fran said nothing until the tea came, in enamel mugs with some kind of government stamp. It tasted wonderful, and she said so.

'So it should,' smiled the policewoman. 'We do grow the stuff here, after all.'

The two women laughed, and Fran found she could smile again.

'Maybe you need some sea air to bring back your English roses. Ladies, let's take a walk,' said the policewoman, surprisingly. 'It's only a few minutes away. You know,' she continued, as they followed her outside with their mugs, 'sometimes this place reminds me of Brighton.' She gave a wry smile, as if remembering something not entirely pleasant. 'Except there's no pier.'

'But you've got some terrific palm trees,' laughed Fran, now feeling positively light-headed with relief. 'You know Brighton? Really?'

'I did six months there, on secondment. Good language schools, too.'

'Obviously,' said Fran.

'And before that, three years doing Sociology at Warwick, on a police scholarship.'

Well now, thought Fran, having almost recovered her wits. So what's a bright girl like you doing behind the counter of a Tourist Police Office, I wonder. Maybe she was head of station. The way she'd ordered the tea and then left with only a quick word telling them where she was going seemed to suggest it. For someone her age, which Fran guessed to be about her own, being in charge of a small office in the upmarket Mount Lavinia area might have seemed like a good career move. Yet Fran had a feeling the woman was bored.

They found a seat overlooking the beach where a rather splendid white neo-classical pile could be seen on a rocky promontory.

'You know it?' asked the policewoman, seeing Fran's interest. 'Our famous Mount Lavinia Hotel – once the out-of-town retreat of the British governor, except that it's hardly out of town any more.'

'It does look rather spiffing.' Fran mimicked a Raj accent, and got a smile.

'Named after the old boy's wife. Mount Lavinia. Maybe not the wisest of names, with a lot of randy young officers about.'

Surprised, Fran couldn't help a snort of amusement. 'I see what you mean.'

Mrs Mario giggled too, but Fran doubted that she'd got the joke.

'So tell me, Mrs Merrick, you say your husband is here on business. Yet he's not with you at Mrs Mario's?'

The question was put almost idly, but Fran reminded herself she was still talking to the police.

'Um, no,' she replied, thinking quickly. 'I'm not particularly keen on big hotels – and they're very pricey. My husband's isn't a big firm, so all the expenses are down to us, but he has to be there to impress clients.'

'Is it a construction firm, perhaps? We have so much going on in Colombo at the moment, what with the Trade Centre and all that. The Fort area is barely recognisable these days. Mind you, as fast as we build them, some wretched terrorist is trying to blow them up.'

There was a real edge in her voice. She's not Tamil;

65

I bet she's the other lot – Sinhalese, thought Fran, wondering where the questions were going. 'Not construction, just boring old finance,' she said lightly.

'Oh, I don't find finance boring at all. I used to be in the Fraud section, you see, until . . .' The voice had lost its edge and tailed off. 'Well, let's say I appreciate the fresh air down here. But I'm still wondering. You didn't have any particular reason to believe that your husband might have had connections with the Blue Peacock?'

The directness of the question caught Fran off guard, but not for long. Evasion – it would have to be. 'I hadn't even heard of the Blue Peacock until – all this.' Ouch, she'd almost said "until last night", which would rather have given the game away. 'What's so bad about the place?'

'Most things,' was the cool reply. 'If people have to let off bombs, I couldn't have chosen a better target myself.'

'So you think this, er, Blue Peacock was the real target? They were hinting on the radio that maybe it was a mistake that the bomb went off just there.'

'I think they meant hitting the bus as well was the mistake. It's not usually the Tigers' style, hitting buses, although God knows they can be inept. It antagonises too many people.'

'Has anyone claimed responsibility yet?'

'Oh, everyone will say it is the Tigers, even if they deny it,' put in Mrs Mario unexpectedly.

'Yes,' said the policewoman with a sigh. 'They certainly will. Well now, I think I had better be getting back, if you have recovered from your fright, Mrs Merrick, or those clowns back there will be handing people back the wrong wallets and cameras.'

'You've been very kind,' said Fran as they retraced

their steps. 'I only hope a Sri Lankan tourist in a similar position back home would be treated as kindly.'

'Perhaps. It would depend.'

Fran nodded wryly. She found she rather liked this woman, and could quite happily have talked more with her – if only she wasn't a policewoman. And yet a friendly face among the police could never be a bad thing.

'This is really a very pleasant area,' she said as they walked back to the office. 'Do you have far to come to work?' There was no ring on the wedding finger.

'I live with an aunt in Bambalapitiya – bit of a mouthful, eh? Colombo 4. It's not very far.' Did the voice sound hopeful?

'You've been so kind . . .' Now was she being really stupid here? 'I was wondering if perhaps you'd like to come over to St Anthony's and have a coffee or something with me this evening. We could talk about Brighton. I have a great aunt who's got a little flat in Hove, so I know it quite well. We often used to go there when my mother was alive. Would it be all right for me to entertain a guest, Mrs Mario?'

Some vigorous nodding suggested that it would.

'And maybe my husband will have shown up by then.'

'I hope so. I'd like that very much. Out of uniform, of course.' She laughed. 'My name is Charmaleine Pereira, but my English friends call me Charlie. *Called* me Charlie. There aren't so many now. As long as I'm back by ten thirty, or Auntie will be calling the police.'

They both laughed. 'Shall we say eight o'clock then?' She would have found Nevil by then. Of course she would.

67

*　　*　　*

By late afternoon, there had still been no more messages, from Nevil or Tony or anyone. As much as anything, it was the thought of having to explain away her missing husband to a policewoman, however informal the visit, that made Fran try the Inter-Continental again. She made her by now familiar inquiry as to whether anyone by the name of Merrick had checked in, and was told not.

'But I think you will soon be hearing from him,' said the receptionist, who sounded like the same one as that morning.

Fran caught her breath. 'What do you mean exactly?'

'Someone came and took the message you left.'

'That's marvellous! What time was that?'

'Let me see – about midday.'

'Oh,' said Fran, so deflated that Nevil hadn't yet called her that she stupidly added. 'You are sure it was my husband?'

'I would not know, madam. Is your husband not European? Part Chinese perhaps.'

'He most certainly is not,' said Fran. What was the man talking about? 'You can't mean that the man who took the envelope addressed to my husband was part Chinese?'

'As far as I could tell, madam. I assumed it was the right person. Or that one of them was. There were in fact two men, both East Asian in looks. They went over to look at the message board after inquiring at the desk for someone of another name, not your husband. Then they went to the message board. One pointed and took the envelope. It was the only one in an envelope today, so I remember, and then he tore it open and read it right there. Then they left.'

68

'I see.' Why on earth did people say that when they didn't see at all. Surely Nevil couldn't have asked someone to go and collect a message for him. Or if he had, whoever he'd asked would have hardly opened and read it.

'You said these people were asking for someone else. You don't by any chance remember the name, do you? Maybe it would help.'

There was a long pause, although whether it was because the receptionist was trying to remember, or whether he was wondering if he should be giving out such information, Fran wasn't sure.

'It was a strange name. English, I think. Something to do with gas.'

'Gas?' Was he making this up? 'Gaskill?' she tried, holding her breath.

'Yes, yes, that was it.'

Stunned, she asked if he was sure, and he said he was. They certainly knew a Brian Gaskill. It was Brian who had tried to e-mail Nevil before he left, but had just missed him, and the message had sounded as if it was connected with the trip.

'And did you have a Mr Gaskill booked in?' Please, oh please.

'No, ma'am.'

Her heart sank again. 'These, er, Chinese people. Were they staying at the hotel? Did you know them?'

'We do not know these people.'

Fran was straining to catch any nuance in his voice. Was he implying that these were the kind of people one would not wish to know? Possibly he'd had his doubts that either of these men was likely to have been the one for whom the message was intended.

How could she put this? 'So these men were

69

allowed to take a message from the board without offering identification?'

That produced a sharp reaction. 'Ma'am, it would have been unwise to ask such people for identification.'

'What do you mean – unwise?' She tried to keep her voice steady. 'I left a message with you in good faith, in that I assumed only my husband would get it.'

'Please.' He sounded quite panicky now. 'You must understand my position. One does not argue with such people. It is not hotel policy. I am over here behind the desk – they are over there. What could I do? Also . . .' He seemed to be pulling himself together again. 'It must be understood that notices are left on the board at the guests' own risk. It is a courtesy service, and we are under no obligation . . .'

'Yes, of course I understand,' she said soothingly. There was no point in upsetting him any further. 'You did what you thought was best. But I am a little concerned. Could you tell me please, in confidence, had you any reason to suspect that these people were not, shall we say, respectable? I am not blaming you in any way, of course, but for example, if necessary, would you be prepared to give a description of these men to the police?' She had nothing to lose now, and this would probably be her last chance to get anything out of this man.

There was a pause, and she could almost hear him trying to think his way out of this one. She'd made a mistake there – asked two questions instead of keeping it to one. No, two mistakes. She, a perfect stranger, had asked him to put himself on the line for her. Hadn't she? The complicated silence told her she was right.

'Would you,' she asked gently, 'be afraid to identify these men?'

'Yes, ma'am,' said the receptionist in little more than a whisper, and put down the phone.

'Oh-god, oh-god, oh-god,' muttered Fran through clenched teeth, sitting bolt upright on the bed. Strangely one half of her was pleased with herself that she handled the questions carefully enough to learn something from the man. But what she'd found had shaken her rigid. Had she got this right? She replayed the conversation in her head again, grabbed a pad and wrote down the essentials of it. Basic office training.

She looked at it again. What it boiled down to was that two men she didn't like the sound of had hijacked a personal message to Nevil, who obviously hadn't got it, or he would have contacted her by now. And they had some knowledge of Brian Gaskill, who knew Nevil, and Brian knew something about why Nevil was here. Where was that e-mail? She rummaged in her bag. *Possible tie-in with funding for above. Take care.* So what was 'the above'? It could only be the title – *Tiger Country*, and she was no nearer knowing what that meant now than when she had first seen it. But somehow, the sudden, almost personal intrusion of the Tamil Tigers into her life seemed to give the phrase a more immediate, more ominous meaning. And was Brian Gaskill really the type to end a very brief message with 'Take care' if he didn't mean it literally?

Fran shut her eyes and tried to conjure up the man she'd met only a couple of times. He was what her father might have called a hard nut. Slightly older than Nevil, thick-set, with the air of one who could handle a bar room brawl just as easily as a board room one. He'd been around, had Brian. Not a 'Take care' type. More a 'Cheers', or 'That's one you owe me'.

Then a chilling thought occurred to her. If those men at the InterContinental were in some way to be feared, they now knew where she was staying. Or at least they would have realised that someone connected with Nevil was at the guest house. On an impulse, she read Brian's e-mail a couple of times to memorise it, then tore it up, together with the notes she'd just made, and flushed the pieces down the toilet. She was a very long way from home, and until she worked out what all this was about, there was no point in taking any chances. She took a leisurely shower and washed her hair. Might as well keep up appearances – but this was hardly the way she'd been hoping to feel when it came to spending an evening with WPC Charmaleine Pereira.

# Chapter Five

Charlie arrived on the dot of eight o'clock, which was just as well, because Fran would probably not have recognised her. She was wearing a pale apricot silk sari bordered discreetly in gold, with a darker toning blouse that caught the light as she approached. Her hair was no longer oiled severely back, but hung in a loose frizzy plait over one shoulder, and her face was unmade up apart from some gloss on her full lips and a flame orange *tikka* mark on her forehead.

'Oh, you look do look nice!' said Fran, feeling rather like an ironing board beside all this rounded exotic beauty.

Charlie made the traditional hands-together greeting and then they laughed and shook hands. 'Just a simple Sri Lankan girl, you see.' In her flat sandals she barely reached Fran's shoulder, and the air of authority so much in evidence earlier had been left behind with the crisp uniform. Now Fran could sense only a warm openness which, in her tense state, she found relaxing.

'I'm so sorry Nevil hasn't arrived yet,' she murmured, hoping it sounded like the most natural thing in the world instead of the most unnerving. 'Shall we sit outside?'

'You were expecting him. What a pity . . .'

'I'm going to be really cross with him when he does show up.'

The wedding party Mrs Mario had mentioned was in full, noisy swing in the main part of the garden, but the waiter carried a spare table for Fran and Charlie through a bougainvillaea-covered arch into a quieter corner of the grounds. They skated gently around the subject of Nevil's non-appearance until Mrs Mario's daughter brought them a jug of iced lime juice which they'd decided upon instead of coffee, as the humidity seemed to be increasing instead of dropping with nightfall.

'Would you like some gin with that?' asked Fran. 'I think I saw a bottle of Gordons in the darker reaches of Mrs Mario's not-exactly cocktail bar.'

'Thanks, maybe just one, if you will too. It'll bring back a few memories. I don't get much chance to indulge these days.'

'So tell me, whereabouts were you in Brighton?'

The easy chat flowed on, with Charlie happy to talk about her digs, then the little flat; the fights they'd been called to in the dodgier pubs on a Friday night; the Ecstasy busts; tearful Spanish students; senior citizens writing off their vehicles or each other because they'd forgotten their specs . . . Then she seemed to grow quite wistful. Maybe it's the gin, thought Fran, pouring her another. Mrs Mario had brought them the bottle and some chits for her to sign as the evening went along. Fortunately, the bottle had a measurer in its cap.

Now the talk was of Sunday afternoons on the pier, shopping in The Lanes and windy walks on the Downs. She's telling me she fell in love there, thought Fran, her own problems temporarily forgotten. Careful now.

'Sounds like you really fell for the place,' she ventured. 'Weren't you sorry to leave?'

'Oh, I fell all right,' retorted Charlie. 'But it wasn't just the place. It was the usual story. Real Mills and Boon stuff, but no happy ending. I managed to get through three years at Uni with my honour intact, and not for want of offers, I can tell you. Then on my first probationary posting after graduation, I was fool enough to fall for a brother officer, and he, I thought, for me.' Her face was calm, as if she had told this story to herself a thousand times, but her hands were clenched tightly round the cheap little glass. 'He told me he was divorced. Said I wasn't just his exotic oriental piece on the side, and I thought he meant it. Then he went back to the wife and kiddy. In the end, I couldn't get out fast enough. Sorry. It's all so corny.'

'It's never corny getting your heart broken,' said Fran, making a mental note to hunt down every married policeman in Brighton next time she was down there and cut off their buttons.

'Not broken,' said Charlie, tilting her chin. 'Just damaged. That's what I am now. Damaged goods, you see.'

Fran sighed. "Surely not" and "It's not fair", didn't seem enough. So it was all still true then; Charlie's chances of making a good marriage back in Sri Lanka were now almost nil.

'And so you came home. But you'll have a brilliant career here, with all your background. And you're bright and smart. You could finish up Chief Commissioner of Police.'

'Hah! In a hundred years' time, perhaps.'

'But you've had women prime ministers – you've got one now.'

'Are police and politics the same in England, my dear? I think not.'

'You're right, of course. It's the same in business, too. That inherent conviction men have that they're born to rule. The green door, the glass ceiling and all that.'

'What do you think I'm doing stuck out at Mount Lavinia in a Tourist Police boutique?' She almost spat the words. 'As I told you, I was in Fraud and doing quite nicely. The International section – big stuff. Until one of the bigwigs, shall we say – insulted me. He had my file, you see. Knew my famous "past".'

'And he made assumptions? How typical. At home, the women PC's say it's often assumed you're either gay or anybody's.'

'Not all the men are bad – just most. Anyway, I applied for a transfer from the Colombo office just to show him – but it was the very time when we were beginning to get on to some interesting stuff. I can't go back to Fraud, so after cooling my heels down here with the stolen wallets, I've applied for something in Special.'

Fran raised her eyebrows. 'How – Special?'

'Anti-terrorism. I'm Sinhala, not Tamil, which gives me an edge. Dirty. But someone's got to do it.'

'Absolutely. Look at today.'

'Ah yes . . .'

There was a pause. Charlie seemed to be concentrating hard on the fast melting ice in her drink, as if uncertain how much to say.

'The Tigers have denied responsibility. That's not general news yet, but it will be soon, provided it suits the powers that be.'

Fran blinked. This was getting interesting. But why was Charlie telling her this?

'Now don't tell me you've got other groups who would do such a thing?'

'Maybe not groups in the sense of other terrorists. But let's say certain business interests.'

'And it might suit the people at the top to let the Tigers take the blame?'

'It might.' Charlie laughed dismissively. 'Who knows?'

You do, thought Fran. Or you have your suspicions. You worked in Fraud. But you're hardly going to tell me, a foreigner and a perfect stranger. Unless . . . you're fishing. Had the traditional clothes, the soft smiles, the relaxed girl-talk all been leading up to this? She glanced at Mrs Mario's chit. Two gins each. That was quite enough for her. 'Do have another one.' She offered the bottle to Charlie.

'Not for me. Already I shall have to chew some mint leaves or Aunty will throw me out.' Charlie looked at her watch. 'I shouldn't be much longer. But aren't you a little worried, Fran – about your husband?'

Here it comes, thought Fran, feeling a churning disappointment in her stomach. She's curious. There's something she wants to know.

She tried a dismissive laugh. 'Isn't every wife worried about her husband?'

Charlie's vivid gaze held her eyes. Dark amber to Welsh slate. Then she smiled and said, as if by way of more casual chat. 'Would you like me to tell you a little more about the Blue Peacock? I wouldn't want you to go home thinking that dear old Colombo is just faded colonial charm with a few bombs thrown in to keep us up to scratch.'

'OK, why not? I always appreciate a bit of local colour.' Why was Charlie telling her this?

'Oh, it's colourful all right. Until a couple of years ago, the Peacock was owned by an Australian expat and was no more than a bar where anyone with business around the Fort district could get an exotic cocktail, imported beer and prawn crackers for a bit less than they'd have paid in their hotels. I'm not saying a few of the local working girls wouldn't hang around on the off-chance, but only the Westernised ones. But the Peacock people paid their licence fee and we didn't bother them. Then there was a small fire – started in the kitchen, they said – the Aussie collected his insurance, and some Chinese types moved in. All in a matter of weeks.'

'You've got a Chinese community here?'

'Hasn't everyone?' Charlie smiled. 'No – these weren't ours. In fact they were avoided by the local Chinese, who acted a little put out by them. They seemed to be from Hong Kong. Well, you know, what with the hand-over, we just thought it was some shrewd types looking for a bolt-hole. Then the money started coming in. Quite big money. They did the place up like Caesar's Palace with coconuts and imported some Miss Saigon ladies, and business picked up. Then the casino arrived, but even all this didn't seem to justify the amounts of money floating around. I was in Fraud at the time, and we began to suspect some kind of laundering operation. They didn't send me to charm school in England for nothing, you know.' She laughed mirthlessly

'I think I've seen enough of this sort of stuff on TV to be with you so far. Are they Triads or Tongs or something?'

'*Too* much TV, my dear. As far as we could learn from our Hong Kong colleagues, they weren't obviously connected with the top gangs. Perhaps it was a case of being tolerated by the big boys rather than actually part of them. The only thing the Honkers police could come up with was a possible link with the trade in animal parts.'

'Ugh!' winced Fran. 'You mean ivory, rhino horn, bears' gall bladders, that sort of thing? All that suffering just for some people's ignorance and other people's greed! I'm sorry – but I hate those bastards.'

'It's a bit more complicated than that.'

'How can it be?' Fran was fast losing any remaining objectivity on the subject of the Blue Peacock. 'Wait until I see Nevil. Fancy even drinking in a place like that!'

There was a pause. Damn! she thought. That's the gin for you. Stupid – stupid! All along, she'd been careful not to mention any connection Nevil might have had with the place. And there she was, thinking that it was Charlie who was saying too much and might be regretting it. Shit!

Charlie was too well-mannered, or too well-trained, to yell, Gotcha, sunshine. But she must have been thinking it. She simply licked her lips and looked away – which, if anything, Fran found even more unnerving, because it meant she hadn't finished with her yet. Maybe she'd even been checking the main hotels before coming here and knew already. Charlie was smart, right enough.

'And you've no idea who your husband might have been meeting at the Peacock?'

'Absolutely none,' said Fran sharply. 'The hotel said he'd taken a taxi there, that's all. When I realised what sort of a place it was, I was surprised. Honestly, that sort of flashy joint just isn't his style.'

'I'm sure it isn't. So is he back at the Inter-Continental?'

Now I've got *you*, my dear, thought Fran, I never mentioned the hotel. I was very careful about that too.

But any squeak of triumph in the wheels of Fran's overworking brain was quickly silenced by the inevitable conclusion. Charlie had definitely been checking up on Nevil this afternoon, or had put someone else onto it. She knew where Nevil had been staying, and that he wasn't there now. For chrissake, what was going on here? Was it all true what they said about the East? It wasn't the smile you shouldn't trust – it was the smile behind the smile.

'I think you already know my husband isn't there,' she said simply.

Charlie looked down, as if caught out – as if almost wanting to be. Some of the brightness had gone from her. She knew the present game of being friends was over and seemed actually sad about it.

'Yes, OK – I'm worried,' said Fran at last. 'Of course I'm worried. But you'll have to believe me. I don't know *why* I'm worried.'

'I believe you,' said Charlie. 'Forgive me for saying so, but you remind me of some friends I had in England. After a while, I knew when they were telling the truth.'

'Then you have the advantage on me.' There was no bitterness in Fran's voice, but she could see the words having the desired effect. Charlie hadn't really sounded arrogant about it, but she wasn't going to let her get away so lightly with all this. 'And what did you mean when you said it was a bit more complicated than just the illegal animal parts trade? You're going to have to believe me when I say that Nevil wouldn't have anything to do with that. He's quite soft about animals really. He wouldn't hurt

80

a fly. Well, not knowingly he wouldn't, she added privately.

Charlie nodded, possibly to conceal similar reservations. 'When you asked me round this evening,' she said, 'I was very pleased – even a little flattered. But also slightly puzzled. It didn't seem to be the action of someone with something to hide. Yet it seemed odd to me that you would be so worried about your husband's safety. I had to ask myself why he hadn't contacted you to say he was OK – especially after the bomb incident. And surely you wouldn't have assumed that he'd been travelling on a local bus.' She smiled. 'Only the bravest of tourists do that. So it seemed reasonable that your concern was in some way connected with the Blue Peacock. And anyone interested in the Peacock is of interest to us, you understand.'

'So you played a hunch?'

'Sorry – I felt I had to. Maybe even for your own protection. You seemed to me like an innocent abroad. In need of a guardian angel, perhaps.'

Fran smiled wanly. 'And of course you also know that I rang the InterContinental, and you were told, as I was, that two men of Chinese appearance had removed a message meant for my husband.' Had all the evening really just been leading up to this?

'Afraid so,' replied Charlie.

'And these men are not likely to be Boy Scouts. So you've guessed that this afternoon I was only a little worried, whereas now I'm wondering if I should be going on for terrified, because these people now know where I am'

'I couldn't have put it better myself. But I could offer a little advice – unofficially.'

'Oh please, don't stint yourself.' She hadn't meant

it to sound sarcastic, but she could guess what it would be: "There's more going on here than is good for you, so fly away home and forget all about this", or something similar. That's how these conversations were supposed to go, when they were on the telly and didn't matter.

'I know you won't go home until you find your husband,' said Charlie, surprisingly. 'So I'd advise – and I can only advise, you understand – that you take yourself down to some nice little tourist place down south – just in case. Kalutara or Bentota – somewhere like that. You'll be less visible down there. Don't worry about tonight, though. I've already got one of my flat-feet lurking discreetly round the gates with orders to stop anyone he doesn't like the look of, until you check out to-morrow. Take the train rather than a taxi. Not all taxi men are reliable, and I don't mean their driving. If you leave after the morning rush hour, you might even get a seat.'

'But . . .' Oh God – the evening had started off barely in control. Now everything was spinning all over the place. 'But I can't do that! How will Nevil know where to find me? So far, he doesn't even know I'm in the country.'

'You'll think of something,' said Charlie. 'Surely your husband will be making contact either with your home or his office, and they could contact you. Make sure the hotel you go to has a fax. Most of them do these days. Obviously you will let me know where you are, and perhaps you could check in every day so that I know you're OK. But don't fax my office, and don't leave any detailed messages. Ask for me personally.'

She means this, thought Fran. She really does.

She's thought of everything, and she has her reasons.

'Meanwhile, try not to worry. I'll get onto some more of the hotels in Colombo. I only tried the big ones. I haven't got much else to do back at base. Your husband will show up, you'll see.' She brightened. 'Maybe he's taken himself off for a trip to Kandy or the hill country. Lots of businessmen do, if they've got a few days to spare. Does he like golf? They go mad to get a round or two in at Nuwara Eliya. It's suppose to be one of the prettiest courses in Asia.'

'Golf!' said Fran. 'Why didn't I think of that?' She felt her hopes rising unaccountably. 'He's a real freak. I bet he's gone off with some buddies somewhere. Nuwa . . . what? Maybe I should go there.' She was only half joking.

'M'mm – a bit far up country,' said Charlie. 'Stick to the coast. You'll be less visible there. Anyway . . .' she looked at her watch, winced and got up. 'Chin up. All this is only a precaution, you understand. Part of the service to our visitors. Let's hope you have some good news soon.'

They shook hands and Fran watched her get into a taxi that had probably been waiting for her for some time.

It wasn't until she got up that Fran realised her clothes were stuck to her for the second time that day. Suddenly she felt utterly exhausted. Were Charlie's clothes stuck to her? She doubted it. Just a simple Sri Lankan girl. Who was she kidding? Altogether it had been quite an evening, and to cap it, somewhere out there where the fruit bats were sailing over the dark lane, was a policeman who'd been put there specially to protect her. But from whom, and from what?

# Chapter Six

Fran knew it would be no good trying to get to sleep until she had a clear plan for the morning. She got out the guide books and brochures she'd brought with her from home and the various maps and leaflets picked up since and spread them in the light of the bedside lamp on the little table in her room. As if by invitation, a dozen moths and other nameless winged things immediately joined her. Outside, the cicadas were piercing the humid night air like so many cooker timers in some vast, steamy kitchen.

Really this was not much different from what she'd planned before she left, she told herself wryly. She'd been looking forward to a trip down the coast. More as a second honeymoon – preferably with Nevil. Possible kidnapping, the Chinese mafia and bombings hadn't figured largely in her calculations. Still – there was a policeman outside supposed to be guarding her, and she had to report her whereabouts to the police – as soon as she had a whereabouts. Jesus, what more could a girl ask?

Now, where had Charlie said to head for? Kal-something or other. Kalutara. There it was. It was nearer than the other place she'd mentioned, looked as good as anything else and the train seemed to stop there. To her relief, the Sri Lankan railway system looked starkly simple. One line ran straight down the coast, and Kalutara was only about thirty miles south of Colombo. The nearest station was Mount Lavinia, so even if the thing had a man with a red flag walking in front of it and stopped at every town, it couldn't take much longer than an hour from this side of Colombo. That was nothing. People travelled that far and further to work every day in England.

Slightly comforted, she put rings round a couple of hotels in Kalutara which looked adequate if not the best, and then tried to get some sleep. As expected, it didn't work. Even the gin didn't help, and if the thought of a personal policeman out there in the dark was supposed to make her feel more secure, well, it wasn't working. That night, she could have sworn she heard each footfall of every gecko and skink in the place.

She was up and breakfasted by eight, and packed and checked out by nine. Mrs Mario called her a local taxi whose driver was related. She said she would be in lots of time for the mid morning Express and told Fran, with much head waggling, to come back to St Anthony's any time. Fran decided that Mrs Mario definitely couldn't have known about the policeman outside. On the way up the lane, she saw him, propped against a wall in the feathery shade of a flamboyant tree, so she made sure he'd seen her leaving and got an uncertain salute in return.

'Can you stop at Mr Silva's on the Galle Road?' she asked the taxi driver, feeling as if she was leaving a place she'd known for weeks.

There were no messages, but she faxed Tony, the office and home, with instructions not to send any more messages until she contacted them with a new number very soon. She added not to worry about the bomb if they'd heard about it because she'd checked Nevil wasn't involved, but pleaded for more information on his whereabouts, all without mentioning him by name. Nobody seemed to sure about anybody round here, and when in Rome . . .

The station at Mount Lavinia was like somewhere along the Bluebell Line which the cleaner had somehow managed to miss for the last fifty years. But the Galle Express was on time and almost full of local families, backpackers, people trying to shine your sandals, or selling peanuts and drinks, and business men with plastic briefcases. Babies dressed in bright nylon were shushed or fed, and wide-eyed children watched her, smiled warily and looked away. No one looked in the least bit sinister, or even vaguely Chinese, but for the first time in her life, Fran had that strange, never-to-be-forgotten feeling that someone might be watching her. Someone who shouldn't be.

At the station, there had been first, second and third class ticket windows, but it hadn't made the slightest difference. Everyone got a second class ticket, and sat anywhere or leaned out of the windows and doors, while beggars who could only scoot along on their hands dodged in and out of the thickets of legs and bags waving their tin cups hopefully. Even they were smiling.

The express didn't only stop at every town, but at almost every village too. Conscious of her hefty suitcase, Fran stayed near one of the doors, praying it would be the right side of the train to get off, and hoping she would spot the station in time. Signs were rather scarce, averaging two in English per station. They all seemed to have at least twenty syllables and be placed where you couldn't see them when standing. The occasional announcement was, inevitably, unintelligible.

'Holiday? Very nice,' said a woman with a child, looking at her case. 'Which place? I will tell you.'

'Oh, thank you very much,' beamed Fran. 'Kalutara.'

The woman's face clouded over with puzzlement. Oh God, I'm on the wrong train, thought Fran. Maybe I'm going to finish up in Kandy or Trincomalee or somewhere. How did I do that?

She tried the name again and the face suddenly cleared. It was like the sun coming out. 'Ah – Kalutara,' the woman warbled happily, making it sound as if all the vowels and consonants had been playing musical chairs.

'That's it,' Fran told her hopefully.

However you were supposed to pronounce it, Kalutara station hove into view and Fran hauled herself off and bagged a waiting three-wheeler autoshaw. Or to be more precise, the driver bagged her. 'How much to the Cinnamon Beach Hotel?' she asked, jamming on her sun hat and resigning herself to five minutes of politely intense discussion on the subject. In the end, she settled for half his original price, which was probably twice what it should have been, but it was too hot by now to argue.

The Cinnamon Beach was more or less what she'd expected, and they said they could manage a third floor room with a view over the pool and sea for a week at a good rate, if she didn't mind the air conditioning not working. Someone was supposed to be fixing it, and would she mind waiting while they swept it because it hadn't been in use. Fran said this would be fine, and told them that she was expecting her husband to join her later in the week from Colombo.

One of her reasons for saying this, she told herself, was that it gave her, a lone woman, a respectable reason for being here, in a country where this sort of thing was still important. Something told her that this was not the place to stand on feminist principles, especially if they could work against you. The other was that if she told enough people Nevil was coming, it might make it come true.

Less than half an hour later, she was settled in and looking over the balcony sipping a cold Coke. There were two low rise blocks of rooms facing each other across a grassed area with plenty of palms and frangipanis. In the middle of this garden area was the pool – nothing fancy, just a turquoise oblong with a little thatched bar nearby. The balconies of the blocks were angled to give each a view of the ocean, which was a glaring, glittering white today, visible through stands of very tall palms and clumpy pandanus that had probably been someone's todi grove only a few years ago.

The only thing that bothered her slightly was that there didn't seem to be any kind of security fence on the beach side. This made her glad she was on the third floor rather than the ground floor where anyone could have got in over the low, open blockwork balcony. The two parallel room blocks were connected by a pleasantly sprawling complex of traditionally tiled or thatched roofs and arched verandas which housed the reception, main bar and restaurant. It didn't look like the sort of place that was expecting trouble, or would be good at dealing with it if they got any, and with Nevil here, it would have been perfect. Although, she thought to herself with a wistful smile, Nevil would have preferred a bigger pool.

Downstairs, the blue water and the wooden slatted sunbeds in the freckled shade of the palms looked very enticing. But should she even be thinking about such things? She wasn't on holiday, for heaven's sake; she was virtually in hiding. Nevertheless, in the midday heat, the urge to strip off for a swim was overwhelming.

Changing into beach gear made her feel more relaxed and normal. She went down to reception with her straw bag and towel and was able to fax her three contact points at home giving all the details including her room number. At least Tony would know now that she was booked in here for the week, which would give him a fixed point of reference when Nevil called in, which he was bound to do at some time. In the arched shade of the veranda she ordered a pot of tea to calm herself down, then, without seeming to make a fuss about it, asked to see the floor manager in his office.

'I'm expecting an urgent message,' she told him with her best smile. 'Maybe several. It's business, you see, and it could be very important to my husband's company. I won't be leaving the hotel, or if I do, I'll let you know. Could I be told immediately if there's a phone call or a fax for me? I'm sorry to treat you as a branch of our office, but I hope this will cover the inconvenience of letting the people on duty know this?'

Hoping she had done the right thing and he wouldn't be insulted, she pushed forward a couple of easily pocketable high denomination notes she had ready – the equivalent of about eight pounds.

The manager didn't seem to be at all insulted. 'We

will treat the matter with the utmost urgency, madam,' he smiled.

'Thank you, and please tell the staff that they'll be something for them if they have to come and find me. Especially if the news is good.'

'Then we wish you good news, ma'am.'

Feeling that she'd done the right thing, she then phoned Charlie and was relieved to get through straightaway.

'No luck so far on your husband's whereabouts, I'm afraid,' Charlie told her. 'We've phoned round the other big hotels in Colombo. Now we're mopping up the smaller ones where Westerners might stay.' She took details of the Cinnamon Beach and asked if it was satisfactory. Feeling a bit deflated by the news that there was still no sign of Nevil, Fran said it was fine, except that she felt conspicuous being on her own. Everyone else seemed to be in pairs or families.

'Well,' said Charlie wryly, 'as my mother used to say, don't talk to any strange men, my dear.'

'Trust me,' Fran replied. 'By the way, I haven't tried my room radio yet. Is there anything else on the bombing?'

'Two rather odd things,' was the reply. 'The forensic people have been going through the wreckage, and they reckon the bomb was a fairly amateur affair. It seems it wasn't technically a car bomb, in that it wasn't attached to the car delivering it. They think the bomber is one of the dead, and it seems to have gone off when he got out with it. He was seen heading towards the Blue Peacock, but it went off too soon and caught the passing bus as well.'

'Rather as you thought,' said Fran.

'Ah, but that's not all. Among the bits and pieces in the remains of the Peacock, they found quite a lot of heroin, which was no particular surprise. But there was also a large haul of tiger bones. They use them for Chinese medicine. Very charred, but that's what they were.'

'*Tiger* bones?' If anything, Fran was more shocked by that part of Charlie's revelations than what had gone before. 'We saw a programme on TV about that. A beautiful animal like the tiger, almost extinct because some wretched old Chinese can't get it up. I'm sorry – but I think that's so appalling.'

'Join the club,' said Charlie.

'But hang on, I didn't think you had any tigers in Sri Lanka.'

'We haven't, that's the point. The stuff's obviously coming in from India. Of course, we knew we had a few elderly Chinese around who might want a couple of pinches of powdered tiger bone for their sex life or rheumatics, or whatever, but it was very small scale stuff. Yet this haul was about sixty kilos of raw bone. That's about four tigers' worth. Not a lot, by their standards, but it's far too much for local use.' She gave a humourless laugh. 'Unless the entire male population of Sri Lanka has suddenly become impotent overnight, it's on its way to China. All highly illegal, of course, and worth a small fortune. But it rather proves our information from Hong Kong, does it not, that the Peacock's new owners had links with the animal by-products trade. Obviously they've gone into the import and re-export business in a very big way and were using the Peacock as a base.'

'Well, it deserved to get bombed then.' Fran was still feeling indignant. 'But it's dreadful about those people on the bus. Anyway, that fixes it as far as Nevil's concerned. He saw the programme too, and if he'd had half an idea what was going on, he'd never have gone near the place.'

'I'm sure you're right. By the way, the bit about the bone haul won't be on the radio. Not yet, anyway. They're still trying to work out where the owners are. No one's come out of the woodwork yet. Better go. Stay in touch.'

Charlie's information left Fran feeling more puzzled than ever. She'd read various things about bears' gall bladders, rhino horn and other animal products being used in traditional medicine, but the TV programme they'd seen had dealt specifically with tigers. It had left them feeling angry, but the actual details she could remember were, to say the least, hazy.

Any ideas of a swim forgotten, she got herself a Coke and sank into a wicker chair on the veranda, deep in thought. That programme about tigers. There'd been something about the bone trade being controlled mostly through Delhi. And what else? She put a hand over her eyes to cut out the jagged glare from the pool. Yes, that was it. The bones would leave India for China in backpacks, mainly through the Tibetan refugee camps in the north. The proceeds from getting one pack through could set a man up for life – but that was as much as she could remember. It had all stunk so strongly of ignorance, desperate poverty, corruption and greed that it made you despair of human nature.

'Have you just arrived too? It must be the jet lag.'

Fran lifted her head quickly at the sound of a man's voice beside her – slightly accented. German? Scandinavian? There were two of them. Youngish, not bad-looking, in good shape. They'd been on the far side of the bar when she'd come through and if she'd registered anything about them at all, it was that they might have been gay.

'I'm sorry?' she said vaguely.

'You must take plenty of liquid for jet-lag, so please let me get you another drink.'

Not a bad line, she thought, and delivered in such a way as to suggest that this was the traditional males-on-the-hunt, double whammy tactic on the lone female. Always worth a try, lads – if she doesn't fancy one, she might go for the other. Not gay, then. No, probably not, in spite of those shorts. Just 'continental.' So please go away – but how difficult to actually say it.

Instead she smiled and shook her head firmly. 'Not just now, thanks.' Damn! Did that sound like an opening for later? She paused, unsure of how to get out of this without elaborate explanations. 'Actually I was going for a swim.'

They accepted this in a civilised enough fashion, as she'd hoped. Encouraged, she added, 'But I'm expecting a message. I wonder, if you'll be here for a short time and the steward comes looking for a Mrs Merrick, would you be kind enough to point him to the pool?'

'But of course. We were about to have a beer. No problem.'

She could feel their eyes were still on her. Not all over her, just curious perhaps to see if she really was alone. But at least she'd got the 'Mrs' bit in.

And if no message came . . . Fran took a deep breath ready for a shallow dive. Maybe they were the persistent kind. Explanations of some sort were bound to follow. Well, they looked quite house-trained, and a week was a long time with only your own thoughts for company.

The water was so warm that the dive was more of a sensual experience instead of the usual tingling shock to the system. But as Fran surfaced through the champagne bubbles into a welcoming warmth of blue air and palms, she was sharply aware of how disoriented she felt. To be here, alone, suspended in this re-birthing tank, isolated from the familiar, adrift in a sea of new sensations. So far she had been too occupied with simply getting herself from A to B, with *doing* things, that her familiar world, her life back home with Nevil, had still been the real world, and this new one more like an illusion. But how strange – for a moment there, it had seemed as if this situation, this place, these people, had suddenly become the real world and her life with Nevil the unreal one. Would there ever come a time when the cross-over became complete?

Shocked, she forced herself below the surface and tried to swim a length underwater, hoping that when she surfaced, things would look more normal again. She bobbed up spluttering, to see a waiter anxiously scanning the surface of the pool.

'Telephone for Mrs Merrick, please?'

'Over here!' yelled Fran, breaking into a swift, splashing crawl. 'Tell him to hang on!' The real world seemed to seize her by the hair and haul her bodily out of the pool. She grabbed her towel and ran dripping after the waiter. The two Viking types gave her friendly grins as she scurried past, which she returned with a thumbs-up sign of relief.

It was Tony. But he was better than nothing.

'Fran – nice to hear you at last!'

'You too. Listen, Tony, what the hell is going on?'

'I might say the same. We had a bit of a fit at this

94

end when we heard about the bomb. Home from home, or what?'

'Never mind that now – Nevil wasn't caught in it, and that's that. But don't tell me you still haven't heard from him!'

'I was hoping *you'd* heard by now.' Tony didn't sound half as worried as he should have been, in her opinion.

'No, I bloody haven't!' She could feel her voice rising. 'Tony, I'm really not enjoying this. Maybe it was my fault for coming out on spec, but where the blazes is he? And there's a few more things I don't like the sound of. For a start, you remember I mentioned a place called the Blue Peacock? Well it now seems a whole lot dodgier than a pick-up joint. Any leads as to why Nevil went there? And another thing. I left a message for him at the InterCont, and two guys waltzed in and took it, if you please. Chinese-ish. Now I've got the police on my tail, and I'm getting a bit pissed off!'

'*What?* Hang on a minute. Let's take it one at a time.'

Good – she'd got him rattled. It was about time somebody out there realised just how she was feeling about all this. She took a deep breath and told him about Charlie's involvement, the tiger bone and heroin finds, and how she'd been advised to move out of Colombo. After that, he went quiet.

'And there's something else,' she added. 'The men who lifted my message for Nev were actually looking for Brian Gaskill. Does that ring any bells?'

She knew it would. Both Nevil and Tony knew Brian pretty well from their time in Saudi. When his name cropped up these days, it was usually in connection with some meet-up in a pub when Brian was in town again. This invariably involved Nevil coming home late by taxi and going into work next day full of Asprin and reeking of garlic. There was always a lot of muttering about the time good old Brian had saved their bacon. She wasn't too sure of the details, and had been more than happy to leave them to a bit of male bonding. Brian had even flown in from somewhere hot and sticky especially for the wedding, and was on their Christmas card list, but no one ever seemed to know quite where he was.

'Brian *Gaskill*? Are you sure? I didn't know he was in Sri Lanka.'

'Somebody seems to think so. And I might not have put two and two together from what the desk clerk at the InterCont said if Brian hadn't e-mailed Nevil just in time to miss him, and it looked as if it was something to do with the trip.'

'Great – so Brian's on-line somewhere. He's never e-mailed before.' There was the smallest of pauses. 'Could I ask what it was about?'

Was Tony just a little miffed that he hadn't been in on this?

'I ate it,' said Fran flatly. 'No, actually, I flushed it down the loo.'

'Christ,' moaned Tony. 'Look, Fran, dearest Hot Legs, old pal, you haven't been at the Pinacoladas, have you?'

'Don't call me Hot Legs,' she retorted automatically. 'And I'm more sober than I intend to be when all this is over, I can tell you. I trashed the e-mail because I realised that the strange Chinesey people who pinched my message and were asking about Brian now knew my previous address, and I didn't want them rifling through my smalls for . . . whatever is was they might be looking for. Oh, what the hell do I know?' she finished, flapping her free arm around helplessly.

'But can you remember what the e-mail said, for chrissake?'

'Of course I can.' She relayed Brian's short message slowly enough for Tony to take it down, including the e-mail address she'd tried to reply to and failed.

'Beats the hell out of me,' was all he said, and there was real annoyance in his voice.

'And you've got no idea at all what *Tiger Country* could mean?'

'None.'

'You see, round here, there are several kinds of tigers. We have the Tamil kind who throw bombs, and we have the stripy kind, or more precisely we seem to have some of their bones around. The Chinese use them for medicine, and some were found at the Blue Peacock place. Am I making any sense? No, of course I'm not.'

'Fran, what the effing hell are you on about? It sounds completely Chinese to me – but I'll try to keep it in mind if it makes you happy.'

How Tony hated being at a loss – or not being in on something.

'I tell you what,' he said. 'This call's costing the old firm an arm and a leg – yes, yes, I know it's important,' he added hurriedly, hearing her noisy intake of breath. 'Don't worry, I'm going to drop everything and chase this up. Find out I what I can about Brian's latest whereabouts, put out a few feelers. You sit tight, and I'll get back to you in one hour exactly. How's that?'

'I'll be right here.' She hung up. 'Patronising bastard,' she said to the telephone.

Through the veranda arches, families with

97

teenagers, couples young and old, the beautiful, the saggy, the bold and the bald, were splashing around in the pool, sipping drinks out of coconuts or sprawling under the palms – a holiday video she could only watch, as if she would never be part of it – and right then, Fran hated it all

# Chapter Seven

An hour. Exactly one hour, Tony had said. For all his faults, Tony was nothing if not punctual. What could she do in an hour to take her mind off things?

Have some lunch. No, she could eat any time, and in any case she was hardly hungry. It had to be the beach. Maybe a few lungfuls of Indian Ocean air would clear her head. It was so warm now, that her skin was already quite dry from the swim. Towelling her hair, she strolled back to her beach bag, which meant passing the two Vikings who were now staked out under a palm tree, deep in paperbacks. The one who had done most of the talking was reading *The English Patient*, in English.

'It was good news for you, I hope?' he asked politely, as she passed.

She paused only a second, wiggling her hand. 'A little mixed,' she replied. The other one's book also looked fairly substantial and its title was definitely something Scandinavian. It was the kind of thing she tended to register automatically, like the time when passing a clock.

'Better luck next time,' replied the English Patient, raising his glass.

You too, she thought, smiling wryly as she scooped up the beach bag and pressed on. But they certainly seemed pleasant enough.

The short wiry grass round the pool was being aimlessly watered by a khaki-clad gardener who gave her a half salute and cheerful 'Ma'am'. For all his efforts, the grass quickly became thin, then patchy, until it finally gave out towards a shallow bank of blown sand which seemed to be the only thing separating the hotel from thousands of miles of ocean. The next stop out there was probably Africa. Hardly pausing in her eagerness to get away by herself for however short a time, she tied on her sarong, jammed on a sun hat and struck out for the narrow, shelving beach.

Immediately, she realised that it was not going to be as simple as that. There was some rustling from a clump of wind-shredded pandanus to her right, and suddenly the whole clump became alive. Brightly dressed, slim dark figures stood up and waved frantically to her, while the palm-like leaves of the pandanus began to sprout vivid patches of cloth like so many jungle flowers. Already two of the women and several small children were bearing down on her with armfuls of startling colours – acid yellows, hibiscus reds, jade and emerald greens and tropical sunset pinks and purples. Damn, the clump must be the undeclared boundary between the hotel and the beach, and she'd walked right into the trap.

It took five precious minutes to detach herself politely from the little gang, with promises to come back tomorrow. Next time she would bring a little cash and buy a sarong or something to guarantee immunity from subsequent assaults – if there was a next time. As she finally out-distanced the last of the pursuing children waving shell necklaces at her, Fran wondered if she was going to be a complete prisoner in the hotel until someone, anyone, made contact.

Now that she was closer to it, the sea was a deep, mysteriously uneven blue, like a billowing shot silk skirt flounced with lace where the curving lines of breakers rippled against the shore as far as the next promontory. There was no one on the narrow strand in front of her. Cautiously, not for fear of the cold, but for some other unguessed at reason, she paddled into the gritty, yielding sand and let the tepid water splash her feet – then wondered if it was her imagination that made this sea so different from the so-familiar Mediterranean. It felt more alive, more ambiguous and profound; promising more to those who ventured in. Or was it threatening? This sea had pearls and sharks; it had coral reefs and deadly snakes, huge clams that could trap a diver's foot, flying fish and forests of giant kelp, and strange things with tentacles that glowed among the shipwrecks in its sudden, plunging deeps . . . *Full fathom five thy father lies; Of his bones are coral made: Those are pearls that were his eyes: Nothing of him that doth fade, But doth suffer a sea change Into something rich and strange . . .*

Fran shuddered in spite of the clammy warmth and walked briskly on. Was this why you swotted up Shakespeare at school – so that it would be there to come back and haunt you at times like this? Her father wasn't a drowned sailor. He was back at home and in good health, as far as she knew. Her husband wasn't floating face down, faceless, in some murky lagoon somewhere – as far as she knew. So what on earth had put that image into her mind?

Her pace had slowed almost to a crawl. The damp

sarong stuck to her ankles as she kicked at the tide ripples of sand, trying to remember. Then she clicked her fingers. Of course. That *Time* magazine she'd bought in Bahrain. It must still be in the zip-flap side of her cabin bag. It had said something about people who betrayed the Tamil Tigers being found floating in the lagoons outside Colombo with their faces mutilated to prevent identification. So that was what had put those haunting lines into her mind. It wasn't any kind of omen, then. No geese were walking over graves: no vultures circling overhead.

Calmer now, she strolled a little further before glancing at her watch. Surely that couldn't be the time! It was already more than half an hour since she'd left the hotel. Abruptly, she turned on her heel and began to hurry back.

Slightly out of breath and hot again from half jogging along the heavy sands, she was all ready and waiting in the lobby in time for Tony's call, which they let her take in a small side room by the main office.

Tony sounded quite pleased with himself. 'I've come up with something on Brian,' he told her. 'But I'm really none the wiser as to how it might fit in. What do you reckon? You remember he used to work for Shell when we were in Saudi?' She didn't, but no matter. 'He wasn't on the drilling end, he was on their security staff – keeping the world safe for the mighty oil business and all that. Well, according to his ex-wife, he then went to Shell Nigeria, and got caught in the middle of all that Ogoni political stuff down in the Niger delta – people getting hanged and shot up, villages burnt and so on. Changed his life, apparently. He bailed out of the oil biz and suddenly went all green with a capital G.'

'What? Brian, all concerned for the environment? I don't believe it.'

'Sounds like it. Sue wasn't too chuffed at the sudden drop of income and the increase in muddy boots, so they split up. I always reckoned she was a bit of a gold-digger myself. Anyway, she reckons he's got some kind of job with Animal World Watch, so I got onto them, but they weren't exactly forthcoming. They said they couldn't just give out contact addresses over the phone, but they did confirm that he was working in their South-East Asian section. I suggested Sri Lanka, and they got a bit iffy and asked why I wanted to know, and was I a journalist or something. Hello, Fran? Light of my life? Are you still there?'

'Yes, I'm still here,' said Fran grimly, aware of a strange feeling in the pit of her stomach, which had nothing to do with the fact that she hadn't eaten since breakfast. 'Tony, did you get any idea of what Animal World Watch actually *do*? I mean, I've heard of them, but what's their particular angle?'

She could almost see Tony shrugging. 'I dunno . . . Watch animals a lot?' Tony was not the sort who spent his evenings watching wildlife documentaries. But then, who would have thought it of Brian Gaskill? Yet here he was, apparently working for AWW, whose logo was – oh God – a tiger. The World Wildlife Fund had a panda, and Animal World Watch had a springing tiger.

'No, idiot.' This was as much to herself as Tony, while she racked her brains. 'Think – what do they *do*.'

'Okay-okay! Aren't they against flogging ivory and all that? Why's it so important?'

'I don't know,' murmured Fran, with a horrible

103

feeling that perhaps she might. AWW – it was coming back now. They were very anti-poaching, and against exotic pets. They'd also run a big campaign a while back against the smuggling of live animals, particularly endangered species. They were just the sort of outfit who might be going after people trading in tiger bones. Certain things were beginning to look as if they might somehow fit together. Normally quick at thinking on her feet, she could feel a kind of fog descending whenever the word 'tiger' was mentioned. Was there any point in trying to talk it through with Tony? No – she couldn't see it clearly enough. Not at this stage. It would sound as if she was rambling or hysterical, and if there was one breed that never stood a chance at Merrick & Baldwyn, it was females branded as hysterical.

'Look, I'm sorry,' she said at last. 'I'm just clutching at straws. I'm cross I seem to keep missing Nev, that's all. I'm sure it's simply that he found Brian was out here at the last minute, and they decided to meet up for a drink or whatever. Maybe they've gone off to play a bit of golf somewhere. You know what they're like.'

'Tell me about it! But I do think he might have rung in to let me know how the Al Masira contract was doing.'

From years of training, Fran had already pulled the big pad of cheap paper beside the phone towards her and was writing down the name. So that's what it was called. She'd been so miffed about Nevil's unexpected trip, and what with feeling broody as well, she deliberately hadn't asked the details.

'So you've been expecting him to ring in and he hasn't – is that what you're telling me?' she asked sharply.

'Well, yes. Al Masira is rather a biggy.'

'Crucial, would you say?' There was a note of resignation in her voice.

'OK, pretty crucial.'

Fran sighed. She'd heard it all before: if we can land this one, we'll be out of the wood; we'll be able to tell the effing banks to get stuffed; no one will be able to touch us . . .

'Just tell me,' she said quietly, but not dangerously enough to scare him off, 'Is the house involved? Our house, your flat?' Nevil had promised, really promised, that he wouldn't use their house as collateral again. She liked that house – had put a lot of effort into it.

'Fran, I'm not supposed to be telling you all this.'

But he had, hadn't he? 'You're such a pair of bastards!' she said through clenched teeth. 'OK, I'll pretend I don't know about it. Let's concentrate on finding him, shall we?' And when she did . . . 'So what can we do next? Try all the golf courses in Sri Lanka?'

'There can't be that many,' muttered Tony morosely.

He sounded really fed up. Christ, how like a man! She'd been swanning around here wondering where Nevil had got to so that they could get on with their second honeymoon, and Tony had been back home stewing in his own juice in case the firm was about to go under. And he'd only just thought to mention it. Even so, she couldn't keep the edge out of her voice: 'Oh well, naturally, I'll get onto it! And for pity's sake, ring me as soon as you hear anything,' she said, and put down the phone.

She didn't get up straight away, but sat for a while in the tiny, neat room staring at a wall calendar.

Being in an office again seemed to calm her. It felt more natural to be at a desk rather than sipping cocktails round the pool when you were puzzling your brains out and desperately wondering what to do next, even when wearing only a two-piece and sarong. Being hungry and in need of a shower was nothing. Most days had been like that at Merrick & Baldwyn.

Sheer force of habit had her doodling on the pad – her usual sprawling, untidy notes with ringings and arrows – to see if something might work itself out.

What had she got so far? Brian Gaskill working for AWW. AWW possibly interested in tiger bone trade. Tiger bone trade interesting to the Sri Lankan police. Sri Lankan police interested in the Blue Peacock and all who dwelt therein. Someone interested in Brian's whereabouts. So – if the people interested in Brian turned out to be connected with the Blue Peacock, and from the InterContinental clerk's reaction, they certainly seemed dodgy enough, then it all chased itself into a nice little circle.

What else had she got that might reinforce this neat model? Or, for that matter, make it go pear-shaped or wobbly. There was Brian's brief e-mail, and Nevil buying the surveillance equipment. How did they fit in? Well, Brian's e-mail mentioned the word 'tiger' and something about funding. That could mean that his work was connected with tigers. And organisations like that were always making appeals and looking for funding, all of which would definitely strengthen the Brian-and-AWW section of the circle. Suppose he'd previously e-mailed Nevil at their home to buy the special equipment and bring it out to him. She never checked their e-mail much herself these days, and Nevil could easily have deleted the message anyway. That would fit, and it would also tie Nevil into the circle. But how tightly?

A polite tap on the office door made her jump.

'Mrs Merrick? You have finished your call? I trust everything is OK.'

'Oh yes, thank you.' She got up to go, tearing off the page from the notepad and tucking it into the waist of her sarong. 'But things aren't quite finished yet. I'm afraid there may be some more of this.'

He ushered her out and locked the door. 'No problem, I assure you.'

'Thanks again. I appreciate it.' They passed through to the veranda, where the afternoon light was streaming in from the sea and embossing the rough terracotta tiles with gold. It would be a good idea to give the man a tip. After all, they'd been very good so far, and this could go on for some time. Damn! Embarrassed, she patted her saronged sides as if looking for a pocket when she realised she hadn't any money with her. That's what happened when you got married. You got used to being paid for. Maybe the patting gesture was a universal one, because the next minute, a familiar accented voice beside her said, 'Maybe I can help?'

It was the English Patient. He had an unbuttoned shirt on over his trunks, and in the top pocket was a wallet which he tapped with an inquiring smile. She could see his friend not far away, still reading. Maybe they'd seen her come in from the beach in a hurry and were following up their earlier interest in this strange woman's antics.

OK, you've caught me fair and square this time, thought Fran. Dammit, this was the East, where money talked as nowhere else, and it was very slack of her not to have been carrying some.

'That's very kind,' she said, trying not to sound either too grateful or too ungracious. 'Thank you. Perhaps you could possibly lend me a couple of ten rupee notes to save me running upstairs? Then you must let me buy you and your friend that drink.' Oh God, what had she let herself in for? But it really seemed only polite to make the offer.

'But of course. I am happy to help.'

Whatever the manager thought of the situation, he accepted the tip graciously and left. Fran made see-you-later noises to her benefactor and went quickly upstairs intent on a shower and something to eat from room service while she was getting her head together. There were still a few loose ends that didn't quite fit.

Nevil. Exactly where did her absentee spouse fit into her little scenario, inconclusive and unverifiable as it was? She got out her piece of paper and tried again. This time she wrote down some dates. Wasn't it a little strange that he'd had from at least the Friday night before she'd dropped him at the airport on the Sunday to tell her that Brian Gaskill was in Sri Lanka and they'd be having a meet-up? It was the kind of thing he usually mentioned. But odder still was that Nevil hadn't told Tony either, which was a little worrying, because they were both quite fond of Brian in that oddly complicitous, what-times-we-had, male sort of way. And Nevil hadn't wanted her to help him pack. This had hurt a little at the time, but was beginning to resonate quite loudly now, since it seemed to confirm that he hadn't wanted her to see the expensive camcorder and mini cassette machine.

Then it struck her that she hadn't told either Tony or Charlie about the spy-in-the-bag stuff. Should she have done? And anyway, how would it have helped find Nevil? Which was the only thing about all this that really bothered her.

Except of course, there was the little matter of the – what was it called? She glared at the unfamiliar name – the Al Masira contract. It sounded like another cliff-hanger for M&B, which was how the firm worked, admittedly. Their speciality was brokering finance for big construction deals, and the commissions could be enormous, but it was rather an all-eggs-in-one-basket way of doing things which Nevil had promised her would change. Obviously he hadn't been honest with her about how much was at stake.

But suppose the deal hadn't come off. Maybe Merrick & Baldwyn were already heading for bankruptcy, and Nevil hadn't been able to face it. Perhaps he'd simply had enough, done a Gaugin, walked into the sea, taken to the hills, 'gone troppo', as Australians called it when a colleague chucked in his job and took to non-stop surfing and coconuts somewhere hot and sandy.

It was the first time such a thought had entered her head, but even as a joke she didn't much like it. Not right now, anyway.

Wrapped in a towel from the shower, she patted herself dry and padded to the balcony. The effects of cold water didn't last long out here, not even when the sun was beginning to go down. Below her, people were getting in a last swim or drifting away to get showered for a sundowner before dinner, and somewhere in all the laid back atmosphere were a couple of civilised Scandinavians who were owed twenty rupees and were expecting her company. And once you had paid the Danegeld, you never got rid of the Dane. She could see it now. If the socialising went well, they might ask her to join them for dinner, and what could she do – say she wanted to eat alone? She couldn't go swanning off into Kalutara looking for something to eat, because she was virtually a prisoner here until Nevil made contact. And if it went *too* well, she might start talking about her problems.

She sighed. It was no good - she couldn't face it. She'd have to stand them up and square it with them tomorrow. Then again, she was absolutely starving. Solution – ring room service to bring something up and tell reception she'd be in her room all evening. Bingo. It would hardly be boring, because there'd been a notice in the lobby about a local dance troupe performing by the pool after dinner, and she'd get a grandstand view from up here. If entertainment was what she wanted.

Later, much later, when the troupe had stamped their jingling anklets and twiddled bejewelled fingers for the last time, to polite applause from those still sitting round the flood-lit pool, she watched the fruit bats gliding over the palms and tried to find the Southern Cross. It was easy to see how people could go troppo round here. Sod the mortgage and the pension, just jack it all in and drift. Only half smiling, she remembered one of his grandfather's stories from his time out here in the war – the one about a battalion of Commonwealth infantry, Nigerians, as she remembered, who'd lost their British officer, or perhaps simply mislaid him somewhere in the hill country, and 'gone native'. Was it even partly true?

But that made her think of Brian Gaskill again. No matter what Tony said about Brian becoming a born-again Green, he wasn't the sort who went round with binoculars watching rare birds. Not the feathered kind anyway. Brian was a trouble-shooter – although she'd once heard them joking rather feebly that Brian would never shoot trouble because he enjoyed it too much. Brian was Action Man. Even a bit of a mercenary, with those shadows behind his eyes. If oil installations needed protection, Brian knew how to get people trained up and where to buy the stuff. Her father always maintained that people didn't fundamentally change – they carried on being the way they were, but for different reasons. If Brian joined an outfit like Animal World Watch, he would be in at the deep end, but this time for a cause he believed in. And AWW hadn't been exactly forth-coming as to what precisely he was doing for them, now had they?

Yet the more she thought about it, the more she was convinced that if she could find Brian she'd probably find Nevil as well. Maybe she'd been approaching this from the wrong end. Some lateral thinking was required. Why not tell Charlie about the Brian connection? Charlie would be able to get some information out of the Sri Lanka office of AWW about Brian's whereabouts, assuming they did have an office here. So maybe first thing tomorrow she should get onto Charlie.

Almost as she had the thought, the lights round the pool went out. It was midnight and time all happy campers were in bed. Seaward, there wasn't a glimmer of light now. Her eyes searched the velvety blackness for the horizon, in vain. Christ, it was dark. What had happened to the moon?

Deliberately, she turned off the balcony light, the only one still on, and returned to her seat. It was something she was going to have to get used to – thinking in the dark. Suppose Brian was actually working undercover for AWW. That would be quite his style. Maybe he was onto the tiger bone smugglers too, and working with the local police. But what if AWW didn't trust the local police? Heaven knows there'd been enough corruption in the Indian police and customs service over the whole of the tiger business – to the extent that the poor creatures were almost extinct. So it was possible, just possible, that if she told Charlie, she might be blowing Brian's cover. A thousand days to save the tiger, that's what they said. Three years, if the killings continued at the present rate. And for what? Ignorance and greed. Could she have it on her conscience to have avoided taking even the faintest risk to help the people who were trying to stop it?

Unwittingly she had been staring out to the sea horizon waiting for her eyes to adjust to the dark, hoping perhaps for some gleam of light for her to get her bearings. About Charlie herself she had no worries. The woman seemed genuine enough. But how could she put this to her without mentioning her own fears and suspicions? Ask to meet her again, perhaps. The phone didn't seem the right tool for this kind of delicate fishing.

Fran leaned forward. There was some light out there. Very faint pinpoints of it, bobbing, reappearing, moving very slowly. They had no pattern, no point of reference, yet there was certainly something there. What were they? Shrimp boats, perhaps. The guide book said you could see them sometimes – tiny local craft made of bamboo and kapok wood, with big, patched lateen sails. Somehow their presence out there in the vast ocean made her feel better, as if she wasn't the only one awake past midnight looking at the stars for guidance.

# Chapter Eight

It was while Fran was getting dressed and bracing
herself to go down to breakfast that it occurred to her
to try the radio. She'd slept late and it was nearly
nine o'clock. Maybe she could catch some news to see
if there was anything else about the bombing.

The radio was tuned to an English language
station, and at nine she was rewarded with a bulletin
which started off with some fairly unintelligible local
political row. But the second item had her sitting, pen
poised. The Fort district bomb, declared the
announcer, had claimed another victim – the young
Australian female tourist on the bus whose companion had been killed outright, had died in
intensive care. The parents had been contacted and
had been at the bedside. The Prime Minister had sent
her sympathies to the families of both the young
tourists as well as those of the other innocent victims,
and promised tough action. The number of dead so
far now stood at 33, but most of the other injured
were making good progress. The funerals of some of
the victims had been taking place, and public grief
and anger were being expressed. No one had yet
claimed responsibility for the outrage, but it was
thought that the bombing was definitely connected
to terrorist activities. A reward was being offered for
any information that might lead to arrests.

Feeling rather sombre, Fran considered all this. Maybe it was natural that she should feel more for the families of the two young Australians, but there were more than thirty dead Sri Lankans as well, only one of whom was not an innocent bystander. Some would have been breadwinners; the women would have had children. As for getting any information about the bombing from the general public, it seemed unlikely. The IRA were bad enough when it came to punishing informers and the like, but the Tamil separatists made them look like teddy bears, or so the *Time* magazine article had implied.

Prompted to have another look at it, she rescued the magazine from her bag and found the relevant section. This time she read the whole thing through much more carefully. After all, when she'd read it on the plane, it had been from an entirely different perspective. She certainly hadn't expected to have a brush with a Separatist incident herself, although to be fair, Charlie had said that the Tigers had denied responsibility. The newscast, she noted, had not mentioned this, as Charlie herself had hinted that it would not. Of course, the part about funding for the guerillas had caught her eye before, because Brian's e-mail was still fresh in her mind. But the article was only mentioning some likely sources from which the Tigers might be receiving funds to keep the supplies of arms coming in over the Jaffna Straits. And those sources included everyone from Colonel Gaddafi to various mafia-type groups in assorted countries where law and order were not all they might be.

At the time it had seemed a laughable idea that Merrick & Baldwyn, or friends like Brian Gaskill, could have any knowing connection with those sorts of people, whether the Tigers themselves or those who might be funding them. She had dismissed the idea on the plane before she'd even landed, and she dismissed it now. But this time it was the last sentence of that particular paragraph which gave her pause. *The (Sri Lankan) government, however, is becoming increasingly concerned that outside business interests are being used to launder funds for the guerrillas.* When she'd first read it, she'd thought only in terms of the 'outside business interests' meaning Western companies, perhaps like Merrick & Baldwyn, and again written off any idea of Nevil or anyone connected with him being involved. The whole idea was ludicrous.

But something Charlie had said was coming back to her. Charlie had also mentioned outside business interests. Not in so many words, but the police were certainly concerned about the Hong Kong Chinese who'd taken over the Blue Peacock and the amounts of money they were bringing in. Charlie had also implied that they were quite ruthless and had possible connections with the illegal trade in wildlife by-products. The haul of tiger bones after the Peacock bombing had rather proved it. What in fact Charlie had said was, that just before she'd had the trouble with her superior and asked for a transfer, the Fraud department was beginning to suspect the whole Peacock operation of being some kind of money laundering scam. Could there be something she was missing here? Something connecting the Tigers with the trade in tiger bones? She could only hope there wasn't. If the Tigers were involved, it would add a further strand of terror and ruthlessness to the situation.

Fran could feel her head beginning to swim again. She needed some coffee badly and, if she didn't get a move on, breakfast would be finished. Then there was the question of the English Patient and his friend. Talking to them right now was the last thing she needed. But maybe they were early risers and had taken themselves off for a ten-mile hike along the beach – they looked the sort.

Still trying to get her head together, she went down to the breakfast room. It was on the first floor overlooking the pool area, striped with lemon sunlight and smelling of croissants and bacon. Its only drawback as far as Fran was concerned was a finely worked batik wall-hanging of a peacock in full spread whose little eye watched her beadily as she filled her breakfast tray. A note attached informed her that this and other attractive designs were available at the hotel shop at competitive prices. No doubt the other designs would also include a tiger.

There were only a few stragglers around and the fresh fruit display was almost finished. For a change of view, she chose a table overlooking the front gardens of the hotel where frangipani trees and rampant bougainvillaea were fighting it out in a riot of purples, puce and salmon pinks to reach the top of the stuccoed walls. She closed her eyes. Peacocks, violent vegetation – it was almost too much at this time of the morning. Nearly ten o'clock. Oh dear. But then, what else did she have to do all day? An obligatory lunch-time drink, a swim perhaps. Not exactly a demanding schedule. It was the worrying that was the tough part.

Dutifully crunching her way through a bowl of industrial strength muesli, Fran returned with great reluctance to the question of who might have been up to what at the Blue Peacock. Money laundering. Where did that get her? It was a subject they weren't exactly unfamiliar with at M & B. Anyone in their line had to know the signs; bank accounts in off-shore tax havens, an economy with the truth when it came to the origins of funds, a distinct lack of up-to-date tax records, and a lofty vagueness which suggested it would be vulgar to press further about any of the above. That was the better, cleverer sort of laundry-man. Others simply had suitcases of cash, and occasionally a suspicious bulge under the arm or a nervous twitch. Both sorts were shown the door, the former, she suspected, less hurriedly than the latter.

If in doubt, eat. Breathing rather shortly, Fran got up, fetched two more croissants and spent a long time breaking them up carefully and playing a messy game of chess with them round the plate. The article had suggested that outside business interests were funding the Tamil Tigers. The people at the Blue Peacock were from outside. Maybe the tiger bone trade was a good cover for shifting their money around, and some of that money was going to the Tamil Tigers in the form of hefty protection pay-offs. What an appalling irony that would be.

She sat back looking at her messy plate. But that didn't make sense, of course. There was nothing, so far as she knew, to connect the Chinese at the Peacock with the Tamil Separatists. On the face of it, it seemed an unlikely alliance. And anyway, why on earth would the Separatists go round bombing an establishment that was helping them buy arms? Of course, Charlie had expressed doubt that the bomb had been the work of the Tigers. But the radio was still fingering them, as Charlie had said they would if it suited the politicians.

'More coffee, ma'am?'

Fran started guiltily. The waiter was hovering with

a pot and trying not to look at the strewn plate. 'Oh, I'm so sorry, I wasn't thinking. I mean – I was.'

'No problem, ma'am.'

No problem? How could they be so polite, she wondered as she got up hastily and went downstairs. Anyone who tore up bread and left it arranged in a circle round the plate, in a country where not everyone had enough to eat, had a problem all right. No wonder she was losing weight. The waist of her shorts felt quite slack. Or perhaps it was the heat.

This time she'd remembered to bring some cash. Perhaps it would be better to find the two young men as soon as possible and get that bit over before she went back to the thorny problem of what, if anything, to say to Charlie about Brian Gaskill. Fran had said she'd phone in every day until Nevil put in an appearance, and of course she desperately wanted to find him, but her gut instinct was now to avoid mentioning that Nevil might be with Brian, just in case. Business had taught her a kind of paranoia that went against all female instincts. In their game, you didn't tell people things that they didn't really need to know unless they were your grandmother. Presumably police work ran along similar principles. Saying she'd heard Nevil might be playing golf with an old friend, and that his partner was expecting him to phone in at any time would surely do – unless this went on for very much longer, in which case, she might have to think again.

The only other men in her life at the moment were in their usual place under the palms, still reading. Bracing herself, she gave them a cheery wave and went over, and was pleasantly surprised when they got up as she approached.

'Oh, please,' she smiled. A chair was quickly

119

dragged up for her. So much for a quick escape. 'I do apologise for not coming to find you last night, but I'm afraid I fell asleep.' Well she had – eventually. She pushed the folded rupee notes forward, and after some polite demurring they were accepted. 'My name's Fran Merrick, by the way.' She was speaking quickly – too quickly perhaps, but she didn't want to lose control of the situation. 'Now, about that drink. Would before lunch suit you? Say at the pool bar around twelve thirty – unless you've other plans?'

'That would be perfect. I am Anders, and this is Klaus. We're teachers – from Copenhagen.'

'Teachers of English, I'm sure,' laughed Fran and took the offered hands. 'I'm glad to know your names. I was privately calling you the English Patient,' she said to Anders, nodding to his book.

He grinned. 'It's very difficult, but worth the effort. I already have a list of questions for the first native English speaker who would talk to me.'

Fran found this bit of information vaguely comforting. Of course, that was what they wanted, a chance to practise, or perhaps show off, their English. God, what a relief it would be to think about someone else's list of questions, even for a few minutes.

'Of course, I'd be happy to help, although I haven't actually read it. Have you seen the film?'

'Yes, twice, but it doesn't follow the book very closely . . .'

Before she knew it they were into an involved discussion about divided loyalties and the nature of betrayal. Anders did most of the talking and was enjoying himself, although Klaus was following eagerly, his main contribution being that he taught engineering, as he called it, and was interested in old aircraft engines. She began to relax. It wasn't at all like talking to businessmen. In fact it was more like being back at college, and she liked the way they listened thoughtfully to what she had to say. Maybe they really were listening to her views about *The English Patient* – or perhaps it was simply that they were listening to an English voice saying it for them.

Either way, sitting there under the rattling palm crowns, Fran found she didn't really care. They were good company, especially Anders, who was also quite good-looking in spite of unnervingly blue eyes and blond hair which wouldn't stay put. Ten years ago, he'd probably worn it in a ponytail, and been into frayed jeans and pop concerts. A thousand years ago, he'd probably have had it down to his shoulders under something with horns on and been into wolf-skin and pillaging. Both images she found acceptable, but surprised herself by preferring the latter.

'Well, as much as I'm enjoying this, I'm afraid I have to make a phone call,' she said, getting up at last. Thank goodness they hadn't even got around to the 'how long are you here for?' question, and she hadn't had to explain anything. Not so far.

'And you'll be back for that lunch-time drink?'

'Of course.' She collected her things and went slowly back to the lobby, picking a creamy flower from one of the frangipani sprays that almost brushed her hair as she passed, and twiddling it under her nose to take in the knock-out blow of its scent. It was like all the suntan oils in the world with some mysterious pheromones thrown in. It was not a scent for the lonely or faint-hearted.

'Mrs Merrick?' A waiter was hurrying towards her. 'Telephone for you.'

'What? Oh, great!' Fran flung aside the flower and put on a greyhound sprint across the remaining few yards to the terrace. It was still too early to be Tony again. Maybe it was Nevil. She skidded to a halt beside the little office where the door was open for her, then bounded in and grabbed the phone.

'Hello, it's Fran,' she gasped.

'I should hope so,' said Charlie's wry voice. 'Did I get you out of the pool? Oh, but I'm sorry – maybe you thought . . .'

'Yes, I did,' sighed Fran, 'but I was just on my way to call you anyway, in case you thought I'd been spirited away in the night. By the way, I caught the news this morning.'

'It's so sad about the girl. And apart from any other consideration it won't do the tourist industry any good. The Australians will be staying away in droves.'

'You're no nearer finding out who was responsible, I suppose?'

'No one's saying anything. The owners of the Peacock seem to have gone to ground, but we don't think they've left the country – not by the international airport, anyway. It would be nice to have a little talk with them to see if they can throw any light on the subject.'

'Perhaps they'll try to claim for insurance. Explaining about the tiger bones could be a little embarrassing.'

Charlie gave a snort. 'Some chance! The reason we think they're still around is that there was a couple of other incidents last night, that you won't have heard about on the news.'

Fran felt her skin go clammy. What the heck was it now?

'There was a fire at the home of one of our own prominent Chinese businessmen. Less of a home,

122

more like a very luxurious fortified compound. Priceless antiques, electronic alarms, the lot. Funnily enough, no one was home. Maybe they were expecting it. We'll be calling it accidental – maybe his wok caught fire, that sort of thing. It wasn't a bomb, but it was definitely arson.'

'Oh!' said Fran faintly. Her brain seemed to be taking a well-earned holiday. What was she meant to think about that?

'Looks like a tit-for-tat, you see,' Charlie explained. 'You bomb our night-club; we torch your house.'

So that was what she was meant to think about that. And our tiger bones. You bomb our tiger bones . . .

'And you say both of these groups are Chinese,' put in Fran. 'They've got nothing to do with the Separatists?'

'Why do you say that?' Was Charlie's voice a little sharp?

'Well, you know – bombs. That's what terrorists do, isn't it?'

'Ah well, like I said, the whisper is that the bomber was Chinese. But it's always interesting when two groups like that are intent on knocking seven bells out of each other in our own back yard, don't you think? As if we haven't got enough problems of our own. The trouble is, we flat-foots haven't got a bloody clue what's really going on.'

'Chinatown and all that?'

'Exactly. So it's convenient to let the Tigers take the rap until someone gets it sorted. Which reminds me. We've also had three more bodies floating in lagoons overnight. Oh, don't worry – none of them is your husband. I just didn't want you hearing it on the news, that's all.'

'Thank you, Charlie. I do appreciate all this. I've been in touch with Nevil's partner, and he's certain that Nevil should be calling him soon. I just wish I had some positive news that's all – so you could forget about me and get on with your work.'

'Me? I'm only chasing lost wallets until I get my transfer. If I ever do. Actually I'm not even in the office today – it's my day off – and I did wonder . . .' Charlie sounded uncharacteristically coy, hesitant, almost as if she wanted a favour.

'What did you wonder?'

'If I could come down and have a chat and maybe a swim in your pool. I do love swimming, and it's so difficult here – you know, a woman by herself.'

'Why, of course! I'm stuck here all day by the phone being stalked by a couple of charming Danes. You could keep me out of trouble.'

'That sounds interesting,' laughed Charlie. 'It's my day off. I'll get a taxi.'

They settled for somewhere between two and three o'clock.

Well, thought Fran as she put down the phone, I wonder what that was really all about. Maybe Charlie actually did like swimming and never got the chance. But could there possibly be some other reason? If Charlie was thinking more of fishing than swimming, maybe she could do a little fishing of her own. About whether Charlie trusted all her own colleagues, for example. Anyway, this time, she would stick to tea.

For rather similar reasons, Fran was careful to stick to one Cinnamon Beach Special cocktail which she ordered for herself for politeness sake when it came to the pre-lunch drink with Anders and Klaus. It came in the inevitable green coconut shell festooned with tiny brollies, twisty straws, chunks of exotic fruit, and a flower or two.

'Skol! Is that right? I don't know whether to drink this, eat it or wear it.'

The two men laughed. 'Careful,' said Anders. 'It looks dangerous.'

'Well, it tastes delicious. Here's to a happy holiday.' OK, it was time to get a few things straight. Not too many things, of course. 'How long are you here for?' There was something in the drink she didn't recognise – possibly it was *arak*, which, if the stories were true, could make you feel as if you'd just fallen out of your coconut tree. Yes, after this one, it would have to be Coke.

Anders said they'd arrived in Colombo last Thursday, with no particular plans except a week or so touring the island, after which they were moving on to Thailand, Malaysia and Bali.

'That's quite a schedule,' said Fran. 'I didn't know you had the long school holidays at this time in Denmark.'

'We don't. I'd like to tell you that we just had enough one day, ran screaming from the classroom and jumped on a plane for the mysterious East, but it's nothing so exciting. If we behave well and don't beat the children, we're allowed a sabbatical now and again. Is that correct English?'

'It would be, if we had sabbaticals,' relied Fran. 'I suppose you could say it's American. How very civilised.'

They chatted on pleasantly enough about their impressions of the places they'd seen so far, and then Klaus said, 'But then we were a little disturbed by the bomb in Colombo.'

Not half as much as I was, thought Fran. As if it

was of little consequence, she explained about being caught in the traffic jam caused by the explosion and worrying about her husband who was in the Fort area at the time, at which she was immediately treated as a heroine. Bombs were, it seemed, not too common in Copenhagen.

'And your husband is still in Colombo?' asked Anders.

'Er, yes. His business is not finished yet.' Well, I hope it's not, she added to herself, wincing at her own unfortunate choice of words.

'It is the English cool,' said Klaus, and ordered another round.

Perhaps it was. But then, what was one suppose to do – run round the pool yelling, 'My God, we could be ruined'? She glanced round at the scene beside the pool. Were there other people here with a nagging aches under their suntans – imminent divorce, serious illness, wayward offspring? They all looked so completely chilled out. But possibly, to the casual observer, so did she.

'I should be hearing from him soon,' she said. 'But I have to stay by the phone. If I'd known, I'd have brought some more books.'

'Oh please, you must borrow some of ours . . .'

She'd quite forgotten the time and was doing her best to explain a tricky bit of dialogue which Anders had highlighted in *The English Patient*, when a waiter hurried up with a folded sheet of paper on his tray.

'Fax for Mrs Merrick.'

Fran almost snatched the sheet in her eagerness, while the waiter hovered. Without fuss, Anders slung a couple of ten rupee notes on the tray.

'Thanks,' she breathed, 'Excuse me – it's from my husband's partner and I may need to reply.' Her eyes

126

devoured the words. *Overnight fax from Nev . . . the deal's gone through. Great . .we're off the hook!*

She couldn't help letting out a whoop as she read on. *So stop worrying. He says he's met up with Brian G. and he's staying with him for a few days. He was using the AWW office in Colombo, return number below. What a pity he didn't ring, the silly sod. Probably didn't want to wake me up. Anyway, we know he's OK and where he is, more or less. So, over to you, sweetheart, for a wildly sexy reunion and give him one from me, nudge-nudge, wink-wink. And while you're at it, have a bottle of champers on the house. Anyone's house, but don't fall off the roof. Meanwhile I'm off to a meeting at Cuthbertson & Farts to tell them what they can do with their merger plans.*

'Jesus!' muttered Fran. It had got that close, had it! 'Excuse me, I really have to go and catch my husband before he disappears onto the nearest golf course.'

It was all she could do not to leap across the grass punching the air and doing heel kicks. And to think Nevil still didn't know she was in the country! Boy, was he in for a surprise.

'Good news, ma'am?' inquired the clerk as she asked to use the fax.

'Pretty good,' she told him, 'and the next news should be even better.'

Since the receiving end would be a public office, the message she sent to Nevil, care of Brian, was quite restrained. It simply told him the why's and where's of what she was doing here, said to say hello to Brian and told Nevil to ring back as soon as possible. Even realising that the chances of Nevil actually being in the AWW office at the time were practically nil didn't stem the surge of elation. Obviously it would take whoever was around a little time to contact him, but now she had a number, she didn't mind the wait. If all else failed, it would be a simple matter to go back to Colombo tomorrow and find the AWW people. Someone would be bound to know what the two men were up to.

By the time Charlie was due, she was still in a mood to celebrate. After all, she'd found Nevil, made some interesting new friends, and as far as she was concerned the Blue Peacock and all who sailed therein could go and stir fry their little Chinese heads. This was where the holiday really began.

Charlie arrived looking different again, hair smartly up, in a cream button-through dress and a cherry red beach bag and sandals. 'New,' she said. 'From the Mount Lavinia hotel shop – in honour of my first swim since Brighton. What do you think?'

'Down to the ground,' said Fran approvingly, who'd made a bit of an effort herself, more on the off-chance that Nevil might just come wondering in to surprise her. It was just the sort of thing he'd do. He might even have Brian in tow, and it could turn into quite a party. One or two heads turned as they paused at the bar to order some tea and then strolled to a vacant table by the pool.

'Now wouldn't that be great!' laughed Charlie, clapping her hands together with pleasure as Fran filled her in. 'I feel it's about time I met this husband of yours. By the way – those two over there with their eyes on stalks. They wouldn't be the Great Danes, would they? The dark one is very much my type.'

'Hey, Charlie! Behave yourself,' giggled Fran. 'Do you want me to introduce you? That's Klaus. His English isn't quite up to Anders' style – that's the blond one – but I'm sure you'll manage.'

'Just kidding,' sighed Charlie. 'This is a small

island. The staff here are all Sinhalese. For all I know, I could have a relative behind every palm tree.'

'You mean you can tell they're all Sinhalese?'

'Normally, if one is, they all are. We call it good staff relations, if you follow me.'

'I follow you. By the way, anything else on the bombing or whatever?'

'Ah well, I suppose you won't be too interested in all that now.'

'Why ever not? We tourists don't often get a chance to hear the low-down on what's really going on.'

'Believe me, neither do we,' said Charlie.

'What? Are you speaking as a police officer, or as an ordinary Jo Soap?'

'Both, my dear. Hey, but it's hot. Let me get out of this rather expensive little number before I crease it.' She unbuttoned the cream dress. Under it was a bronze satin one-piece costume which set off a classical South Asian body that wouldn't have disgraced an erotic temple frieze.

'You make me feel like a bean-pole,' grinned Fran.

'Ah, but you have the thighs, my dear. Just think – after four children and too much curry, I'd be like a barrel of lard – but you'd still be an elegant bean-pole.'

They chatted inconsequentially for a while, with Fran thinking quite regretfully that she would really miss Charlie's warmth and flirty frankness. She could sense that beneath it was someone who could love intensely, who would have dearly liked a husband and family, and it angered her that here was a perfectly good woman who would make a lot of men happy going to a kind of waste because of local custom.

'But you were saying,' said Fran, determined not to give up too easily on how Charlie saw her future with the police. 'Is there a lot of corruption here? How would you say it compared with England?'

'I wasn't in England long enough to run up against it there, and I'm not just being tactful. Here?' She waggled her hand. 'India is worse, so they say. But I do feel there are things happening here that are new. There's too much money around, and as usual, it's the wrong people who have it. Drugs; this tiger bone business, for example; it's beginning to stink.' She wrinkled her nose. 'Come on, let's swim.'

Charlie got up and took a smart header into the pool. Fran followed with gusto, noticing as she did so that the two Danes were already in the pool.

'Race you,' yelled Charlie, striking out into fast crawl. 'Five lengths, OK?'

'Right, England v. Sri Lanka, Women's Free-style,' gasped Fran turning turtle to follow in Charlie's foaming wake.

'Too narrowly nationalistic. Can Denmark join in?' called Anders. 'We'll give you ladies a length start.'

'That's sexist,' yelled Fran. 'But go on then, if you insist.'

'And racist,' laughed Charlie, getting on her marks. 'OK – go!'

The two women shot off down the pool, with Charlie taking an easy lead. As they reached the other end, the two men started, together with a German couple who seemed keen to join the fun. Other bathers took to the sides to watch. By the third length, Charlie had lapped Fran, while the others, after a good start, were not making much progress against Charlie's barrelling strokes.

'Don't tell them I was the South of England

policewoman's champion, they'll only say it's not fair,' gurgled Charlie, changing from a furious crawl to an impressive butterfly as she passed Fran.

'No kidding!'

'Did she say she is a policewoman?' spluttered Klaus. 'Madam, I'm drowning. Please arrest me!'

Charlie won of course, to a round of applause from the nearby tables, although not by much with the men's handicap. They hung onto the sides, laughingly getting their breath back. 'Now, for the honour of Denmark,' said Anders, 'Klaus will astound you with some high diving, and myself with some belly flapping, is that right?'

'Flopping!' they both laughed.

'See, you are even affecting my English!'

The men strolled off to the diving board to avenge themselves.

'Maybe you should have joined Air/Sea Rescue,' said Fran to Charlie, still puffing. 'Or the Marines.'

'What, and have to identify drowned tourists who don't know the meaning of a rip tide, or have to go round fishing mutilated bodies out of lagoons? No, thank you!' She paused. 'Actually Fran, that was one of the reasons I came down this afternoon. But now you know your husband is safe, it didn't seem important. One of the bodies we found last night was a European male – British, actually – and I didn't want you having a heart attack if you heard it on the radio. It's OK, I know for sure it wasn't your husband. It was someone who's been working out here for some time. The odd part is, it looks like a Tiger killing – his face, and so on, which is a bit weird. They can't release the details yet until they notify his people in England, but it'll probably go out as a car accident . . .'

131

In spite of Charlie's reassurances, Fran felt her chest tighten unaccountably . . . *Of his bones are coral made* . . . 'What was his name?' she said quietly.

'Now let me think – Gaskill, Brian Thomas, 32, unmarried . . .'

*They are pearls that were his eyes* . . . Fran felt her head begin to spin. She couldn't get her breath, and there was no strength in her fingers trying to keep their grip on the pool side. Suddenly she felt very cold, as if a blue icy stream had engulfed her, and then there was red – then only blackness.

# Chapter Nine

Fran's next impression was that she was trapped under some great weight which was pressing the life out of her. Maybe if she could somehow manage to groan, it would take pity on her and stop. But to groan, you had to be able to breath, and she couldn't remember how. Then something which must have been another part of her managed to work it out, and her body gave a great choking heave, followed by a dreadful gurgling groan that didn't sound like her at all.

Miraculously the pressure on her chest stopped and she heard a man's voice saying urgently, 'She's OK. She's breathing.' The voice wasn't Nevil's. It wasn't Tony's, either. It couldn't be Brian Gaskill's, because Brian was dead – dead in the water – face-less . . .

'Oh my God,' she gasped, 'Brian!' and tried to sit up.

'Who's Brian?' she heard someone ask, as several arms tried to support her. 'Is it her husband? Anyone here called Brian?'

Why were there suddenly so many faces around?

'No, I don't think Brian's here,' said Charlie's voice. 'She'll be all right now. She's just had a bit of a black-out, that's all. It must have been all the extra exercise. You'll be all right now, Fran, won't you?'

Fran looked up at her vaguely. Charlie, the police-woman, was ordering her to be all right, to pull herself together. Charlie was smart. Charlie had worked it out.

She gave a few experimental coughs and then her head flopped again. She felt sick, as if she'd swallowed a bucketful of bleach. 'I'm OK,' she managed to say. 'Just give me a minute or two.' Then maybe it would all go away. Brian wouldn't be dead after all. Nevil would be here at any moment and everything would be fine again.

With polite murmurs of concern, the crowd of faces slowly receded. Anders and Klaus still seemed to be there, helping her to a chair. The effort of not thinking about all the horror made her feel light-headed again. If Brian really *was* dead, where did that leave Nevil? He was supposed to have been with him.

'Perhaps you'd like to go for a lie down,' Charlie was saying. 'I'll come with you, and we'll get some tea sent up. I won't go until I'm sure you're feeling much better.'

'No, don't go,' muttered Fran feebly, as Charlie got her to her feet. This woman was the only thing between her sanity and whimpering terror.

'Perhaps we may check later to see how you are?' she heard Anders say from far away.

'What? Oh yes, thank you, please do.' Was this what they called shock – when you wanted to scream and nothing came out except perfectly ordinary, silly words, and you felt clammy all over?

Charlie collected their things, and then took her arm as they walked slowly upstairs. Fran thought she might be sleep-walking, and was almost at the edge of the cliff. Hoped she was, in fact. Perhaps it was one of those dreams where if anyone spoke, you died.

Only when the door of the room was safely closed did she let go and collapse in a heap, sobbing and shivering on the bed.

'I'm so sorry,' said Charlie, stroking her hair. 'So very sorry. You were brilliant about it. I had no idea – no inkling at all that you could have known that poor man.'

'I know,' wept Fran. 'But it's not just the shock. I keep thinking that if only I'd mentioned Brian's name, told you everything, this might not have happened. And then, if they can do this to Brian, what might they do to Nevil? He could be dead already for all I know!' She could feel hysteria like a coiled spring inside her.

'Don't!' Charlie was shaking her shoulders. 'Just don't think about it.'

'Why not? I have to. Somebody has to. Oh God, why is all this happening . . .'

'Oh thank heavens, here's the tea.'

'*Tea?*' Fran's voice was rising unbidden. 'Is that all you can think of - tea?'

'Sh'sh, my dear, while I open the door, or they'll think I'm giving you the third degree. That's better. Right now, tea's all we've got.'

Strangely, the sheer effort of having to sit up to drink it stopped Fran going to pieces again.

'Now why don't you tell me all about it?' Charlie's voice was soothing, almost motherly.

'But I don't know where to start . . .' She was losing it again. Wanted to lose it. Didn't want to be found. Wanted to hide . . .

Charlie gripped her arm as if afraid she might suddenly fly away. 'OK, let's start with 'they'. It's as good as anything. You said "If they can do this to Brian". Who are *they*, Fran?'

'Oh come on, Charlie. Jackie Kennedy said that too, you know. She said, "They've shot Jack." Then everyone wanted to know who *they* were, and she didn't know, did she?' How the shit should I know who *they* are?' The anger was helping to drive away the fear. 'It's just a figure of speech, that's all. I thought you were supposed to be the expert. Suppose I ask *you* a few questions, like how exactly Brian died. Or wouldn't I want to know?'

Charlie, the professional, took the outburst on the chin. 'Fair enough,' she said softly. 'It was like this: we think he must have been in his car. It was found abandoned just outside the northern suburbs of Colombo, on the road he usually took home from the AWW office.'

'Are you absolutely sure there was no one else in the car with him?'

'Well yes, we're pretty sure.' Charlie's eyes widened. 'Surely you're not suggesting that your husband might have been with him?'

'Read that,' said Fran hoarsely. She grabbed Tony's fax from the bedside table and pushed it at Charlie.

'I see.' Charlie let out her breath as she read it. 'No, we're sure he was alone. The secretary at AWW said he left by himself after working late. He was on his way back to the rented bungalow he shared with the local AWW representative who'd already gone home. It was when this man reported Brian missing and we'd got an unidentified European body from the lagoons on our hands that we were able to put the two and two together.'

'And now you're going to tell me Brian was killed immediately, with a nice clean bullet in the back of the head.'

'I would tell you that if I could,' said Charlie, and

136

Fran saw she was near to tears. The whole mess had obviously shaken her up too, especially since she could now see that Nevil might easily have been with Brian that night. Fran almost felt sorry for her, and there seemed no point in making this harder than it had to be on either of them.

'I see,' she said, suddenly icy calm. 'So they tried to get some information out of him in the good old-fashioned way – no, don't tell me, I can't bear it. And then they killed him and carved up his face. Bastards! Animals!'

'Tigers, of the Tamil kind,' replied Charlie without irony. 'It looks like their work, and if it wasn't, it was meant to look like them.'

'You mean you're not even sure it was the Tigers?'

'They don't exactly hand in signed confessions, you know. I'm sorry, I didn't mean to sound flippant. It's just that it doesn't seem to make sense for the Tigers to do such a thing. This sort of killing is usually a punishment for police informers or some other form of betrayal, and it seems highly unlikely that your friend could have been in any way connected with them. All I'm saying is, that given all the circumstances, it might suit certain other people to make us think it was the Tigers.'

'Who, for chrissake?' She badly wanted to say something like, 'Exactly how many other groups of sadistic, murdering bastards do you have around here?' Anything to hurt.

'Look, I think we have to assume that this killing is somehow connected to the Blue Peacock affair. Your friend was working for AWW, and we now know about the tiger bones at the Peacock. So we have to admit a strong possibility that he was killed because he was getting to close to the bone trade. Now that's

137

not Tiger business. This killing means that it's doubly important for us to find the owners of the Peacock and sort out what's really going on. Believe me, people of that kind could easily get rid of someone and then make it look like the work of the separatists just to put us off the track.'

Fran put her head in her hands to stop it splitting. If she didn't get hold of herself, the seething brew of anger, fear and guilt would splatter everywhere. 'Right, you've answered my questions. Thanks for that. I know the police don't have to, and I appreciate it. Sorry I snapped.'

Charlie nodded and patted her arm.

Fran had to make a conscious effort to relax. 'OK, I'll tell you absolutely everything I can to nail who-ever did this. Then you can make your own mind up and take it from there.' This wasn't going to be easy, and she didn't want to leave out any seemingly un-important details this time. 'Here's all I know about any tie-in Brian might have had with any this.' She quickly told Charlie about the e-mail she'd destroyed, the surveillance equipment, the men asking for Brian at the InterContinental, and as much about Brian's background as she knew.

When she'd finished, Charlie breathed in deeply, as if she was preparing for a dive.

'My God,' she said at last. 'I think I'm beginning to see. I missed it, didn't I?'

Fran didn't dare say a word. Charlie seemed to be staring into space, outwardly calm. But it felt as if there was an electrical current coming from her, and it was enough to make the fine hairs prickle on the back of Fran's neck. Perhaps they were both under some kind of evil spell that was drawing together and fusing their worst imaginings.

With what felt like her last reserves of strength and will, Fran got up to find her notes and the *Time* magazine and threw them onto Charlie's lap.

It had the desired effect. Charlie jumped like a shot rabbit, but at least it brought her to herself again.

Yet in the end, it was Fran who had to say it. 'It *was* the Tigers, wasn't it? *They* killed Brian because he was onto the bone trade. That's the link. It's the bone trade that's been giving the Tigers a fresh source of funding. I can't see it clearly, but I can smell it. It's all tied up with the money-laundering at the Peacock. The Chinese owners are using the Tigers, or the Tigers are using the Chinese. Or more likely they've got some kind of ghastly mutual interest deal going. Am I getting warm?'

'You're smart,' replied Charlie tonelessly. 'You should have my job.'

'But Charlie, it hasn't been your job to put all this together, not lately anyway. You didn't have the facts. I didn't know myself what I was sitting on. But it all ties in, doesn't it? If only I'd said something earlier – but it all sounded so far-fetched and paranoid.'

'Look, don't blame yourself for Brian's death. Even if you'd told me, I wouldn't have been able to see far enough into this to prevent it, and there are still so many loose ends. But do you know what's really worrying me? If we two can make these connections, who else might already know about it?'

Fran closed her eyes and tried to work out what Charlie was getting at. Did she mean politicians with secret Tamil separatist sympathies, or commercial interests in on the financing side of it – banks, perhaps? Or even her own colleagues in the police force.

Suddenly the complications and ramifications of it

all were too much for Fran. It wasn't that she didn't care – she *couldn't* care. She'd had enough, and had nothing else to tell. Brian was dead, and no one could bring him back. They could keep their bloody bombs, bones and torture, their filthy money and corruption, their political shenanigans and all the rotten rest of it. All she wanted now was to know that Nevil was safe and get the hell out of this place for ever. The whole lot could sink into the sea for all she cared.

'What will you do now, Charlie?' she asked, her voice strangely calm for all the turmoil inside her.

The answer surprised her. 'Take a shower, if I may. No, it's not to help me think, but I'm going to have to make a call, and I'd rather not do it in my cossie.' Maybe Charlie too had had enough, looked too far into the depths for one afternoon, and wanted to believe they were both wildly, stupidly wrong.

'Sure,' murmured Fran. 'Use anything you want.'

She got up stiffly and walked to the balcony. Her legs felt wobbly and her face taut and dry. Below was the same peaceful scene: people strewn about like big untidy flowers on the grass, kids kicking like drowning dragonflies in the pool, waiters in white *saramas* dispensing coloured drinks, and the sudden wink of a polished metal tray. Not peaceful. Surreal. Because someone she knew was suddenly and horribly dead. How long was this weird situation going to last? Maybe she'd be stuck here for ever, like a mad tourist version of the Flying Dutchman, doomed to spend eternity in strange hotels waiting for a message that never came, from a man she thought she was married to, but only in her dreams.

A mosquito had been experimenting with her ankle bone. That was real enough. It itched. Down there, Anders and Klaus were in their usual place and she drew back, hoping they hadn't seen her. How long before she told them? She supposed she would, eventually. Eternity was a very long time.

Dressed again, Charlie declined the offer of the room phone and went downstairs, saying she hoped she wouldn't be too long, but sometimes it took a while to reach the right people. As Fran showered, she wondered if it was just courtesy or the need not to be overheard that had sent Charlie to the office phone, and who the 'right people' were. Listlessly, she found herself looking round for something suitable to wear. Holiday glad-rags didn't seem right when someone had died. It was a matter of respect.

When Charlie came back, she was sitting on the bed drying her hair, but the minute she saw Charlie's face she knew that it hadn't simply been courtesy that had sent her downstairs to make the call, and that Charlie at least was in touch with horrid reality.

'What is it?' she asked, not really wanting to know the answer; shocked that she'd almost said, irritably, 'What is it *now*?'

'Fran, you may never speak to me again, but I have to ask you to do something. You don't have to. You're not a relative. But it would help us to clear up the formalities.'

Fran looked away, half guessing what was coming. Brian hadn't had much of a family. She'd told Charlie so herself. 'Who actually identified the body?' she asked warily.

'No one, officially. Not yet.'

'Oh Christ,' muttered Fran. They couldn't do this to her. They couldn't.

'You see, in cases like this, where someone's from abroad, we're in a kind of Catch 22 situation. We should really have a positive identification before we notify the next of kin. Because of the distance, it's only fair. But it's difficult to get a proper one when people here don't really know the deceased intimately.'

'But couldn't the people at AWW do it?'

'There were only two of them, both local – the secretary, and the other man, the one who was sharing a bungalow with Brian – and they haven't known him long. The AWW rep. did identify a blood-stained piece of a shirt in the car and the shoes found on the body as his. It was a start, but it wasn't a formal identification. Now he's disappeared. So has the girl, and the office is locked. I guess after what's happened, they're both absolutely terrified.'

'Or dead,' said Fran bleakly.

'No, we think they've gone to relatives. It could take a while to find them. This whole island is full of relatives, not all of whom are what you might call co-operative, which is to say, entire villages will lie through their teeth if they think it's necessary. So you see, you've known him longer than anyone here, and it would help us enormously if . . .'

'I can't. I mean, I've never . . .' Fran's voice was no more than a hoarse whisper.

'It'll be made easy for you, I promise. You won't have to see the face. Can you remember his hair? Or anything else at all that might help?'

Fran was quite numb now, and yet she was being asked to think about more impossible things. It wasn't fair, when you couldn't grasp anything clearly, yet somehow the answers were coming.

'He had sort of sandy hair.' Her voice sounded flat as an answerphone. 'Almost crimpy. He usually had it cropped. And he'd had his ears pierced when he was younger. I remember Nevil saying he'd been a bit of a punk in his youth. But Brian wasn't the earring type any more. You could still see a scar on one lobe. Perhaps it went septic or something.' Her voice trailed off meaninglessly.

'That might be all we'd need. With you present and a signature, we can get onto the people in England to notify his next of kin. I expect he was insured with AWW so that'll take care of the body being flown home.'

'And of course you want me to do this as soon as possible.'

'So you'll do it, then? It would help us a lot.'

'Charlie, what real choice do I have? It's the least I can do for a friend – make sure he can be sent home for burial. I just wish Nevil was here, that's all.'

As Fran wept again, Charlie came and put an arm round her. 'One last bad thing. I'm afraid I can't come with you, Fran. I have my reasons. Don't ask me yet. Will you trust me?'

Tears still flowing, Fran nodded, barely hearing her. 'Christ,' she muttered, in a desperate attempt to staunch herself with black humour, 'some holiday this is turning out to be.'

'It took me some time to realise,' said Charlie, gripping her shoulder, 'that often when the British are ironic, they're really being brave. You only have to say the word and I'll cancel it, but I took the liberty of making an appointment for you since I had the right people on the other end. A car will pick you up at 9.30. You'll be taken straight there and the visit itself will be very quick. You should be safely back here by three o'clock at the latest. And then I swear, all the stops will be pulled out to find Nevil for you.'

\*   \*   \*

After Charlie had gone, Fran sat for a long time trying to come to terms with what had happened. It got dark, yet she couldn't bring herself to put the lights on. If only Nevil would ring, she told herself for the hundredth time, all this would be more bearable. For one thing she wouldn't have to break the news to Tony that Brian was dead. If he was. Suddenly she sat up rigid in the darkened room. Maybe it was all a horrible mistake and it was some other poor sod lying in that morgue without his face.

They call this denial, don't they, she thought, almost cheerfully. I'm in denial. And I'm bloody going to stay in denial – at least until I'm sure it's him. Why upset Tony unnecessarily? Yes, that was the right thing to do. Don't believe it until you have to. Look at Doubting Thomas. He'd been in denial, although at the time they'd probably called it something else, like lack of faith, and that had turned out all right. Was she going mad? Probably not, but how could she know for sure?

Hastily she put on the light and ordered a sandwich, if only to get her teeth unclenched again. There were so many things Charlie had said that she'd wanted to ask about, but now she couldn't remember them. Almost certainly they would come back to her with a bump at about two in the morning, and she wouldn't get a wink of sleep. Maybe some whisky would help. But too much to drink usually made her sick, and the thought of having to visit a police morgue with a hang-over and a grotty stomach was enough to put her off any such idea. Tomorrow night would be the time to forget.

When the tray came, she was touched to find that the manager had sent up a basket of fruit with a compliments card, and there was a neat little marigold garland round the carefully garnished sandwich. But she couldn't seem to swallow, however hard she chewed. Her jaws felt like steel clamps and there were knots in her shoulder muscles. She was listlessly trying to peel one of the hard, yellow-skinned oranges from the basket when there was another knock at the door, and Anders' voice cautiously asked if she was feeling better.

'We saw your light come on,' he said as she let him in, quite pleased for the company. 'Klaus sends his regards, but we thought two noisy men might disturb you. Perhaps if you are well enough, you would like to join us for dinner.'

'You've all been so kind,' she said, feeling near to tears again. Oh, what the heck - she needed someone to talk to. 'I wouldn't be very good company, I'm afraid.' How was she going to explain her obvious distress without getting in too deep? 'You see, it wasn't just the swimming. You remember Charlie saying she was a policewoman? She happened to mention the name of an Englishman who'd just been killed in a bad road accident outside Colombo. It turned out that he was a friend. Well, a friend of my husband's, really, and of course she had no idea we knew him.'

'And that was the name you said – Brian. But that's terrible! What a tragic thing to happen on holiday.'

'Actually he'd been working here.' She had to say that, because it might be in the papers or on the TV soon, and both were readily available in the hotel. People often watched the TV in the bar out of sheer curiosity, and most of it was in English.

'Was he driving or walking? The roads here are so very dangerous.'

145

'He was driving. I'm sorry, I can't talk about it.'

'I have distressed you. Please forgive me.'

'It's not the talking about it,' she said when she was able. 'It's what I have to do tomorrow that's getting to me,' among other things, she badly wanted to add. 'They've asked me to identify the body.'

'But that is quite appalling! Is there no other way? Your husband, perhaps?'

'He can't,' said Fran a little too quickly. 'He's away. I mean, he's not in Colombo.' She was beginning to sound incoherent.

'But of course, I understand.'

No you don't, she wanted to scream. *I* don't understand. Nobody understands.

'You will have to do this alone?'

She nodded dumbly.

'Would you let me come with you? It would perhaps make the travelling easier.'

It was quite uncanny. How was it that this man always said exactly the right thing? His offer was so unexpected, so tactfully put, and so very welcome. She explained about the car being arranged, adding that she'd still be very glad of his company.

Yet almost as soon as Anders had gone, Fran regretted accepting the offer. It was a long way to Colombo, and after what she had to do, it would be an even longer way back. Charlie had already warned her not to expect LAPD Blue standards, and she had no idea how she was going to take the experience. Could she trust herself not to say too much to Anders? Perhaps she was actually adding to her ordeal by allowing herself to be with someone as naturally sympathetic as he seemed to be.

But then, she was still in denial, and it wasn't going to be Brian, was it? It was going to be some total stranger. And she wasn't going to have to tell Tony, and Nevil would be here soon. And the moon tonight would be a weird shade of blue, and pigs would fly like fruit bats over the darkened sea.

# Chapter Ten

Afterwards, Fran wondered if that night had marked some kind of transition in the process of growing up, or at least of getting older. She'd been quite young when her mother had died and for all the pain and tears and aching sense of loss, she'd felt strangely uninvolved in the whole process. There had been so little she could do, or ever could have done in her short life, to prevent it. That was twenty years ago, and when she thought about it, she'd come to associate death with a kind of hopeless, helpless remoteness. Having once been wounded by death when most of her contemporaries had not, she'd hoped the avenging angel had done his worst, and she could afford to relax a little.

But this time it was different. So different that it had caught her on the raw. This time she was being asked to get involved. This wasn't something from the impartial world of illness and disease. Someone had done this to Brian – ordered it, carried it out, quite deliberately. At first it had shocked her that Charlie had presumed to make the identification appointment without even asking. Did Charlie really have that much faith in her, or had she just crossed her fingers and hoped? Somehow, it mattered.

She chose her attire with care the next morning: a long, dark brown cotton sun dress, the strappy top disguised with the short-sleeved linen jacket she wore for travelling. For some reason, she felt she ought to wear a hat, and wound a silk scarf that matched the dress round her fine straw sun hat to make it look more stylish. Brian had liked women to look what he called smart, and it only seemed right to do her best for him. The only possible bag she had that was big enough and matched would have disappointed him. It was now crammed with tissues, bottled water, a cologne stick, insect repellent (she did not want to think about why she'd put those last two in), her passport, refresher wipes, disprins, stomach settlers, sunglasses, a notebook and pen, and lots more totally unnecessary bits and pieces to convince her that she had thought of everything and was going to cope. Nevil, in happier circumstances, would no doubt have suggested adding chewing gum, string and a hot water bottle, and just then she would have taken any amount of his teasing.

She thought she'd better eat some breakfast, if only to stop her feeling faint later. It didn't seem the sort of day to stop for lunch. Anders was waiting for her in the lobby in good time for the car, and she was touched to see that he too had abandoned his usual beachwear for light slacks and a plain shirt. He wasn't carrying a camera, although it must have been tempting for him to bring one, because she'd noticed that he liked to go for oddly angled shots round the pool, or of blossoms, or the tiny chipmunk-like creatures as they darted after fallen seeds between in the trees.

At the desk, she left a message to say she would be back by three o'clock and that if her husband rang he was to be asked to come to the hotel as soon as he could. It was her last attempt to persuade herself that all this was just some particularly foul nightmare, and that Nevil would be waiting for her in the bar with Brian and their golf clubs when she got back.

The car that came wasn't a marked police car, rather to her relief. It was a well-kept sedan with tinted windows, air conditioning and a sliding glass partition to separate them from the driver, who was young and smart. Fran thought he looked like an off-duty officer, or perhaps a plain-clothes one. As she expected, policeman or not, he drove like Grand Prix winner on acid.

To put Anders and herself at ease, she said she'd never felt the need for air conditioning and tinted windows in places like this, and he agreed wholeheartedly. In spite of the seriousness of the occasion, or perhaps because of it, they chatted on, about his teaching, places they'd been and anything of interest that they happened to pass. She could not, she felt, have asked for a better companion in the circumstances, challenging and bizarre as they were, and at least she'd provided him with one more tale to tell when he got back home to Copenhagen. 'The day I took a mysterious Englishwoman to the police morgue in Colombo' did have a certain ring to it.

Yet the last thing she wanted now was to be mysterious. All she could think of as the car sped along was that being Fran Merrick, boring housewife and company asset, would do nicely for the rest of her life.

'May I ask, was your friend married?' Anders' voice made her jump. Deep in her thoughts, she'd almost forgotten he was there.

'He was once,' she replied. 'And it took him long enough to get round to it. He was always on the move, you see. But in the end I don't think marriage suited him. There were no children. He never mentioned his mother. She left when he was very young, and I'm not sure about his father. I think he spent some time in care, but I seem to remember he has a married sister somewhere.'

'Will she want to come out here, do you think?'

'I've never met her, but I'd say it's unlikely. She's got young children. He sometimes mentioned his nephews. He seemed quite proud of being an uncle.'

'It is a relief, I suppose, that there is no widow. You say he worked out here. His colleagues will surely be very upset.'

'They're more than upset. They're terrified.' She hadn't meant to say it, but the well-meaning remark had caught her off guard. Unsure of how much the driver could hear, she lowered her voice. 'Actually, Anders, this wasn't a simply road accident. Brian was killed because they wanted some information out of him.'

'Do you mean industrial spying? But who would do . . .'

She'd turned to him and given an almost imperceptible warning nod towards the driver, who fortunately was preoccupied with trying to overtake a coach. In the tinted light of the car interior, Anders' eyes were grey, but she saw the spark of quick intelligence at work that had stopped him in mid-sentence.

'Let's call it that, and talk about the weather,' she said briskly

But the slip worried her. It was what they called in racquet sports an unforced error. There was no reason for her not to trust Anders. That wasn't the problem. But if she was going to tell him anything more, it had to be her choice, not her mistake. Bugging was not something to which she'd ever given much thought, but it was quite possible the car was fitted with some sort of device for listening to the conversation in the back, perhaps with a disabling switch for passengers in the know. A couple of days ago she would have dismissed any such thoughts as pure fantasy, but what Charlie had said about not being with her at the identification had kept her wondering ever since. If she'd read the signals correctly, Charlie didn't trust some of her own people, and that was enough to make her bite her tongue.

The traffic in Colombo was as bad as usual, but it least it was moving today. With a kind of sickened resignation she took no notice of where they were heading, although Anders was intent on following their route on his map. She did not want to know where they kept the bodies in this town, and taking no notice was her way of reassuring herself that she would never have to go anywhere near the place again.

Somewhere in a leafier part of town, they pulled into a kind of compound with the inevitable peeling stuccoed walls and a wire gate. A policeman let them through on a nod, and the car stopped at one of a collection of buildings inside. It all looked a bit piecemeal, as if some older colonial structure had been stretched until it had podded into single-storey replicas of itself. Some Sixties concrete blocks had been added as an afterthought, and part of it seemed to be a hospital. On the whole, she thought it didn't look too bad, considering Charlie's warning.

Clutching her bag, she turned to Anders. 'I can't ask you to come in with me,' she said firmly. 'I have no idea what to expect, and it wouldn't be fair, under the circumstances . . .' Her voice faltered. 'It's enough that you've come, and that you'll be here to catch me when I come out.'

'I will come with you,' he replied and opened his side of the car while the driver opened hers. Then he came round and offered her his arm. 'As far as they will allow me.'

Outside the office for which they appeared to be heading was a straggling queue of people. In fact there were queues of various lengths outside all the blocks. The people looked mainly poor and depressed, and stared at her with listless eyes. Some of the women had their faces covered with the edge of their saris as if in grief, and somewhere in the queue a baby was wailing, a thin, desperately insistent wail.

The man with them ignored the crowd and led them through into an office where a lot of uniformed police were typing and generally bustling about, but for Fran the details were becoming blurred.

The driver did most of the talking. Log books were consulted, piles of forms shifted and metal filing cabinets were opened and shut with clangs that did her already frayed nerves no favours. Would the body be in a drawer or on a table? She couldn't suppress a shudder, and felt Anders tighten his grip on her arm. Only a fraction above her head, the helicopter blades of a huge ceiling fan stirred the air. For a brain-twisting second it seemed as if everything was upside-down, and the room was about to spin out of control and plummet from the sky into some unseen canyon below her feet.

Automatically she showed her passport and signed something they said she ought to sign, desperately hoping that this might be all that was required of her.

'Would you come this way, ma'am?' asked a

female voice, and for a moment, Fran hoped it was Charlie. But there was no resemblance. The woman was very slim and dark and had the kind of legs that started at the edge of her khaki skirt. Fran thought she would remember those legs for some time. Anders was told firmly to take a seat, and she followed the woman and her clipboard out of the side door into a hot, bleached-out courtyard with weeds in every crack of the concrete. This time there were no queues, but she could still hear the baby's penetrating cries.

Across the baked out yard was a modern, featureless block that could have been anything. There was no notice on the door, which was wide enough for trolleys, but the smell, as the woman opened it for her and they passed through another set of doors into a dark corridor, was enough to tell her where they were.

'Everything is ready,' said the policewoman. 'Do not be alarmed.' Her eyes were on Fran. Probably she was wondering if she might have hysterics or faint, which was what Fran had been afraid of all morning.

The room was very cold, but the smell of formaldehyde and disinfectant almost made her retch. It wasn't over-large, and with all the tiling, it looked more like an old-fashioned public toilet than a medical facility. At the end was a heavy door marked REFRIGERATION, KEEP OUT. There was enough room for a row of instrument cabinets and a working surface, several sinks and a lot of hose-pipes, and three steel-topped tables. Two of the tables were empty, but on the middle one was a long mound covered with a rubber sheet.

Brian? The name seemed to be wailing like a banshee trapped inside her skull.

She couldn't move.

'Please come round this side,' said the woman, glancing at some notes in her hand. 'I will take back the sheet to the shoulders. The face will remain covered. Please observe the hair and right ear.'

'Thank you.' Inexplicably, Fran found herself whispering. She swallowed hard, took a deep breath and moved to the head of the table as the sheet was rolled back. The face was covered by a blank white plastic mask. Fran felt her hands clench on the tissue she was clutching. The details were so clear that she knew they would stay with her for the rest of her life. The hair was sandy, but longer than she remembered. It had been washed and combed, but there was still a streak of mud just below the right ear, as if a little boy had washed his neck and left a tide mark. Her fingers twitched. She wanted to wipe the mud streak away. Until she saw why the woman had led her round to this side. On the other side of the head was some taped surgical gauze where there should have been an ear. There was only this ear, with its pathetic muddy streak. Christ, he only had one ear . . .

She felt herself swaying and the woman put out a thin arm to steady her. The ear had a tiny dent in the lobe where once an earring might have been. It must have been the missing ear that had carried the larger scar, but she knew now it was Brian.

Steady – don't pass out, said a faint echo of her father's voice. She'll never hold you. You're bigger than she is. You'll end up on the floor.

'It's him,' she gasped, fighting down the nausea. She wanted to hold onto the steel edge of the table but couldn't bring herself to touch it.

For a second, she didn't know what to do. The

woman was watching her, hawk-faced. Then suddenly Fran knew what was right. She gently touched the stiff, sandy hair, and bent closer to the ear they had left him.

'Don't worry, Brian,' she said quite clearly. 'We'll get them. Rest in peace.' Then she turned on her heel and followed her escort to the door.

Her courage, if that's what it was, didn't last much longer. There could be no more denial now. As the door shut behind them and the tropical warmth hit her, she felt her knees start to buckle. It was a strange sensation, like tripping over a wire, but as if from behind, and in the dark. Instinctively she put out her hands and felt herself supported by each arm. The falling stopped and she was able to right herself. The afternoon heat was suffocating, but she forced herself to breathe deeply to get rid of the clinging formaldehyde smell.

'I've got her,' said Anders voice. 'Is it the bad news?'

'It is the bad news,' replied the woman, and Fran realised as her feeling came back that they had done her the kindness of letting Anders come through to meet her. Or maybe he'd insisted that he came. It was wonderful to have something that wasn't cold and dead to lean against, and she let out a choking, grateful sigh.

They'd told her she'd have to sign something else, and to get herself out of there she would have signed almost anything.

'This way, please.'

Anders held her for a little longer, gently, rocking her, murmuring that it would soon be over. They followed the clicking shoes down the corridor and into a tiny side room where there was almost nothing

156

except a metal chair and a chipped table on which were some forms interleaved with carbon papers, and a ball-point pen. The only other thing in the room was a low wooden stool in a corner, on which was some kind of shrine with a marigold garland and white jasmine flowers in a small brass vase. Their scent was strong enough to reach her, and the humanity of whoever had placed them there went a little way to calming her mind.

She signed the formal identification papers in several places and in triplicate. There was something else, also in triplicate, and she had just enough presence of mind to check that she wasn't consenting to take formal possession of the body for burial. It looked like some kind of release form stating that the police had fulfilled their duties. The woman tore off a copy of each and handed them to her.

'Our sincere condolences,' she said, unsmiling. 'That is all. Please follow me.'

They were let out by a side entrance straight onto a wide road, to face yet another silent crowd full of sad, staring faces. The covered heads leaned forward hopefully, then sank back disappointed. At least the car was there, waiting in front of a queue of taxis, three-wheeler autoshaws, and rickety bicycles. There was even a bullock cart or two, a food stall and the inevitable beggars. Some of the bicycles had long canvas stretchers with tattered, hooped canopies attached to their sides.

For a second, Fran faltered. Was this where the dispossessed of the city came to collect their dead – and took them away *on bicycles*? As she stopped, a thin dry hand touched hers. A squatting, leaf-like woman, perhaps no more than middle-aged, was looking up at her and smiling. She clearly wasn't a beggar. Touched, Fran stooped and grasped the hand with both her own. The next woman made the hands-together gesture and Fran returned it. The crowd stirred and murmured. She could feel their sympathy reaching out to her, and wanted so much to thank them for it. They were making it more bearable for her, as Charlie had promised they would, saying that they were all the same when it came to this. Yet the air-conditioned car waiting for her, and the bicycles with their tatty, barely concealing stretchers, said that even with death it was not truly so.

The car shot off, and all Fran wanted to do was close her eyes and forget the horror that she'd seen on the table in the morgue. Anders passed her the water and she drank deeply to get rid of the vinegary, acrid taste in the back of her throat, grateful to have him to lean against. 'People work in those places all day,' she said almost lightly. 'Can you believe that? Can you smell it?'

'A little,' he replied. 'They say it stays a while. If it would help, we could dismiss the driver and go somewhere for lunch; somewhere cool and quiet. We can always take a taxi back. Maybe we could try the InterContinental.'

Fran almost choked on the water, and he had to pat her back.

'I do appreciate it,' she said at last. 'but not there. You see, I have to get back in case my husband rings. I don't even know if he's heard about Brian.' Please God, Nevil didn't know, which would mean that his contact with Brian had been only brief. A drink, perhaps. An arrangement to meet later. But if Nevil did know, why hadn't he already contacted her? And why hadn't he, either way? She'd sent a fax to the

AWW offices herself. But Charlie had said the AWW offices were now locked. Had he even received it?

She jerked bolt upright in her seat. Jesus, what an idiot she'd been. Why hadn't she asked the driver to go straight to the AWW offices, to check if anyone was there?

Alarmed, Anders pulled her back into the crook of his arm and held her. 'You have seen the ghost? See, I will soothe it away.' He put his fingertips on her forehead and massaged it gently. 'It will soon leave you in peace. You have done what you can.'

'No, no, it's not a ghost,' she said, willing herself not to relax against him again. 'It's something else I should have done – I'm not sure . . .' The dark, cloudy headache was back. Why couldn't she think straight? She rapped on the driver's compartment. 'Could you pull over for a moment, please.'

With a stylish twist of the wheel and squeal of brakes that surprised even the taxi behind, he obeyed. Perhaps he thought she was going to be sick. Suppose she asked the driver to turn back and some-one was actually at the AWW office. What could she learn by talking to them that she couldn't find out on the phone? All she wanted to know was if Nevil had got her message. The office could be anywhere in Colombo. In the time the detour took, she could be back at the Cinnamon Beach to see if there was any news from Nevil, and if there wasn't she could phone the office herself.

'It's all right, please drive on,' she said at last, pray-ing she'd made the right decision. If she had, at least she wouldn't have to make another one in this bloody place, unless it was whether to sleep or swim. Nevil could do the rest. He could tell Tony that their old friend was lying cold on a slab with no face and no ear, and God knew whatever else they'd done to him. Suddenly she felt utterly drained.

'I'm sorry,' she said, sinking back into the safe, comforting seat. Anders' arm was still there and she was glad. 'One day I'll explain all this to you. Right now, I'm so tired. I didn't sleep much last night.'

'I can wait,' said Anders, settling her against him. 'Sleep is best.'

# Chapter Eleven

Anders had to shake Fran awake when they got back
to the Cinnamon Beach. She came round suddenly.
Perhaps her brain hadn't really switched off, because
everything was suddenly there again in that un-
welcome rush back to total clarity, right down to the
smell on her clothes.

Before they had even collected their keys, Fran saw
the manager emerge smiling from his office and
come towards her with a message pad. For one whole
wonderful second she thought Nevil might have
rung.

She almost grabbed the paper from his hand, but
her hope vanished as she read it: *Message for Mrs
Merrick, Room 306, Charlie called while you were out.
Please to call back.*

Oh no, she thought, not more trouble, please. Or
perhaps Charlie just wanted to know if it had gone
smoothly.

'I can't thank you enough for today,' she said to
Anders, taking his hand. 'I'm afraid I have some
rather painful calls to make.'

'Please – it was nothing. I hope you will ring our
room any time, day or night, if I can be any further
use.'

Fran watched him go and turned heavily towards
the office. Would Anders and Klaus be moving on

soon? She realised she hadn't even asked them their plans and had simply taken it for granted they'd still be around when she needed company.

Back in the familiar little office again, she looked at the phone, willing it to ring and there would be Nevil on the line. The silence went deep. She sighed. Well, it had better be Charlie first.

After only one ring, Charlie answered, saying how sorry she was, and how grateful for Fran's help. All very kind and correct, and it was a comfort, because she knew Charlie meant it. Yet there was a note in Charlie's voice which sharpened Fran's attention.

'There's something else, isn't there,' she heard herself saying.

'I'm afraid so. No news, just another request. Have you called your husband's partner yet?'

'Tony? Not yet. I was just plucking up the courage.'

'Fran, I can't ask you not to tell him, but could I ask you to be, er, economical with the truth?'

'What? You can't be serious.' What was the woman talking about? 'You mean I can't actually tell him what happened – what they did to Brian?'

'That's it, exactly. Thank you for understanding.'

'But Charlie, I *don't* understand! I want to talk about this, with someone who knew him.'

'I know, and I'm sorry. But yes, you do understand. I can't talk too long, I'm on duty.' There was real intensity in the voice. 'Do you see what I mean?'

'God almighty,' she said, staring at the receiver. She must mean that somehow this conversation wasn't safe.

'You could try Him,' said Charlie, almost angrily. 'But I don't think He's in.'

'I see.' How could she phrase this without knowing

162

where Charlie thought the problem might be. Was it just someone in her office that she didn't want to overhear, or did it go deeper than that? Did Charlie think her office line was being tapped? 'Can't we meet and talk?' she asked, completely at a loss.

'I'm not sure. Shall we try and do the same as before? Well, perhaps not a swim this time. It won't be today.'

'Yes, whenever. I'm not going anywhere.'

'Fine,' said Charlie and put the phone down abruptly.

Fine. *Fine?* Now they were being bugged, and were down to one word at a time. Shit! Just when you thought the worst might be over, they threw something else at you.

Fran sat with her head in her hands trying to sift through the permutations. She'd been doing a lot of that lately, only there always seemed to be more of the little buggers. What on earth was she going to say to Tony? She was beginning to wonder whether it was wise to contact him at all. If she phoned and found him in, she'd have to lie unconvincingly about some kind of car accident. Tony would get upset and want to know all the details. If she sent him a carefully worded fax, he'd only keep phoning back until he got her.

She stared at the wall calendar, distracted by the weird, psychedelic oranges and pinks round the picture of the Kandy tuskers in procession. How strange it looked to her today. Quite out of key.

Yet she had to face this rationally. Her only reason for letting Tony know about Brian was to share her bewilderment and anger. Tony would feel exactly the same, but what good would it do? It wouldn't help her find Nevil any faster, and that was her only priority now. It might even muddy the waters still further in some way Charlie could foresee, but she could not. Perhaps even the AWW people in London were being asked to keep quiet about the real cause of Brian's death. No – on the whole it was better to keep the lines free in case Nevil tried to get through, and let Tony contact her if he had any news. And if he did, she'd just have to think on her feet.

It was a tough decision, but having made it, she felt slightly better, or at least less shaky. But then, climbing the three flights of stairs to her room, it began to feel as if she were tackling a hill of sand, and a leaden tiredness dragged at her feet, at her calf muscles, even her clothes. Once safely inside, she sank onto the bed and closed her eyes, grateful that the cleaner had drawn the curtains against the midday glare. Her nap in the car, curled against Anders, childlike and dreamless, had made up some of the sleep lost last night. Now she just wanted to lose herself completely for at least a week, bury herself somewhere dark and deep and soft were nothing bad could reach her.

But you can't do it, hissed some part of her mind, all the while tossing and twisting her body on the bed as she looked down on it. The bad things won't let you.

With the balcony doors closed, the room was too warm, and for once she regretted the lack of air conditioning. But getting up to open them required an effort she couldn't make, and all she would hear would be the unthinking, callous sounds of people who hadn't seen what she had seen this morning and, if they were lucky, never would. She felt marked, damaged by that sight. She wanted to get undressed and shower, but couldn't find the will. What was the point? The mark wouldn't wash off. It wasn't a label or a *tikka* spot. It was permanent, like a brand or a tattoo. Or pierced ears . . .

The sound she made woke her briefly. A choking, nightmare cry. And then the body was back on the bed again not curled childlike, but wreathed in sweat, flexing, worming, in its need for oblivion.

The dreams that came had strange densities of colour. There were pungent, forbidden scents, words that were not hers and sounds with no name. Anders was there, riding naked like a Hindu deity on the back of a painted elephant which strode towards her from the gaudy pages of the office wall calendar. Anders was waving two of his six arms, beckoning her. Then he pulled her up in front of him with another pair that were braceletted with pearls, and onto the mountainous, warm back.

She giggled at the strange excitement of it. The third pair of arms, banded with gold, held her round the waist as the great animal moved mysteriously forward. The prickles of its shoulder hair were rough and loofah-like against her thighs, while the middle pair of hands had found her breasts. She too seemed to be naked, held firm, skin to glistening skin, her back tingling against the finely muscled chest behind, and she found herself swaying unbidden to the rhythm of the elephant god. For their further pleasure, a sacred peacock stepped delicately forward to dance before them, its breast feathers catching blue-green fire from the setting sun. It bowed and strutted, then fanned its fabulous tail erect, shaking it into ripples with a sound like wind rattling the high palms, while its hundred magic eyes watched and winked at them.

It was then that the tiger sprang, with a roar of rage that sent her tumbling from the elephant's back and out of Anders' arms – a full-grown Bengal tiger in its prime and it was coming in for the kill. But there was no one to save her. Nevil should have been there, but he wasn't. It was so close she could feel its hot breath on her face . . . She woke up with its roar in her ears, fighting off the pillow she had been clutching.

In the dark, for several frightening, disorientated seconds she'd lost all sense of where she was, and when she pulled round at last, was shocked at herself. To be dreaming of Anders, in *that* kind of way. What had come over her? Of course he was an attractive man. She didn't need her dreaming subconscious to tell her that, and she'd have had to be brain-dead not to notice that he'd been genuinely caring, yet so amazingly unintrusive. For a man.

The thought worried her. She remembered how at first she'd wondered if he and Klaus were gay. Even with people who spoke such good English, it was possible to misread the signals, but she'd soon felt that the body language and chemistry were wrong and dismissed the idea. Neither had Klaus' reaction to Charlie gone unnoticed; nor if she was honest, had Anders' attention to her. It wasn't the obvious, flattering kind, but she couldn't help but *be* flattered by it. Yet she'd felt perfectly at ease with him, without really thinking about it. Too much so, perhaps. Maybe Anders was not just the safe erotic deity of the dream, but also the tiger waiting to pounce.

Come on, she told herself: *Them old dreams are only in your head.* Echoes of Bob Dylan, about a hundred years ago, and never mind Freud. Yet she still couldn't shake off the idea that she was missing something about Anders. Muzzy and bewildered, she tore off her damp clothes and headed for the shower.

The light coming in through the curtain chinks was no longer knife bright, but golden syrup trickling down the walls. It was nearly six o'clock. Damn! She'd slept far longer than she'd intended. Now she wouldn't be able to sleep tonight, and worse, no one had disturbed her to say that Nevil was on the phone. She had a pain in her stomach, and knew some of it at least was hunger. But she needed action – violent, strenuous action to tire her out and make her sleep again.

There were still some bananas in the fruit basket, but she couldn't face them. She felt hollow, insubstantial as a ball of knotted string. A swim. She would swim round the pool till she dropped, then eat, and get a few whiskies inside her.

Without caring what she wore this time, she pulled on a crop top and a bikini bottom that didn't match, and tied on a beach sarong. Everything about her felt board-like and tense. Her stomach was very flat and she was beginning to hate it. She wanted to be pregnant. Very pregnant, waddly and content, and away from all this.

As she reached for her towel there was a tap at the door and Anders' voice said, 'Fran, are you all right? I was worried that you sleep so long.'

'Come in,' she called wearily.

'Please open. I have brought you something to eat.'

She went immediately to the door, almost at a loss over his thoughtfulness.

'Why are you so kind to me?' she asked as he put the tray on the table. There were a couple of Heinekens, bowls of tahini and mixed salad, some chicken satay, and cutlery for two.

He laughed, surprised at the question. 'Because I'm good at it,' he replied, as if it needed some thought.

'And it pleases me. There, you see. I have no ulterior motive. Is that correct?'

'If you say so,' she smiled, amused at the ambiguity. 'Anders, you puzzle the hell out of me.'

'Sometimes I puzzle the hell out of myself. Don't you puzzle the hell out of yourself?'

'No, not often,' she replied truthfully.

The answer seemed to disappoint him. 'Ah,' he said. 'But you haven't eaten all day. You must eat now. And then you should take some exercise or you will not sleep. It is very important, after such a shock.'

'I've been drinking lots of water and taking my vitamin pills,' she told him straightfaced, to see if he understood her tetchy humour. Had he taken a course in trauma counselling, for goodness' sake? 'And I was just going for a very long swim.'

'That is good.' A quirky smile flickered in the colourless eyes. 'If you will permit me . . .' He went to slide back the balcony door and open the curtains, and as he turned back to her, his eyes went very blue. Shouts, squeals and the sounds of splashing filled the room. 'Unfortunately you are too late. It's the water polo evening. Staff versus guests, Germany versus the rest of Europe, Australia against everybody . . .'

'OK, you've made your point. Let's eat.' She so wanted to enjoy this, to feel relaxed and happy again, but nothing was functioning properly.

They took the food onto the balcony and to please him she tried to eat. Down below, the games continued with ferocious intensity, turning the pool to spume. She managed half her beer and passed him the rest. 'Were you ever married?' she asked suddenly.

'Oh yes,' replied Anders, 'for five years. We had no children. I guess it wasn't right for me.'

What wasn't – marriage or that particular marriage? she wanted to ask. But then he hadn't asked her anything too personal, perhaps because it seemed obvious what her position was. She was waiting for her husband. Yet she sensed now that Anders knew there was more to it than that, and she was also beginning to wonder if there was a reason for his lack of asking. Was he holding out, making sure that it was she who broke first and told him the dark secrets? Perhaps she should put the record a little straighter, in case he was getting his wires crossed.

'I want children very much,' she said. 'I came here looking forward to a second honeymoon. And now this.' She was choosing her words carefully, so as not to imply that Nevil's non-appearance was connected with today's events. And why shouldn't she tell him she wanted a baby? At least it would make it clear, if it wasn't already, that she was unprotected and in no way prepared for sex with anyone other than her husband. All her life she'd been left in no doubt that men in general were opportunists. Nevil, Tony, the men she'd worked with, even her father, had all said as much at one time or another, joking or for real. It came with the kit and, while she would have sided vehemently with any other female who bemoaned this fact, or even questioned that it was so, Fran's personal belief was that basically you could only hope to curb rather than destroy it. But what you shouldn't do was pretend it didn't exist.

Has she said too much? Anders had taken this with little more than a thoughtful nod. Then he turned to look at her and said: 'You are still very tense.'

'Damn right I am,' she almost snapped. What the hell did he expect? 'It's been that sort of day.'

'You British,' he said, and it sounded like a reproach.

'I know. If I was Latin or Arab or something, I'd be out there now, wailing to the moon and feeling much better for it.'

'If you cannot swim, perhaps you could jog. Do you like to jog? Maybe that would help.'

'OK, Doc.' She almost smiled. 'I get it. I'm the English Patient. 'I don't mind jogging. Where do you prescribe? Along the beach?'

The notion seemed to please him. 'I think so. It'll be quiet now. They're all tired out after their little games.'

'How much daylight have we got?'

Anders got up and squinted at the sun and then his watch. 'About forty minutes.'

'You're on,' said Fran, hitching up her sarong. 'I'd be glad of the company. I don't think they understand women running round in the twilight by themselves out here.'

They went downstairs and started a gentle trot past the pool where Klaus seemed to be organising a game of piggy-back volley-ball that involved a lot of the girl riders finishing up squealing in the water.

'Let's look professional now,' said Anders, and they picked up speed to pass the sellers and the touts who in any case seemed to be on the point of packing up.

He let her set the pace, her strides almost matching his, and unhesitatingly she chose the opposite direction to where she had walked the other day and been confronted by those strange poetic lines of loss and

170

watery death. Had it been a premonition? She pushed back her shoulders and breathed deeply, not allowing herself to be seduced again by the poetry of it in case the reality penetrated her instead.

They were facing more towards the sunset this way and there was only one last hotel before a stretch of open fairly beach. They jogged on in silence for what must have been almost a mile, not speaking, concentrating on getting the breathing right. Then something caught Fran's eye on the wet sand ahead where the barely lapping tide was on the ebb. It was rounded, and at first she thought it was just another washed up coconut. But it was too white.

She pulled up short of it, her breath gone. It looked so much like a human head. Suddenly she couldn't help herself. Transfixed to the spot, she let out a kind of wailing scream. Half her mind was telling her it was only a lump of coral rounded by the sea, but it was too late. She couldn't stop, and the sounds she was making shocked her. She raised her arms, clench-fisted to the sinking sun and yelled, raged, howled, cried, 'No, no, no . . .'

'Fran, what is it?' called Anders in alarm, turning on his heel and sprinting back. He looked down. 'It's only an old piece of coral, see . . .'

He caught her as she swayed there, distracted, with the sudden, awful pain in her chest and throat. The scream that wouldn't come had come at last, and she didn't know how to stop. He held her face into his shoulder until the sound became a convulsive heaving, stroked her hair while she choked on the words. 'They tortured him,' she sobbed. 'I can't bear it any more. They hurt his face. They wouldn't let me see it. He only had one ear.'

Anders muttered something to himself that wasn't

171

English and held her closer, waiting for the storm of sobbing to pass. She wanted to hurt something back, beat his chest, bite into his shoulder, anything to release the coiled spring of pain inside her. When at last she had exhausted herself, she raised her head and said, 'Thank you,' still shivering and gulping for breath.

'This will help.' Releasing her for a moment, he picked up the lump of coral, then took her hand. He led her unresisting to the edge of the water and threw it with all his strength into the receding waves. 'And so, I think, will this.' He let go her hand and placed himself behind her, hands on her shoulders and very gently began to massage them with expert fingers. 'Let it all go', he said soothingly. 'Just let it go.'

*Nothing of him that doth fade, But doth suffer a sea change Into something rich and strange.* Slowly she felt the taut muscles of her jaw and neck responding. He started on her backbone, thumbs each side, kneading lightly and then more firmly. When her breathing had returned to normal, she heard him say, 'Breathe deeply now. Don't think, just breathe,' and she willed herself to do as he said, not to obey, but because she knew it was working.

'You're very good at this,' she murmured, her face towards the dying cusp of the sun. Streaks of crimson and orange were already backlighting the duck-shell blue of the western sky which deepened almost to emerald where it touched the sea horizon. Across it, streamers of trade wind cloud hung motionless, and nothing moved but the ripples of the waves and Anders' skilful fingers.

'It's a gift I have. Now I give it to you. Ss'sh – don't ask me why. I told you.'

172

Her toes were sinking into the soft wet sand, imprisoning her there, but it didn't seem to matter. The movements down her spine stopped fleetingly, and she almost groaned, but then he returned to her shoulders. He slipped down the straps of her top and went deeper, round and under her shoulder blades, coaxing her to flex and relax them.

'That's wonderful. Don't stop.'

'I'll stop when you say.'

He moved down over her hips, letting the sarong drop, and feather-tapped the backs of her thighs and calves, kneeling as he did so. Without rising, he came to kneel in front of her and took her hands. 'You are Venus on the half-shell,' he said, 'rising from the waves. I will give you this gift and want nothing except that you take it for your pleasure.'

Unbelieving, she looked down at him, and read it in his face. If women were from Venus, this man did not come from Mars like other men. He was from a different place.

'Put your hands on my shoulders,' he said.

She thought she might faint. This couldn't be happening, but it was. She couldn't move, but didn't want to. He smoothed his hands over her hips, easing down the silky lycra of the costume. Then he began to move his mouth over her stomach, lower and lower, and she knew she wouldn't stop him. She took his head in her hands and held it gently to her, stroking his hair.

He didn't hurry, and she didn't want him to. Once, he raised his head as if to tease her. 'Women taste of the sea,' he said, but she hardly heard him for the ripples of pleasure suffusing her. When she came, it was strongly, easily, on a high note, her head thrown

173

back, her mouth soft with delight, hands entangled in his hair.

The aftershocks held her there, gasping, while the waves washed at their feet. Over the sea, was one bright star, and she wondered if it was Venus.

'That was a better sound,' he said.

Laughing in sheer disbelief at him, herself, the crazy sunset, all of it, she stooped and cupped her hands into the waves to wash his face, then wiped it with her sarong. He kissed her lightly on the forehead, and since he hadn't kissed her there before, it surprised her. Then with a cheerful shout, he ran into the surf and took a dive into the waves.

Fran didn't follow, just stood there watching him looping about like a dolphin. The sky was now a furnace red where the sun had slipped away, and the sea was turning to molten copper. For the moment, she did not care how she would feel about this tomorrow. It was enough that the crippling pain had gone, and that she was glad to be alive again.

They walked back to the hotel, not strolling as lovers do, but quite at ease, jogging where they could see far enough ahead in the deepening twilight. She stopped only once to catch her breath, and saw the first glimmerings of the shrimp boats. It was only then that she knew what it was she was feeling, and it was as strong as the nameless fears that had been preying on mind. Anders was not the tiger, and somewhere out there in the darkness Nevil was alive and wanting desperately to come to her, she was sure of it.

'You will sleep again now, my English patient, and tomorrow will be different,' said Anders as they reached the clumps of pandanus that marked the way into the hotel.

'I think so,' she said, and wondered if he could see her smile as they passed through the darkness under the palms and into the floodlit garden.

# Chapter Twelve

The gardens, the pool, the reception block – the phone. It was all there again, but now she could cope. And this man? To Anders it all seemed so easy, but she still couldn't fathom him. Couldn't fathom either of them, in fact. Not at all.

'Anders,' she said, 'I have to check for messages, but if there's nothing I have to do, may I come and sit with you and Klaus for a while? Maybe he thinks you've been neglecting him.'

She went to the office, although she'd already guessed there would be nothing new. No one came hurrying out to meet her. It was like being caught in a web, and for the moment she'd stopped struggling to free herself, was resigned to it. Tomorrow it would all start again – the worry, the decisions . . . For now, though, she would have to let it go if she was going to be any use to herself or anyone.

They found Klaus looking far from neglected, chatting to a couple of French girls and teasing them about their English. As soon as he saw they were back, he came over to join them. Was Klaus from Mars? she wondered. Or was he from the same strange planet as his friend? Watching them together, she envied their companionship, sensed it was somehow different from anything she'd come across before, and was still puzzled by it.

Klaus made no comment about her ordeal of this morning. One thing she was sure of now, was that it wasn't lack of concern. Possibly Anders had told him all he needed to know, and she was thankful.

'How long have you two known each other?' She had to ask it eventually.

'You mean, how long have we been together?'

The phrasing threw her temporarily. 'Well, yes.'

'Since before I was married. My wife knew, of course. It wasn't Klaus that broke us up. We just grew apart, you know, in our heads.'

'I can imagine.' But she couldn't quite. Not yet. Was she hearing this right? 'You have, let's say, a very open approach to life.'

He shrugged, and Klaus smiled, looking down at his feet, but it was a relaxed and knowing smile. There seemed to nothing hidden or furtive about them, nothing camp or smirky. That was part of their otherness. The otherness of the true bisexual, perhaps. She had them now, safely in the palm of her hand, and held it to her, feeling a strange relief.

'Maybe in Denmark we don't like to put ourselves into too many compartments,' was all Anders said. Had he assumed she'd known the situation? Perhaps he thought she had. It explained a lot.

'I haven't met many Danes before,' she said, smiling at them both. 'Now I see what I've been missing.'

They both laughed.

'We're a small country,' said Anders. 'We like to extend our frontiers.'

'So's the Vatican,' she replied. 'But I don't notice them extending theirs.'

'Maybe you haven't looked in the right places. And talking of places, I'm sorry, I had almost forgotten.

Tomorrow we're booked for a two-day trip to Kandy. We could ask them to transfer it, if you wish.'

'Oh no, I wouldn't hear of it,' Fran said, trying not to show her disappointment. 'I'll be fine. But I'd really appreciate it if you'd lend me some of your books.'

Anders smiled. He knew which one she meant. 'I'll go and get it,' he said. 'And we have others. Do you like thrillers?'

'No,' she said quickly. 'I don't think I could read a thriller just now.' Write one, maybe, she thought, after all this has become history.

A group of traditional dancers had arrived and was setting up nearby. Even if she went to her room, she couldn't have slept, so they had a couple of drinks and watched the show. Fran tried to let the whisky and the hypnotic music lull her, but every time she looked at the dancers, they reminded her of Charlie. When would Charlie come? But that was for tomorrow.

When the show was over, she rose, told them she was sure she would sleep, and lightly kissed them both goodnight and wished them a good time in Kandy. It seemed as good a way as any to end what had been the most bizarre of days.

Anders and Klaus had left very early that morning. Sitting on the terrace with her breakfast papaw and lime, Fran looked round and knew she was going to miss them. It seemed simpler to think of them as a couple – an un-jealous couple, bound by mysterious ties of chemistry, affection, shared experience and need. For them, which came first? She tried to imagine how their relationship might be, and gave up. There appeared to be no complications, no tension between them. It was also a relief that Klaus didn't seem to resent her in any way, although he must have been aware of a new bond between her and Anders. She'd always believed that men who were from Mars, even when they were good friends, didn't talk much to each other about such things. These two were different.

Last night after she'd left them, much to her surprise, she'd found she didn't at all mind the idea that Anders and Klaus might even then have been in bed together or involved in an intense discussion about her, or possibly both. Yet the idea of this being so with almost every other man she'd ever met would have appalled her. What worried her was that she had no idea why she should feel this way. Was it delayed shock perhaps, or some part of growing up that she hadn't realised was still there to do? Or was it something more insidious – the beginnings of a kind of corruption of the soul? She felt adrift. Somewhere east of Suez. And all she had to steer by was the wake of so many others who had drifted on the current down this particular sea lane.

Lingering over breakfast wasn't going to get her through the day. Reluctantly she finished her coffee and went up to her room. It was no use wishing Anders and Klaus were around to take her mind off things. Of course she'd been disappointed when Anders said they would be away for a few days, but she knew she shouldn't get too dependent on him. That, she felt sure, had been part of the gift. He hadn't tried to *possess* her, not her body or her soul. Would Nevil ever understand all this? She knew one day she would tell him, and that when she did, it would be when he was capable of understanding it. That would be her hostage to fortune, her promise to herself – eventually to tell him. But first she had to find him.

Fran had never been much good at doing nothing. Normally her instinct was to act, take the initiative if there was a problem. In business they called you pro-active. The rest of the world called you impatient. Just to sit and read, swim, get a drink, read again, doze in the shade, face down on a sun bed underneath the peacock-tail rattling of the palms – that's what she'd wanted, but for them both; not to be alone and drifting like this.

As soon as she thought that offices would be open, she called AWW in Colombo. But each time she tried, there was no reply, nor was there a recorded message. She couldn't ring Charlie, and shouldn't ring Tony. There was nothing about the so-called accident on the radio or TV news, and nothing in the papers. She was stumped, utterly stumped. Beached, abandoned, forsaken and seething with impatience.

In the end, what got her through the day was forcing herself to think every time she got restless and fretful, of all the people in the world who would have willingly given their eye-teeth to be doing exactly what she was doing, in surroundings like these – namely, nothing. But even that barely kept the lid on her frustration.

It was the day after Anders and Klaus had left when the call came. She was reading under the big frangipani tree with a banana daiquiri beside her, giving a deceptive impression of relaxation, when one of the waiters appeared, calling, 'Mrs Merrick, telephone, please.'

She lurched to her feet. 'Man or woman,' she asked urgently as she passed him at a trot. There had been so many false alarms now, that she hardly dared hope.

'Man.'

'Did he give his name?' Tony always did. Until now, he'd had no reason not to.

'No, ma'am.'

So *could* it be . . .? The trot became a sprint. She snatched up the phone, listening acutely even as she spoke for that special silence that would tell her it was Nevil. Was it the way people breathed that told you who it was before they spoke?

'Hello?' She paused. It was *his* kind of silence. 'Nevil?' She could hardly say his name.

Like music, the silence turned into his voice. 'Fran, sweetheart, is that really you? Thank Christ for that. Listen, I can't talk long, I'm in a call box on the Galle Road, and you never know with these things.'

'Darling, are you all right? Where are you, for goodness' sake?' The little-wifey words just wouldn't stop. 'I've been worried out of my head.'

'Yes I'm all right, really,' he replied tersely. 'If you call scurrying about keeping my face out of people's way all right. No, listen . . .' He must have heard her sharp intake of breath prior to another barrage. 'It's OK, I'm with a friend. He'll show you where. We haven't got to where we're going next, if you see what I mean.'

She waited, closing her eyes, trying to conjure up his face; straining to catch a hint of his usual laid-back humour. The absence of it was her only clue. For pity's sake, what was going on?

'He's going to come to the hotel and pick you up. We think it's better if I don't come myself. As soon as he's dropped me at the house, he'll come straight there. It'll take him about an hour and a half because

181

some of the road is a bit ropey. We've only got one night before his people come back, but at least I'll be able to see you, and it'll be better than the other place.'

What other place? Did it matter? The nightmares of fear and confusion were back. 'When?' was all she managed to say.

'He'll collect you around four o'clock, and take you back tomorrow, early-ish. His name's Vesak, and he's been great. He'll be able to do some filling in. We'll just have to take it from there. Is that OK?'

'I love you.' she said, sensing that as soon as he knew she understood he would hang up. 'I'll be waiting.'

'That's my girl,' he said, and the line went dead.

This time Fran didn't allow herself the luxury of sitting for a while in the office trying to work out what it was all about. Her brain was already in overdrive as she left and bolted for her room. With the door safely locked, she sat slumped on the bed, shoulders hunched, arms pinned between her knees to stop the shaking. 'He's all right, he's all right', she repeated tonelessly to herself. It was pretty obvious that nothing much else was, except that by some miracle she'd be seeing him soon. Seeing him. Touching him. But she'd heard his voice. He really was *all right*.

When the shaking subsided, she drank half a bottle of water and tried to pull herself together. It was nearly half past one. He'd said they were at a call box on the Galle road. Or could that could mean the Galle Road with a capital R, which meant that he was still somewhere in Colombo South. But this far down the coast, the Galle road also meant exactly that – the trunk road from Colombo straight down to

182

Galle, which was almost on the southern tip of the island.

She snatched up her map, anxiously scanning the tear-drop shape of Sri Lanka. So where could he be? Suddenly it seemed desperately important to have some idea where he might be heading. Because of the traffic it could take at least two hours to get the nearest part of Colombo, which almost certainly ruled the capital out. So it had to be the Galle road they were on. That was a start.

Using the distance to south Colombo as a guide, she drew an arc from Kalutara using her fingers. That narrowed it down a little. Arbitrary as it was, it gave her a few possibilities. He could either be further north along the trunk road, perhaps in one of the resorts towards Colombo, or further south along it, again in the resort strip, maybe even as far as Galle. But there was another possibility. The Galle-Colombo road branched north of Kalutara, to the inland town of Ratnapura, off which were some unmetalled roads and jeep tracks, and Nevil had said some of the road was bad. It certainly looked hilly. Maybe Nevil was holed up somewhere towards Ratnapura. It made her feel less useless to imagine that she'd got her calculations right.

The prospect of actually seeing him again, in whatever circumstances, left her breathless. Four o'clock. Only another two and a half hours to wait. No, it was more like two and a quarter now. She jumped up, knocking the as yet unopened book from the bedside table onto the floor in her excitement. Scooping it up, she smiled at the title. She was still the English Patient, and she knew what she had to do. Ten laps of the pool at full stretch, something quick to eat, and then a luxurious bath, followed by everything she could think of to make herself look and feel terrific.

By a quarter to four she was in the lobby, trying to stay calm and unruffled. Several people asked if she'd fully recovered from the pool incident, and she could tell by the way they looked at her clothes that they were wondering what she was up to now. This time it had to be the suede silk jade: tailored, sleeveless, button-through. Just the touch of it against her skin made her feel coolly sexy. On a sudden impulse, she rummaged for a notepad and dashed off a note to Anders, keeping it as open as possible. It said, *'Some good news at last. I should be back the same day as you. With love.'* She decided not to sign it, and watched while it was put into his key pigeonhole behind the desk. The last time she'd tried to leave a message in a hotel . . . But that was something she didn't want to think about. Nevil would have all the answers.

The man who came to collect her was youngish, tall for a Sri Lankan, and slim. Apart from rather prominent but very white teeth, he was good-looking in an intense sort of way, and greeted her energetically with a handshake that was firm and cool, in spite of the humid heat. He was in local dress: a loose shirt, striped cotton *sarama* and flip-flops, but smelt of what she thought might be sandalwood.

'Mrs Merrick? I'm Vesak Thomas. I work for Animal World Watch. Please come with me.'

'Fran, please. You've been taking care of my husband – that's good enough for me.'

He led her out to a banged-up old Peugeot pick-up and tucked her politely into the front seat. On his own seat was what looked like a folded sunflower-yellow sari, a red hibiscus flower attached to a hair clip, and a battered sun hat. As he got in, he put on

184

the sun hat, and handed her the folded cloth and the flower.

'Please do not be alarmed,' he said, 'if I stop when we get nearer and I ask you to cover your head.' Used to Charlie's excellent English, Fran had to adjust to the rapid staccato of a strong local accent. 'Nevil wants us to take no chances.'

'Whatever you say,' she said faintly. 'How far is it?'

'About half an hour fast on the main road, and then off it and bumpety-bump a little longer. It is my uncle's country house. He is a gem merchant in Ratnapura, and the family have gone away to a wedding for two days, which is very fortunate. I was sharing a bungalow with Brian Gaskill, you see. It is a terrible thing . . . terrible.' His confident manner began to crumble in front of her, and he seemed at a loss to carry on.

Fran sighed. 'So you're the person Brian was staying with. It must have been an awful shock for you.'

'In a way I blame myself. We were working on the same case, and I feel it should have been me. Why was it him they picked? He was a foreigner, working here only. It was not his war, this business with the Separatists and these filthy Chinese . . .' He stopped, as if he might have said too much.

She knew it was no good pushing him. He was driving a vehicle that would have failed every test in the book, on a road full of others which didn't look any better, and needed all his concentration.

'You mustn't think like that,' she said gently. 'Brian chose the life he wanted to lead. He wasn't afraid of taking risks. In fact, I think he enjoyed danger.'

Vesak's hands were clenched on the wheel. 'I have thought about this so much,' he said. 'That one night, Brian stayed late, and he was alone.'

'So where was Nevil at the time?' Fran couldn't help interrupting. How close had he been to this horror? She had to know.

'He had been at the house all day. Brian was going to take the next two days off so they could go and play some golf together at Nuwara Eliya.'

'Nevil was *staying* with you both when this happened?' Suddenly she felt quite sick. But then logically, where else would he have been, for heavens' sake? He certainly hadn't been at the Inter-Continental or the Blue Peacock – she couldn't help a shudder at the name – and Charlie had checked most of the other hotels.

'Oh yes. Nevil had been helping us, you see.'

'Helping you? You mean AWW? How, exactly? ' Christ, had he got himself even further into this than she'd thought? The stupid, irresponsible . . .

Vesak must have sensed her sudden anger. 'Maybe Nevil should tell you himself,' he said unhappily.

'Oh, I know about the equipment he brought out,' she said, trying to make light of it. 'I only came out here to persuade Nevil to take a break, because he was under a lot of stress. What a joke! But I'm sorry – you were saying about Brian being alone in the car that night.'

'Yes indeed. So now I am thinking that they wanted a European in particular, to make AWW take notice. A local man would not have been so high-profile. Maybe AWW would have thought, oh, he is only a Sri Lankan, so perhaps he was also a police informer in the problems with the Separatists, and that's why he was killed. AWW would not have got the message, do you see? Killing Brian was a warning to them and similar organisations of what happens when people interfere with the tiger bone trade.'

'I suppose it makes a ghastly kind of sense,' she agreed bleakly. She paused, wondering if there was still something she was missing. 'But wouldn't it also signal to AWW, the police and everyone else trying to stop the tiger bones trade, that they were on the right track? Wouldn't they simply redouble their investigations?'

For a brief moment, Vesak took his eyes of the road to look at her, intensely, urgently. 'Think now, dear lady. Do you have some sympathy with our aims?'

'Saving the tiger? Well, of course! I love tigers. They're fantastic animals, I don't want to see them extinct any more than the next right-thinking person. But when it comes to friends being mutilated and killed, and my husband being only one step away at the time, you'll forgive me if I feel a little less gung-ho about it.'

'My point exactly. These people have now shown themselves to be completely ruthless on this matter. But would *you* die to save the tiger? That is what all AWW operatives are now having to ask themselves. Myself included.'

Seeing only too well what he meant, she bowed her head. 'I'm sorry,' she said, 'but I'm frightened, and I know you are, too. Really frightened, for the first time in my life. But surely now this whole thing ought to be turned over to the police. They're already trying to find the owners of the Blue Peacock, not to mention the bomber of the wretched place and the ones who torched that Chinese businessman's house. It's all connected, isn't it?'

'Spotting the connection was Brian's greatest contribution to all this,' said Vesak, grinding the gears to get round a lorry. 'From AWW's point of view anyway.'

'Of course! That e-mail Brian sent which just missed Nevil. It really *was* a warning that things might be more dangerous than he'd led Nevil to believe. Tiger Country! I spent ages trying to work out which meaning I should have taken from it. Now I see. He meant all three – real ones, terrorist ones and danger, pure and simple. Clever old Brian. I keep thinking, if only I'd said something earlier, maybe . . .'

A particularly deep series of ruts had Fran almost out of her seat. It felt as if every bolt in the old pick-up was working loose.

'But what could you have done about it?' yelled Vesak above the din. 'As soon as Nevil arrived, Brian told him anyway, so that Nevil could make his own mind about how far he wanted to come in.'

And he *is* in, thought Fran grimly. Up to his bloody neck, I know it. He's a chancer, which is part of why I love the silly sod . . . But Vesak isn't going to tell me how far. Loyalty, or what!

'Excuse me, soon we will turn for Ratnapura.' His eyes were on the rear-view mirror. 'I don't think we're being followed, but can you watch to see who else makes the turn?'

'You bet,' replied Fran, fighting back an instinct to close her eyes as they cut dangerously fast across the stream of oncoming traffic.

They got an indignant blast from a pick-up full of veiled woman. But the only things that followed them onto the Ratnapura road were some trucks, a tourist coach and assorted cyclists wobbling under their bulky loads of fodder and sugar cane.

When Vesak was satisfied they weren't being tailed, he said, 'You mentioned the police. Now here we have a problem.'

Wouldn't you know it? thought Fran. Nothing would have surprised her now – not the involvement of the CIA, the FBI, the IRA, Interpol and old Uncle Gaddafi and all.

'You see, we were coming to the opinion that the police must have known about the connection between the Tamil Tigers' funding and the tiger bone trade even before Brian worked it out for himself. Ironical, is it not – the Tigers abusing tigers in this way?'

'You can say that again. So why didn't the police at least alert AWW to the danger their operatives were in? Are you suggesting that someone in the relevant police department is being paid off?'

Vesak shrugged helplessly. 'Maybe they were being blackmailed. Maybe it is political. Who knows? All we know is that the attitude of the police to this has been two-faced. It could even be that the information we passed onto them was the cause of Brian's death. It was to do with the money-laundering side of it. And now all his files have gone.'

'Oh no! Were they stolen from the office?'

'Unfortunately, he was bringing the most important items home with him for safety the night he was killed.'

Fran stared at the road ahead. Why were things always worse than you thought they could possibly be?

'Vesak, could you still tell me what you've got so far? Then if anything happens to you . . . I'm sorry, do you see what I mean? I need to be clear about it, because if necessary, we can go and talk to various people when we get home.'

Which will be soon, I sincerely hope, she added privately. Why didn't she just collect Nevil right now? Then she could grab her stuff from the Cinnamon Beach and they could be off on the first plane out of here.

'First let's get off the main road,' said Vesak. 'Then I will ask you to put on the sari and cover your head. It's better that people round my uncle's place don't see a European lady. They always gossip, and you never know who might come asking.'

They took an almost-concealed left turn and no one followed them. Before long the road deteriorated to little more than a dirt track, with dense vegetation on either side as it began to climb. There were stretches that were virtually jungle now. Even the village rice fields were fringed with palm thickets and groves of papaws, while bananas thrusted and sprouted all higgledy-piggledy, like fantastic weeds. Here and there, forest giants with buttress roots straight out of a wildlife documentary were looped together with mauve-flowered climbers.

'Don't bother stopping, I'll manage,' said Fran, opening out the yellow sari and wriggling around to trying a few experimental twists. 'So tell me about the tiger bone trade. Why did they choose Sri Lanka?'

'Most of the remaining territory of the Bengal tiger is in northern India. The trade used to be controlled mainly from Delhi, with the bones reaching China through the Tibetan refugee camps on the Indian border. It's high country. Very difficult to police.'

'I can only imagine,' said Fran, struggling with the folds of cotton.

'The problem is, one tiger produces about fifteen kilos of bone, which one man can carry in his backpack. Even that amount is worth many years' earnings for these people. The World Wildlife Fund, the Wildlife Conservation Society, Traffic India, the

Environmental Investigation Agency and ourselves of course, have been campaigning about it for ages.'

'But wasn't it beginning to work?'

'Up to a point. In spite of corruption in high places in India, some of the key people went to gaol. So the Chinese end decided to switch to Colombo instead. Perhaps Sri Lanka looked an easier option, you know, with the trouble in the North.'

'So that's where it's coming in!' It was beginning to make sense now.

'Exactly so. The bones don't hang around Delhi any more. The parcels are moved south, usually by private car or truck. The drivers would probably be Tamils with Separatist sympathies. From the south, it's a simple matter to get the goods across the Jaffna Straits by fishing boat or whatever.'

'I suppose if the government patrols can't even pick up all the arms shipments, they're hardly going to notice a few bags of bones.'

Vesak nodded glumly. 'To make it worse, the dealers have begun to specialise.'

'Sorry,' said Fran blankly. 'How do you mean?'

'You see, all tiger bones are very costly when they are ground up and put into Chinese medicine. But some bones are worth more than others.'

'You mean, they're bigger? Denser?'

By now they were being bounced around without respite, with the bottom of the pick-up constantly scraping on the sandy ridge in the middle.

'No, not that.' Vesak seemed reluctant to explain. 'You see, unfortunately, the male tiger has a small bone in a certain part of his anatomy that is con-sidered to be far more, ah, potent for male complaints than all his other parts.'

Fran shot him a startled glance. Had she understood him correctly? 'You're saying the tiger has a bone in his . . . Good grief!'

'No bigger than a finger bone, but that is the case,' said Vesak, with some relief that he didn't have to spell it out. 'And these are truly worth a small fortune.'

Fran stared out of the window at the deeply rutted road and ever thickening jungle. The whole thing was so utterly grotesque. Barbaric. And more than anything, it was so bloody *ignorant*.

'As long as I live,' she said, 'I'll never understand men.' And poor Vesak, wrestling with the bucking steering wheel, was so flustered that he agreed with her.

She made one last attempt to make the sari stay put, but with no waistband to tuck it into, it was almost impossible. In the end, she simply wrapped the three meters of cloth round and round herself until she felt like a cocoon, and used the end to cover her head. The jade silk dress top made a passable blouse.

'Is this OK?' Her antics broke the tension between them. 'And the flower – like this?' She stuck the bright hibiscus in her hair so that it peeped out coyly from the sari. By now she was being gently stewing from the waist down. She also felt faintly ridiculous.

'To keep it close to the face, hold the cloth with your teeth. That is what the country women do. Now we are a farmer and his wife on the way back from market.'

'It's a good job I'm not a stunning blonde and that I've been working on my suntan,' she said. 'Now a *tikka* mark, for luck.'

Another convulsive lurch had her hanging onto

the front bar, but she managed to find her melting lipstick and draw a smudged spot on her damp forehead. Did she really believe she was doing this? A ring in her nose would be next. But then, she'd have even gone as far as that, if meant keeping Nevil safe.

# Chapter Thirteen

The track twisted and turned through countryside that was like some vast abandoned estate where the jungle was creeping back to claim its own again. Fran had lost all sense of direction. They passed one village a little larger than the rest. It was beside a wide river whose shallow bed was thrown into relief by clumps of great, smooth boulders which looked for all the world like families of elephants taking a dip. Then one of them moved, and Fran stared. It really *was* an elephant, and there were three more of them, wallowing peacefully among the perfect camouflage of rounded stones, while their mahouts and a gaggle of children looked on. One man had a yard broom and was scrubbing his elephant's back.

She sighed, pulling the sari tighter round her face, relieved that the children hadn't even given her a second glance. She must really look the part.

The idyllic scene fell behind them as Vesak took a sharp right-hander uphill that had her clutching the bar again. The track flattened slightly at the brow of the hill, and ahead she could make out a shallow-pitched, red tiled roof and square metal water tank, a peeling stucco wall, and the by-now familiar shapes of flamboyants and frangipanis, which usually meant a better kind of habitation.

'My uncle's family compound,' said Vesak with a touch of pride.

'This is it? Oh, that's terrific.' She was aching all over from being bounced about, and wouldn't really have cared if she'd found Nevil shacked up in a pigsty. 'How long have you been here?'

'Only since this morning we were driving down from Colombo. Before that, we were in the apartment of a friend, but there is only one room.'

'Really?' A thought struck her. 'So how long has Nevil known I've been in the country?'

Vesak grinned and seemed to relax now that he was nearing familiar territory. 'It was only last night. When I knew that this place would be free from today, I went secretly very late to the AWW office to see if there was anything I could find that might be useful, and to check the mail and so on. That's when I found your message. By the time I got back to my friend's flat, it was too late to telephone. To be safe, we found a call box off the beaten track on our way here.'

'What did he say when he found out?' She could feel the tension mounting inside her. 'No, don't tell me. Poor Nevil, on top of everything else, to have to cope with his wife. He must have had a fit.'

'He was laughing, crying, everything.'

Fran swallowed hard and pulled her veil closer. The barred double gates were chained and pad-locked. Vesak sounded the horn. An elderly bearded man in a *sarama* and singlet emerged from a tiny pan-roofed shack to one side of the house, and shuffled towards them holding a huge bunch of keys.

'He's the old gardener,' said Vesak. 'He's really retired now, but he still lives here. It's all right, he's the only one, and he's completely loyal to the family.

I have told him you are the cook from my Colombo house, and you have relatives in this area. You will be cooking and cleaning for us tonight, and then I am taking you back to your village until I return to Colombo with my visitor.'

'Well, thanks a lot,' laughed Fran into her sari, as the old man saluted them smartly and shut the gates. 'Not much change there, then. Was that Nevil's idea?'

'I'm afraid it was mine. Nevil doesn't understand how traditional it is round here. So please be careful how you greet him.'

'Does he know you're bringing him a Sri Lankan bride?' She was so keyed-up she couldn't help giggling, but Vesak's warning was only just in time. The front door opened and there was Nevil, peering out anxiously.

'He knows,' replied Vesak, and as he said it she saw Nevil's face break for an instant into a huge smile of relief which he quickly hid again behind a casual wave. Even from this distance she could sense his elation.

The pick-up slithered to a halt in the sandy drive. There was a wide flight of steps on a projecting plat-form to the heavy teak front door. While Nevil did his best to walk sedately down to meet them, Fran sat stock still, trying to get her legs working inside her yellow cocoon. 'Help,' she said faintly. 'I can't move in this thing.'

Mindful of the gardener still pottering back to his quarters not far away, Nevil let Vesak help her out of the pick-up. Keeping up the pretence, he put out his hand for her to shake. Speechless, she took it, staring at him, holding the sari to her face to suffocate a gurgle of near-hysteria. 'Is that all I get?' she managed to say through the folds, 'After coming all this way.'

'Your sister is very beautiful,' he said to Vesak. 'I hope she can cook.' He looked ready to explode with excitement.

Vesak agreed that she was indeed very beautiful and worth several elephants.

'Now will you get me up these steps, you daft bastard?' she hissed.

'In our country, this is the customary greeting of a wife to her husband after a long absence,' explained Nevil, as they helped her mince up the steps one at a time. Fortunately the gardener had disappeared into his house. 'And this,' he said, closing the door behind them and yanking her towards him with a whoop, 'is what we do next.'

She fell into his arms and reached for his face, laughing, kissing, gasping. Vesak tactfully looked the other way. Eventually she found his ears and held them, feeling them gently as if they were a new and strange kind of silk, while she held his face away and blinked at him through easy, happy tears.

'What is it, love?' he said softly, stroking her hair.

'Your ears – you've got two of them,' she said. 'They're so beautiful. Poor Brian.' Then the sobs really broke loose.

Vesak brought in a tray of tea, and soon she felt a little better. They sat on the sofa in the main room as close as two people could get, trying to piece together at least some of what had happened. It took some time, because neither of them was particularly co-herent. The strain of keeping their hands off each other with Vesak there was almost too much.

'Who's Charlie?' asked Nevil suspiciously at one point.

'She's a woman. Very much so. You'll love her. Actually, she's a policewoman. She's got a mind like a heat-seeking missile and she swims like a champ.'

'Sounds just my type,' said Nevil dubiously.

'If you ask me, she's our last best hope. That's if we want to get out of this in one piece. I'm sorry. I'm not making much sense, but I still can't seem to think straight.'

'Neither can I, and I don't want to, not yet.'

Vesak got to his feet. 'If you will excuse me, maybe I should find us something to eat. There is a house in the village where they will cook us some food. It might take a bit of time if you would like something special.'

'We would like something very special,' said Nevil without hesitation.

Vesak smiled. 'Then I'll collect the containers and be off. It could be dark by the time I come back. I'll sound the horn three times, so you'll know it's me.'

'What a brilliant idea,' said Nevil.

They stood by the door, Fran hovering just out of sight, to watch him go. It seemed to take forever. Before the door was even closed, she was beginning to tackle the sari.

'Why don't you let me to that?' Nevil took over, slowly unwinding it while she stood there, enjoying the novelty of it. 'It's like Christmas morning, this.' He didn't start to kiss her until the last fold of yellow cloth was on the floor. Then he took his time unbuttoning the jade silk dress with a kiss at every button. When that too was on the floor, her legs wouldn't hold her any more, and he scooped her up and almost ran with her to the sofa. It was a very large sofa, family-sized, soft, covered in dark crimson velvet, and it was the last thing she remembered before she gave herself up to him completely.

Afterwards, they went and had a shower together in the half dark. The master bathroom, like the rest of the house, was a curious mixture of traditional and kitsch. There were odd touches of luxury which seemed to have fallen off the back of container ship from Naples bound for Hong Kong, like the orchid-mauve, gold-tapped bathroom suite. But the floor was unfinished and there was an odd lack of mirrors.

They decided they'd better make love again in case they'd missed out on anything the first time and went to Nevil's room, which seemed to belong to one of the older women of the house. There was almost no furniture and the bed was very narrow and simple, just a thin mattress on a traditional wooden frame, but it hardly mattered. On the wall was a fan of peacock feathers. There seemed to be no escape from the things. 'Which reminds me,' she gasped, not wanting him to stop. 'What were you doing in the Blue Peacock?'

He raised his head. 'How do you know about the Blue Peacock?'

'My spies are everywhere.' And Nevil was here. 'OK, later,' she said, and pulled him back to her.

An hour and a half had gone by, and Fran suggested reluctantly that they'd better get dressed again, so they sat on the sofa smooching like teenagers waiting for the parents to come home.

When the horn sounded three times, they sprang apart almost guiltily and smoothed each other down. 'Here comes the take-away,' murmured Fran as the last button was fastened.

'They probably had to catch it,' said her husband

nibbling her ear. 'Good old Vesak. Anyway, I don't care if it's curried skink, I'll eat it.'

Vesak apologised for the delay with a smile. 'It's goatmeat,' he said. 'Very young and sweet.' He put the neatly stacked enamel bowls on the low table and they pulled cushions round. There were no plates, but Vesak found some spoons and forks.

'Right,' said Fran. 'Now we're sitting comfortably, you can finally tell me what you were doing at the Blue Peacock. Unless it's embarrassing, of course.'

She saw Vesak almost imperceptibly shake his head at Nevil. She knew that game. Men, she'd found, were expert at it. Even here, it seemed. It meant, I've been a good boy like you said. I haven't told her. Until she'd mentioned it, Nevil had probably been hoping that she already knew why he'd gone there, and got used to the idea. And whatever the reason, Fran knew now that she was not going to like it.

'So tell me how you knew about the Peacock,' said Nevil.

This was the boyish charm approach. Delaying tactics. It must be bad.

'OK, that's it!' Only half-joking, Fran slammed the lid back on the curry. 'Nobody eats until I get the whole story. And this time, I mean the lot. I want to know how far you're into this thing, and no bullshit. Just cut the mushroom-growing techniques. If we're all going to die, I think I'd prefer to know why.'

'No one's going to die, love.'

'Nobody else, you mean. I had to identify the body, remember?'

The two men looked at each other. They seemed to be asking each other's permission. Again, that almost-nod.

'OK, you win,' said her husband.

Reluctantly Fran removed the dish cover. 'Shoot,' she said as they began to eat.

'I suppose you could say it started way back in Saudi.'

'*What*? It's been going on all that time? Don't tell me Tony's been in on it too! Why, you set of scheming . . .' She almost choked on her first mouthful. She was really angry now.

'Hang on, Fran. You know that wouldn't add up. Brian was still doing his Securicor bit at the time, keeping the world safe for the mighty petro-dollar. No, what I mean is, when we were there, Tony and me, that is, we hit a spot of bother and Brian did us a favour. A pretty big favour, actually. It was getting political, if you know what I mean, and he got some really nasty people off our backs. You know how dodgy it can be out there.'

Fran shut her eyes. This was getting beyond her. 'If this involves anything about hand-lopping and Saudi prisons, I don't want to know,' she said sharply. All those meet-ups in London, reminiscing about the good old days. No wonder they hadn't invited her along. 'What you're saying is, ever since, you felt you owed him one.'

'Right - a big one. But honestly, all Brian asked when he knew I was coming out to Sri Lanka on the Al Masira contract, was that I should bring the special recording equipment. That and a bit of checking up on the backgrounds of various companies. He didn't say what it was for. I got one brief phone call, and the details were by e-mail.'

'Which you wiped, in case I spotted it.'

'See what you get for having a smart wife?' said Nevil to Vesak. 'I'm sorry, love. I should have told you, but I knew you'd be mad enough about the Sri Lankan trip without Brian being involved as well. You'd have thought I was cooking up a boys-only golfing spree.'

Fran ground her teeth at him.

'The whole thing surprised me actually, because the hardware cost a bomb and I could see it was surveillance quality. We all thought he'd given up the rough-tough stuff when he jacked it in at Shell. I knew he'd gone all Green and done some kind of conservation course, but I didn't even know who he was working for.'

'So what about the e-mail I did spot – that guff about tiger country and funding for the above? What was he asking you to check up on – the Tamil Tigers' personal pension funds?'

Nevil snorted. 'Do you know, the crazy part is, you're almost right, although neither of us knew it at the time. He sent me a list of all kinds of outfits – banks, holding companies, off-shore people, you know the kind of thing, mostly with a foot in Hong Kong and China. What he was looking for, was any which had developed recent links with Sri Lanka. If you remember, there'd been something about the trouble in the north – government forces making a push on Jaffna, that sort of thing – and knowing him, I'd jokingly asked if he was anywhere near it. And he'd just laughed and said, "Oh that's tiger country up there." At first, I don't think he was on to any actual connection with the guerrillas. Working for AWW, it was the bone trade, pure and simple, that he was after, but I didn't know that, of course.'

Fran's frown of concentration deepened. She'd hardly touched the food. 'But by the time the last e-mail arrived, he was on to the fact that the guerrillas were being partly funded by the bone trade.'

'Exactly. He explained all this when I arrived, but the e-mail was a kind of warning that things were much more complicated than he'd thought.'

'*Complicated*?' Her voice went up to the danger level. 'Is that what you call it? I'd call it downright life-threatening. So what did he ask you to do?'

'Well, after I'd done my bit for England and M & B, we met at Vesak's place and that's when he came up with Plan A. By then he'd rumbled that the Blue Peacock was being used as a cover for the tiger bone trade and he strongly suspected that the owners were giving a cut of the profits to the Separatists.'

Just look at him, thought Fran. He can sit there eating while he's telling me all this. She noticed how quickly the curry was disappearing and tried to eat some, if only because she was now very hungry.

'You see, what Brian needed was video proof,' continued Nevil, quite unruffled. 'He'd already set himself up as a dodgy arms broker, and got himself an invite to the Peacock.'

'Oh yeah – I can imagine! He certainly looked the part. And then I suppose he thought he'd drag you along for good luck.' She sighed. 'What are friends for?'

'It was belt and braces, really. He reckoned he'd get more out of them if I was there. The idea was to bring me along, with their agreement of course, as an old Gulf hand who knew his way round the financing of arms deals. No one said who the arms were for. It could have been half a dozen places. You know what it's like these days. There are plenty of Russians and other ex-Eastern bloc types who'd sell their spare Kalashnikovs and Semtex to anything that moves, provided it pays in hard currency, and the Gulf is the in-place to meet them.'

'And you used your own name for this? Nevil, honestly . . .' Fran closed her eyes tight and sat back hard on the cushions. Any minute now she was going to hit him.

'Had to. We knew they'd check. I'd been at the InterCont on legitimate business with the Al Masira people anyway. Perfect cover, you see. Brian booked in for one night too, as if he'd just blown in from somewhere with a dodgy human rights record, and bingo! We'd check out of the InterCont, get a taxi to the Peacock meeting, and then go back to Vesak's place with it all on tape.'

'Then waltz off for a few rounds of golf, I suppose. Nevil, there are times when I don't know whether you're daft or just plain crazy. And did you get it?'

'Oh yes, we got it all right. 'It's all over there, locked in that cupboard.'

'What?'

He pointed to a dark, elaborately carved monster of a dresser, the only big piece of furniture in the almost spartan living room, apart from a large television set and the sofa. She stared at it across the expanse of floor tiles.

'Do they know you've got it? My God, but of course they do! Or why all this?'

'We can't be sure. What we do know is that someone tipped them off after the meeting that Brian and, by implication, myself, were not quite who they thought we were. We think it came from the police. They were the only ones who knew that AWW were going after the tiger bone dealers. What we can't know for sure is what they got out of poor Brian before they killed him.'

'Christ . . .'

There was a long, sober pause.

Nevil swallowed hard. 'So we have to assume the worst. And that's why we both ran for cover. We haven't even been able to play the stuff yet to see exactly what we've got.'

'I'm sorry about that,' groaned Vesak. 'One reason I was so pleased we could use this house was that I knew my uncle had a video. But see?' He waved at the television where Fran now noticed an obvious space and some wires beneath it. 'He's taken it to the wedding, so everyone can see the pictures. And he doesn't have a tape machine for such tiny audio cassettes.'

'Could we buy one?' put in Fran. 'At least we could hear what the recorder picked up.'

Nevil nodded. 'We'll see what we can do on the way back to Colombo tomorrow. Trouble is, we were terrified of being watched and giving the game away.'

'But between the recording and the video do you think you've got enough to nail the whole thing down?' she asked hopefully. 'Then we can all go home. Now wouldn't that be great?'

He reached over and briefly took her hand. 'It would, if we had. But we haven't,' he said flatly. 'Even assuming that what we think we've got has come out clearly. It's all good stuff, but what we're missing is something to tie in the people we were talking to with the way the bones are brought in from India and sold on. Naturally, the bones weren't mentioned at the Peacock meeting. It was none of our business to ask where the money was coming from, and we'd no idea at the time that there were was a haul actually on the premises.'

'Oh come on! Surely if the police now know about the bone haul, that's enough to connect it to the club owners?'

'To the owners, yes, but not to the guy who really ties all this lot together.'

'Aagh!' Fran clapped her hands on her knees with a yell of sheer exasperation. 'Wouldn't you know it? Now you're going to tell me there's a Mr Big behind all this. And you're not coming home until you get him. OK – fine. You and whose army?'

'Fran . . .'

'All right, carry on. I can take it.' She knew she was behaving badly, but didn't much care.

'Right – according to Brian's information, there's one guy who liaises with the Tigers to bring the stuff in from India across the Jaffna Straits. He's also the one who gets it shipped on again to China.' Nevil fished out a tiny ball of paper from his pocket and smoothed it out to peer at the minute writing. 'No joke, this is so that I can eat it if I have to. I've got his aliases and account numbers down here. His name, if you can believe this, is Xavier Michael Cheng. He's part Sri Lankan, part Chinese, and his friends call him Zavvy.'

'Does he have any friends? Sounds like a mission boy gone wrong to me.'

'Oh he's got friends all right, just about everywhere. Hong Kong, Macao, Shanghai, Bahrain – all the usual sunny places for shady people.'

'But he wasn't at the Peacock meeting?'

'Actually, he was. At least we think it was him from the description Brian had, but he was only in the background and didn't say anything. He left before we got down to business.'

'That's a start, I suppose. If only we could see the

tape. What does he look like, this Zavvy?'

'I'd like to say he's old, bald, fat and inscrutable, with a heroin habit that's rendered him toothless and impotent. As it happens, he's thirty-something and really fancies himself. Often has his hair in a ponytail. He's married, but uses prostitutes for purposes you wouldn't want to know about. Let's just say it's rather specialised. He's a vicious little bastard, apparently.'

'Oh yuk!' Then suddenly she sat upright, her eyes wide. 'Part Chinese! The desk clerk at the InterCont said one of the men who came looking for Brian was part Chinese. I assumed he meant the other part was European. How silly of me! The clerk was Sri Lankan. He most likely meant part Sri Lankan, part Chinese, and he was certainly scared stiff of him.'

Nevil sat up with a jolt. 'My God, Fran, what did you put in that noticeboard message? Maybe they know about you, too. If you get dragged any further into this, I'll never forgive myself.'

She tried to laugh. 'Years of working with you lot have left me deeply paranoid. Largely thanks to Charlie, I could already smell something when I left that message. I had to leave the address of St Anthony's, or you'd never have found me at all, but I just signed it 'F'. I thought it might slow them down if they didn't have a sex or a surname to go on and the desk clerk who knew me wasn't around. Unfortunately, it was the same one, so it's possible they might have asked him who'd left it.'

'Jesus! So they could know my wife's in the country, and what you look like?'

Fran bit her lip. Had she been lulled into a false sense of security by her move down the coast?

'Nevil, I simply don't know,' she replied unhappily. 'But forget the guilt trip. Nobody asked me to come. Anyway, Charlie's smart enough for both of us. She must have spotted that possibility, which is why she suggested I move. But I'm sure they can't have traced me to the Cinnamon Beach.'

'I hope to hell you're right. But the whole point is, my darling, we can't be sure of anything now. Like who's after us, just for starters. Are we talking about the Peacock crowd here, or the police? And doesn't Charlie reckon there's something bent at the police end too?'

Fran nodded bleakly. 'She's worried stiff. Right now, she doesn't know who to trust and she's more or less freelancing. You two suspect it was one of Brian's police contacts who betrayed him, and we've no idea how far up it goes.'

'What is most worrying,' put in Vesak, 'is that they could be watching the airport. It's a simple matter here. Security is tight because of the Separatist situation. If you are thinking of sending the tapes out by airmail, parcels can easily be screened. One nod from the right person . . .'

'God, is it really this bad?' Nevil had his head in his hands.

Fran watched him almost clinically. So far, it was as if he'd been running on adrenaline. Maybe he'd simply been in shock after what had happened to Brian. Now it was all beginning to come home, and having her around was just one more worry for him.

'Look, suppose we all just left, taking the tapes.' He was casting around desperately now. 'What charge could they hold us on?'

'You must understand,' said Vesak, almost angrily. 'If they want to, they can cook up anything at all. For you, maybe something about currency, or they'd claim the tapes were pornographic. Even plant drugs.' He shrugged expressively. 'For me, something worse. In the end, they'd have to let you go. You have the British High Commission. I do not. Then we'll have lost what proof we have, and there will be no hope of stopping this terrible business.'

'And Brian's death will have been for nothing.' Nevil was making an effort to pull himself together. 'That's not on. Brian really wouldn't have liked that.'

'Well,' said Fran. 'What with bent police, airports being watched, and that bunch of murdering sadists from the Peacock, we're really up against it, aren't we?'

'Just one thing, though,' she said, to break the grim silence that followed her observation. 'I want to nail these bastards as much as you do. They kill our friends, they blow up buses, they destroy people's lives with drugs, and soon there won't be a tiger left on the face of the earth. So if you're about to suggest that I go home and leave you to it, forget it. I'm not going back without you, and that's that.

Nevil sat up and took her hand again. 'I think it's going to be a long night,' he said.

It was gone two o'clock, and the table and floor were littered with bits of paper covered in notes, circles, arrows and crossings out. To get some order into the chaos, Nevil suggested that they each took it in turns to write down what facts the other two knew. There were names, addresses, numbers, and maps. Vesak did an elaborate flow chart tracing the possible routes of the arms, money and bone trade, and then they made lists of unanswered questions and tried to thrash out a way of getting some answers.

Fran was in favour of memorising as much of it as

possible and then getting rid of every bit of paper except the most essential and difficult material in case any one came snooping. They recited names, addresses and dates to each other like school kids swotting for an end of term exam. No one so much as hinted at the possibility that they might be caught, or they might have gone to pieces.

They were dead on their feet by now, and for all their deliberations, they hadn't come up with any clear answers as to their best course of action. Vesak was already asleep, sitting on the floor, propped against the sofa.

'We'd better try and rest,' yawned Nevil, standing up and reaching for Fran's hand to haul her to her feet. 'Maybe I could get Tony to do a bit more check-ing for me. There are still a few names I'd like him to work on, and it'll be a damned sight easier from London than from here.'

'Fine. You can't exactly go swanning into the Inter-Cont and ask to use their business centre, now can you?'

'Oh Christ!' said Nevil, suddenly awake again. 'We haven't even told Tony about Brian.'

Back home it was only about nine o'clock in the evening, so they tried phoning, but it was the week-end, and Tony obviously wasn't in. Nevil decided to he'd try again late tomorrow morning before they left for Colombo, when Tony should be getting up. It would have been cruel to wake him in the middle of night with such grim news.

Nevil glanced at the sleeping Vesak. 'Poor guy,' he said softly. 'He must be scared witless. We can't just leave him to cope with all this on his own, can we?'

They both shook their heads helplessly and she

leaned against him, almost too weary to be frightened.

'Are you going to leave the tapes in that cupboard overnight?' she asked, as they aimed themselves in the general direction of the bedroom door. 'Maybe we should take them to bed with us.'

Nevil unlocked the cupboard, and she looked at them with a kind of awe. Brian had died for these. 'Wouldn't it be safer if I took them?' she asked, her mind suddenly clearing.

'*What?*' said Nevil. 'I couldn't possibly let you take that kind of risk. Over my . . .'

She put her hand quickly over his mouth. 'I've been thinking. Look, of the three of us, I'm the safest. No one but Charlie knows I'm at the Cinnamon Beach, except the young cop who picked me up for the identification, and he must have been OK, or Charlie would never have chosen him for the job. What I'm hoping, is that they'll think I've gone home. No one will be looking out for me. Let me take them until we work out what to do for the best. Maybe if Tony comes up with something really interesting about some of these people's sordid little connections, we could just turn the whole lot over to Charlie and go home.'

He shook his head. 'If you think I'd dream of putting you to any more risk . . .'

'But can't you see? It makes sense.'

'Not another word. Sleep.'

And still in their clothes, they fell onto the narrow little bed and slept with the cassettes under the pillow.

# Chapter Fourteen

Although they'd been through it all a thousand times, the parting that morning made them utterly miserable. It would not have been sensible for them to stay together, even if it had been physically possible. Hotels were out of the question, and the two men's best chance was to lie low in Colombo at Vesak's friend's flat. The flat had only one room, with three men already in it, and Fran was the first to agree that it would have been pushing hospitality as well as their cover beyond the bounds of safety for her to stay with them.

Over a hurried breakfast the question of the tapes came up again, and this time Fran put up a real fight.

'Just give me the wretched things,' she said in exasperation. 'Why not? We can't stay together, and I'm going to be stuck at the Cinnamon Beach at least until Charlie makes contact again. Right now, there may be a lot more going on than we know about. I bet they'll just about fit into my safe deposit box. That way, if there's been any break-through, I can just hand them over to Charlie and let her take it from there.'

Reluctantly the men agreed.

'After all, I'll be able to come down there now and again for the odd conjugal visit,' said Nevil, in an attempt to cheer themselves up.

'Not at the hotel,' replied Fran morosely. 'It had better be the beach, or there's a couple of little restaurants in the town that would do.'

'OK, just because I'm paranoid, it doesn't mean there isn't anyone following me.'

'Ha! The old jokes are the best.'

Fran could sense Nevil's increasing frustration at his own position. He seemed to feel he had no role except to lie low and wait for more information from Tony in the hope that something crucial might turn up to help them nail the bone traders. Meanwhile they were both acutely aware that, with all their other problems, the matter of finalising the details of the Al Masira contract had been almost forgotten. Yet the future of Merrick and Baldwyn depended on it, and that was no mean consideration. Nevil was now virtually forced to stick around Colombo, where he could get to a fax at some quiet little shop like Mr Silva's.

With obsessive care Fran packed her overnight bag, putting the bigger video cassette into a hastily emptied sponge bag. The tiny audio tape she tied firmly into a scarf wound round her sun hat. With the help of a belt and some advice from Vesak, they made a reasonable job of getting her into the sari again. Then they all just stood there looking at each other, unsure how to say goodbye, knowing that time was pressing if Vesak was to make the return trip before his family arrived back and found a stranger on their doorstep.

'Group hug?' sniffed Fran. If the old gardener who was pottering round with a hosepipe outside had looked up, he might have been rather shocked to see his employer's nephew, his cook, and a young European male in a huddle trying to smile and dabbing at each others' faces.

They composed themselves and Vesak opened the door. Fran negotiated the steps in slightly better order this time. Vesak gave three toots on the horn as they drove away, which prompted wistful memories of the last time she'd heard him do that.

Vesak drove the pick-up to its limit. The elephants by the river had gone, leaving only the litter of rounded storm boulders. Had she only dreamt they'd been there?

They covered the distance in an hour and a quarter without actually killing anything. Before they got to the hotel, Fran quickly got herself out of the sari, folded it and put it under the seat. The red hibiscus flower she had worn yesterday had collapsed like damp silk, but she put it in her bag just the same.

Vesak dropped her about a quarter of a mile from the entrance. They parted with the briefest of hand-shakes.

'Look after yourselves,' she said listlessly, and walked back to the hotel. The thick sand coated her sandalled feet in seconds, slowing her down, and the strip of tar looked ready to melt and trap the unwary like flypaper. If anyone was watching, she didn't see them. But then, as she told herself, if they were any good at their job, she wouldn't, would she?

She went through the usual ritual of checking for messages at the desk, and got a welcoming smile from the manager. The tapes, carefully wrapped, she put in her deposit box with a small prayer for their safety. Presumably, the management would not allow the box to be opened, even by the police, without her being present.

The Kandy excursion wasn't due back until the evening. As Nevil might have said, it was going to be another tough day, and the irony of it almost made her smile as she went up to her room and changed for the pool. How many lengths would it take to keep her sane today?

It was very late when the Kandy group got back. Fran had spent the rest of the day with only her own thoughts for company and at times they became overheated and confused. Why hadn't Charlie made contact? Had Nevil managed to get hold of Tony yet? And where was Nevil now? The idea of his being confined to a one-roomed flat in Colombo with two other men made her almost smile. Nevil wasn't very good at that sort of thing. He liked his space, but east of Suez the word 'privacy' was not in the dictionary. But then, she wasn't very good at waiting, and they were world class at that out here.

Dutifully she took her vitamins and malaria tablets, did her pool lengths, slept a little, ate properly and tried to read. *The English Patient* sat still unopened by the bed. On the back, the reviewers were calling it a novel of love and confusion, about a group of shell-shocked characters – a net of dreams. No, she wasn't ready for that yet. In it, people who had loved deeply had died alone, that much she remembered. Klaus had lent her *Pride and Prejudice*. That would have to do instead – all graceful snobbery, refined feelings and soothing English temperaments. Maybe that would cool her down.

But by the time Anders and Klaus appeared, she was bursting to tell them at least part of what had been happening. They greeted each other like long-lost relatives. Anders inquired after his patient, and was delighted when she told them she'd found Nevil. They accepted without comment that he'd had to go back to Colombo on business, and she was only

215

too happy to hear all about the great time they'd had in Kandy.

'You'll be moving on soon, though,' she said sadly. 'I know there's a lot more you want to see.'

Anders looked at Klaus. 'There is no hurry,' he said.

Two days passed before Charlie made contact. Even as Fran sprinted across the grass to take the call and the waiter said it was a woman, she wondered if something was wrong, because Charlie had said she'd simply turn up, not phone. But then, Charlie didn't know the good news.

In the office, she snatched up the receiver and grabbed a chair. 'I've found him,' she carolled excitedly. 'I didn't ring because you said not to.'

'I'm so glad he's all right,' said Charlie. She sounded strained, tense. 'He's not with you, is he?'

'No – we thought it best not. He's with friends.'

'Thank God for that. Don't tell me where. Now listen, my dear, I think you may have to move on.'

'Who, *me*?' Fran was on the edge of the chair, all the elation gone. This was red alert and no mistake. When was this craziness ever going to end?

'Apparently, Mrs Mario has been trying to get hold of me, but I've been off station. I've just been talking to her now. She was most concerned as to whether she'd done the right thing. Some men who said they were police arrived at the guest house and asked to see the register. They began asking questions about one guest in particular – you. What you looked like, what your business there was and where you were going next.'

'I don't believe this! Thank heavens I didn't know exactly where I was going when I left.'

'But think – you must have mentioned Kalutara to Mrs Mario. You remember, the train?'

'My God, of course!'

'At first she thought that maybe they'd found your husband and was eager to help. Then one of them said that they were looking for him too, making it sound as if you were both criminals. That began to worry her, so in the end she came round to see me.'

'Oh, my lord,' groaned Fran.

'Unfortunately I was out all day, but she kept coming back, bless her heart. I wouldn't like to say how long it might take them to check out all the hotels down your way, but I'd leave right now and move much further south. Try the hippie place, you know where I mean. There are beach shacks and whatnot. Then ring me at my aunt's and leave a message if necessary. Have you a pen?'

Fingers numb, Fran scribbled the number down. The hippie place. That was Hikka-something. She'd find it. It was all done at breakneck speed, as if Charlie was hoping to fool someone who might be in the next room and didn't have her flow of English.

The call ended in a flurry of terse goodbyes. As Fran rushed from the tiny office, her only thought at that second was that this would be the last time she would be leaving it with yet another nightmare situation hanging over her head. Half way across to the stairs, she came to skidding halt on the tiles. The tapes! Suppose the police turned up before she'd packed and checked out. Above all, she had to keep them safe.

Quickly she backtracked to the office and retrieved them from the safe deposit box. Now what? She could hardly stuff them into her costume. Anders, of course. He was reading in his usual place, Klaus beside him, that slightly amused smile around his lips. Had he been watching her latest imitation of a headless chicken?

Trying not to break into a gallop, Fran went over to them. 'Anders,' she said breathlessly. 'You've have been so good to me. Could I ask you one last favour?'

'Of course, but not the last, I hope.'

Soon she was going to have to tell them she was leaving – as soon as she had packed, in fact – and that was going to hurt more than she wanted to admit. But in the meantime . . . 'Please could you take these and look after them for me? It's just a video and stuff. It's to do with my husband's business and it's quite valuable – to the right people.'

Praying no one was watching, she passed Anders the brown paper bag with the tapes. He took it without a word and slipped it under his towel, looking at her quizzically with his Baltic blue eyes.

'I won't be long. Actually, I don't know how to say this, but I'm going to pack. I have to leave, you see.' She was trying desperately not to look over her shoulder at the reception area.

'You mean, you're going home?'

'I wish I was,' she said heavily. 'I'm going south. I don't know where, but I have to leave here right now.'

'But that's amazing! Klaus and I were just discussing that it is about time we moved on – to Galle, maybe, or Hikkaduwa. You know, a bit of surfing, a bit of clubbing.'

'You're kidding!' For a moment, sheer relief made her want to sit down right there with them, relax, believe everything would be all right. But she didn't dare.

'Kidding? Not at all. See? Here is the guidebook, already open. Klaus was keen, and I was saying that maybe now that you are all right again, the doctor could move on . . . What is it, Fran? You are seeing ghosts again?'

She had suddenly frozen. Two men, one a policeman, had walked through the main entrance and were making their way purposefully to reception. Her eyes narrowed. There was something about the civilian which didn't look typically Sri Lankan. Quickly she pulled up a chair and sat down before her knees gave way.

'Anders, Klaus,' she said, her voice fearful. 'Tell me quickly. Do you like tigers? Bengal tigers,' she added, seeing the mystification on their faces.

'Why, yes . . .'

'Then please listen carefully to me. Don't look round, but some police have just come in and any minute now, someone is going to come over and say they want to talk to me. All this isn't about my husband's business, it's about saving tigers. If they don't take me away, I'll explain everything to you, I swear. If they do, get onto the British High Commission, then call these numbers.' She turned her body to conceal what she was doing, and wrote down Charlie's and Nevil's phone numbers quickly on a table napkin, followed by Tony's home address. 'Give it two days, and if I'm not back, please post the package to that address, registered.' Even if airmail packages were being checked, it was worth the risk. 'And can you scribble down your home address for me? I'd hate you never to know what all this is about.'

Anders managed to move his jaw from the half-open position, his normal air of relaxed amusement quite blown away. 'I wrote it inside the book,' he said. 'For you to keep.'

'Anders, you're a wonder. Now let's talk about Kandy until they come for me.'

She was only just in time. A waiter came hurrying across the grass, exactly as she had predicted. The two newcomers were watching from the veranda. She acted politely bemused, turned to look round at them as if only just aware of their presence, and then shrugged and got up. 'We'll have that drink later,' she said, and followed the waiter at a pace as casual as her stalling legs would allow. Hope was still flickering. Maybe she was panicking unnecessarily, and this was only something to do with Brian's identification process.

'I'm Mrs Merrick; can I help you?' she asked brightly. Perhaps she could charm her way out. The policeman was tall and his uniform seemed to have shrunk in the wash. The other one was slight, light-skinned, and shorter than she was. That usually annoyed them. Then she saw his eyes. They were almost black, and quite without expression. Not a spark.

'We can go to the office, please,' he said, in an accent that could have been almost anything Asian. What was he? *Who* was he?

'Fine.' She tried a shrug and followed them. 'I suppose you're a policeman, too?'

He didn't reply immediately, just sat down in the only chair, rather too relaxed. Not a good sign. She could feel herself beginning to sweat. Those eyes. Predatory. She didn't dare look more closely. They said if you looked an animal born to hunt too closely in the eyes, it felt threatened. Then it got angry.

'We are looking for your husband,' he said at last, as if it bored him to state the obvious. This man looked as if he never sweated.

Giggle. Go on, giggle for your life. 'Looking for my husband? Whatever for?' In her present state, it wasn't going to be that difficult to play it all silly and girlie. 'OK, but don't tell me if you find him, *please*. You see, we've had the most *awful* row.'

This seemed to throw him. 'You do not know where he is?'

'No, and I don't care.' She was warming up now. 'He might have gone home for all I know.'

'He has not left the country.'

Shit. So Vesak had been right about them watching the airport. 'Oh, hasn't he?' she prattled. 'Well, he can come back when he's ready to apologise. Sorry I can't help. Oh,' she added almost casually. 'I suppose he's all right, is he? He's not had an accident or anything?'

Dumber still and dumber. It was like being in a West End farce. Fortunately, neither came up with the classic retort: 'If we knew that, Mrs Merrick, we'd hardly be asking you,' which was encouraging. Any minute now the manager would walk in and say, 'Anyone for tennis?' Some other part of her brain was wondering if slapping your own face when you got hysterical would actually work.

'According to our information, he has some illegal pornographic material in his possession.'

'What? Oh come *on*.' Another giggle. Careful, don't overdo it. Although considering that the reference to the porno material meant they probably knew about the cassettes, she was doing well not be downright hysterical. 'He's no angel, but he's not really the type.' Try hurt pride. 'Anyway, I'd have noticed.'

'We have to search your room. Also, may we have your safe deposit key?'

'Well, that's a bit much.' Not too indignant; just enough. 'Now let's see – have I got it on me? Oh, silly me. It's in my bag, and that's over by the pool, being looked after by those two nice men over there. I don't know what they're going to think, I'm sure.'

'He will go with you.'

"He" opened the door. Strange – that uniform didn't really fit. Sri Lankan police were usually ultra smart. Got you, you bastard, she thought, walking airily across the grass. It's not yours, is it? Stolen, borrowed, hired? Not really a problem, if you knew the right people.

Anders and Klaus were reading with expressions of intense concentration, but several people looked up curiously as she passed.

Maybe this one would loosen up. He didn't look quite such a hard case as Snake-eyes. 'My room's awfully untidy,' she rattled on. 'It might help if I knew exactly what you were looking for. Is it maga-zines or something?'

'We cannot say.'

'Oh well, I expect you'll know it when you see it, eh?' The sarcasm was wasted on him. Fortunately, he didn't seem too bright. Maybe he was just one of their foot-sloggers. Were these the people who had called at the guest house? If not, how many did they have at their beck and call, for heaven's sake? But whoever these people were, it had shaken her to the core to find she'd been so wrong about them not being able to trace her. Thank heavens for Mrs Mario's commonsense. That was one she owed St Anthony.

'Hi, guys,' she said as reached Anders and Klaus, who did a brilliant job of looking surprised to see her with a policeman in tow. 'Would you believe? This gentleman wants to see my safe deposit box.' She picked up her bag and handed over the key with a touch of drama, making sure the man knew other people had seen what was going on. 'Can't think why. I've spent nearly all my money. Then they want to check my room. Embarrassing, or what! There's obviously been some mistake. See you later.'

Leaving Anders and Klaus silent with amazement, Fran and her escort collected the other man and trooped round to the safe deposit office with the manager firmly in tow. The more people who had seen all this the better. Just then, it seemed like her only defence against what might happen next. Should she ask to see a search warrant or something? Did they have them out here? And if they did, would it make any difference? Better not push it. Dear God, she prayed, don't let them take my passport.

But when the box had been opened, to reveal nothing but a small amount of cash, her travel documents and some travellers' cheques and credit cards, they only flicked through it, and she began to breathe again.

'And could I ask you to come with us to the room?' She beamed at the manager. 'We wouldn't want any misunderstandings, would we?'

The room search was embarrassingly thorough, but then, of course, it would be. What a relief that she hadn't started to pack, or it might have looked more suspicious. Maybe they really would write her off as a dizzy daisy who hadn't a clue what her husband was up to, and didn't really care.

'Oh, do be *careful!*' she squeaked once or twice as

her possessions were methodically rifled, shaken and turned inside out.

Tutting with petulant irritation, she flounced onto the balcony, and noticed that Anders and Klaus were packing up to go in. Anders had the towel rolled under his arm. She hoped they'd thought of keeping an eye on the entrance in case they took her away, which seemed at least a possibility. What would she have done without those two? At least they'd be able to sound the alarm if it came to it.

The search had produced nothing, and they couldn't really plant anything because the manager was hovering about showing signs of distress.

When they finally ground to a reluctant halt, she said, all merry and bright, 'Well, if that's all. Oh please, don't bother trying to put it all back . . .'

Strangely, they seemed unsure what to do. Having found their quarry, they'd obviously been hoping for more. Perhaps they wanted some sort of let-out for whoever had sent them. Some kind of resolution. It would have to be the cock-up theory. That was the best she could do for them at such short notice.

'It must be some mistake,' she said comfortingly, as if the whole thing had absolutely nothing to do with her or her errant husband. 'I do hope you catch them. I think pornography's so disgusting, don't you?' she added, ushering them towards the door like a hostess speeding tiresome guests on their way. 'By the way, Merrick is quite a common English name, you know.'

'But you are tall,' said the policeman sullenly.

Various stinging retorts to this apparent non-sequitur raced to the edge of her tongue and had to be swallowed down hard. She chose the least harmless and played to the gallery.

'Do you think so?' she cooed, turning to the manager. 'For a foreigner, I mean?'

The manager's head performed some very satisfactory waggling. His whole body seemed to join in.

Snake-eyes sighed. He was clearly getting tired of this.

'Still, they can't arrest you for being tall, can they?' Watch it, she told herself, don't go over the top or you'll blow the whole thing. 'I'd keep on looking, if I were you.' Keep them moving, that's the way. 'It must be awfully difficult with all the tourists about.' Get them downstairs. There we go, one step at a time, still smiling away . . .

Nevil always said she was good at babbling. After this, she could babble for England.

Phew – they'd made it to the lobby. She waved to Anders and Klaus, who had installed themselves by the television and seemed to be taking great interest in a football match. I love them, she thought. I just hope they're enjoying this, that's all. Any minute now, she'd be able to rush over and buy them the biggest Singapore Slings they'd ever seen. Then she was going to get the hell out of here . . .

Too soon. Snake-eyes had paused at reception.

'We'll have to take your passport, of course.'

'*What*?' Her yelp made several people turn round, including Anders and Klaus. 'You can't do that!' Oh yes they can, said a warning voice. People like this can do whatever they like.

Snake-eyes didn't even bother to correct her. He just smiled and held his hand out for her safe deposit key.

Bastard – making her think she'd got away with it! Was he trying to get her rattled? Better be consistent.

'But I told you, I was planning to go home straight

225

away. I've simply got to teach him a lesson this time, or he'll never take me seriously.' Tears. Quick, find some, you silly cow. Think of Brian on that slab. 'Really, this is awful!' Sniff. Reach for a tissue. 'This whole holiday's turned into a complete nightmare. I'll get it back soon, won't I? You'll give me a receipt or something?'

A small crowd was gathering.

'It is just for checking. It will be returned.'

'Well, I certainly hope so. What with one thing and another, I've had just about enough.' How very true.

Once more they traipsed round to the safe deposit office with the manager watching unhappily as the box was opened. Her brain was into overdrive. If she made too much fuss or refused to let them take it, they'd probably get rough and say they were taking her in for questioning. Better keep up the charade.

'Oh, all right,' she simpered, as if she had a choice. 'If you can't trust the police, who can you trust? But could I possibly have it back tonight? I'd really like to go home tomorrow.'

'But of course.'

Not daring to raise her eyes to his, she took a last longing look at her passport as he tucked it into his jacket. She knew exactly what she'd see in those eyes. They hadn't got the slightest intention of ever giving it back. If they needed her again, they knew she couldn't leave the country without the hassle of reporting it lost and getting a replacement. That could take ages. And if they didn't need her, why should they worry about causing her some in-convenience?

It seemed to take forever until the two men were safely outside. She hovered at the entrance, her ears straining for the sound of their engine reversing. Then came the surge of the accelerator . . .

They'd gone. All she wanted to do now was sit down and howl with relief that they hadn't taken her away. But she was supposed to be feeling outraged about the passport. Squaring her shoulders, she took a shaky breath and turned to face the inquiring faces still lurking near the entrance in case anything else dramatic might occur to enliven their pre-lunch cocktails.

'Well, I don't know what all that was about,' she declared to the lobby at large. 'Mistaken identity, I suppose. What a laugh!'

The message went round, translated into several languages. 'All a mistake . . . nothing to worry about . . . no problem . . .'

Now the immediate crisis was all over, her hands were shaking and her knees felt wobbly. She sat down quickly. Not only was she very frightened, she was also angry with herself. How could she have been so confident about taking charge of the precious tapes? It had been touch and go whether she'd lost the lot and ended up being the next one in the nearest lagoon without a face. Christ, it was even possible that they might get a thick ear from whoever sent them for not bringing her in, and come back for her.

Panic forced her to her feet again and she made straight for Anders and Klaus.

'You see what I mean?' she said, keeping her voice well down. 'Look, you two have been so fantastic. If you really are going to Hikkaduwa, there's nothing I'd like better than to go with you. You're like my guardian angels. But I've got to leave right now. Maybe we could fix somewhere to meet.'

'Are you packed?' asked Anders, imperturbable as

ever. 'We can pack in ten minutes, isn't it so, Klaus?'

Klaus held up five fingers with a grin. 'You see? Why waste a taxi? It's a long way.'

Fran wanted to hug them both. 'OK, if you're sure. I'm just so frightened they'll be back, and not with my passport, either.'

'Is it really that bad?'

She put her hand over his so he could feel it shaking. 'It'll take me most of the journey to tell you what all this is about. I'm going to have to think of some way of getting out of here. They may have left someone outside.'

'Suppose we all leave together,' ventured Anders. 'Maybe they wouldn't l look closely at three people. No, better if all three of us leave together, but you do not look like you . . .'

'What? Oh no, not the sari again,' she groaned.

'I'm sorry? You have a sari?'

'No, I left it in the car. I'm sorry, I'm not making sense, am I? But I will, Anders. Trust me. What had you in mind?'

There was a rapid discussion in Danish which seemed to amuse Klaus no end.

'Do not be offended, dear Fran,' said Anders. 'But we think you would make a lovely, slim-hipped man. You know - my pants and hat, with Klaus' precious Armani jacket . . .'

'Now look, you two, this isn't funny any more.' But then she saw that they meant it, and that it might even work. No bra, scarf to tie everything down, hair in ponytail, her Gucci loafers . . . 'Wait a minute – I've already scandalised the entire hotel. I can't check out dressed as a feller. Round here, there's probably a law against it. I don't need the real police as well.'

'They were not real police? Oh my! This is getting

serious. Well then, what we do is this. First you go and tell reception you are checking out and going back to England while we go and pack.'

'OK, I'll say I've had bad news or something. It might put them on the wrong track if they come back. And for the moment, you'd better keep the tapes, just in case.'

'Fine. I will bring you the clothes. Then we will check out and have a taxi waiting a little way from the gate. Then *you* check out, but you wear only enough to look like you. When you leave the entrance and can't be seen from reception, you tie back your hair, then – hat, jacket and sunglasses. See? I will be waiting, and walk with you to the gate. By that time, if anyone is watching they will see only two young men joining a third in the taxi. You will have become invisible, isn't it so?'

'You really think I could pull it off?' She was stunned by the sheer gall of it. 'I saw something like that in a film once – The Pink Panther. It was Inspector Clouseau's wife. She went down in a lift, and by the time she reached the bottom, she was a totally different person.'

'It happens like that many times on a Friday night in Copenhagen,' chuckled Anders. 'Only usually it is the men coming out dressed like women. Maybe some places in London, too.'

'My God, I've had a sheltered life,' said Fran. 'But I'll give it a go.'

The entire crazy charade took less than twenty minutes. Fran went round the room like a whirling dervish scooping armfuls of scattered belongings into every available bag space. Anders brought the clothes, and by the time she got as far as checking

229

out, the sweat was running between her breasts and down her backbone inside the scarf she'd wound round to flatten herself out.

The check out went smoothly and she made sure to leave the staff a generous tip. As planned, Anders was waiting for her, propped against a huge pot of canna lilies, half hidden in the dense shade of the drive. But the minute she saw his face, she knew something was wrong.

'You look great,' he said. 'But they are still outside, further up the road. And another car has just arrived. They're talking.'

'Jesus!'

'Keep calm. You can do it.'

In his agitation, he tried to take her big case, but she stopped him in time, letting him take the smaller bag instead.

Walk tall, she reminded herself, hoping it would stop the quaking.

They headed for the gate. Not thirty yards up the long dusty lane leading to the main road, two cars were parked carelessly on the wide verge, side on. Neither was a police car. In the back of one she caught a flash of a khaki shirt and peaked cap. There were three men in the other, and there was definitely a conference going on. One man was leaning casually out of a window watching the entrance while the others talked. The hotel was a dead end, and their taxi would have to pass them to get onto the Galle Road.

Somehow she reached the taxi and all three got in the back, with Fran in the middle.

'Off we go,' said Anders gaily, as if they were going on a picnic.

Stiff with fright, Fran stared straight ahead as the

driver slipped the brake and they moved forward. Klaus was chatting to distract the driver whose English was pretty basic, and what with the bumping and rattling from the rough road surface, it seemed unlikely that he was aware of the drama going on behind him.

'Tell me what they look like, the new ones,' she said through clenched teeth.

Klaus, who was on the left side, had a good look as they passed. 'The driver and the man watching, probably Sri Lankan,' he reported softly. 'The one in the back? Hey – not bad! Mixed race. Very good looking.'

But she'd spotted it already. The ponytail. Just as they'd passed, the man in the back of the nearest car had half turned.

'I think his name's Zavvy,' she hissed, cringing in her seat, even though they were safely past. 'And believe me, Klaus, you wouldn't want to know him.'

'But there's a lot we do want to know, dear Fran,' said Anders gently. 'But maybe not now.' He nodded almost imperceptibly to the driver. 'Can you find us a good place to stop for lunch?' he asked him, raising his voice. 'It's a long way to Hikkaduwa.'

The driver replied cheerfully that he could find a very good place.

'Oh God, I feel so bad about this,' she couldn't help saying. 'Getting you two involved, I mean.'

'Why should you feel bad?' asked Anders. 'We have never had so much fun on a holiday before. Not even in Miami.'

She glanced at his face in the driving mirror and, to her utter amazement, realised he meant it.

231

## Chapter Fifteen

*'It's a long way to Hikkaduwa; it's a long way to go . . .'*

They were actually singing – Anders, Klaus, and the taxi driver. The relief at making her escape was making even Fran light-headed. She would have liked to join in, but had to content herself with mouthing the words. The situation was weird enough without her wobbly soprano giving the game away. The driver found it a huge joke that people from Denmark knew the song but, had he spotted that the one in the middle at the back was not quite the man 'he' appeared to be, the atmosphere might not have been so cordial.

Half way to Hikkaduwa they had taken a break at a tiny shack which served snacks, chosen for the perverse reason that it didn't look as if had any toilet facilities and they could all disappear into the bushes. Then, over a spicy coconut *sambol* served on banana leaves under a cashew tree, she'd taken time explaining to Anders and Klaus the bizarre series of events which had led her here, dressed in their clothes, and heading for heaven knew where without her passport.

They'd absorbed it all as she knew they would by now, calmly and thoughtfully. Yet she couldn't shake off the feeling that deep down, for them, all this was still part of the holiday. They seemed to be revelling in the fact that fate had handed them a ready-made little adventure, one they could walk away from whenever they wished. But to compensate, there was an almost telepathic understanding between the pair and it touched her that, every now and then, they seemed to let her tune in.

Back on the road, between the Danes and the driver, the repertoire was eccentric and at times hilarious, which for Fran, slowly dissolving inside her all-concealing layers, was a welcome distraction.

*'Yesterday, all my troubles seemed so far away . . .'*

And wasn't that the truth, thought Fran, as the recital trailed off at the first sight of Hikkaduwa. Anders rummaged for his guide book.

' "Sri Lanka's biggest hippie hangout," ' he read. 'This is our kind of place, I think.'

'You want cheap room or cheap-cheap?' asked the driver.

'Cheap-cheap,' they chorused, like birds in a nest.

Hikkaduwa, a straggling strip of low-rise habitation between the eternal Galle Road and a curving beach of fine golden sand, was not so much a town, as a way of life. It seemed to have no recognisable centre and no obvious limits. To Fran, it looked exactly what the guide book said it was – one end of the great Sixties hippie trail that began in Istanbul, where the travelling people who couldn't make it to Bali had run out of money and beached themselves, along with their few remaining possessions and their dreams. The indiscriminate smatterings of European languages, the names and hop-head artwork on the tiny bars and tacky stalls said it all – The Tangerine Dream, Carnaby Street, Mellow Yellow, and inevitably, The Pink Elephant. Was there a Sunburnt Arms here too? Probably. But for all the attempts at ultimate cool, there was a feeling that the real action had long since jetted off elsewhere.

At Anders' request, the driver took them to the southern fringes of the town. Here, any attempts at regular buildings had long since given out. From the car, it looked as if the flotsam from some long-ago pop festival had taken root among the palms. There would be no questions here. It was, quite literally, the last resort.

To be extra safe, they had politely turned down all the driver's suggestions for accommodation.

'Here would be fine,' announced Anders suddenly, and they pulled over where a track left the main road beside a vast peepul tree. Under it was a small thatched bar called, with scant regard for accuracy, Unter den Linden. The words COLD BEER beckoned like a desert mirage.

There was no one about as they paid off the driver. It took only a moment for Fran to dive behind the huge tree trunk, slip out of the jacket, shake out her sweat-soaked hair and wriggle free of her bindings inside the damp shirt. Only now, she told herself wryly as she rejoined the other two, could she really appreciate the fortitude of those Victorian women who'd coped with things like the Indian Mutiny and exploring the Calabar Coast while still firmly restrained by their corsets.

Under the peepul tree, Anders and Klaus were dug in with the suitcases and were setting up the beers. Wondering if sweating like a man was going to make her drink like one, Fran tackled her first lager with the gusto of an England scrum-half after a win against the All Blacks. Three more cans were quickly produced by mine host, an ex-Berliner with a gleaming brown pot belly which made Fran feel slightly queasy. She decided two lagers were enough and switched to Cokes.

Anders was dispatched to find somewhere to stay. His brief was to find a quiet place where he could pay for two rooms for one week, with cash in advance. That way, they reckoned he would only have to show one passport, and Fran could go down under her maiden name. If anyone asked, she was Anders' girl friend, with a divorce pending. Another requirement was that the rooms should be close enough to facilitate any shunting around, which would be doubly important if Nevil showed up. Hikkaduwa did not look the kind of place that specialised in nosy landladies, but there was no point in appearing too outrageous.

She needn't have worried. At the place Anders had chosen for them, it probably wouldn't have mattered if they'd all had a sex change and swapped partners twice before breakfast. After a short taxi ride further along the beach, Fran found herself squinting into the late afternoon sun at a quite extraordinary construction. The front, if that's what it was, consisted of two ancient wooden boat prows upended on the dunes, with a lot of bamboo, old fishing nets and palm matting, all apparently held together with some kind of flowering creeper. Whoever had designed the thing, then christened it The Sydney Opera House, had at least a sense of humour.

This turned out to be a wiry, chain-smoking Australian called Baz, of indeterminate age, with skin like a sun-dried tomato. Baz not only looked as if he'd seen it all, but tried most of it and only just survived, and Fran thought she could get to like him if he'd give her half a chance.

Not exactly proudly, Baz showed them to their

rooms, which were in a palm thatched extension on stilts backing down to the beach. To reach them, there was a splintery but surprisingly sturdy ladder arrangement of split palm trunks. In between the floor boards, 'solid teak, off a liner', Fran could see sand, a line of drying sheets, some engine parts, and piles of crates and cooking gas bottles.

'I don't let it in the Wet – place leaks like a tub,' announced Baz, cigarette dangling. 'Only house rule, don't smoke in bed, or she'll go up like a ghost gum on Bonny Night.'

Even Anders needed a translation of this one, and then Baz left them to it. Amazingly, there was electric light – not much of it, but enough for one bulb per room. Later, when she asked about a phone, Baz said she could use the one in the office. An *office*? Fran couldn't wait to see it. In fact the only drawbacks to life at the Sydney Opera House, as far as she could tell, were the lack of a fax, and a tendency for small items to slip between the floor boards and finish up on the beach.

By the look of it, the office was also Baz's living space, and occasionally the kitchen. A hammock was slung in one corner, clothes hung limply on nails, and the phone was on top of a 'fridge which had frequent attacks of the shakes. The best Baz could offer by way of a safe for the precious tapes was a lockable metal filing cabinet of great age, which he assured her was termite-proof. For guests to register their phone calls, he showed her an egg timer and a greasy notebook.

As soon as Baz had gone, to catch, as he put it, something to barbie, Fran rang Charlie's home number, where she lived with her aunt. Rather as she feared, Charlie wasn't in, but the aunt sounded

236

pleasant and reliable enough, so Fran crossed her fingers and left the new number with her.

Then it was Nevil's turn, and this was going to be difficult. Bracing herself for an onslaught of indignation, recriminations and panic, she dialled the number of the Colombo flat. Since the place had only one room, they had little trouble finding Nevil. There was lot of background noise, against which she was surprised to hear some relieved cheering as Nevil took the phone.

'Look, Nev, I'm sorry about this . . .' she began, only to be interrupted by half a dozen questions of the 'what-the, where-the, who-the' variety.

Once she'd convinced him that she still had the tapes, hadn't been kidnapped or arrested at the airport and was quite safe, she quickly understood the cause of his outburst. He'd rung the Cinnamon Beach that morning, only to be told the alarming news that she'd checked out saying she'd had enough and was going home, after a police raid during which her passport had been confiscated. The atmosphere in the little apartment had been pretty desperate ever since.

'I got it wrong, I'm sorry,' she said again. 'I couldn't believe it when Charlie said they were on my tail.'

He said she'd obviously handled it brilliantly, even chortled about the disguise, and when they'd both calmed down, they got around to Tony, and this time there was some good news.

'I actually managed to get hold of him at last and fill him in,' Nevil told her. 'Naturally, he was devastated about Brian. Apparently it's not been in the papers at home. Then he came up with the best idea of his life. He's going to come out here himself,

237

with anything he can dig up about the various companies these people are using.'

'But that's fantastic! No one will be watching out for someone like him. He'll be able to take home the tapes.'

'Not to mention the Al Masira stuff. I'll be glad to get that all signed, sealed and delivered, I can tell you, or we won't have a firm, or a house, when we get back. *If* we get back . . .'

'Nev, stop it,' she said sharply. 'Meanwhile, any ideas on how I get a new passport?'

There was some quick consultation at the other end. 'It's OK, Vesak's got the number of the British High Commission. They're bound to fix you up with something temporarily.'

'Oh yes, eventually. If I can show how I lost it. Having it pinched by two suspicious characters posing as police who searched my room for pornography is going to sound very plausible, isn't it? And if I go to them, it would have to be issued in my real name, which right now doesn't seem a good idea.' She sighed. 'And by the way, Vesak was right. They knew you hadn't left, so we have to assume they're watching the airports. Nev, how are we ever going to crack this and get out of here?'

'I see what you mean. What about your friend, Charlie? Could she swing a fake passport for you?'

Fran clapped her free hand on the 'fridge top, and it gave a loud burp. 'Brilliant idea! But I'm still not going without you. Meanwhile, let's hope good old Tony comes up trumps and we can interest someone trustworthy in arresting a few of the nasty people round here. Which reminds me, I think I saw that Zavvy guy this morning.'

'*What?*' Nevil sounded as if he was going into

shock. 'Fran, I told you, he's poison. He's a complete psycho.'

'Don't worry, he didn't see me. Actually, I think Klaus rather fancied him.'

'For chrissake, Fran!'

'OK, it's been a tough day. God, did we ever used to say that and think it was true?'

When Charlie didn't call that evening, Fran felt only slightly uneasy. But by the time it was getting dark the next day, and there was still no word, she was beginning to feel quite ill with worry. At first she tried to hide it from Anders and Klaus. Then even Baz noticed it. He'd turned out to be something of a wizard at barbecuing freshly caught barracuda over half an oil drum on the beach, and was quite indignant when she left most of hers for a second evening. She knew she'd lost weight, even in the last couple of days, and put it down to anxiety and the heat.

Baz suggested it might be a touch of dehydration and plied her with Cokes and iced water until she thought she would burst, but all that afternoon, when she'd insisted that the other two go off and see the reef, all she wanted to do was sleep.

At half past four she was woken by something she thought for a moment must be crickets, and then realised it was Baz's phone. Thick-headed and out of sorts, she stumbled down the makeshift steps, only to find the room locked and no one about. The phone rang on and on, demanding attention like a crying baby. Was it Nevil or Charlie, or some long-lost crony of Baz's? Hanging on the door was a chalked sign made from a beer carton – a piece of pure school room art which read, GONE FISHING. Seething with frustration, Fran stumped down to the beach and went for a half-hearted paddle to calm down.

It was still very hot, and soon a kind of listless depression took her over as she wandered along the water's edge. Further into the sun and standing in the surf, were some curious contraptions unnervingly like half-finished gallows. Then she noticed some turbaned men squatting nearby, preparing hooks and bait: stilt fishermen, about to start their evening vigil. One by one they waded out and climbed into position, then hung there with their lines, a crucifixion scene in silhouette; a picture on a thousand postcards home. But for Fran just then, they seemed more like victims of some ghastly ritual sacrifice to the ocean. Beyond them, due south, the blueness simply carried on until it turned to ice. Next stop, Antarctica. She was out on a limb here, isolated, and it was beginning to get to her.

But then she'd reckoned without Baz.

'Hey, Franny!' he bawled.

She spun round with relief to see him waving a bunch of small silver fish at her, and thankfully went to meet him.

'Someone called while you were sacked out. So I said you was a bit crocked. Sounded like a local lass to me.'

'Charlie - at last! What did she say?'

Baz blinked at the urgency in her voice. 'Nothing much. Said she'd call same time tomorrow.'

'Oh shit,' said Fran fervently.

Baz grinned. 'She'll be right,' he said, scratching his armpit. 'Another bloody day in paradise.'

Fortunately for Fran's sanity, Charlie's call came around midday. She was sitting in the deepest shade she could find, under the balcony overhang among the beer crates and engine pieces, clutching a mineral water and staring out to sea, when Baz gave her the shout.

'Is it safe to talk?' was Charlie's first question.

Fran said that it was, while keeping an eye on Baz, who was washing a basket of fruit under the stand-pipe at the back. 'Thanks a million for the warning,' she added, and briefly explained about the incident at the hotel.

Charlie was relieved that it hadn't been worse. 'Don't worry too much about the passport,' she said. 'I can probably wangle something for you if I have to, although I'll need a photo and a bit of time to fix it.'

'You don't know how happy that makes me,' Fran told her. 'But where have you been, Charlie? I was getting really worried.'

'So sorry, my dear, but there've been several inter-esting developments, one of which meant that I didn't go back to my aunt's the other night. I just rang her to say I wouldn't be home, and didn't get your message. You see, we picked up some working girls who were hanging round the Mount Lavinia Hotel. It turned out that they'd been bombed out of the Blue Peacock and had been ordered to take their talents further afield. I decided to stay late, and agreed to let them off this time, on condition they did some talking. They were very afraid, I can tell you. The guy who runs most of the Colombo girls is a real horror.'

Fran caught herself looking round automatically. 'The one they call Zavvy?' she asked bleakly.

'You know about him? Ah – through your late friend's investigations, I suppose.'

'Right. So what did the girls have to say?'

'Apparently, the Peacock crowd has had to find some new premises pretty quickly. Nothing too flashy this time, just somewhere in the back streets where they can set up meetings and store the tiger bone consignments until they can be shipped on.'

'Do you know where this place is?'

'Not yet, but I'm working on it,' said Charlie. 'I'm going to keep in touch with those girls, if I have to go under cover to do it. And listen to this. After talking to the them, I rang a former colleague from Fraud and asked if I could stay overnight with him and his wife. I'd had an open invitation for some time, and I knew a lot of things were worrying him. He's a great guy. Older type, and I trust him. Never got promotion because he refused to turn a blind eye to certain things. Anyway, he'd heard about the new place, too, but said they'd been told to leave it alone.'

'What, for keeps, or until they can set up a raid or something?'

'The impression my friend got was that no one was going to do anything about it. He reckons his seniors are either too scared, or they've been paid off. And guess what? One of them is my old boss – the charmer who made a pass at me and made sure I got myself transferred out of harm's way. I fell for it, but I can see it all now.'

Fran leaned heavily on the 'fridge top. 'So what do we do now, Charlie?' she asked. The whole thing was such a bloody, unsolvable mess.

There was a thoughtful pause. Then Charlie's next words almost knocked Fran sideways. 'Does your husband still have that surveillance equipment?' she asked.

'I think so,' said Fran warily. 'It's probably in the

flat where they're staying. I don't think it was in the car with Brian, or Nevil would have said. Charlie? You're not thinking of . . .'

'Hush, my dear,' was the reply. 'Just as long as I know I can borrow it, if I need to.'

'But couldn't you use police equipment?'

'Most of it's pretty old stuff. Then I'd have to go into all sorts of explanations when I sign it out. As you know, I don't trust anyone these days.'

'OK, just take the damn' stuff. I'll tell Nevil to bring it down here, and you can pick it up. It's caused one death already. But not you, Charlie, please. You will be careful.'

'Oh yes,' said Charlie, 'I'll be careful. I'll ring again in two days; same time. Fran, are you all right? You sound a bit under the weather.'

'It's probably Baz's cooking,' said Fran. 'You wouldn't believe this place. It hasn't even got running water, unless you count a couple of taps in the yard, and the sea.'

They hung up on a promise that Charlie would ring in two days' time.


But it wasn't Baz's cooking. Next morning Fran slept late, and felt dizzy when she finally got out of bed and wandered across to haul in the bucket of water that Baz left outside, morning and evening, for her ablutions.

The strangest of sensations assailed her as she looked out at the glittering blue beyond the reef. It felt like a hangover, and she'd had a few of those in her time. But she hadn't fancied anything alcoholic for days. It wasn't so much that the world was different, but that her own perception of it had somehow slipped a couple of frames. She felt a curious detachment, as if nothing out there mattered, and only she was real.

It's stress, she told herself. It's wind. It's that time of the month. It was certainly due, but she'd been too preoccupied to think about it. Or was it the onset of malaria or some ghastly tropical disease?

To her considerable relief, it didn't last long. But next morning it was back, with some optional extras. This time she felt sick when she was cleaning her teeth and her stomach heaved. The smell of the toothpaste had suddenly become quite obnoxious. Transfixed, she stared down blankly into the washing bowl on the wicker table. Looking down made her want to retch again. She fought it, grabbed for her diary and started counting. She was a whole week overdue. That had never happened before.

'Oh God!' she breathed aloud. 'I *can't* be. Not now. You can't do this to me. I'm not ready yet.'

'Did you say something, Fran?' called Anders from the other side of the slatted palm-leaf wall.

'Just saying my morning prayers,' gasped Fran, swallowing hard and willing herself not to retch again.

The next few days would tell. In fact, what with one thing and another, even getting through the next few days was going to be a bit of a bitch. The strange part was, she *knew* she was pregnant, and she also knew, with a clarity she hadn't felt for days, that she wasn't going to say a word about it to anyone.

# Chapter Sixteen

Whatever Fran was feeling, there was no doubt that Anders and Klaus were finding the laid-back Hikkaduwa lifestyle very much to their liking. With their usual mixture of solicitude and playfulness, they tried to draw her into their activities, most of which involved getting very wet, often at considerable speed. Wind surfing, water skiing, snorkelling, or sailing with the local fishermen kept them busy for most of the day, and sometimes half the night.

Normally Fran would have joined in whatever was on offer. Now, she was more than content to sit on the beach, distracting herself by trying to spot them through Baz's ex-Navy binoculars. For once she was glad they weren't around, as she had a feeling Anders might soon start wondering if it wasn't just general anxiety that was making her so passive.

Last night, the pair had rolled in from a beach party at some unearthly hour, which meant they were sleeping late this morning. This suited her well, because it gave her time to get herself together before Nevil rang, hopefully with news about Tony's arrival.

After a shaky start, Fran was doing her level best to act normally by tackling her breakfast fruit with the gusto expected at the Sydney Opera House, when Anders appeared looking not the slightest bit hungover.

'We met some great people last night,' he said, coming over to her table with a plate of scrambled egg and red peppers, regarded as Baz's speciality. 'You should have been there, Fran. They were saying we should try parascending. So we have fixed it up for this afternoon. You must come. The view over the bay is fantastic, and you can see the reefs under the water.'

She looked up at him, blinking. Being pulled along in mid air, looking down on all that water below – the very thought of it made her feel giddy.

'I don't think so, Anders.' It took all her concentration to fight down a wave of nausea.

'But you said you always wanted to try it.'

'That was – before.' How long was she going to be able to keep this up? They'd be insisting she went to see a doctor soon.

The phone rang, and she stiffened.

'Fran, are yer there?' bawled Baz from his lair. 'It's your old man.'

Was she going to make it to the phone? With the forced nonchalance of a drunk hoping to look sober, she aimed herself at Baz's quarters, only to find he was cooking up more scrambled egg. She swallowed hard and leaned on the 'fridge, trying hard not to think what Nevil would say if he could see her now.

Fortunately, asking after her well-being wasn't the first thing on his mind

'Hey, Fran – Tony's coming out the day after tomorrow. Isn't that great?'

'Terrific! Is that Thursday? I've lost count. Where are we going to meet?'

'I reckon it's too far to drag him all the way down to you. But he's going to avoid all the usual Colombo business watering holes, and not use the firm's name at all in case someone picks up a mention of Merrick. We thought somewhere like your Mrs Mario's.'

'Maybe not there,' said Fran quickly. 'She's a lovely woman, but she might get curious if a whole gang of us shows up, and I'd hate to have to explain.'

'OK. But in any case Vesak reckons it's best not to meet where Tony's actually staying, just in case. There's a little place in the Mount Lavinia area which has private rooms for lunch and so on, so we're booked in for the afternoon. Unfortunately, it doesn't do accommodation, so can you make it up here by midday on Thursday?'

'You bet,' said Fran, doing some hasty calculations. Since she wouldn't have to go through Colombo, about two and a half hours by taxi should do it. Compared with home, the cost would be peanuts. 'That area will be handy for Charlie, too.'

'I'm looking forward to meeting this Charlie.'

'You'll like her. But I'm worried, Nev. She was asking about the surveillance equipment. Have you still got it?'

'The mini recorder was in the car with Brian, so that's gone. But we removed the camcorder from Vesak's place before they searched it. It's here, well wrapped up and hidden in a sack of rice. I'll bring it with me. In fact I'll be glad to get rid of the damned thing.'

'Not half as glad as I'll be to pass over the tapes to Tony,' said Fran fervently, glancing at the metal cabinet in the corner.

'It's coming together, isn't it, love? Chin up. A few more pieces of this bastard little jigsaw, and we'll soon be out of here knowing we've done our bit. Then, I promise I'm going to make all this up to you, starting with a *real* holiday, somewhere cool and green and safe.'

'How about Iceland?' muttered Fran, swaying slightly and fanning herself with Baz's greasy message pad.

'Iceland it is. By the way, did Charlie say why she wanted the camcorder? My God, she's not planning a bit of freelancing, is she? Against *those* animals?'

'I'm trying not to think about it.' Yes, Iceland would be fine. And when they got there, she would think up some suitable way of impressing on Nevil that this sort of thing must never, ever, happen again.

'I'll bring it, anyway. Just leave it to Charlie. Have you got a pen?'

Fran stopped fanning long enough to scribble down the venue address, told him to take care, and said she'd see him on Thursday.

'Well, if don't want the scrambled eggs, how about the fish kedgeree?' asked Baz as she put down the phone.

'Not just now,' gasped Fran, and ducked round the back and out of earshot just in time. Jesus, how long was this going to last? Pregnancy? No problem. In nine months, she'd be as right as rain.

Once the morning queasiness wore off, Fran felt almost human again. In fact once she'd got used to the idea of being pregnant, she felt ridiculously proud of herself, not to say downright smug about it. She would have loved to tell them; couldn't help imagining how pleased they'd all be, even Baz, in his taciturn way. But this would have to stay her secret. She'd read somewhere how pregnancy could make you feel you had suddenly become the centre of the universe. There would be no more contemplating of the navel with a Mona Lisa smile. All that was going to have to wait.

Charlie rang that evening, and was delighted to hear about the meeting with Tony.

Next day, while the others were out, Fran carefully composed a deposition addressed to the AWW offices in London, stating what she knew and what she suspected about Brian's death. Then she wrote a covering letter asking for an immediate inquiry and saying she'd contact them the minute she got home to offer every possible assistance. She enclosed the pathetic bit of paper they'd given her at the morgue, and sealed the whole lot into a rather grubby envelope cadged from Baz. Tony was flying home on Saturday evening, so with any luck this material would soon be in AWW's head office in Coventry, together with the tapes.

Fran slept most of the way to the Thursday meeting, stretched out as best she could in the back of the taxi. As they neared the southern outskirts of the capital, the traffic inevitably thickened and the stops became more frequent.

Then the driver gave a cluck of annoyance and slowed to a crawl again. Yawning, she looked at her watch. It was still only half past eleven, so there was plenty of time She sat up to have a drink of water and see what the trouble was. There was a double line of assorted vehicles ahead, and only the occasional one oncoming, but slowly, as if the vehicle hadn't yet had time to pick up speed.

'Is it an accident?' she asked the driver.

'Road block,' he replied, reaching into the glove compartment for his papers.

Bloody hell. Things had been going just a little too well this morning.

'Military or police?'

He shrugged. 'Maybe both. There are always road blocks after bombs. You have passport or ID, ma'am?'

'What? No, I haven't. How silly of me. I left it back at the, er, hotel.' She could feel her pulse beginning to race. Until now she'd assumed her lack of a passport would only be a problem at the airport or checking into hotels. But lots of countries with security problems expected foreigners to have their passports with them at all times. Damn! Even if this was just a routine road block where weapons and explosives were the prime targets, and not anyone called Merrick, she could be in trouble. Meanwhile, the tapes were burning a hole in her bag and it was too late to try and conceal them now.

Ahead, several trucks were being unloaded and searched, and a bus full of passengers was emptying onto the verge while figures in khaki prodded round the haphazard piles of baggage on the roof. It looked as if they meant business. Even a bullock cart of fodder was getting the treatment.

Suppose this wasn't the only road block around Colombo today, and the others had been stopped too. Maybe she'd arrive at the Lime Tree Inn and find no one there. The prospect was so appalling that she dismissed it immediately.

It was fifteen minutes before they began to move slowly forward, and Fran looked anxiously at her watch. Any minute now it would be amateur dramatics time again, but at least she'd had time to think what to do.

At last they were beckoned forward. There were four of them, all uniformed police, smart, if perhaps a little bored, but they were all armed. To one side, under some mango trees, was a police car and a military jeep in which a young officer was watching the proceedings and talking into a phone. Were any of these men in the pay of Xavier Michael Cheng? Brought up in a climate where, if you had nothing to hide, you should have nothing to worry about, it went against the grain to be feel this kind of panic. But this wasn't the local high street back home.

A face appeared at the driver's window – a blur of sweating brown skin and strong white teeth. There was an exchange which quickly turned to English when the driver indicated Fran sitting in the back, meek as a nun. She caught the magic words 'tourist' and 'England', and nodded gravely. But she was out of luck.

'Will you get out of the car, please, ma'am?'

Rather stiffly she complied, clutching the bag with the tapes and her sun hat, and trying to look as if the sudden heat and glare were too much for her.

'Today they are searching all vehicles,' grunted the driver, going round to open the boot, which was empty.

'You are a visitor. May I see your passport?'

'I'm so sorry,' she said faintly, fanning herself with the hat. 'I left it at the hotel for safety.' Please, don't let him ask its name. The Sydney Opera House might have needed some lengthy explaining. 'I didn't think I'd be needing it. I'm meeting up with some friends for lunch, that's all.'

'You should carry your papers at all times, for your own protection,' retorted the officer mechanically. 'We can question anyone without papers during the emergency. Your bag, please.' He held out his hand.

For a second, Fran hesitated. His manner seemed very much to be, 'I'm bored, stuck out here in the sun, so I might as well give people a hard time', but with those tapes in there, she wasn't taking any chances.

'May I take out the water bottle? I've been feeling a little car sick – you understand.' She clutched her stomach to stress the point.

The policeman surveyed her dispassionately. Either he didn't understand, or he had his orders.

'Oh goodness, do excuse me.' She gave a groan and turned aside, hand to mouth. To her amazement, the mere thought of retching made her performance very convincing indeed.

The face of officialdom softened a fraction.

'You may proceed,' he said, and waved them hastily back into the car.

'You OK, ma'am?' said the driver, looking at her in the mirror as they drove away. To her surprise, he had a smile of pure relief on his face. 'Me, I am very happy. No licence. He no catch me.'

*Where there aren't no Ten Commandments* . . . Suddenly Fran wanted to throw back her head and laugh at the insanity of it all.

'Now we stop and I get you medicine for vomiting in vehicle. Very good – local medicine.'

'Thanks, but I'll be fine once I've had some water,' she told him. 'Cheers!'

'Chin chin,' said the driver, still chuckling at his luck.

She looked down at her ridiculously flat stomach. That's your first good deed, kid, she silently explained to the new occupant. I don't think I could have done that without a bit of help. One day you'll be a hero – or a heroine. Or just another head case, like your Ma and Pa. Was this what they called bonding? If so, it felt like a good start.

They got to the Lime Tree Inn at around twenty past twelve, which Fran thought quite reasonable, considering the distance and the circumstances. It certainly wasn't late enough to have started Nevil worrying.

Set back from the Galle Road in an old citrus grove, the Inn was a post-independence version of St Anthony's, with a similar air of dustiness and un-hurried, peeling charm. There seemed to be no one about, and there wasn't a vehicle to be seen. But then, she reminded herself, the others would have used taxis too. Everyone did.

She paid the driver half the agreed rate for the day and told him to come back at four o'clock. As arranged, she asked at the desk for the lunch party in the Kandy Room, and breathed a sigh of relief when she neared the door, to hear Nevil's quite un-mistakable laugh over Tony's excited voice.

A burst of noisy, elated welcome greeted her as she went in, and there were kisses all round. Everyone was at extra pains to assure everyone else that they were fine, but Fran couldn't help noticing that beside Tony's gloss of well-groomed business bonhomie and Charlie's exotic charm, Nevil looked peaky and strained. She was sure he'd lost weight, but if he thought the same about her, he gave no sign of it. Perhaps he was as grateful as she was to let the chemistry of the other two's presence lift their spirits. The gang was all here. Or nearly all here. Things would be easier now.

'No road blocks, then?' she asked eventually, when the euphoria had settled.

They shook their heads, suddenly quiet again. 'I

never thought of that,' said Nevil, biting his lip. 'I hope Vesak's OK. To be ultra safe, we took separate taxis fifteen minutes apart. But the traffic's always dreadful round our way. How did you manage without your passport?'

'I threatened to be car-sick all over the officer's best boots,' said Fran, almost truthfully. 'It was easier than I thought.'

The laughter erupted again. It was a heady brew they were running on, and one basic ingredient was fear.

They gave Vesak until one o'clock. Then Nevil went to phone the flat, and Fran had a moment to observe the other two. Her impression of a powerful chemistry in the room was right, except that she'd overlooked another of its ingredients. Tony and Charlie were getting along remarkably well. In fact they were striking sparks from each other. Charlie was a model of understated chic, in a short-skirted, olive green linen suit, and cream silk shirt with tiny touches of gold which set off her golden skin to perfection.

Glad to detach herself for a second or two from the serious business in hand, Fran watched them with their heads together over the wad of computer print-outs Tony had brought with him. By some mysterious instinct, Charlie had chosen just the kind of look, which, after years of Tony-watching, Fran knew he particularly went for. But then, with Tony's general penchant for women, and the warmth of Charlie's personality, the effect might well have been the same if she'd turned up in a plastic bin liner. Now he was getting the full benefit of her intelligence as well. Fascinating, thought Fran. Would Nevil spot it too? Probably not. He'd be far more interested in what was in those print-outs, and rightly so.

Nevil came back looking not so much worried, as thoughtful.

'Vesak's still at the apartment,' he told them. 'He's quite OK, but his cab took a different route, and they hit a road block. He saw it in time and told the driver to turn back. Would that have attracted anyone's attention, do you think?'

'Not necessarily,' replied Charlie. 'Lots of people do it if they spot the tail-back soon enough, and they're in a hurry. Rather defeats the object, of course, so the block positions keep moving in case the tail-back gives the game away. It's probably clear by now.'

'Even so, I've told him to stay put. I can always fill him in when I get back.'

Over lunch they got down to business, the key to which was the print-outs Tony had brought.

'Wonderful things, company searches,' he began with a grin. 'Unfortunately, as with most things in life, it's a huge help to know what you're looking for in the first place. But if you don't . . .'

Fran gave a groan. She'd had to do a few company searches herself while at Merrick & Baldwyn. Both Tony and Nevil had learnt the hard way to check up on who owned what, who was under whose umbrella, and what kind of holding companies couldn't even hold water.

'You see, as far as companies registered in the UK are concerned, it isn't that difficult,' Tony explained for Charlie's benefit. 'You simply get onto Companies House, and if it looks complicated or time is short, there's an army of smart little outfits who specialise in that sort of thing who'll do it for you.'

'But if the companies aren't registered in the UK?'

'That's when the canny operators with the contacts really come into their own. They weren't cheap, but they save a lot of leg work. What I did was throw a few names like your Mr Ah Fat of Blue Peacock fame, and Zavvy Cheng, at my army of elves and let them do some serious digging. The chief elf, that's Benny Goldsmith at Finders – you may remember him, Fran – got very excited when I told him to go after arms companies trading with the Gulf. He loves that sort of thing.'

Fran nodded. Benny was a nervy, balding type, an Internet freak, and something of a hacker on the side. He was very bright, and inclined to drop things into the conversation, such as that he had an uncle in Tel Aviv who'd once worked for Mossad.

'Sure enough, Ah Fat's somewhat unforgettable name cropped up in connection with a holding company which had recently got control of *this* bunch . . .' Tony grabbed another sheet and stabbed at a name half way down. 'Benny's come across them before, and they certainly sell on arms from the old Eastern Bloc countries, no questions asked, to whoever's buying. Benny doesn't like them at all.'

'Where's the holding company based?' asked Charlie. 'Don't tell me. Hong Kong. That would figure.'

Tony shot her an approving look. 'Spot on,' he said. 'The main nominee is a bank with considerable Chinese connections. Not one of the big boys, but big enough to know better than to let itself be used for a money-laundering scam on this sort of scale. And that's what's going on here, isn't it?'

'Among one or two other things,' remarked Nevil dryly. 'I'm sure Ah Fat isn't the only crook in Hong Kong who's looking for ways of sneaking his ill-gotten gains out of harm's way in case Beijing goes for a massive clamp-down. Fortunately, not all of them want to get involved in buying arms for terrorists and the extermination of the tiger population.'

Charlie's eyes were gleaming. 'This material is fantastic, Tony. If only we'd had access to this sort of stuff when I was in Fraud. It's what I suspected, what I was looking for, even, but we simply didn't have the facilities.'

'You've got to hand it to old Ah Fat,' said Tony, waving an arm at the mass of material on the table. 'Picking Sri Lanka as a base must have seemed like a smart move. Centrally placed for all the to-ings and fro-ings, not especially sophisticated financially, a northern shoreline outside government control . . .'

'Fanatical terrorists, corruptible police,' added Charlie unhappily.

'Most places have got a few bad apples in the police. I was going to say that he'd reckoned without the good ones like yourself, and outfits like AWW.'

Charlie bowed her head. 'And the dedicated people they employ, like your friend Brian. And as for the ones like me, my dear, what good am I now? They didn't teach us computer hacking at the Police Charm School. Apart from one or two still useful friends with only limited access to what's really going on, I don't know who to trust. What's keeping me going is that if anyone was really on to me, they'd probably have picked me up already, and I'd be minus a few vital parts, including my face.'

The effect of this on Tony was electrifying. 'My God, what are you saying, Charlie?' He reached across the table and caught her hand. 'They wouldn't. Not a woman. I mean . . .'

'Tamil Tigers regard women as expendable,

wouldn't you say?' Charlie gave the hand a squeeze before returning it to its horrified owner. 'You remember? It was one of their women who strapped a bomb round her belly and embraced Rajiv Gandhi at a political meeting. Afterwards, they had trouble working out which bits were whose.'

'Jesus, don't say things like that.' Tony had gone quite pale.

Fran found herself instinctively wrapping her arms round her stomach. Don't listen to this, she told the baby. Stick with me, kid, and one day I'll explain everything.

'I'm sorry,' said Charlie. 'Forgive the dramatics. It won't get us anywhere, but your friend Benny just might. You say he's a hacker. How good is he at getting into people's bank accounts?'

'They haven't caught him yet,' replied Tony, taking large gulps of water as if trying to wash a bad taste away. 'But even if half the things Benny claims he does for fun are true, I'd say he could probably come up with the goods on Ah Fat if he knew what he was looking for and had enough time.'

'As usual, it's time we don't have,' said Nevil.

Charlie gave a discreet wriggle and produced a tiny notepad from inside her blouse. 'OK, here's what I'd like Benny to do.' She grabbed a sheet of paper and started copying from the pad in a fast, neat hand. 'Starting with Ah Fat's and Zavvy Cheng's known aliases and accounts, and moving on to some of their buddies in Hong Kong. I've got stuff from last year here – some transfer payment with dates, how much they declared for tax, and what went through the proper exchange control channels. I'd like to know what didn't, and where it finished up. And that's just for openers.'

*    *    *

It was nearly half past three by the time Tony and Charlie were satisfied that they'd each got enough information from the other to set Benny on Ah Fat's devious financial trail. Fran was able to follow most of it. Links were what they needed. Clear proof that money from China coming into Ah Fat's Hong Kong bank was connected with the tiger bone trade, and then being used to buy arms.

As they all agreed, the worrying part was having to find all the pieces. Networks like this were like a cancer. You had to know where every bit of it was, so it could all be cut out at once. Anything that remained would quickly re-establish itself and soon become just as deadly. But were they putting too much faith in Benny Goldsmith? It was a lot to ask, and no one could be sure how long it would take.

A couple of times, Fran felt Nevil looking at her as if something about her was puzzling him, but there was nothing she could do to ease his mind. At this stage of the game, toughing it out was the only way.

'I wish you weren't so far away down there,' he said quietly. 'I miss you like hell.'

'Me too. It's a shame I've got to get back tonight, but it won't be for much longer.'

'You are OK down there, aren't you? It sounds a bit primitive to me.'

She laughed. 'Oh, that's just the plumbing. The water sports are really high-tech. My two handsome Danish bodyguards tried to get me parascending the other day.'

'Just tell them, if anyone's going to get you into a wet suit and harness, dangling fifty feet over the Indian Ocean, it's going to be me.'

'Kinky!' said Tony, who caught the end of the

conversation, and they all laughed. 'Right, guys, I reckon that's about it. Is this where we make the drop, as they say in all the best spy rings? Who's got the goodies?'

Nevil hauled up a battered hold-all from the floor and Fran reached for her handbag.

'One video cassette and two mini-audios,' she said, 'with love from Brian. We haven't even played them yet, and we didn't dare get them copied here. I hope they're good.'

Tony took them thoughtfully. 'I'll get multi-copies the minute I get home. Trouble is, they won't mean anything to me without one of you guys to say who's who. But one set of these goes straight to AWW, right?'

'Together with this,' said Fran. She produced the battered envelope and showed them what she'd written.

'Brilliant job. I'll get a zillion copies of everything, and I'm not taking any chances. I'll take the whole lot up to their Coventry office myself, and talk to whoever I can. I should be able to do that by Tuesday, or Wednesday at the latest.'

'And then there's a small matter of this little lot, old pal,' said Nevil, and handed over a serious looking file. 'The Al Masira stuff, just in case you'd forgotten.'

The two men looked at each other. 'Good work, Nev,' said Tony. 'You smooth-talking old bastard. Is there anything I need to know?'

'One or two things,' replied Nevil. 'Have you got a couple of hours?'

Fran sighed. Her driver was coming back at four, and he'd made it quite plain that he wanted to be back before dark.

260

'I have to go and call a taxi, ' said Charlie, 'or Auntie will be having fits. Come with me, Fran?'

'Of course.' Fran now had a strong feeling that Charlie wanted to speak to her alone.

The two women got up and made for the door.

'Nearly forgot,' Nevil called after them. 'I believe you wanted this, Charlie.' He produced something else from his bag - a compact bundle wrapped in a piece of striped local cloth. 'Just promise me you're not going to try using this yourself.'

'It's quite all right,' said Charlie soothingly, looking from one to the other. 'I'm going to give it to a friend who's much braver than I am.'

As she put the camcorder in her bag, Tony looked as if he was dying to grab the thing away from her, but didn't know how. 'Promise?' he said. Then, almost desperately. 'Charlie, why don't I take you to dinner tonight, if you're not on duty or anything. What about that Mount Lavinia place? I'm a sucker for all that old colonial charm.'

Charlie gave him her best Sri Lankan head waggle and a coy smile. 'I'm sure you are,' she said. 'Back in a moment.'

'Bit of a charmer, isn't he?' said Fran, as the two women walked to the reception.

'Is there anything I should know, my dear?' asked Charlie.

'Plenty,' answered Fran. 'I know, why don't I ask my driver to make a little detour and drop you home? He's from down south and his English isn't good, so it'll be safe to talk.'

'Good idea,' said Charlie. 'A lot of the drivers round here aren't to be trusted. They get their licences from the wrong sort of people and owe them favours, if you know what I mean.'

'This one hasn't even got a licence, but I'm sure you won't hold that against him.'

'We are a lawless people,' Charlie sighed. 'But I really want to talk, and not only about Tony. I've had a little idea, you see, and I wanted to try it out with you first.'

'I can't wait,' said Fran, eyeing her curiously. 'That's my taxi coming into the drive. Shall we go and say the goodbyes?'

# Chapter Seventeen

For Fran, it was a strange goodbye, because in a way she was the only one leaving. Nevil and Tony had ordered some beers and were staying put at the Lime Tree for a thorough debriefing on the Al Masira papers. Charlie was going home to freshen up for dinner later with Tony, by which time Nevil would be safely back at the apartment with Vesak, and she herself would be half way to Hikkaduwa.

As she hugged Tony and wished him good luck, she couldn't help noticing that he felt to her more like Nevil used to feel before all this had happened – solid, breezily confident, raring to tackle any problem with a good dose of black humour. Twenty-four hours of being here hadn't touched Tony in the way she and Nevil had been touched by what had happened to them in this place. After this, they would be different, but Tony would remain the same old Tony.

And as for Nevil . . . 'Now whatever you're thinking, just stop it,' she said as he held her tight. The other two laughed, as she'd meant them to do. 'Don't forget. Next stop, Iceland. We'll book the minute we get back.'

'Don't worry about Fran, Nev, she's tougher than she looks,' said Tony.

'Sod that!' replied Nevil. 'She's tougher than *I* look.'

                              *        *        *

Fran negotiated a bit of extra mileage with the driver,
who remained cheerfully unaware that there was a
policewoman in the back, and they set off in the rush
hour traffic for Charlie's place.

'OK, ' said Charlie, keeping her voice low. 'I'd
better come clean. The reason I wanted the camcorder is that I've now found out where our friend
Zavvy is setting up in the bone business again.'

'But that's marvellous!' Fran was doing her best
not to look hopelessly confused at this turn of events.
'So why didn't you say? Now, Charlie, you promised
you weren't going to do anything silly.'

'I never said that, my dear,' said Charlie wryly. 'I
said I wanted it for a friend. And the reason I didn't
mention it back there is because what I really meant
was, I wanted an accomplice.'

'You can't mean you're thinking of filming that
little weasel on his own premises.' hissed Fran.

'No, listen. I'm not completely insane. Zavvy's got
a fancy house, complete with razor wire, nasty dogs
and still nastier guards. Everyone in town knows
where that is, but even he's not cocky enough to
store the bone consignments or the arms in there.
The thing is, our Zavvy likes to party. The other night
he had the nerve to hold a little bash over there for
half the low life in Colombo, to which my working
girl friends were invited, in a purely professional
capacity, of course.'

'Sounds like a fun evening.'

'You wouldn't want to know,' replied Charlie
seriously. 'The man is deranged. Even the girls think
so. No, what I had in mind was something much
simpler than getting myself invited in there. According to the girls, Zavvy's taken over a run-down

property in the Pettah district. The front is a little shop selling spices and traditional medicines, where anyone who knows the right words can buy whatever they want in the aphrodisiac and general deviancy department, be it animal, vegetable or mineral.'

'And here you mean animal, and tiger parts in particular?'

'Oh yes, but that's just the front. I drove past the place yesterday for a look-see. It wasn't easy. That area's never been hot on town planning. At the back of the property there are all sorts of little outbuildings, and from what the girls said, I reckon that's where the stuff is being held until they can find somewhere safer.'

Fran stared out of the window at the jostling, honking traffic. 'Can't you nail him for simply owning the place?' she asked, momentarily distracted to see that they had just passed the turn to St Anthony's. Instinctively, she found herself looking for Mr Silva's shop. How long ago all that seemed. But the little grey cow was there, thin-flanked now, still munching patiently, and beside her was a calf.

'Oh come on, Fran!' Charlie's voice jolted her back to a harsher present. 'On what charge? Sure, I was able to check the property deeds by waving my ID around, and Zavvy's the owner all right, under one of his aliases he doesn't know we know about.' She tapped the notebook inside her blouse. 'But can you imagine the scene? By the time a raid is set up, someone on the inside tips him off, and we draw yet another blank. It's hopeless.'

'Unless someone you can really trust helps you get some kind of transaction on video?'

'That would certainly be an enormous help,

especially when combined with Brian's material and whatever Tony comes up with at his end.'

'I still don't like the sound of it, Charlie. Have you got someone you can really trust?'

'No,' said Charlie shortly. 'I was thinking of asking Nevil. But I wanted to ask you first to see what you thought. OK, I'm sorry. Forget I ever mentioned it.'

The look on Fran's face was an answer on its own. Neither said anything for what seemed like too long.

Fran knew it was up to her to break the silence. 'I know you wouldn't ask such a thing unless you were desperate,' she said at last. 'The crazy part is, Nevil would do it, just to make sure we get out of here. Oh Charlie . . .' She put her hand over her eyes as if soothing a headache. 'You've got me, haven't you? Fair and square. If he'd do it to get us out, I can't really stop you asking him, can I?'

'If I could think of any other way . . . But it's been such a break to find out about this place, and it may only be temporary. What's more, I can't rely on much more from the girls. They're already terrified they've been seen with me.'

'OK, tell me how you're going to set it up. I'm sure you've got it all worked out.'

'It goes like this. I do myself up as a giggling tart and drag Nevil along to the emporium as a really sicko client who wants something special to put a bit of lead in his pencil. He's prepared to pay quite a lot for the real thing.'

'The real thing being what, precisely?' put in Fran warily.

'A tiger's penis bone, my dear. The idea is, it's so expensive that they keep it whole to make a sale so that the client can see he's getting the genuine article. Then it's ground up on the spot.'

'Holy God! And Nevil's somehow going to film this disgusting operation?'

'I distract the salesman and do the patter. Nevil holds the bag with the camcorder, acts dumb and pays up.'

Just then the driver broke in with a question to Charlie, who rattled off some directions. It sounded as if they were nearly there.

'All I can say is that I'll ask him,' said Fran helplessly, 'I think it's crazy. Maybe Nevil will too. Maybe we're all crazy.'

'But it might work. I'll do my homework thoroughly, I swear it. It's my life too, remember?'

They drew up outside a pleasant little bungalow with its porch almost hidden by a mass of deep red bougainvillaea.

Charlie gave her shoulder a squeeze. 'I'll phone around nine tomorrow evening, after you've had time to talk to Nevil.'

'Take care,' said Fran as they touched cheeks. 'Which reminds me, I didn't even get a chance to warn you about Tony. Have a lovely evening.'

'With Auntie around?' retorted Charlie blithely. 'We wouldn't dare.'

As the taxi moved away, Fran turned to wave. A pretty, round-faced woman in a pale blue sari was greeting her niece beneath a drift of blossom. It all looked so peaceful, so suburban. And yet she'd just been asked, so charmingly, if it was all right to borrow her husband for something so dangerous that it took her breath away.

Her return to the Sydney Opera House was greeted with a barrage of questions which took most of the evening to answer.

As they sat out under the stars, Fran listened carefully for any hints that Anders and Klaus might be wanting to move on. They'd paid for a week, but it was obvious they wouldn't be staying here indefinitely. So far, her needs and their plans had shown a remarkable degree of compatibility which was surely too good to last. Being Anders and Klaus, they'd showed keen interest in the situation between Charlie and Tony. But knowing them as she did, Fran guessed it was their way of distracting her from the scenario Charlie had in mind for Nevil. On that subject, they'd kept very quiet.

She didn't sleep well that night, but now that she knew what was likely to happen the minute she got out of bed in the morning, she was learning how to control the queasiness. If she didn't bend down or move around too quickly on waking, then avoided Baz's fry-ups and kept to toast and fruit, she didn't feel too bad. But by now there was no doubt that it wasn't her imagination.

A lot of that day was spent gearing herself up to the prospect of putting Charlie's request to Nevil. So when he didn't phone after six o'clock as arranged, a feeling of anti-climax began to crawl over all her other anxieties, which she then had to hide from Anders and Klaus who were going out in search of some serious clubbing. Baz had also disappeared on some mysterious errand of his own, which was enough to convince Klaus, fascinated as ever by people's sex lives, that he had a woman somewhere.

Alone with her thoughts, Fran first tried convincing herself that the frustrating silence from the Colombo apartment must have had something to do with Tony's departure. After all, he was flying home that evening, and it was possible they'd met up somewhere for a final drink and briefing. This time, maybe Vesak had gone too. Which should have left two other men in the apartment. But then, it was Friday night, so perhaps they'd gone out on the town, or joined the mad exodus from Colombo to see their families.

To add to her frustration, Charlie was supposed to phone around nine o'clock for Nevil's answer. But the phone stayed silent. To stop herself fretting, Fran took a brisk walk along the starlit beach between her attempts to phone, but couldn't go too far in case she missed a call.

With Charlie, there wasn't much point in trying the house, because if Charlie was there, she would have called as promised. So where was she? There was always the long shot that things had gone particularly well with Tony last night and she'd gone to the airport to see him off. But they had phones at the airport. No, that's not like her, thought Fran, kicking at the sand. It was far more likely she'd gone out on a call, and phoning was awkward.

But for all her attempts at reasonable conjecture, Fran was fighting panic by the time Anders and Klaus returned that night. It was gone half past one, and she'd sat up for them, wanting to have them tell her with alcohol-induced confidence, that there had to be a dozen perfectly good reasons why no one had phoned.

The rattling of a vehicle slowing down on the rough verge in front of the Opera House made her jump up from the deck chair where she'd been dozing under the stars. Shouts, whoops, snatches of song and doors slamming rose above the sound of an idling engine, and by the headlight glare, she could see two figures being helped down from a pick-up loaded with clubbers. Another cheer urged the little truck on its way, and with a lurch it regained the road and disappeared into the night, leaving Anders and Klaus making their unsteady way round to the staircase.

'Hey, you two,' she called from the darkness, and they stopped, peering towards the light of her torch. To put it mildly, they were flying high. 'Do you want some coffee?'

'Fran, my darling!' carolled Anders, coming over. 'Why are you not sleeping?'

'Because I'm worried sick,' she replied tartly. But they were too far gone to take anything really seriously.

She warmed up the coffee pot in Baz's little room and took them a mug each.

'We were saying earlier,' said Anders, 'that tomorrow we would talk to you. Now it is tomorrow.'

'No, it is not. It is still today, isn't it?' put in Klaus dreamily. 'We talk about moving tomorrow.'

'You want to move on *tomorrow*?'

Anders shook his head in affectionate irritation. 'No, tomorrow we *talk* about moving. That is correct, isn't it? Klaus, do not speak of this.' There followed a brief altercation in Danish, which Anders seemed to win. 'Dear Fran, if you are worried, we will come and sleep with you,' he continued. 'We will rock you like a baby.'

'We will, we will rock you. Boom-boom, rock you,' droned Klaus. 'Why did Freddie Mercury have to die?'

'Thanks, fellers, but I think I'll go and rock my own baby,' replied Fran, too frazzled to stop herself saying it. She stood up and looked down at them. They didn't seem to have heard. She could always say it was an English joke. But by the sound of it, what she had been hoping wouldn't happen was now very much on the cards. Her guardian angels wanted to move on. But did it have to be so soon?

They were all still asleep when the phone rang at seven o'clock next morning – even Baz, who must have returned on his old bike as quietly has he'd left. The first Fran knew about it was a disgruntled yell from Baz. She lurched to her feet, swallowed hard and aimed herself at the door.

'Coming!' she yelled back, steadying herself on the hand rail and taking in large gulps of sea air.

'It's that bloody hubby of yours,' mumbled Baz, wandering out to the beach shower in his undershorts. 'There's never any peace round here.'

'Nev!' Fran grabbed the phone and steadied herself against the 'fridge.

'Sorry if I woke anyone,' said Nevil tersely.

On the 'fridge top, under a cloth, was some dry bread. Gratefully, she broke off a piece and started chewing hard.

'Now don't get excited, love,' Nevil went on, 'but there's been a few developments . . . I'm afraid we've had to move on.'

Fran stiffened. The background noises were different. It didn't sound like the apartment, more like a call box.

'Move on?'

'It's OK, it's another of Vesak's friends, but there's no phone. Can you take the address?'

She dropped the crust and snatched a ball-point, writing on her palm. The name of the road was long and complicated and the postal district, which was even longer, had to go on her wrist.

271

'Got it,' she snapped. 'What happened?'

'We're still not sure, but Vesak thinks it might have been the driver he used. You remember, Vesak asked him to turn back when they hit the road block? He must have got curious, maybe talked to my driver, put two and two together and reported it to some-one.'

'Charlie warned me about taxi drivers.' Christ, what was Charlie going to say about this, in view of her plan to use Nevil? 'But they didn't pick you up . . .'

'No, thanks to some quick thinking by Vesak's mates. It must have been about five o'clock. One of them spotted a couple of cars pulling up, full of the sort of people he didn't like the look of. He yelled to Vesak who got out the back with his bag. We each kept a bag packed, just in case. Then he beat it, and didn't stop running until he got to another friend's place.'

'Oh my God . . .'

Baz put his head round the door. 'You all right, Fran? Here, park your bum.' She looked round at him, wild-eyed, as he pushed a metal chair under her collapsing knees.

'Obviously he phoned the Lime Tree as soon as he could to warn me, but we'd left by then to drop Tony at the Mount Lavinia. They said they were police and turned the place over, but by then, the other lads had chucked my bag up a mango tree in the back garden. They gave them a hard time, but left when they couldn't find any trace of us. The first I knew about it was when my taxi slowed to turn into the lane and Ferdie from the apartment jumped out of the bushes waving my bag. I really owe those guys. Fran, are you still there?'

272

'Just about,' said Fran. 'So Charlie and Tony don't know about all this?'

'Right. After all that, I didn't dare take another taxi, so Ferdie and I walked to the new place. It took us two hours. By the time we got there, Vesak was in a bit of a lather, I can tell you. I thought I'd better leave Charlie to you, and Tony won't be home by now. Just let him know whenever you can. I've got to keep out of sight.'

'But you can stay there for a while. Oh Nev . . .'

'It's OK. Everyone's being just brilliant. But every minute now, I can't help feeling that I'm endangering people simply by being around.'

'Nev, just stay out of sight until we can think of some way to get you home. You promise?'

'I don't have a choice, do I? Look, there's a queue, and I'm feeling conspicuous. Fran, I've got to go. I love you.'

'Me too,' she said staring blankly at the wall as the line went dead. Then she picked up the abandoned crust and sank her teeth into it.

'Trouble?' asked Baz, looking at her curiously. 'You sit tight. I'll get some tea.'

Charlie. She had to tell Charlie. And not just to explain about the enforced move. It was quite impossible now to use Nevil in any kind of undercover operation, however carefully Charlie set it up. Nevil was a big man, in a country where Westerners of average height stood out down a busy street. In any case, he'd always been the sort that people noticed. It wasn't something she'd given much thought to before, but considering it now, she saw with a jolt how distinctive he was. Some people were like that. So Charlie would have to understand that it simply wasn't on.

She swallowed the tea Baz had put in front of her in grateful gulps, then stood up to steady herself for the trip back to the room to get Charlie's number, aware that Baz was watching her. Sheer fright, she decided, might not be the recommended treatment for morning sickness, but it seemed to work.

There wasn't a sound from the other two's room. Where would they be going next, she wondered. Thailand, perhaps, or Malaysia? Bali? A couple of times she'd heard them talking to Baz about Australia.

She glanced at her watch and quickened her pace, thankful that the nausea was under control and that Baz hadn't yet set to work with the frying pan. If Charlie was home, she'd be getting ready for work now, and probably thinking of phoning in to say why she hadn't done so last night.

Baz's greasy log book was becoming full. Crossing her fingers, Fran set the egg-timer, and dialled Charlie's home.

'If it is urgent, I will call her,' said the aunt.

'I'm afraid it is,' replied Fran, but Charlie was there already.

She sounded sleepy. 'Sorry not to have called, my dear,' she yawned. 'I had rather a late night. Interesting, though. Thank heavens I'm due a weekend off. I think we have to move fast.'

'Hold it, Charlie,' said Fran. 'Things aren't so good from this end.' Briefly she explained about Nevil and Vesak almost being picked up, and heard Charlie's gasps of dismay.

'Bloody taxi men,' she exploded. 'Quick, have you got his new address and number?'

Fran looked at the words on her hand and, for

once, hesitated. 'Charlie, you can't still be thinking of using him . . .'

'I'm not completely irresponsible, my dear. I was just wondering if I could think of anywhere safer for them. Maybe I should get him moved to Auntie's. She'll think it highly irregular, and I hate the thought of frightening her or putting her at risk, but it might be the only way. She hates my work, but at least I can trust her. So why don't you tell Nevil that if he gets at all worried again to go straight to Auntie's at any time of the day or night.'

'I can't. Not until he rings again. There's no phone, and I've told him to stay inside.'

'Then for the moment that might be best. Do you know, I was hoping that after what I'd set up for tonight, I'd have enough material to put the tin lid on these bastards. Very soon, Tony is supposed to be faxing everything he's come up with at his end to a friend I have on a newspaper in town.'

'It's OK,' Charlie continued, to Fran's squawk of alarm. 'She's an old school friend. She's been expecting this. At the same time, I was going to go to the very top with the tapes and some witnesses in tow, and dump the whole thing on them. Blitz everyone at once. Go on local radio, get AWW on the line, call the British High Commission, everything. What a dreadful pity. I really needed that part of it on tape. Now things will slow down again until I can think of something else.'

Fran stared out at the brilliant early morning sky where a jet's vapour trail was fastening the blue together like a silver zipper.

'Charlie, what exactly was it you'd set up for this evening?' she asked almost idly. It was odd how you took planes for granted – until you desperately needed to be on one and knew you weren't going to make it.

'I really think it would have worked,' said Charlie sadly. 'Last night I was taking lessons on how to be a tart from a couple of experts on the subject. I let them think the police were going after a nasty little pimp who'd given a friend of theirs a beating. We'll get him too, of course, eventually. They even lent me some of their clothes. My dear, you should have seen me. On any good street corner, even Auntie would have passed me by.'

'But you wouldn't get kitted up and leave from home, surely.'

'Good heavens, of course not. One of the station sergeants in town knew about the pimp, and told me I could use them as a base for the evening. I said I'd be bringing a former colleague from England who was on holiday over here, as an observer, to show them how we did things in good old downtown Colombo. Busman's holiday, and all that. But I said I didn't want anyone to get into trouble, so I'd let him in round the back.'

'That's rather good, Charlie.'

'The sergeant seemed to think it was quite funny. I said I'd owe him one, and we'd square the paperwork later.'

There was a pause. The jet was heading south. That meant Australia. Wrong way, but never mind. Up there, hundreds of people were crammed together complaining about airline breakfasts, discussing cures for jet-lag, and moaning that they'd already seen the in-flight movie. For a very long moment, nothing seemed real.

'I'm going to do this, aren't I, Charlie?' said Fran, hardly believing her own ears. 'I'm coming with you

276

to hold that bloody cam. That's what I'm going to do, aren't I?'

'Oh, come on!' Charlie was laughing in disbelief. 'This may come as a surprise to you, my dear, but we don't have too many European hookers in this town. And certainly none that are ten feet tall. Someone would have noticed, I can assure you.'

'But they won't be seeing me, you sweet-old fashioned thing,' retorted Fran. 'They'll be seeing a feller.'

'Jesus, Mary and Holy Joseph,' squealed Charlie. 'Sorry, Auntie. Fran, are you serious? You'd do it dressed as a man?'

Baz was looking at Fran curiously from the door. What on earth would he be making of this end of the conversation?

Fran made a face at him. 'I have it on the best authority that I'm quite good at it,' she replied calmly. 'But I may need some extra coaching. Hey, Baz, go and get those two up, will you?'

'You'd really do it?' asked Charlie breathlessly.

'I'd do anything if there's a chance of getting us out of here. OK, Charlie, let's have some times and places.'

Everything would be all right now. They'd soon be going home. Wouldn't they?

When a rather sheepish Anders and Klaus finally surfaced, it was to find Fran sitting at their table under the papaw tree, settling her bill with Baz.

'Fran, what are you doing?' asked Anders in alarm. 'We were so drunk last night. It was very bad of us. But we have discussed it, and if you need us around, we can stay a few more days. It is no big deal.'

'Where's next on your itinerary?' she asked thoughtfully.

'We thought Bangkok and then Jakarta. We have open tickets, so we would have to stay a night or so in Colombo to confirm the onward flights. But really, there is no hurry.'

'There is for me,' said Fran. 'I've got to get back to Colombo tonight, and you won't believe what Charlie has got in mind by way of light entertainment.'

Baz went off to make their breakfasts and she quickly told them what was going on.

'I need some coffee,' said Anders, as she finished off with a request to borrow their clothes again. 'You would do this? That stuff we were smoking last night – it is stronger than I thought. No, really, are you crazy?'

'Didn't I do it right before?'

'But Fran, you only had to walk down a path and then keep very quiet in the taxi. In Copenhagen on a Saturday night, you would have fooled nobody. They would think you had come as Marlene Dietrich.'

'Oh,' said Fran, rather deflated. One bit of amateur dramatics had clearly gone to her head. They were right, of course. Even allowing for the range of possible peculiarities in a man who would go with a prostitute to buy exotic aphrodisiacs, she was going to have to do better than last time if she didn't want to endanger the operation, not to mention their lives.

'OK, where do I start?'

'How long have we got?' grinned Anders.

'I have to be at this place by seven o'clock this evening.' She pushed a sheet torn from Baz's notepad towards them. 'It's a police station somewhere in the Pettah district. The trouble is, I'm a little nervous of taxis now, after what happened with Nevil and Vesak. That was too close for comfort. But Charlie reckons if I get one from down here like last time, it should be safe enough.'

There was a hurried consultation in Danish. 'We think we should hire a car,' said Anders. 'Under my name, so there is no risk to you.'

'Hiring's very pricey round here,' put in Baz. 'Unless you're desperate. They don't trust people to bring them back, you see.'

'Believe me, I'm desperate,' said Fran. 'This one's on me. We'll sort out the money later, because I'd better not risk using my credit cards.'

'Same with the hotel,' said Anders. 'We'll book two rooms for a couple of nights while we sort out our tickets, and you can come and crash in with us whenever you want.'

'Crashing around with you two has been the highlight of this trip,' she told them with a wry smile. 'As a grand finale, I don't suppose you'd fancy driving a get-away car, would you?'

The two men looked at each other and grinned.

'OK, now we're really impressed,' said Anders, and for once, he actually looked it.

I'm mad, thought Fran. Completely mad. But it was too late now.


'I've had some weirdoes through this place in my time,' declared Baz as he watched them load up the hired car. 'But I reckon you lot take the biscuit.'

They'd ordered the car for two o'clock to allow plenty of time for Anders to adjust to driving on the British side of the road all the way to Colombo, in conditions where he had to be ready for almost every hazard except snow drifts.

'I think,' said Anders, as they drove away with a final wave to the Sydney Opera House and its bemused owner, 'that I drive this thing like an old lady going to church on Sunday.'

From the back seat, Fran nodded. The last thing they wanted was any kind of accident where they would have to stop and make a statement. As far as road blocks were concerned, the story was that her passport had been lost and they were on their way to collect a replacement from the British Consulate. Meanwhile, she was Mrs Baldwyn, divorced and travelling with friends.

In the event, they reached the outskirts of Colombo without incident at around five o'clock, and began the search for a quiet hotel with some parking, within reasonable distance of the chaotic Pettah district. Fran stayed out of sight in the car while the two men checked in, taking all her luggage with them except a bag containing an outfit put together by Anders and Klaus with as much care as a Paris spring collection. Before leaving, they'd had a dress rehearsal, and she'd made a few subtle alterations with her sewing kit so that give-away curves were concealed. Then they'd given her a crash course in walking and general body language, and she'd practised what they described as typically Scandinavian male grunts, the idea being that she spoke almost no English and left all the talking to Charlie. Amid hilarity which the seriousness of the operation hardly warranted but certainly alleviated, they decided that being macho was not on.

'Clearly you are a deeply troubled, inadequate young man of low vitality,' Anders had declared.

280

'With shifty eyes,' agreed Fran. 'And acne. Can I have acne?'

Anders had considered this for a moment. 'No, the instant suntan cream will do. But you need a strong bladder. No mistakes there, please.'

But now that the time for putting it all into action was approaching, Fran had to admit that she was getting seriously jittery, and there were still a few things she needed to buy. Charlie had said she'd be responsible for fixing up a bag for the camcorder, but told Fran to buy a detailed street map of the area. Also, they'd agreed that the sun hat she'd borrowed before might look odd at night, but she still needed something with a brim to shadow her face. The Gucci loafers had been discarded as not masculine enough, and the other two's shoes were too big for comfort. Hefty trainers seemed like a suitable compromise. At least she would be able to run in them, if, perish the thought, running became necessary.

They went to the Pettah bazaar and found what they wanted with very little trouble, then got something to eat at a place calling itself an ice-cream parlour. Over toasted sandwiches that tasted like sawdust, she studied the map of the district with mounting unease. The whole of Pettah was a maze of alleys and lanes, most of which either didn't have names, or if they did, the names were long and almost impossible to pronounce. Eventually they located the police sub-station where Charlie had told her to arrive at the back entrance, but it looked as if the access to it was too small to be marked. Marching in the front door and asking for Charlie was definitely not on, so the idea was to get as close as possible and hope to spot the back way.

'And once Charlie's let me in,' said Fran with a

confidence she was far from feeling, 'I'll suggest that you two act as a back-up with the car. She was going to pick up a taxi to get us there, and then tell him to wait. I think I'd sooner it was you two waiting for us on the way back, maybe at a slightly different spot from where we're dropped. It should only take a few minutes to sort it out with her. Are you sure you're still on for this?'

'We wish to be in at the kill, is that right?' asked Anders.

'Don't say that,' said Fran. 'It makes me nervous. Correction – terrified. Do you know what I'd really like now? To go and find Nevil's new hide-out just to make sure he's all right.'

'And if you were able to see him, what do you think he would say to all this?'

'That's a very good point,' said Fran, biting her lip.

# Chapter Eighteen

For a nightmare, the first part of the plan went comparatively smoothly. Thanks to some inspired map reading, they found the police station with ten minutes to spare and while there was still enough light to see that a particularly grubby little alley led round the back.

Fran gave a shiver of distaste. It looked like the kind of place where people who hadn't made a satisfactory job of helping the police with their enquiries were put out with the rubbish, of which there was plenty.

'I won't be a minute,' she said, and set off gamely into the gathering darkness between the glass-topped, man-high walls, with several mangy dogs for company. She found the single, sheet metal gate with spikes on top that Charlie had said to look for, and gave it a couple of sharp raps.

'Charlie?' she called hopefully.

To her immense relief, the gate ground open with a gothic creak, and Charlie was there with a huge smile of relief, ready to pull her inside.

'Wait,' hissed Fran, and told her about her plan for using Anders and Klaus.

Charlie jumped at it. 'Now let me think,' she said.

They looked at the map under the one light at their end of the overgrown courtyard. 'OK, here's where I want them to be. There's a mini-market called the St Francis Baking and Grocery on the corner of Goptal Street. Here, see? There's usually enough room for a couple of cars. Tell them to be there by nine o'clock and to wait until midnight. If we're not back by then . . .'

There was a thoughtful pause. 'Tell them to call the police?' suggested Fran dryly.

'More like an ambulance. But seriously, they must check their hotel in case you've got back some other way, and if not, they should ring this number. It's my old friend from Fraud. They'd have a lot of explaining to do, because he's not in on this. Nobody is. But don't worry, my dear, it won't come to that.'

Charlie scribbled it all down and Fran traipsed back up the lane with it, pursued by an ever increasing pack of hopeful curs.

'James Bond does not get chased by stray dogs,' joked Klaus, as she handed over the instructions.

'Don't be so fussy,' retorted Fran. 'In a low budget production, this is as good as it gets. And this is also where you wish me good luck, and I say we'll see you later outside this St Francis Baking place, hopefully with no dogs, or anything else, on our tails.'

Charlie led her down a cracked path round the outside of the tangled yard that might once have been a citrus orchard. In the far corner was a low building, the smell from which, rising above the evening scents of orange blossom and frangipani, identified it as the lavatory block. They went into the women's side and then looked at each other.

'Race you,' said Charlie gaily, and went into one of the cubicles with her bag.

Fran looked round bleakly at the broken tiles and

uneven floor, the crude neon lighting and exposed plumbing. What had she expected – fluffy pink loo paper and air freshener?

She found another cubicle and started peeling off.

'I don't think I could get to like this,' she called, removing her bra and winding the silk scarf round herself tightly. Her breasts had felt slightly tighter and fuller lately. Typical, she thought, something you'd always wanted, just when you could do without it. Then Anders' checked, long-sleeved shirt, altered for sleeve length. Even without Klaus' linen Armani jacket she was sweating, but that had to go on too. Anders' slacks; the new trainers. She'd bought good ones. People noticed things like that. And if she had to run? She hadn't been a bad sprinter at school, and still went for the odd jog round the village at home – but in this heat? Better not to think about it.

Bundling her other clothes into a plastic bag, she left the cubicle and studied her face in the mildewed mirror, twisting her jaw the way men did when they shaved. The instant tanning cream had been a good idea. Eyebrows roughed up and blackened just a little. Don't overdo it. But was she ever going to get away with this? To stop the spider runs of panic, she slapped at her stomach, then remembered. Sorry, she whispered. Go back to sleep.

Now for the hair, slicked back with some gel so that it looked almost black, and into a low, stubby ponytail. Now wouldn't Zavvy be flattered, she thought grimly. The very thought of the man made her flesh crawl.

Rustlings and exclamations of annoyance were coming from Charlie's cubicle.

'How are you doing in there?' called Fran taking a

few practice strides across the dingy concrete floor and trying to remember Anders' coaching.

'It's this bloody push-up bra – it's too tight.'

'Now there's professionalism for you.'

'Coming, ready or not,' sang Charlie at last, and flung open her door.

Then – 'oh my God's' and giggles as the pair faced each other. If Fran had been at pains to flatten herself out, Charlie had gone to the other extreme. Her shiny mauve skirt was too short, her heels too high, and the neckline of her sheer, frilly blouse too low for Asian modesty. She'd also shaken her normally sleek hair loose, so it was wild and crimpy.

When they'd got over the shock, Charlie surveyed Fran critically. 'The hair's fine,' she declared, 'but you definitely need the hat.' At the market, they'd rejected a baseball cap as too unisex and gone for a cotton drill bush hat with a brim. 'M'mm – top shirt button done up, I think. No Adam's apple.'

'I'll suffocate,' sighed Fran, but obliged, squaring her shoulders and setting her chin.

'Don't try too hard, my dear,' said Charlie. 'Remember, you're a young man, spoilt, with money, on your first trip to the mysterious East. Danish, but with enough English to know what's going on.'

'Fine. I've been practising my Nordic grunts and shrugs in case anyone speaks to me.'

'I'm Chula, by the way. Makes me sound Thai. They think that's sexy. Now, shall we have a look at the spy-in-the-bag?'

Fran could only admire Charlie's handiwork. It was a small canvas hold-all with a tiny hole cut under the leather tab trim at one end. Charlie opened the zip a fraction, to reveal some striped cotton *sarama* material, a towel, a man's handkerchief and a wallet.

286

'Mostly wadding to deaden the sound,' said Charlie, 'But it's actually very quiet. It's inside a sponge bag, held in place with tape. It's all set up. You'll have the remote control in your jacket pocket. Here you are.'

She showed Fran a smooth, black matt plastic object no bigger than a child's watch face. The only thing on it was a tiny button.

'Click on, click off. That's all there is to it. See?'

Fran watched fascinated as Charlie held the control concealed in her hand, aimed casually at the bag on the floor. Her thumb gave an almost imperceptible twitch, and they both held their breath, straining to catch any sound. All Fran could pick up was the very faintest trace of a whirr.

'That's brilliant,' she said. 'It's like listening to a mouse thinking.'

Charlie gave a throaty chuckle. 'A little beauty, isn't it? So don't worry about noise. As you may have noticed, this is not a quiet country, and the cicadas and frogs haven't even started up yet. Let's try a few practice passes.'

The technique, Fran quickly learned, was to enter the building with the machine running, aperture to the front, to get a good view of the place and who was in there. Then you changed hands casually to get a good sweep, before resting the bag on some convenient surface pointing in the best direction. If you weren't satisfied, it would be possible to move it a little, but the less movement the better. If the angle was still wrong for getting the main part of the action, fumbling for the handkerchief or checking the wallet allowed you to tilt the bag for a better shot.

Fran nodded and gave it a try. It seemed so simple when someone showed you how. No problem at all, in the niffy, neon warmth of a police station loo. No problem, when the strong brown hands of a woman you now barely recognised were turning up the collar of a jacket that wasn't yours, so you could smell her sweat and your own through the cheap scent she was wearing. Was it pure blue funk that was making every sensation suddenly so acute?

'I'm sorry,' said Fran suddenly and sat down on the bench with a flop. Disturbed by the impact, a couple of cockroaches scuttled across the floor. She watched them without blinking.

'I'm frightened too.' Charlie sighed, and came to sit beside her.

'We're not frightened enough,' retorted Fran. 'Or we wouldn't be doing this, would we? I've just realised – I've never been *really* frightened in my life. I only thought I was.'

'It's like sea sickness. You get used to it. At least that's what they tell you at the police college. Oh, by the way.' Charlie tore a page from her notebook and handed it to Fran. 'This is the address of the man who can fix you a passport. It won't be a brilliant job, but it'll get you out of here. Just mention my name. It stinks in here. Let's talk outside.'

As a final touch, Charlie slipped some vicious looking chunky rings onto her right hand and bunched it into a fist with an evil grin. Then she bundled their belongings into a locker and they stood in the yard by the narrow walkway which led to the main building. It was pitch dark now, and a high tangle of bushes screened them from the ghostly artificial glare of the windows. Insects of all sizes buzzed the garish neon strips, then fell out of the air as if they'd suddenly had enough and wanted only to join the flittering, dying heap on the ground below. The air was no cooler outside, but the heavy smell of frangipani blossom made her want to break off a spray of the pale, waxy flowers and hold it to her nose. But a man wouldn't have done that.

Quietly they rehearsed the drill. Fran would leave first. She'd walk round to the metalled road at the front, go to the corner of the third side street on the left and wait, looking as if she might want some action. Then Charlie would come along in a taxi, the beat-up up sort used by her kind, but driven by someone the girls said could be trusted not to ask questions. She'd yell a few of the usual phrases at Fran who, after some obvious haggling, would get in, and they'd head off downtown. But once they were inside the cab, the game would be on. The driver would think it was all quite genuine, and have no idea where they were going.

Walking the three blocks to the pick-up point, Fran tried not to clutch the bag too tightly. Instinctively she'd pushed her arm through the handles, but quickly returned to holding it the way a man would. In her back pocket was a wad of grubby notes which Charlie had signed for from police funds.

Fran stuck her other hand into her side pocket, lengthened her stride slightly and prayed. Suppose she did something daft, like pointing the bag the wrong way. Forgot something crucial. People always did. Hands – that was it. Her hands, when it came to passing over the money. Damn!

Fortunately she never kept her nails very long. Cursing her own slackness, she stopped briefly to rough them up on some old mortar under the window ledge of a travel ticket booth.

There were still lots of people about, on foot or on bicycles, while a stream of traffic jostled past. The street lighting wasn't up to much. Then something strange struck her. No one was taking any notice of her at all. She'd become invisible. Were men *always* less visible, more anonymous, than women? Or was it just here, where a European woman by herself at night would certainly have attracted some looks. So far, so good.

Too good. A car had slowed down beside her, and a voice yelled, 'Hey, darling! You looking for a friend?'

Fran stiffened in her tracks while a prickling surge of adrenaline ran away with any ideas about taking up undercover work as a hobby. This wasn't the right corner – and it wasn't Charlie. The face leering out from the crawling car was crudely painted and the voice hoarse. Was it even a woman? Talk about mix 'n' match.

'Not tonight, love,' she called, keeping her voice low and gravelly. Go away, please go away . . .

A coarse cackle came from the battered Toyota which, to Fran's intense relief, kangarooed off into the night. Had they homed in on something sexually ambiguous about her? Was it hanging over her like a cloud?

The sweat was running between her breasts now, and she'd have given anything to have slipped off the jacket and fanned herself with the hat. Then another car slowed down beside her just as she reached the appointed corner, with such perfect timing that it took all her concentration not to greet Charlie with a whoop of relief.

They went through the pre-arranged patter and Fran got in the back with her. Unseen by the driver, Charlie reached for her hand and squeezed it briefly. 'So let's go and buy you something to make us

290

remember tonight for ever,' she said loudly, with a wink in the mirror at the driver, who gave a toothy smirk.

My God, thought Fran, right now I'd settle for a guarantee that we'll still be here tomorrow to remember anything at all.

'OK, let's try Goptal Street, by the old fruit market.'

Once off the main roads, it felt as if the unending streams of people and vehicles were simply being squeezed into narrower and narrower spaces. Everything slowed down, even your breathing; the clogged streets couldn't cope any more.

For a moment Fran thought she'd stopped sweating, but when she heaved her shoulders, she realised her shirt was soaked. The only reason she hadn't felt it was because everything in the car was at blood heat.

'Nearly there, dearie,' said Charlie sharply, sensing her distress.

The car lurched into a big night market area, and the driver began muttering to himself about and looking for somewhere to drop them.

'Here!' yelled Charlie above the din from the market, and they bundled themselves out into the market detritus to the sounds of indignant hooting as she paid off the driver.

'See Colombo by night,' she muttered, after answering what sounded like a coarse comment from a couple of male idlers with an even coarser one. 'Stick with me, darling, and I'll show you a good time.'

Like chewing gum, thought Fran, ploughing through the filth.

With Charlie teetering along in her high heels and tight skirt, they walked two blocks down, until they passed a name Fran recognised – the St Francis Baking and Grocery.

'That corner,' said Charlie, swinging her little white fake leather purse on its cheap gold chain. 'Your friends will be there. If for any reason we get separated . . .'

'No chance,' said Fran fervently.

They turned off Goptal Street into something called, unbelievably, Ponnambalam Arunatchalam Road.

Fran sighed. 'Who thinks of these street names?'

'Sorry,' smiled Charlie. 'One of our heroes in the struggle for independence.'

'I'll try to remember that.'

Once they were round the side, it was obvious from the smell that the St Francis mini-mart had a sideline in another home-made product as well as bread. A silent, furtive queue of men were shuffling into a back entrance and coming out with second-hand bottles filled with something that smelt like sweetish varnish remover. Hooch. Her sainted namesake would not have been impressed. The alley at the back smelt of urine, goat, old tyres, curry and diesel.

Along the impossibly named street, most of the booths were still open, and the odd stall keeper who was not too busy called shrilly to them as they went past. As they got further into the alleys, Fran could see women hanging round doorways, some in tawdry saris, but mostly in cheap, ill-matched European clothes.

Soon there wasn't even a nod towards street lighting, and there were rats about – small, but definitely rats. By now Fran had almost lost count of the turns they had made from Goptal Street. In one doorway a couple writhed under a filthy blanket, and she quickly looked away.

'Nearly there,' said Charlie, taking her arm. 'When I give a squeeze, start the cam.'

A women passed them, saying something to which Charlie replied and got a harsh, throaty laugh in return. But the woman was rickety thin, and her remaining longish teeth and sad, vacant eyes made her look painfully donkey-like. Were ever men that desperate, wondered Fran. Maybe. These women certainly were.

Charlie gave her arm a squeeze, and as she fumbled to press the control button in her pocket, Fran found herself being steered towards an un-marked archway just big enough for a car to pass. Had the cam started? She had to believe so. If it had, and she pressed it again, it would stop.

The littered earth yard inside was like so many others they'd passed, but fortunately not completely dark. Here and there, in what looked like an attempt at security, some ugly strip lights had been recently installed. There were grills over the tiny windows of the out-buildings, and new padlocks on several of the corrugated iron doors. Over the only door that was open to the courtyard, was something sign-written in what Fran now knew was Tamil script, and under-neath, in uneven English, were the words, MEDI-CATIONS FOR ALL AILMENT AND SEXUAL PROBLEMS, WELCOME.

At any other time, Fran would have smiled, even risked a photo. But with a jolt she realised she was already doing exactly that. Suddenly she was acutely aware of the bag. It felt alive, emitting a strange in-audible pulse like some tiny tropical insect in search of a mate. Fortunately there was a distant wailing of local pop music coming from across the way. Without breaking her stride, she gently angled the bag round the dimly lit yard to get it all in. These could be store rooms - probably were, she told herself. Please don't let the music stop.

The shop, if it could be called that, didn't look anything out of the ordinary. Beside the doorway was a kind of display counter – a ramshackle rectangle of light and clashing colour in a wall of mud bricks that showed their age through filthy, crumbling plaster. A corrugated iron awning was propped up from below by wonky poles, presumably so that it could be flapped down and padlocked.

As they approached, a man in a loose striped shirt and *sarama* shuffled to his feet and greeted them. For all his slightly rat-toothed smile, he looked no more sinister or depraved than the thousands of his fellow citizens selling everything from wing nuts and washing powder, to false teeth and gold dust at similar stalls all over the city. Maybe . . . maybe, thought Fran in a desperate burst of optimism, it really was going to be this easy. She'd just casually hitch the bag onto the tin counter; Charlie would say, 'Half a pound of ground tiger bones, for this impotent tourist idiot, my good man,' and they'd waltz off into the night with the proof on film. Then they could all go home.

She was trying to follow the proceedings with what she hoped was a credible mixture of casual interest, young male arrogance and embarrassment, when the pop music stopped. Fran's heart began to thump. By now, to her over-sensitive ears, the cam seemed to be making as noise as a small lawn mower, and worse, there was nowhere to put it down while still keeping the counter in shot. Temporarily paralysed, she realised that unless she got the bag into a better position, all they would get would be a view of Charlie's legs and the floor. And things were moving fast.

After a rapid-fire discussion, various bottles and ointments were plonked on the counter and dismissed by Charlie after some critical sniffing. Old shoe boxes and twists of paper full of dried wisps and scraps of lord-knew-what kinds of creatures were produced from cubby-holes and explained in detail with gestures. There was even something that could have been powdered bone. Fran held her breath.

'Here, darling, tiger bone, you see?' announced Charlie gleefully and beckoned her closer.

Should she just plonk the bag on the counter? It felt too risky, but otherwise, she couldn't get it in shot.

Charlie was ahead of her. 'This is real tiger bone?' she repeated to the man, who nodded, and Fran was able to lean forward appreciatively to examine the goods, while the cam picked up his voluble reply in Tamil. It was a start, but it wasn't enough.

'Maybe we'll buy,' said Charlie airily. 'But he's rich, this one. Look at him, isn't he handsome?' She grinned back at Fran. 'He needs to be strong tonight. Something special.' Then she giggled something in Tamil to the man. 'Another girl, Yo-yo – I think you know her – she told him you've got the best goods in town.'

At first the man seemed to be denying it, but Charlie persisted.

'Come on,' she wheedled. 'He knows it won't be cheap. We won't tell the boss if you let us have a peep. Don't let me down. Let's see what you've got back there.'

For the first time, the shop keeper looked at Fran. It felt as if her heart was trying to escape, and only the tight silk binding was holding it in. With a desperate bravado that seemed to come from nowhere, she half winked at him and patted her pocket.

Amazingly, it seemed to work. They were beckoned in, and followed him down a dark, narrow passage leading to a tiny back room. She didn't stop the machine because Charlie had said continuity was important. In the best Baz tradition, the room seemed to be a store, office and family living space. Hardly daring to breathe, Fran eyed the low, oilskin covered table longingly, but couldn't decide whether to place the bag on it there and then, or wait until the goods were produced, in case she put it down facing the wrong way to catch the action.

The swishing of a sari and scuffle of sandled feet in the corridor told her that someone had probably just vacated the rumpled, shelf-like bed against the wall. Clearly, whatever these people were selling, they weren't getting rich on it. Outside, a baby was crying as if it was past caring what happened to it.

Then things happened fast. The dealer pulled a small, grubby cloth bundle from under the bed. Sensing this might be it, Fran tracked his movement slowly by turning herself round with the bag to watch as he put the bundle proudly on the table. With a certain sense of occasion, the man dragged a metal folding chair from behind the door and offered it to Fran, who declined it with a lordly wave to Charlie.

Charlie promptly sat down with an 'Ouf!' that was supposed to be relief at taking the weight of her high heels, but was most likely because she'd spotted that if Fran kept standing and holding the bag, there was a brilliant angle onto the low table.

The bundle was unknotted with a flourish. Craning forward, Fran stared.

There were only four of them - each hardly bigger than a finger. So small. They were lying there on a piece of almost white cloth inside the striped wrapping. Fine – they'd show up better. *Bastards* . . . Ignorant, stupid . . . This was why tigers were dying. She mustn't blow it now.

She counted. Ten seconds focus on the objects on the table. Now, move back, as if in the excitement of the moment, to dump the bag on the bed. There we go, oh so casually. Now, step forward. You're keen to buy, but don't block the view. Perfect.

The other two were talking at the tops of their voices, obviously haggling. The man picked up the smallest of the obscene little objects as if weighing it, and the shouting match continued while he fetched a knife and a tiny pair of brass scales. 'Grammes', and '*lahks*', the unit for a thousand rupees, were the only words Fran could make out.

Suddenly Charlie clapped and held out her hand almost impatiently to Fran in the universal flick-finger gesture that meant, 'Hand over the cash, sucker'. Fran reached into her back pocket, and with a questioning shrug passed the grubby wad to Charlie, who snatched it greedily. Show him the money – that was the game. How much there was, or what they would have to pay, she had no idea. What was a tiger's penis worth today?

Conscious of the machine still filming, she stepped back and sat on the bed beside the bag, as if the matter was now out of her hands. In fact she was desperate to cover the next move. It was very important to show the hand-over of the goods.

Under cover of taking out the handkerchief to mop her brow, Fran panned the bag round as the man produced a stone pestle and mortar. With an elaborate show of cutting and weighing their purchase, the man kept up a sing-song litany for their benefit. Charlie nodded her agreement over the weight, then started to count out the money onto the table, reciting the amounts as she went.

At the last few fifty rupee notes, she hesitated and giggled. My God, she asking for a cut, thought Fran, whose knees were trembling so badly that it was a relief to push the handkerchief back and stand up with the bag. She was just in time. With a waggle of his head and a show of reluctance, the man slapped some of the notes back into Charlie's hand, and she immediately tucked them into her bra. Then almost reverently, he placed the morsel of bone into the mortar and reduced it to a kind of dry paste in seconds. It was all Fran could do not to wince.

The contents of the mortar were carefully scooped into a spill of brown paper and given to Charlie, who popped it into her chain purse. 'We know what to do with this, big boy, don't we,' she winked to Fran. 'Let's go and have some fun.'

In a daze Fran offered her hand to the dealer, and he took it with a wolfish grin. For a second she wondered whether to put her hand straight back into her pocket to stop the recording, but in that instant there was a disturbance outside. Some kind of vehicle had slowed down and sounded its horn, and then there was an impatient scrunch of tyres in the yard.

The effect on the dealer was startling. He aimed a string of desperate words at Charlie, punctuated by oh-my-Gods as he scooped up his equipment. Then he rushed to the door with the bundle, calling urgently to someone, presumably the woman, because a frightened female voice answered, accompanied by more wailing from the baby.

'Jesus, he says it's the boss,' hissed Charlie. 'Don't say a word. I'll get us out of this. If I say run, run.'

'But you can't run . . .' The *boss*? What was she saying? Oh no, please, it couldn't be. Not Zavvy.

She felt it then, the way a cornered animal feels it, the weirdest of sensations; her hair, wet from sweat, plastered down and under a hat, was standing on end, just like they said it did. The urge to run when you couldn't was so strong that it did *this* to you . . .

Still panicking, the dealer returned, minus the bundle, to urge something incomprehensible to Charlie.

'He says we must say nothing about this and leave.'

'Suits me.' Fran's jaw was so tight she could hardly get the words out. 'After you.'

With Charlie leading, they got almost as far as the outer door before the first man from the big estate car in the yard reached them. He blocked their way with the kind of leer which suggested this was his main function in life. Behind him, Fran could make out three other men, one of whom had stayed to open the hatchback. The second man strolling towards them turned briefly, as if checking on the others, and she was near enough to Charlie to hear the rasp of breath in her throat as they both spotted the elegant ponytail together.

'Who are these people?' The voice was educated, almost unaccented; the question asked as if it were hardly important, even boring.

The nearest man rapped out something in Tamil, but Charlie had barely time to open her mouth before the dealer, hovering behind them in the corridor, let out a frantic stream of explanation and repentance.

Zavvy ignored him and stared hard at Charlie. 'Out here, under the light,' he ordered.

Charlie trotted forward with an attempt at a simper, leaving Fran feeling totally naked in the neon glare.

'This isn't one of mine,' remarked Zavvy, to no one in particular. He might as well have been talking about a stray dog. Then suddenly the focused menace in the amber eyes was full on her. 'Hey, bitch, are you working my patch?'

'No, please! I work up Negombo way – tourist hotels,' Charlie countered, in a cringing sing-song of fear.

'But you know who I am?'

'Yes, Mr Cheng. All the girls know who you are.'

'And you've got the nerve to come here?' The idea seemed to intrigue rather than anger him. 'Who's he?'

'A tourist, only. He's from Copenhagen.'

'Has he got a tongue?'

'He doesn't speak much English. He wanted a night in Colombo. That's all, I swear.'

'OK, come here.'

The other man shoved Charlie forward. Petrified beyond amazement, Fran watched as Charlie made a show of shaking him off, and presenting herself to the tall figure almost flirtatiously.

Zavvy grabbed Charlie under the chin and Fran saw a subtle change come over the eerily handsome face. 'Well now,' was all he said. Then again, that flick of a hidden switch well calculated to jolt all their nerves. 'Has he paid you yet?'

Without waiting for a reply, he reached with both hands for the front of Charlie's low frilled blouse. His expert downward wrench tore at the buttons and dragged her forward so that she overbalanced against him, blouse gaping. Fran felt as if Charlie's stifled gasp had come from her own throat.

'What's this, loose change?' he rapped, taking his time to remove the notes Charlie had stowed in her cleavage. The other two men were now openly staring. 'You're underselling yourself, bitch. You've got class. You could double that if you come and work for me.'

Charlie cocked her head at him, and Fran had to stifle a gasp at her nerve.

'Triple,' she said, swinging the white purse teasingly and easing down a bra strap. 'I'm good.'

The other men sniggered. Even they seemed impressed by her sheer gall.

No, please . . . prayed Fran. Don't do this, Charlie. I can't help you. Please. While all the time the machine that could still kill them both was sending its tiny pulse through the bag handles clenched in her tingling fingers.

The finely arched eyebrows showed little more than amused surprise. 'Triple? Ha! That's for the special stuff. A bit of kink, a bit of rough?' He turned to the other men now near enough to paw Charlie if he'd given the word. 'You think she's worth a try?'

'You want her first, boss?' called the fat man still by the open hatchback. He'd paused in what he'd been doing, which was lifting a bulky bundle wrapped in hessian from the car. Now it was balanced on the back, while he eyed Charlie with open lust.

'When I know she's clean,' said Zavvy. 'Put her in the car.'

The third man made a clumsy grab at Charlie, who drew back indignantly at just the wrong moment so that he broke her bag chain. Fran blinked in horror. The contents of the purse had spilled on the ground, the twist of brown paper among them.

Ignoring the other bits and pieces, the man was on it like a cat. He snatched it up and handed it to Zavvy, who sniffed it.

Fran saw his eyes narrow, and after that it was chaos. Zavvy yelled something which galvanised all three men into action. Drawing a knife, the first pushed past Fran and rushed into the shop after the dealer who must have known what was coming next. A door slammed, and muffled thumps and sharp cries followed from the back room.

The second man's reaction to his boss's voice was almost too fast to follow. He hit Charlie across the mouth and punched her in the stomach so that her legs buckled.

'Not her face, you fool,' growled Zavvy.

Utterly helpless, Fran wanted to cry out as Charlie was almost dragged to the car and pushed in.

The man who'd been unloading the wrapped bundle quickly manhandled it into one of the storerooms and came puffing back to join in. Fists bunched, he looked at Zavvy hopefully, and then at Fran, like an overweight old dog wanting to be useful.

But Zavvy seemed to have other plans for him. 'Pick up that crap,' he snapped, kicking at the sand where the contents of Charlie's bag lay scattered.

Only Fran and Zavvy didn't move. Fran, because she couldn't. The amber eyes had her transfixed.

Yet every muscle in her body was yelling at her to run.

With a disappointed grunt, the man squatted down to obey. At that precise moment, the car erupted into indignant banging, cursing and squealing as Charlie put on a wild-cat act to vie with the sounds of the beating in the back room.

'And shut that bitch up, can't you, while I work out what the fuck's going on round here,' snarled Zavvy to the man who'd been leaning against the car.

In that second of Zavvy's indecision, Fran's brain kicked in. It was so clear now. He actually didn't know what to do with this gawky, silent tourist standing there, mouth open, watching all this. And Charlie must have seen the fat man bend down. Now she was distracting the others to give Fran one last chance to bolt for it.

An echo of Charlie's voice was screaming in her head: 'When I say run, *run*', and it was all Fran needed. In a fear-fuelled explosion of energy she took off towards the archway and was out into the darkened alley and running for her life before anyone had time to pull a gun.

She had to get out of the line of fire. Choking, gasping, still clutching the precious bag, her feet stumbled over ruts and rubbish, mud bricks and sand ridges. She swerved round the nearest corner and didn't stop until she'd rounded the next one. Fighting for breath, she paused for a split second, cowering against a wall behind a heap of rubbish.

A car passed the end of the lane, and she froze. There was no way of knowing if it was them. Hardly daring to move, she stopped the camcorder, then stuffed the hat and jacket deep into the stinking rubbish. Then she opened her collar and wriggled free of the restricting scarf binding, took a deep breath and plunged on again.

All she could remember was to keep dog-legging downhill through the interminable alleys. Eventually, she would run across Goptal Street where Anders and Klaus would be waiting, but the names she could see meant nothing to her, and there seemed no way out of the labyrinth. Just as she was ready to collapse, a smell she recognised above the others made sudden sense. Like sweetish paint-stripper. Hooch. She emerged from a blind corner and saw the lights of a metalled road. The St Francis place must be nearby.

With a thankful gasp she forced herself on towards the sickly smell of fermentation, and saw she'd emerged from the warren on the right, not the left side of the St Francis block. Anders and Klaus would be past the store, on the very next corner.

Klaus was on the look-out, and ran to catch her when he saw the state she was in.

'They've got Charlie,' she sobbed, the breath rasping in her lungs. 'And I don't know where they're taking her.'

# Chapter Nineteen

That Saturday night was the longest of Fran's life, and she spent it curled up and exhausted between Anders and Klaus in their hotel with the cassette from the camcorder under the pillow. Distraught at the thought of what might be happening to Charlie, the first thing she'd done was to phone the home of Charlie's friend in the Fraud department, explaining briefly that she'd disappeared on a secret operation in the Pettah district and asking for all possible police help in looking for her.

The man had been bewildered at first, and wanted more details. Fran said all she knew was that Charlie might have been taken to the town house owned by Xavier Cheng. At the other end of the line, the name had caused a disconcerting silence.

'Please, if you can't do something, won't you at least tell me where Cheng's house is?' pleaded Fran.

'And who are you, ma'am?' asked the officer, very politely. 'Do you have a special warrant, or are you intending an armed raid personally? I have no power to organise this kind of operation, which, believe me, some of us have been urging for some time. But there are many problems, you understand.'

'But don't *you* understand! We can't just abandon her. They might even kill her.'

'Please calm yourself. Sergeant Pereira is trained in undercover work and knows how to defend herself. She has great personal courage, and may try to escape if she thinks it's possible.'

'But how can you simply not do anything. You're her friend.'

'I am indeed, and for that reason, we must do nothing to endanger her further without special assistance. And I did not say I would take no action. I will now go myself to this place and see what signs there are, if the place is fully occupied and so on. I can also alert all patrol cars to watch for any woman in distress in that area and see she's brought in immediately.'

'Thank you,' breathed Fran. 'And you will let me know the minute you hear anything?'

'Of course, but you must understand that I can't divulge the address of this place, even assuming she has been taken there. Any encroachment on that property must be properly co-ordinated, or it could be a disaster.'

She'd given him the hotel number, and at least the call had made her feel slightly less guilty about running away. In fact Anders and Klaus had spent half the night trying to convince her that she'd had no choice. But the thought of Charlie in Zavvy Cheng's hands was pure torment. In the end, Anders had insisted they got some rest. Fran had complied, mainly because she was afraid his next suggestion would be that she should leave the country with the cassette the minute the fake passport was ready.

She was jerked out of a nightmarish waking dream by the chirp of the bedside phone, and had to reach over Klaus to pick it up.

'Sorry to wake you, ma'am,' said the polite voice of

the receptionist, 'but the police are here and wish to speak with you.'

'Oh my God,' said Fran automatically. Up to now, almost any police except Charlie had been very bad news indeed. On her other side, Anders had shot bolt upright, and Klaus was trying to listen in to the receiver. He mouthed something to Anders, who immediately went to the window and lifted a curtain to peer out. Then he shook his head and drew a finger across his throat. No way out, and they were on the second floor anyway.

'I'll come straight down,' she said.

Anders and Klaus nodded to each other and began putting on their shoes. They were coming too.

'What about the tape?' she whispered.

There was a pause, broken by Klaus. 'I will stay here and put it in my pants. Only Anders will go with you.'

'Brilliant,' said Fran, at a nod from Anders.

'And if they search me, I scream for the Danish Embassy.'

Oh God, just once, give me a break, prayed Fran as they went downstairs. Let it be someone to say they've found Charlie, and I swear I'll never bother you again. God-bothering had become rather a habit lately.

Two men were in the lobby, and this time, they both looked like policemen. They were smart, correct and relaxed. The first one even saluted and smiled as he wished her good morning. Anders must have sensed it too and hung back. Through the glass front doors she could see the blurred image of a police car.

'You are Mrs Merrick?' For a fraction, she hesitated. It seemed like weeks since she'd dared to think of herself by her real name.

She nodded, waiting.

'Our orders are to accompany you to the General Hospital. A friend of yours, a Miss Pereira, is asking to see you.'

'You've found her? gasped Fran. 'But that's wonderful. What happened? Is she badly hurt?'

'There was an accident. I am sorry, I have no more details.'

For a second, Fran hesitated. It might be a trap, but if so, it was an elaborate one.

'May I bring a friend?'

When the policeman raised no objection, she felt some measure of reassurance. Anders quickly phoned the room to tell Klaus what was happening, and they got into the waiting car.

Fortunately, Colombo at this hour on a Sunday morning was fairly quiet. She tried a few more questions, but it was obvious that if these men knew anything more, they weren't free to say. The details of the pick up were being relayed over the car radio, but it was only when she saw the first sign to the hospital that she was able to relax.

The patrol car dropped the officer with them at the main entrance. They were immediately whisked to reception desk where she caught the words 'intensive care' and began asking questions urgently again.

'We have no details for this patient,' said the clerk. 'They will tell you there.'

Numbly she followed the officer's boots into a lift and down endless corridors. At the door of the ITC unit sat a policewoman, and for a moment Fran's heart stopped.

'Her condition is stable,' was all she said. 'You may enter.'

A nurse beckoned them into a big airy room with a

series of curtained cubicles. The only sounds were their shoes on the squeaky clean floor and the hushed humming chorus of monitoring equipment.

'There is a hairline fracture of the skull, broken ribs and left ankle, with severe blood loss,' said the nurse, and seeing Fran's stricken face, added, 'The surgeon said she's been very lucky.'

'Is she conscious?' whispered Fran.

'Conscious, but she may be sleeping. Please do not stay too long.'

At last Fran was able to part the curtains and felt her throat catch at what she could see of Charlie through the maze of bandages, plaster, pulleys, tubes and an oxygen mask. Her head was completely bandaged, her eyes were closed, and both arms had drips and were propped on pillows.

'Oh Charlie,' she whispered going to the bed but afraid to touch her. 'What did they do to you?'

The body on the bed gave a barely perceptible start and the eyes opened dreamily. 'Nothing I can't live with, my dear,' said a muffled, cracked voice. 'Just slip the mask down, will you? I feel like Tutankhamun's grandmother in this thing.'

'But . . .'

'Go on, I'm not going to peg out – they said so. And they took it off to give me a drink.'

'OK, maybe just for one minute.' Fran slipped the mask down, watching the monitors nervously to see if anything went haywire. 'Can you time us, Anders?'

'I wish I could say they did all this,' said Charlie, a little more distinctly now. 'Truth is, I did most of it myself when I jumped out of the car. Dived headlong, actually. I wanted a dark bend where they'd have to slow down, but I didn't see the culvert wall in time. Remind me to get all culverts painted white when I get out of here.'

'So they didn't even get you to the house? Thank God for that.'

'I'll say. I didn't want to be responsible for what I might say if they rumbled who I was and really got to work. Those guys are specialists.'

Fran shuddered.

'Anyway, I was at the back in the middle, and one of them was playing with a knife and telling me what fun we were going to have. Fortunately, Zavvy and the driver were strapped in. I started to come on to the one on the off side, in a way, being an ex-convent girl, I'd rather not describe. Then I applied maximum manual pressure to the relevant organ in the manner described at training school, while lashing out with my best right backhand at the knife man's face.'

She gave a dry chuckle and winced. 'The rings fetched him a good scratch, and at the time, all I felt was a burning down my back as I threw myself across the other one and got the door open. That's when I caught my head on the culvert and rolled right down into a storm ditch. I went out like a light. I don't even know if they bothered to look for me.'

'Time up,' said Anders, and Fran put the mask back on in spite of Charlie's muffled protests.

Her voice had almost gone by the end of it and Fran glanced guiltily towards the curtains. Any minute now, someone would come in and throw them out.

'Don't speak for a bit,' Fran told her. 'Just nod.'

'I can't bloody nod . . .'

'Charlie, I'm so sorry. I shouldn't have left you like that.'

'Don't be silly,' wheezed Charlie through the mask.

'Listen to me, Fran. Promise me you'll go home straight away. Just get your passport today and go.'

'But Charlie, I can't. Not without Nevil, and with you like this.'

The dreaded face appeared at the curtains. 'Time to go, please. The doctor will be making his rounds very shortly.'

Fran got up and beckoned the nurse outside. 'She is going to be all right, isn't she?' she whispered.

The nurse nodded, checking her watch. 'She should be nearly finishing her fifth pint of blood. It was the knife wound in the back mostly. They said some children running after a ball found her when it got light, or she could have bled to death. After the doctor's visit we will probably be moving her into a general ward. Also, the ankle may need some more attention, and the stitches. Three weeks, maybe. Now please . . .'

Fran went back in to find Anders with his head close to Charlie's.

'I'm telling him to make you go,' said the faint voice. 'He'll say why . . .' The last word was no more than a sigh, and she closed her eyes wearily.

Fran bent over and kissed her forehead.

'Don't go soft on me now,' murmured Charlie. 'Just go.'

'We'll be back this evening if they'll let us.'

'No, I mean it. Go home. But one last thing. Please Fran, don't tell Tony about this. It will only upset him.'

'But . . .'

'Out!' said the nurse.

\*       \*       \*

311

Back at the hotel, they held a council of war over a hasty breakfast. The men were in total agreement with Charlie that Fran should leave immediately, while she fought them all the way with every excuse she could think of.

Finally, tearfully, she had to concede that whatever happened now, the only way of solving the whole mess and getting Nevil out safely was to take the material back to London and immediately attack things from that end.

She was resolved not to tell Tony about Charlie's injuries, on the grounds that there wasn't a thing he could do to help her condition, and if, as she strongly suspected, he'd taken more than a fancy to Charlie, it was quite on the cards that he'd hop on the next plane. This would only have complicated matters further. Charlie, she decided, would fairly soon be able to handle things her own way, which clearly mattered a lot to her.

In the event, Fran's deliberations on that score were premature, because it was about four o'clock in the morning in England when she rang, and all she got was Tony's answerphone. All she could do was leave a message asking him to phone the hotel immediately if Nevil had made contact, adding that she'd decided to come home and would let him know the details.

'I think we should now go straight away and see this man about your passport,' declared Anders. 'Then we go to the airline office and buy you a fresh ticket in your new name. You could even be on a plane for London tonight.'

'I've got a better idea,' said Fran. 'Suppose they still have someone watching the London departures. Even with a false name, they might still spot me because I'm tall and on my own. Why don't I get a ticket for Bangkok. Then I could check in with you two, and fly home from there.'

'Brilliant idea,' cried Anders, and sprang to his feet, as if he feared any delay might cause her to change her mind.

If you knew the right people, thought Fran as she watched Charlie's friendly 'document expert' at work, getting a false British passport in Colombo was not as difficult as she'd assumed. In other circumstances, she might have described it as depressingly easy.

Her photo was taken with her hair tight back and lots of eye make up, which was how she'd decided to travel, on the grounds that it changed her looks just enough to fool someone not really concentrating on the Bangkok check-in queue. After that, it didn't really matter.

Then, in the small back room, she watched a man with a jeweller's eye glass putting the finishing touches to her new identity. He was painstakingly re-etching the minute background pattern on the paper from which someone else's details had been carefully removed, and she couldn't help wondering about the original owner. Man or woman, dead or alive? Had it been lost, stolen, sold to a dealer? Whatever, it was a pretty battered specimen of the traditional kind, and the previous owner had certainly been something of a traveller.

'Catherine Mary Ryan,' she replied when he asked for her name, and wrote it down for him to copy. It was her mother's maiden name, but the other details were her own.

With the heat embossing of the photos, the whole thing took about two hours.

'Not bad for just under a hundred pounds,' she said, when they had time to admire the careful handiwork. 'I should have asked if he was any good at airline tickets.'

When they got back to the hotel, Fran felt suddenly deflated to realise that Tony hadn't rung. She tried his number again with the same result, comforting herself that he could well be round at Benny Goldsmith's for one of his famous hacking marathons.

Since it was Sunday, the main airline offices were closed, so they phoned the airport offices from the hotel. It was now around two o'clock, and when Anders told her they could all get on a Bangkok flight at ten o'clock that night, she almost got cold feet, but reluctantly told him to go ahead and book. He paid for it with his credit card, and they checked out immediately, although the hotel let them leave the bags behind the desk until they were ready to leave. The precious tape, they agreed, would go in Anders' bag through the security check, just in case anything went wrong at the last minute. All being well, Fran would then reclaim it when they were safely through to the departure lounge.

All they had to do now was kill some time as inconspicuously as possible, because Fran certainly didn't want to be waiting around the airport longer than necessary. The obvious thing to do was visit Charlie again and let her know things had worked out very well so far.

Back at the hospital, they had the first setback of the day.

'She's being prepped for surgery,' the nurse told them. 'No, it's not serious, but the ankle needed further attention. Tomorrow, she'll be back on the general wards.'

All they could do was write down what they were planning, and leave it for Charlie when she woke up.

'I think we should phone Charlie's home and talk to Mrs Senaratna,' said Fran as they walked disappointedly back to the car park. 'She's probably very upset, and it's always possible Nevil might have phoned there if Baz has told him we've left Hikkaduwa.'

Outside the hospital at visiting time was not the best place to do it, but it seemed preferable to searching the streets for a payphone. They had to queue, and when at last Fran was able to dial, the number rang for ages. Then, just as she was about to give up, a quiet, nervous voice answered.

'Mrs Senaratna? My name's Fran Merrick, and I'm a friend of Charlie's . . .'

'Oh dear, this is terrible, terrible,' said the voice, and Fran could imagine the distress on the soft, round face of the woman she'd seen greeting Charlie only a few days ago.

'I know, it must have been a dreadful shock to you. But Charlie's so brave, and she's going to pull through . . .'

Again, the tearful interruption.

'What is brave? One minute she is at death's door only doing her duty, and the next there are officers telling me I cannot see her and she is being suspended. I don't understand it at all.'

'I'm sorry, did you say suspended?' The noise round the booth was considerable, and Fran was desperately hoping she'd misheard.

'They said there will be an inquiry and maybe disciplinary action, and her so poorly.'

'But that just doesn't seem possible. Did they give any reason?' Fran could hear alarm bells beginning to

315

ring. Poor Mrs Senaratna sounded quite distraught.

'They would tell me nothing. And what about this? Some people I don't know from Adam telephoned me. They said to tell Charlie urgently that some men staying at their house have left very quickly. One of these men is British. They did not understand anything either. It is all very confusing. What should I do about this, now I cannot see Charlie?'

Fran felt the colour going from her face. 'Please, Mrs Senaratna, one of the men might be my husband. Did they decide to leave, or did someone take them away?'

Beside her, Anders and Klaus stiffened and tried to listen in.

'I told you, I don't know what happened or who these people are. I don't understand who has gone where. I only know the people who rang me were afraid also.'

'Oh my God!' muttered Fran. 'Mrs Senaratna, please may I come round and talk to you straight away. This could be very important.'

'I know nothing. I cannot say any more until they let me talk to Charlie. Excuse me.' To the sound of weeping, the phone was hung up.

Anders had to take the receiver out of Fran's hand. 'This can't be happening,' she said in a daze. 'Not now. It looks like Nevil and Vesak have had to move house again and she couldn't tell me why. She can't mean Zavvy's lot have got them, can she?'

'Surely not. Maybe they just had to move for safety, like the last time.'

'I hope you're right,' said Fran grimly. 'Christ, this is just appalling. What am I supposed to do, go home without even knowing if they're all right?'

The queue outside rustled politely.

'I can't go, I can't,' Fran said through clenched teeth as they led her back to the car.

Neither of the men said anything. They let her sit for a while with her head in her hands, desperately trying to think, but when the answers came, they were always the same. Suddenly the rules had changed. She'd gone from hunter to hunted again in the space of a few confused words over the phone. The net they'd been so carefully constructing to destroy the enemy was now turned against them and was closing in. She had to break out, and pray Nevil would make it. If she didn't go home with the evidence right now, they might never get another chance to crack the whole rotten thing wide open. This time, it was now or never.

# Chapter Twenty

Fran had prepared herself for a big police presence at the airport. It had been there when she'd arrived, and the situation had only deteriorated since then. What she hadn't really taken on board was the thought of having to go through so many checks on a passport which wasn't hers, the very possession of which was enough to put her in jail.

The police checks started even before they got out of the car, and she looked longingly at the tourist coaches full of tanned relaxed faces being waved through with little more than a head count and a cursory nod to the courier. Any other vehicle got much more thorough treatment.

'That's two down,' she breathed as she and Klaus unloaded the bags while Anders completed the formalities for returning the hire car. But how many more would there be inside?

They'd timed their arrival for about a quarter to eight, which was the latest they could reasonable leave it for a 21.50 flight, and it was now gone eight.

She willingly left it to Anders to collect their tickets and nervously scanned the departure screen with Klaus. Relieved, they exchanged smiles. So far there was no sign of a delay for the Bangkok plane. The desk was open and a queue was already beginning to develop as they waited for Anders to return with the tickets.

At the far end, the London charter flight check-in was in full spate, occasionally locking trolleys with the Lufthansa queue next door. Patrolling the lines of oddly wrapped, bulging parcels, from which protruded brightly painted shapes of devil masks or wooden tusks, touts offered hard currencies for unused rupees. One up-market French contingent were kissing their courier goodbye and being handed cling-wrapped sprays of orchids. If only . . . thought Fran, while here she was, hardly daring to raise her eyes in case a saturnine, ponytail figure should suddenly materialise through the plate glass from the darkness beyond, like the very essence of evil.

Anders came back with her new tickets, made out to Catherine Mary Ryan. Colombo-Bangkok, and Bangkok-Heathrow, blessed word. The flight time to Bangkok was just under three and a half hours, and the Heathrow departure was 07.40. Allowing for the local time difference, that meant less than five hours to kill in transit. That was nothing, and infinitely preferable to even an extra five minutes spent here.

She tucked the tickets into her passport and clutched it tightly. There was one more thing to do. While Klaus was parked in the queue with all their bags on one trolley, Fran and Anders did some hasty calculations as to how much she owed them. Then she had to find a Cirrus cash point that would take her Switch card. The money came out in rupees, and one of the touts was only too pleased to change it into American dollars for a hefty commission.

'This is only money,' she said as she handed it to Anders with a hug. 'The rest I can never repay. Now get me onto that plane, Doc, before I change my mind and start screaming.'

When their turn came, the clerk's expression didn't change as he checked the name on the worn passport against her ticket.

You have packed these bags yourselves? Yes. You have not left them unattended at any time? No. The usual litany flew by. You have read the regulations concerning the export of endangered animal products? Fran almost choked on that one.

'And we'd like three seats together, please, non-smoking,' said Anders calmly, and somehow a boarding card arrived in her nerveless fingers as the cases disappeared into the black hole beyond.

That only left passport control. But as they strolled to the counter, the two men joking loudly about who was going to have the window seat, a dreadful sensation suddenly hit her in the pit of the stomach. The number of the passport hadn't been changed. Suppose it was on the list of rogue numbers which lurked behind every immigration counter these days. The sweat was prickling under her drawn-back hair. If it made her heavy eye-make up run, she'd look like a panda . . . Was there a picture of a panda in the rogue's gallery behind there? Or a tiger? Hysteria. Stop it.

The official looked her in the eye. She heard his intake of breath, knew he was going to speak. She met his gaze and forced herself to smile.

'Safe journey,' said a voice that couldn't have been real. 'And come back soon to Sri Lanka.'

'Thank you,' she breathed. 'I'm sure we will. It's a beautiful country.'

\*       \*       \*

Whether it was simply fear, or the whole compelling ritual of boarding the plane that made it seem impossible at any point actually to turn back, Fran was never able to decide. Possibly it was some strange alchemy of the two, because it was only when she felt the plane leave the ground that the enormity of what she'd done came home to her.

The plane made its turn for the north-east over the dark ocean, and as Fran looked back at the receding light patterns of Colombo, the feeling of being wrenched away, of abandoning what was down there, was almost physical. She had left Nevil when he was quite possibly in danger again, after she'd sworn not to leave without him; run away twice now when Charlie was in trouble; not even thought about Vesak. If that wasn't enough, she was travelling on a false passport, and would be soon be saying goodbye to two people who had come to mean such a lot to her.

For a while, the weight of it all was overwhelming. Anders and Klaus seemed to realise how she was feeling and left her to her thoughts. Yet up here there was a feeling of rising above it all, of elation that she had somehow got this far, and when Anders reached into his bag and silently handed her the tape, her spirits began to revive. There was so much more to do if the crazy, painful events of the last few weeks were to achieve anything at all.

At Bangkok, it was all so quick. She'd already told them not to wait around to see her off but, not knowing the airport, hadn't reckoned on the TRANSIT PASSENGERS ONLY sign looming so soon and forcing them to go their separate ways.

They said their goodbyes at the side of the corridor. The other passengers streamed past trying not to look at the strange, huddled threesome, apparently caught so completely unawares by their emotions.

The two men waited until she reached the door of the transit lounge and turned for a final wave. They'd promised to phone regularly, and said they'd come back before their intended six weeks was up if there was anything they could do by way of giving evidence.

The clock in the transit lounge said it was 03.10, which didn't mean a great deal when you felt as wiped out as this. Fran fiddled with the zone change button on her alarm and set it for three hours' time. Then she curled up on some seats and slept without stirring until it woke her.

She slept on the London plane too, fitfully, between the half-eaten meals, the rounds of duty-frees, the flickering in-flight movies; determined to lose the mysterious seven hours of time difference that would plunge her into a London Monday in mid-afternoon, after being in the air for nearly twice that time. You sat, you ate, you slept. You filled in your embarkation card, with your real name and passport number, and did exactly what they told you. The minute she landed, she would make for the phone, and Tony. Nothing else could happen now. She was home. It was even raining out there. Perfect.

Except for one last little detail.

Instead of the usual quick glance and a genial wave through, the man behind the immigration control desk had taken her passport and was flicking through it thoughtfully. Then he started at the beginning again and his expression changed to something that was almost a smile. Jolted from her fantasies of England welcoming its own, Fran suddenly realised what it meant. It was the look of a man whose whole life was geared to moments like these.

'Excuse me, madam. May I ask you to confirm that this passport is in fact your own?'

Fran blinked at him foolishly. She'd never seen anyone stopped in the 'EC Passport Holders Only' queue before. Things like that only happened in the 'Others' queue. Fascinated, she watched herself from somewhere on the ceiling as she carefully considered her reply.

'Oh yes, it's definitely mine,' she said cheerfully. 'I bought it – in Colombo, actually. It cost almost a hundred quid.'

The ominous silence from the desk was accompanied by rustlings and sighs from the queue behind. She saw his hand go to a buzzer, and one of the airport police by the wall slipped out of his comfortable air of benign professional boredom and into something more appropriate for the occasion.

'Got a wrong'un?' asked the policeman, giving Fran a stare that made a stone wall look transparent.

For some reason, it made Fran want to laugh. This was terrific. She wanted to make them all laugh.

'I'll say,' said the man behind the counter. 'A real beauty.' He had a pleasant face, she decided. Almost avuncular. Until he'd suddenly realised he could be looking at either a complete head case, or the kind of woman who could plant a bomb in a crowded supermarket and not think twice about it.

'In that case, would you care to accompany me, madam?' said the policeman. And she knew, without any previous experience on the subject, that to have moved one unnecessary muscle at that point would have been a very bad idea indeed.

'I'd be delighted, officer,' said Fran calmly. She felt utterly relaxed – positively carefree. 'And if I didn't think you'd have me in an instant arm lock, I would very likely try to kiss you.'

Afterwards, considering the gravity of what she'd done, Fran was keen to tell everyone that the experience of being completely turned over by the entire Heathrow security staff wasn't really that bad. They were at least coldly polite and clinically efficient, and listened patiently enough to what she had to say.

'Well, I'll say this – it's different,' said one officer shaking his head.

The worst part had been when the rubber gloves appeared, but a sharp claim that she was pregnant and a request to make her one regulation phone call got the examination put on hold.

The problem was, who to phone for maximum effect. Tony might have been at the office, at Benny's or even on his way to the AWW offices in Coventry. In the end she decided on her father, since he was now semi-retired, likely to be at home, and had a long-term friend as a solicitor.

'Hello, Dad,' she said when, after a two-hour drive through the evening rush hour, he arrived with the solicitor in tow. 'It's been quite a trip.'

'And now you're going to say it was all my idea,' said her father hugging her. 'Now will someone tell me what to do to get you out of here?'

It took a lot more time and paperwork, but eventually Fran could sense an easing of the atmosphere as the impact of all she'd been saying sunk in. Everyone was still very cautious, but slowly she dared to believe that she might soon be released and on her way home.

When the solicitor explained the conditions of release, she almost laughed. She wasn't allowed to leave the country, and had to keep herself available for questioning.

'I can't wait to answer more questions,' she declared. 'And as for leaving the country, I haven't got a passport.'

'That didn't stop you last time, love,' retorted one of the younger officers with a welcome glimmer of humour 'How much did you say you paid for that thing?'

Fran told him and he laughed. 'You were robbed. Never mind, it'll do a turn at the training sessions. Next time, get it done by the CIA. They're expensive, but they're good.'

'I'll try and remember that,' she replied as they got up. 'But I don't think there's going to be a next time.'

'Oh, I don't know,' he said pensively. 'The most surprising people get a taste for it.'

The next few days were full of frantic activity. Some of it included getting the pregnancy confirmed. Her own delight was reflected in her father's face, and the thought that she'd soon be able to tell Nevil gave her a terrific boost of energy and enthusiasm for the rest of what she had to do. The next priority was getting the precious tape copied and finding out what Tony had come up with at his end.

Processing the tape copies so that it could be viewed on a normal video machine took a whole day, even at express rates. When she was finally able to view the results with her father and the solicitor, the tension was almost unbearable as the memories of that night came flooding back.

The shop, the dealer, Charlie's giggle, the pathetic little objects on the cloth and the whole obscene exchange in the stifling back room – it was all there. And then – 'That's him, with the ponytail,' she hissed, craning forward.

'Amazing,' said her father curiously. 'He looks almost civilised.'

'He's so damned civilised, he could still wriggle out of the rest of it. I hope to God Tony's come up with enough stuff to tie him in with the Tigers and the arms trade. Then they'd be able to put him away for life. The thing is, though, I don't really want him in jail.'

'Sorry?' Her father looked at her blankly.

'I want him dead. Right here, on the carpet, in my front room,' said Fran. 'That's the real trouble with people like him. It's the effect they have on you.'

When she finally managed to get Tony on the phone, it was at the head office of AWW, and they were both beside themselves with excitement.

'Fran, my darling, you made it! And another tape – you and Charlie? I can't believe it. There's me sitting here fooling around on a keyboard, and you two doing the real heroics. How's Charlie? My God, I'm nuts on that woman. I haven't stopped thinking about her since I got back.'

'Glad to hear it.' Fran gulped. 'She sends her love. So tell me what you've got.'

'Listen, it's just incredible. That Benny's a wizard. He actually hacked into the bank where dear old Ar-Sole or whatever his name is has a controlling interest, and got into Zavvy Cheng's accounts as well. You're not going to believe this, but Benny reckons Cheng could be ripping off Ah Fat.'

'That wouldn't surprise me.'

'It's going to surprise Ah Fat, though. Benny's a bit of a joker. He faxed the bank pretending he's an auditor, quoting chapter and verse. It looks as if Zavvy has been siphoning off bits here and there and building himself a nice little bolt hole on the shady side of Cape Town.'

'You're kidding!'

'Not at all. If only half of what Benny's put in that fax is true, Zavvy Cheng is going to find himself answering some serious questions, probably under a naked light bulb with the assistance of nasty men with baseball bats. And that's *before* the police get to him.'

Men, when they got on a high! 'Tony,' said Fran warily. 'You haven't let Benny do anything stupid, have you? Like putting the wind up the pair of them before the case is watertight?'

'Would I do that? Benny's just making a bit of mischief, that's all. It could take them a week to sort it out, and they won't have a clue where it's come from. Seriously, though, you should see what he's got on Zavvy's connections with the arms trade and China. The AWW people are ecstatic. I've got Mike Paulsen right here. He's the boss, and he's been dying to talk to you. Oh hang on, before I pass you over, where's Nev? I assume he's around somewhere?'

'He's not with me,' answered Fran. Suddenly she couldn't bear to admit to Tony that she'd actually left without him. 'Did he say when he was coming?'

There was a heartbeat's pause in all the excitement.

'Tony,' she said. 'You have heard from Nev, haven't you?'

'Actually, not a word. I assumed you had. The minute I knew you were back I stopped worrying.'

'I see,' said Fran, utterly deflated again. 'Perhaps we'd both better start worrying about Nev.'

On Thursday morning, the day after AWW had gone public with the truth about Brian's death, and all the material collated by Tony had been faxed to Charlie's newspaper contact in Colombo, the door bell rang.

Thinking it was probably the post, Fran answered in her dressing gown, to find a policeman and a WPC on the doorstep.

'Good morning,' she smiled. 'You haven't come to take me away, have you? I'm not even dressed.' But the smile died when she saw their expressions. This time it wasn't stone-faced officialdom. It looked very much like sympathy.

'Are you Mrs Francesca Anne Merrick?' asked the woman constable kindly.

Fran nodded, still not quite realising what this form of visitation might mean.

'Please may we come in?'

Still it didn't click.

Afterwards, in the kitchen over a mug of tea, the policewoman told her that people sometimes fainted when they saw two policemen on the doorstep. That meant they'd guessed, which made breaking it to them easier.

But Fran hadn't guessed. Everything had been going so brilliantly well, that even when the policewoman told her Nevil was dead, that there was no mistake, that he'd been shot trying to escape from the house of a Xavier Michael Cheng - even then it made no sense to her. Nevil simply could not be dead, and that was that. People like him were *not* seen running

328

from the back of the Cheng compound, waving frantically to a police car which had been watching the place. People like Nevil did *not* get a couple of bullets in the back and die in the arms of a policeman, gasping, 'Help him, for Christ's sake, he's still in there.' They made it to the car. They helped rescue their friend. Then they came home a hero.

Except when they didn't.

'Had he been . . .' She had to ask.

No, they said. Just tied up, probably for a day or so. But the other man had not been so lucky.

'Is he dead too?' she whispered. 'His name is Vesak Thomas.'

Sadly yes, they said. That was the other name given by Interpol when the message came through. Fran bowed her head. She didn't want to know the details. Couldn't cope with that now.

But even as she vainly covered her eyes as if to ward off the dreadful images rising behind them, the policeman was saying something else – it might help her to know that a later message had confirmed the death of Xavier Michael Cheng and several of his men. But not in the raid on his premises, when they'd found the body of Vesak. Cheng had died of knife wounds after some kind of confrontation with his boss. The police had found him dying in a ditch with two of his men dead beside him.

Fran said yes, it did help her to know. Just a little.

The policeman took out some papers and checked something. Ah Fat was the name of the man who had been arrested in connection with the attack, and there were also other charges pending. Chinese, was he?

Then he stopped, embarrassed by his own professional curiosity.

But Fran wasn't listening any more. 'I'm sorry, I'm

so sorry,' she whispered, her arms tight round her stomach, rocking gently. 'Your Dad never knew about you. But I'll make it up to you somehow.'

It was, they all agreed, a very moving memorial service. The funeral had been private and local, but after talking to Brian Gaskill's sister and Vesak's family in Colombo, Fran decided they should have a joint service for all three of them six weeks later. She chose the church nearest the offices of Merrick & Baldwyn, and a Friday afternoon, so that Nevil's City friends and colleagues could be there. A central location was also more convenient for those coming from abroad.

The place was full. Charlie was there, of course, still limping, but smart in her uniform, and accompanied by two senior officers. With them they'd brought three wonderful wreaths of Sri Lankan orchids. One of the police officers had told Fran quietly that a decoration for Charlie's part in the operation to clean the tiger bone dealers out of Colombo was in the pipeline. She'd already been promoted, and was back in the Sri Lankan equivalent of the fraud squad.

Anders and Klaus had flown in from Denmark looking tanned, but clearly feeling the emotion of the occasion, and Fran had invited them, along with Charlie, to stay with her for as long as they wanted.

But of them all, thought Fran, as she listened to the tributes from Nevil's friends, the AWW and the police, of all those who had been closely involved, it was Tony who had changed the most. He'd been to Sri Lanka twice to see Charlie in the intervening time, and it hadn't taken Fran long to realise that he was deeply, painfully, in love.

There were no other flowers in the church apart from the orchid wreaths. At Fran's request, donations had been sent to AWW. There was talk of friendship and love, of duty, courage and commitment to a worthy cause, of heartfelt sympathy. They spoke about the way Nevil laughed, of the good times, and hope for the future.

Fran thought of endless golden beaches and brilliant sunsets and wished them for her husband. She thought of peacocks, of bright jungle flowers, and the majestic creatures with coats that rippled like sunlight on tall grass – and prayed that when her child grew up, there would still be tigers in the wild where they belonged, for people to wonder at their untamed power and regal beauty.

THE END

Aspire Books are available from bookshops, super-markets, department and multiple stores throughout the UK, or can be ordered from the following address:

Aspire Publishing
Mail Order Department
8 Betony Rise
EXETER EX2 5RR

Please add £0.50 PER ORDER for postage and packing, irrespective of quantity.

# Aspire Publishing

# 1 UNIT

## No. A.001

### SAVE 10 Units

and exchange them for any **1** Aspire
book of your choice

### SAVE 20 Units

and exchange them for any **3** Aspire
books of your choice

## THIS OFFER IS VALID
## INDEFINITELY

Redeemable at any stockist of Aspire books
or by post to:

**Aspire Publishing**
16 Connaught Street, LONDON W2 2AF

For the name of your nearest stockist
telephone, fax or write to:

**Aspire Publishing**
*Voucher Redemption Dept.*
8 Betony Rise
EXETER EX2 5RR
Tel: 01392 25 25 16
Fax: 01392 25 25 17

ASPIRE
1 UNIT
No. A.001